No. 1 *New York Times* bestselling author **Christine Feehan** has had over ninety novels published and has thrilled legions of fans with her seductive Dark Carpathian tales. She has received numerous honours throughout her career, including being a nominee for the Romance Writers of America RITA and receiving a Career Achievement Award from *Romantic Times*, and has been published in multiple languages.

Visit Christine Feehan online:

www.christinefeehan.com
www.facebook.com/christinefeehanauthor
@AuthorCFeehan

Praise for Christine Feehan:

'After Bram Stoker, Anne Rice and Joss Whedon, Feehan is the person most credited with popularizing the neck gripper'
Time magazine

'The queen of paranormal romance'
USA Today

'Feehan has a knack for bringing vampiric Carpathians to vivid, virile life in her Dark Carpathian novels'
Publishers Weekly

'The amazingly prolific author's ability to create captivating and adrenaline-raising worlds is unsurpassed'
Romantic Times

By Christine Feehan

CHRISTINE FEEHAN

DARK WHISPER

PIATKUS

PIATKUS

First published in the US in 2022 by Berkley,
An imprint of Penguin Random House LLC
First published in Great Britain in 2022 by Piatkus

1 3 5 7 9 10 8 6 4 2

Copyright © 2022 by Christine Feehan

The moral right of the author has been asserted.

A CIP catalogue record for this book
is available from the British Library.

Hardback ISBN 978-0-349-43237-3
Trade Paperback ISBN 978-0-349-43238-0

Printed and bound in Great Britain by Clays Ltd, Elcograf S.p.A.

Papers used by Piatkus are from well-managed forests
and other responsible sources.

MIX
Paper from
responsible sources
FSC® C104740

Piatkus
An imprint of
Little, Brown Book Group
Carmelite House
50 Victoria Embankment
London EC4Y 0DZ

An Hachette UK Company
www.hachette.co.uk

www.littlebrown.co.uk

For Elizabeth Castellos.
With love.

Stockport Libraries
and Information Service

You should retain this receipt.

Customer ID: **********9908

Items that you have loaned

Title: Dark whisper
ID: C2000003267647
Due: 31 July 2023

Total items: 1
Account balance: £0.00
Borrowed: 4
Overdue: 0
Reservation requests: 0
Ready for collection: 0
10/07/2023 12:46

Thank you for using Marple Library

www.stockport.gov.uk/libraries
Tel: 0161 217 6009
@SMBC_Libraries
Facebook: Stockport Libraries

FOR MY READERS

Be sure to go to ChristineFeehan.com/members/ to sign up for my private book announcement list and download the free ebook of *Dark Desserts*. The recipes offer so many wonderful, yummy desserts! Join my community and get firsthand news, enter the book discussions, ask your questions and chat with me. Please feel free to email me at Christine@ChristineFeehan.com. I would love to hear from you.

ACKNOWLEDGMENTS

As always, there are so many people to thank: Diane Trudeau and Sheila English, for helping me with edits. Brian Feehan, for keeping me on track. Denise, for going beyond the call of duty every day, all day, when so many things were happening. Cheryl Wilson and Elissa Wilds, for helping me find April. April Lark, for answering my SOS at the very last minute and helping me with tarot readings. I appreciate all of you so much!

THE CARPATHIAN FAMILIES

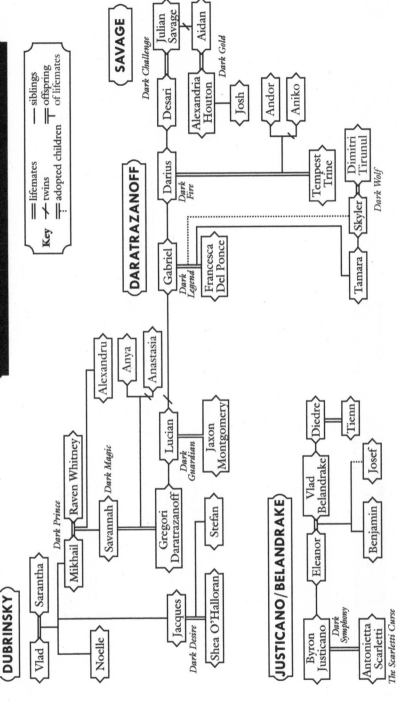

Key:
═══ lifemates
↗ twins
═ adopted children
— siblings
┬ offspring of lifemates

SAVAGE

Julian Savage
Dark Challenge
Aidan
Alexandria Houton
Dark Gold
Desari
Josh
Andor
Aniko
Darius
Dark Fire

Tempest Trine
Dimitri Tirunul
Skyler
Dark Wolf
Tamara

DARATRAZANOFF

Gabriel
Dark Legend
Francesca Del Ponce

DUBRINSKY

Vlad
Sarantha
Mikhail
Dark Prince
Raven Whitney
Noelle
Alexandru
Anya
Anastasia
Savannah
Dark Magic
Gregori Daratrazanoff
Lucian
Dark Guardian
Jaxon Montgomery
Stefan
Jacques
Dark Desire
Shea O'Halloran

JUSTICANO/BELANDRAKE

Byron Justicano
Dark Symphony
Eleanor
Vlad Belandrake
Diedre
Tienn
Antonietta Scarletti
The Scarletti Curse
Benjamin
Josef

THE CARPATHIAN FAMILIES

Key
- $=$ lifemates
- $\curlywedge$ twins
- $\overline{\overline{}}$ offspring of lifemates
- $-$ siblings
- Y cousins
- V parents not lifemates
- $\sim$ offspring
- $*$ monastery ancients
- $\wedge$ converted male

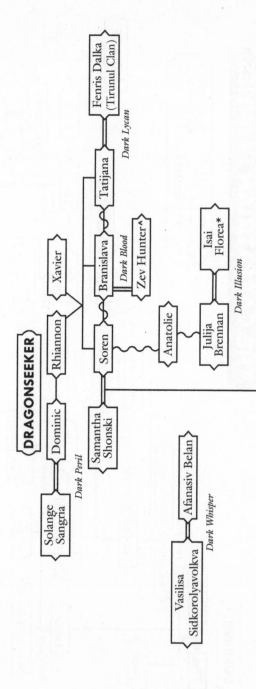

DRAGONSEEKER

Solange Sangria — Dominic = Rhiannon ⅄ Xavier

Dark Peril

Samantha Shonski — Soren

Branislava — Tatijana — Fenris Dalka (Tirunul Clan)

Dark Lycan

Dark Blood

Zev Hunter^

Anatolie

Julija Brennan = Isai Florea*

Dark Illusion

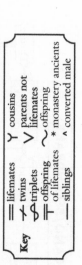

Vasilisa Sidkorolyavolkva = Afanasiv Belan

Dark Whisper

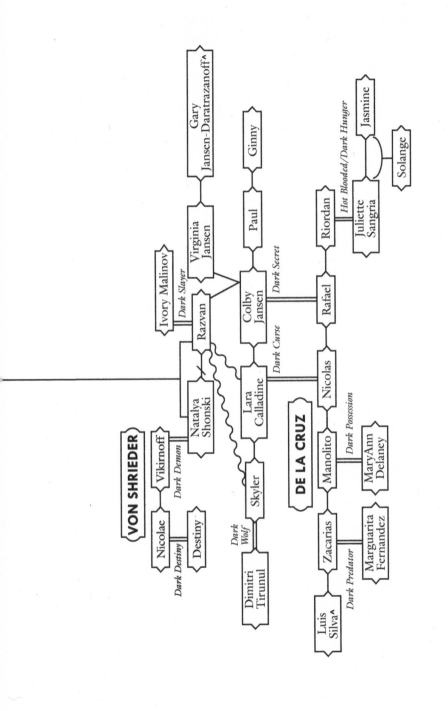

VON SHRIEDER

Nicolae — Destiny
Dark Destiny

Vikirnoff — Natalya Shonski
Dark Demon

Dimitri Tirunul — Skyler
Dark Wolf

Ivory Malinov — Razvan
Dark Slayer

Lara Calladine — Colby Jansen
Dark Curse

Virginia Jansen — Gary Jansen-Daratrazanoff^

Paul

Ginny

Dark Secret

Nicolas — Rafael

Riordan — Juliette Sangria
Hot Blooded/Dark Hunger

Jasmine — Solange

DE LA CRUZ

Zacarias — Luis Silva^

Manolito — MaryAnn Delaney
Dark Possession

Marguarita Fernandez
Dark Predator

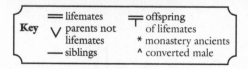

OTHER CARPATHIANS

Key
= lifemates
∨ parents not lifemates
— siblings
⊤ offspring of lifemates
* monastery ancients
^ converted male

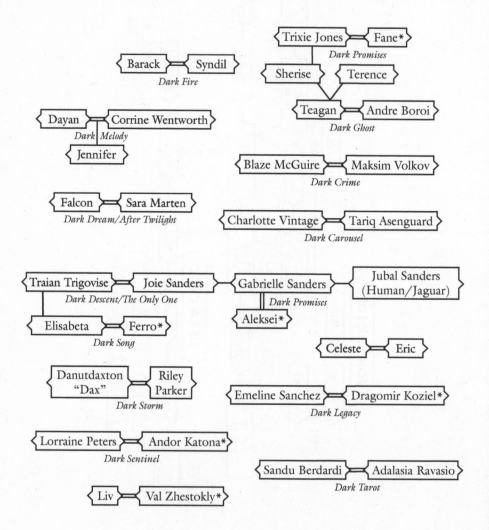

Trixie Jones = Fane*
Dark Promises

Barack = Syndil
Dark Fire

Sherise — Terence

Teagan = Andre Boroi
Dark Ghost

Dayan = Corrine Wentworth
Dark Melody
Jennifer

Blaze McGuire = Maksim Volkov
Dark Crime

Falcon = Sara Marten
Dark Dream/After Twilight

Charlotte Vintage = Tariq Asenguard
Dark Carousel

Traian Trigovise = Joie Sanders — Gabrielle Sanders — Jubal Sanders (Human/Jaguar)
Dark Descent/The Only One
Dark Promises

Elisabeta = Ferro*
Dark Song

Aleksei*

Celeste = Eric

Danutdaxton "Dax" = Riley Parker
Dark Storm

Emeline Sanchez = Dragomir Koziel*
Dark Legacy

Lorraine Peters = Andor Katona*
Dark Sentinel

Sandu Berdardi = Adalasia Ravasio
Dark Tarot

Liv = Val Zhestokly*

dark whisper

THE GODDESS

PART ONE

VII

THE CHARIOT

CHAPTER

1

Vasilisa Sidkorolyavolkva stood for a long moment staring up at the sliver of silver moon in the dark bluish sky. She loved this time of night, when millions of stars were scattered like a blanket across the sky, and it was clear and perfect. She inhaled to take in all the scents around her, a habit ingrained for self-preservation, taught from the time she was a toddler.

The pavilion was empty, a mixture of black and white squares where others often came to dance and party late into the night, but that hadn't happened for a long while. She knew her family wanted her to settle for a husband, and during every ball, they pushed eligible bachelors at her. She detested the disappointment in her brothers' eyes, especially her eldest. She knew if she didn't cooperate soon, he would demand she comply with his choice—and she knew she wouldn't.

Andros, ruler of her family, was running out of patience with her. He thought she would do as he said, mostly because he was used to everyone doing as he said. Her other brothers—the twins, Garald and Grigor—knew her so much better. They knew her stubborn streak, and they watched her carefully after each ball. The more Andros pushed her, the more they kept their eyes on her.

She had to smile to herself. She had her ways of sneaking out of their palatial home, and her brothers had never caught her. Not once. Not in all the years she'd been doing it.

They lived in a small community in a very remote area in the Eastern Siberia boreal forest. The community had existed for hundreds of years. More. They had kept to themselves for generations, although now, the younger ones had left the villages to seek employment and service in more modern settings. They blended in seamlessly.

The villages dated back so many centuries that they still considered themselves ruled by a monarchy rather than acknowledging the government, although every man and woman served in the military for the experience of it. Vasilisa came from that monarchy, and her brother Andros was the current ruler.

Vasilisa had been extremely uneasy lately. Restless and moody. Edgy. She always maintained her serene composure. She was too skilled in battle technique to give anything away. That cool exterior didn't mean she wasn't burning hot with passion deep down. She needed an outlet. She knew she desperately needed out from under her brothers' watchful eyes. They'd felt it, too—that unrest in their land—which was why they were even more vigilant watching over her.

She was particularly terrified of what that edgy, moody, wanting-to-snap-at-everyone-just-for-looking-at-her-wrong feeling actually meant. She had no power over the things that were changing. Things that could directly affect her. She needed a friend to talk things over with. Someone she trusted who would never betray her confidence. That fire inside her was growing, right along with the terrible dread she tried not to examine too closely.

She moved with quick, silent strides down the wide steps onto the snow-covered path that led to a trail into the forest of larch trees. The path was well used by members of her family to travel to the small inn where locals gathered in the evening to drink and gossip. A roaring fire in the great stone fireplace kept everyone warm in spite of the bitter cold. The more bodies packed inside, the warmer the interior.

The inn was owned and operated by Kendal and Odessa Balakin. The older couple had been around for as long as Vasilisa could remember. They were unfailingly friendly and welcoming to everyone in spite of the fact that the villagers could be a superstitious lot and were often suspicious of strangers.

She glanced at the moon again as she wound in and out among the thick trees. A few brave mice scampered across the vegetation lying on the snow, hurrying to grab the seeds and burrow deep under the branches that had fallen on top of the snowpack so they wouldn't be spotted by the owls on the lookout for food. Snowy owls, great gray owls and pygmy owls occupied the larch forest and hunted relentlessly.

A snow-white mountain hare suddenly emerged from behind a tree trunk and stopped moving abruptly, rising up on its hind legs. She froze as well. The two simply stared at each other. Her heart began to accelerate, the blood circulating with a hot rush through her body. The little rabbit thumped its back foot on the thick bank of snow, a warning to the rest of its extended family that they weren't alone in their pursuit of food.

"Be at peace, little sister. I'm not hunting," she spoke softly to the animal.

The rabbit cocked its black-tipped ears at her, turning them this way and that as if it could understand everything she said. She spoke in her native language, and who knew? Maybe the rabbit was that intelligent. It had survived long enough to grow to adulthood. Many didn't. She ignored it and continued along the narrow trail winding through the larch forest to the inn. It was a good distance from her home, but she welcomed the walk. Sometimes she felt as if she were a prisoner in her own home. She had needed to get out, and the night air was the perfect antidote.

She wore a long coat of white fur that fell to her ankles and a matching white fur hat that covered her ears to keep the cold from sneaking into her bones through her scalp. Her gloves were white as well. If she needed to disappear into the snow, she blended easily, even with her choice of lipstick and her blazing blue eyes. Her coat, although slim and looking as if it hugged her figure, hid a multitude of weapons. She wasn't a woman who trusted. She had been raised to defend herself. Her lessons had taken place early, and she had been expected to take them very seriously. It had been drilled into her by her mother that there was no room for mistakes—everything was about life or death.

Strangely, her brothers were never invited to those daily training sessions, and she was cautioned never to discuss anything her mother taught her with them or her father. As she grew up, she realized why—her mother had passed a legacy to her, one that had been handed down from mother to daughter. She felt the weight of that legacy every waking moment. Lately, she knew the weight had increased, pressing down on her, because something had changed.

There had been a dangerous shift, a seismic tremor that had opened a fissure deep within the earth somewhere. She was certain of it. She felt the dread of it, the constant danger surrounding her beloved people. Little things were suddenly going wrong. Small animals had been found savagely eviscerated miles from the village, and that had been enough to alarm some of the hunters, who had gone out to track the culprit. There were tracks, of course, very small ones they weren't familiar with, as if an unknown animal had come up from below and then burrowed back into the ground after killing several rabbits and squirrels.

Vasilisa had been unsettled ever since. Nightmares affected her ability to sleep. She rarely slept at night, preferring to rest during the day, but even with the blackout curtains at her windows and her music on, nothing seemed to help. She had an ominous feeling that continued to get worse as the days went by.

The inn was completely lit up, as it often was, with a cheery, bright radiance that threw a glow across the snow through the uncovered glass of the big windows in the lobby of the bar. Travelers seeking a room could check in, but mostly, the inn was full of locals who came for their vodka, tea, kvass and warm black bread.

She pushed the door open, and the swinging wolf-head bells on a rope announced her arrival. She stomped on the outside snow mat, trying to remove the worst of the mess on her boots while she caught her breath. It was difficult to adjust to the heat after the brisk cold of the night.

She had been inside the Wolf's Retreat hundreds of times, yet this time it felt different. This time it *was* different. Her breath caught in her throat, and she glanced toward the stairs leading to the rooms Kendal and Odessa rented out. Her hand crept protectively to her throat. Already she could feel the invasion. A scent reached her first. Something wild. Completely feral. Not wolf. She was used to wolf. Something even wilder. Further back than wolf. They had tigers in Siberia. No, she shook her head. Not tigers. Something even more dangerous.

She tried not to inhale, but she couldn't help herself. It wouldn't have mattered. She was being surrounded. Enfolded. More scents invaded, but this time through her pores. Branding her. Cedar. Birch. Spring water. If she crossed the threshold, she felt as if her world would instantly be changed, and there would be no going back.

She wanted to turn and run into the night, but she knew if she did, whatever had settled around her, slowly invading through her pores, going deep—bone deep—she would take with her. She forced herself forward and held on to her smile because she was no coward, and she had been waiting all her life for this night. It was just that dreaming of it and the reality of it were two very different things.

"Vasilisa." Odessa broke into a huge smile. "I should have known you would be in tonight. It's that kind of night. Full of surprises."

Vasilisa ignored the men who were seated around the curved bar and had turned to face her as she walked all the way into the room, pulling off the white gloves covering her hands. She pushed the gloves into the deep pockets of her coat. "Surprises? You've had surprises tonight, Odessa? I didn't think there were many surprises in our village anymore."

Odessa put tea service on a tray. "Ordinarily, I would agree with you. Skyler and Dimitri have been coming around. You know Dimitri. He's been around for years. He avoids people, much preferring wolves. Now he's got himself a wife. She's young, too. I think Skyler's too young for him, but who am I to say? She does all those wolf experiments with him, or whatever it is he does."

"He set up a wolf sanctuary to make certain the wolves have a safe place to go as the forest shrinks in other places," Vasilisa explained patiently, as she'd done so many times before.

Dimitri Tirunul was a prime example of how mistrustful the locals were. Dimitri had been coming there for years. He'd helped them countless times, but he was still regarded as an outsider, and he wasn't trusted in the least. He had a residence there. Vasilisa had met him often in the forest. He had skills that rivaled her brothers', and that was saying something, because few could match her brothers' skills. Of course she knew Dimitri was married.

"That's the surprising news? That Dimitri has a young wife?"

"No." Odessa laughed merrily as she added to the tray. "We had strangers come to the inn. That's the surprise. Four men. They looked very dangerous." She lowered her voice, although the room was packed and the strangers were either out of the inn or upstairs. The noise level was loud. "They came asking for Dimitri."

A chill went down Vasilisa's spine. Dimitri may not have been born in their village, but as far as she was concerned, he was one of them. He protected the wolves, the same as they did. "What did you tell them?"

"I certainly didn't know where Dimitri would be. He goes wherever he wants." Odessa gestured toward the forest. "It's a big place out there, and he runs with the wolves. Let them try to find him."

Vasilisa tried not to openly wince. Even that last little bit might have been too much to say. She had to warn Dimitri. Often Dimitri and Skyler would stay out in the woods for weeks on end, and no one would see him or his new wife.

There had been a terrible incident that had nearly taken Dimitri's life. Rumors swirled about it, and she knew the truth was far worse than the locals even realized. He had been a very handsome man. He had scars now, although they were faded to thin white lines dissecting his face, neck, arms and hands. She hadn't asked him about the scars or rumors. She hadn't wanted to bring up anything unpleasant, but her family had been briefed on the entire disturbing and horrifying event. It had made all of their people look bad.

Dimitri had always stayed away from others, but since that incident, even after marrying, he avoided everyone even more. She couldn't blame him. She was well aware that the two people he had saved from certain death had betrayed him and then had him tortured and hung up in front of others to die a slow, painful death. Young Skyler had saved his life.

Vasilisa didn't understand people. Maybe she never would. She didn't think she wanted to go out into the busy world where so many of the younger crowd wanted to go. She wouldn't fit in. Even at twenty-eight she retained the old-fashioned values and ethics her mother had instilled in her.

"I think I'm a dinosaur, Odessa. I don't fit in anywhere."

"You fit in just fine right here, Vasilisa," Odessa assured her. She leaned over the counter, looked both ways again and nearly whispered, "There's more. I was hoping you would come in. It made me happy that your friend was here to see you. You always seem to show up when we need you the most."

Vasilisa frowned. She could tell that Odessa wasn't being dramatic. She was concerned. "What is it?"

"Government men. They're pretending not to be, but they are. I can smell them a mile away. I've seen too many of their kind. They're here to cause trouble for us."

Vasilisa's stomach instantly knotted. That was the worst possible news. The one thing the villagers tried to do was stay under the radar. Most of the time, the government ignored their existence. They were up too high in the wilderness. They lived off land no one else really wanted. They kept to themselves and didn't cause trouble.

"Did they ask for Dimitri, too?" She hoped not, but it wouldn't surprise her. Dimitri was a man who went his own way. He had to work with the government to get permits for the protection of his wolves and the lands he wanted to safeguard.

"No, but they were asking about your brothers, Andros in particular."

Vasilisa's breath caught in her throat. "Thank you, Odessa." She didn't have to ask if Odessa or Kendal had spoken to the government agents about her brothers. They never would, nor would any of the villagers. No one would ever betray the monarchy.

Odessa pulled back a little and put a smile on her face. "There now, I don't want to ruin your time with your friend. She doesn't come to see you often. She's waiting in her usual spot in the corner. You know how difficult it is to see her when she doesn't want to be seen. Have a lovely time with her, Vasilisa."

Vasilisa took the tray and moved smoothly through the crowd, mostly because the men and women parted for her the moment she got close to them. She had known Sorina as long as she could remember, and she'd always looked the same. Tall, gorgeous, impossible to tell her age with her very thick ice-blond hair and generous mouth that always seemed ready to smile. Sorina stood up and took the tray immediately.

"There you are. I thought I might have to come looking for you. You get lost looking at stars, Vasi."

Sorina's voice lifted Vasilisa up, making her feel lighter. She instantly wished she'd asked her to come visit earlier. Some of the dread that was overshadowing her mind dissipated just listening to the musical quality of her voice, allowing Vasilisa to think more clearly.

"What is it, Vasi?" Sorina asked. "I can feel your concern."

Vasilisa shook her head. "I want you to reach out and see if you can find something on your own without me saying anything. I don't want to color whatever you might get." She poured the tea into the small glasses, added milk and set the glasses in the gold filigree containers.

"I have already been uneasy, and just coming here tonight has confirmed that something is wrong." Sorina studied her face with her dark, knowing eyes. The combination of blond hair and dark eyes was striking.

"Odessa told me that there are strangers at the inn. Four men came looking for Dimitri." Vasilisa couldn't keep the worry from her voice.

Sorina smiled. "There is never a need to worry about Dimitri, Vasi. On his own, he could take on any enemy or number of enemies. He is back to full strength after the treachery he faced. He has his wife, who is a force on her own. With them right now are Razvan and Ivory. They are training young Skyler and Dimitri to hunt vampires with wolves. Ivory and Razvan are legendary, known in our world as two of the most famous vampire hunters alive."

Vasilisa couldn't help the little spurt of excitement when she heard the names. "I certainly know those names. They're here? Close by?"

Sorina took a sip of her tea. "They could be anywhere. The point is, Dimitri is safe. He is surrounded by an enormous pack of wolves who accept him as one of their own. He has Ivory and Razvan with him, and his wife, Skyler. I think he is safe from any intruders who might wish him harm."

The relief Vasilisa felt was tremendous. There were so many other things she had to worry about. She didn't want to think she might have to rush out and check up on Dimitri's well-being. She would look for him eventually, but she was going to put him on the back burner until she discovered everything else that was going on—and she feared it was quite a bit.

"And the government men were asking about my brothers. Specifically Andros. All three of my brothers served their time in the military, and there are records. They are known to the government. They served with honor. It scares me that these men are here asking questions. Especially now."

"Why especially now, Vasi?" Sorina asked.

"Did you feel the tear in the earth? The tremor? There was a large seismic event a few days ago. It woke me up, nearly threw me right out of bed. The moment I went outside, I felt the tear. I heard wails of the dead. There is a vent open somewhere, and I have to find it, Sorina. I have to find a way to close it."

"You aren't telling me everything. I hear something in your voice. A reluctance to speak of it aloud."

Vasilisa sighed. She fiddled with the gold filigree on the small glass holder. "There is a prophecy in my family, handed down from mother to daughter, a very sacred one we never share with any other. Not a male sibling. Not our father. No one else." She looked up at Sorina. "My mother told me that a man would come to claim me, that he was my true mate. If he doesn't appear to claim me within a certain time period, and I'll know when, then I must marry a good man and pass the soul I guard to my daughter."

Sorina continued to look at her for a time in silence. She didn't object or say Vasilisa was crazy; she simply asked her a straight question. "Are you guarding a man's soul?"

"Yes. I feel him sometimes. He's close now. Very close. When I walked into the inn, I knew he was extremely near and that he'd been here."

Sorina let out her breath and reached across the table to touch Vasilisa's hand briefly. "You must be frightened."

"Very. Why aren't you telling me I'm insane?"

"Because I hold the other half of a man's soul as well," Sorina explained very calmly. "It's the way of my people. I know it isn't the way of yours. You know I'm Carpathian, and if your people knew who and what I am, they wouldn't accept me here. They're very superstitious.

Still, I've been coming here for a very long time, and we've been friends since you were a young child. I grew up with you. I'm not quite certain how you happen to carry a soul as well, but if you were told by your mother that you do, know it is very real, Vasilisa."

"My mother said it is my duty to guard his soul against any and all who might seek to take or destroy it. That if it is taken from me, he could destroy the world. He might be that powerful. Is that true as well?"

Sorina nodded slowly. "You're aware of vampires. You've seen the destruction they cause. You know what we guard together. That's even worse. Whoever you're lifemates with could be an ancient who has been in this world far too long. He might not be able to be contained by other hunters should you give up his soul. It would be a disaster. You have a huge responsibility."

Vasilisa nodded, running her finger along the rim of her glass. "My mother drilled that into me."

"Have you consulted the cards?"

"I live by the cards. You gave your blood to keep the cards alive and allow me to help you guard the gate, Sorina. I am very careful of the cards. I consult them daily. Today I drew the chariot. It was upright, staring right at me. It's a card of determination. Inner strength. It also can signal change, and in this case, I think it's screaming change."

Sorina smiled at her. "The attributes sound like you. You're always determined, and you have more inner strength than anyone I know."

"When I dealt the cards today, I realized the hand wasn't for me alone. The chariot was for *him* as well. He has determination and inner strength. His willpower is strong. He is so strong I *felt* him as I was laying out the cards." She pressed her hand over her heart where the goddess card was protected at all times. "Sorina, I know he was aware of me. He *felt* me. We somehow connected. He's that strong. I didn't understand how he could have connected with me when I wasn't looking for him or expecting to find him."

Sorina's white teeth bit down on her lip. Vasilisa noticed that two of her teeth appeared just a little sharper than the others. Instead of detracting from her looks, the teeth only enhanced her beauty.

"Why do you look so worried? You need for this man of yours to be strong. You're in an untenable position, Vasi. You have to protect everyone, and suddenly you've become vulnerable through no fault of your own. You are going to need help. His help. All along, you must have known this. Your mother must have told you when she said he was coming."

Vasilisa pushed back her dark hair. "I had my girlish fantasies," she admitted. "It isn't the same thing as facing a real living man in the flesh. For all I know, he could be a raving madman bent on ruling me. You know that's not going to happen."

Sorina smiled. "I know he might try. He's Carpathian. The males were born with an attitude. They speak the ritual binding words and you're stuck together. That gives them an advantage."

"Carpathian?" Vasilisa all but spat the word at her. "I don't want him to be Carpathian. Do you know how much trouble I have as it is hiding what I am from my brothers? From my people? Can you imagine what it would be like trying to hide it from him? I don't think you can have secrets from Carpathians."

Sorina shook her head. "You're right about that. For one thing, he wouldn't stand for it, and for another, he'll be able to read your mind."

"Just great. I mean, that's just great." Vasilisa slumped back in her chair. "As if I didn't have enough problems. I'm going to avoid him."

"What does the chariot mean as far as the relationship goes?" Sorina sounded curious.

Vasilisa looked at her suspiciously. "Did you just read my mind?"

"No, of course not. I promised you I wouldn't unless you gave me your permission. It's just that if you're going to believe in the cards, you have to actually believe everything, not just pick and choose what you want to take from them."

Vasilisa waved her hands in the air. "It doesn't always work like that, Sorina. Card readings are never absolute."

"Most cards readings aren't, because they aren't *your* card readings," Sorina corrected. "You don't want to tell me."

Vasilisa sighed. She didn't want to tell her, but she knew she was going to, so she might as well get it over with. "Fine. It's time to move forward with confidence in my relationship. But that could mean our relationship. My relationship with my brothers."

Sorina's laughter was bright. Joyous. Musical. The sound, although soft, dispersed the blanket of negativity in the room, replacing it with cheer. The flames in the fireplace responded, leaping and springing higher, throwing orange and red figures dancing on the walls. The competing conversations vying for air space grew animated and happy, voices soaring with enthusiasm.

"You don't lie very well," Sorina told her.

Vasilisa flung herself backward in her chair again. "I know. I've never been able to tell a decent lie. I used to try, but I always got caught. Fine. I've got this impression of a massive man. Not in terms of his body but his brain. One who is very intelligent, quick-witted and stubborn as hell. He goes his own way." She frowned, concentrating. "I just got a small glimpse of him, but his mind is a minefield."

"What does that mean?"

"All joking aside, he's scary, Sorina, and very dangerous. I just caught a glimpse of what he's capable of."

"When a Carpathian male is born, his soul is split. He retains the darkness, and the light is given to the female to protect. It is his responsibility to find her. He loses his ability to see in color and feel emotion when he is around two hundred years old. Sometimes it happens to him much earlier, depending on the circumstances. He hunts the vampire and searches for his lifemate. There is only one woman who can restore color and emotions back into his life. If he lives for centuries, can you imagine how difficult it would be killing old friends or even those he grew up with in his family? Seeing people from his village die? It wouldn't matter if he had emotions or not, it would still register somewhere."

Truthfully, Vasilisa couldn't imagine such an existence. "Why in the world would fate complicate his life even more by matching him with someone like me? I'm the absolute worst of the worst as far as matches go."

Sorina shrugged. "You may think that . . ."

"I *know* it. He'll be under such scrutiny. The moment I show any interest at all in a male, my brothers are going to study him with a magnifying glass. You know they will. Then it will be the villagers. Not one or two, *all* of them. And we don't know if we're compatible. I've become someone different. He might not like that."

Suddenly, a headache came out of nowhere, her temple pounding. It came on fast, a hard punch over her left eye that felt as if someone had shoved a hot poker into her skin, right through her bone. It was excruciatingly painful, so much so that she clapped her palm over the offending spot with a soft cry.

"What is it?" Sorina asked.

"Pain," she managed to gasp out. "It's bad."

Sorina reached out and gently removed Vasilisa's hand to place her two fingers over the pounding spot. She closed her eyes and inhaled sharply. "Vasi, let me in for just a moment."

Vasilisa hesitated and then opened her mind to her friend. The pain was so bad she knew she needed help. She didn't want to cause a scene in front of everyone. At the moment, they were in a secluded corner where no one was paying attention to them, but if she began vomiting, everyone would look.

"This isn't your pain," Sorina said. "This is his. You have to disconnect from him. You're feeling a kind of echo of what he's enduring."

"His pain? What's happening to him? What do you mean, echo?" If she was feeling just a portion of what he was feeling, he needed help. She had to find him. She kept one hand pressed tightly over her eye.

"He's in some kind of battle. Sit down, Vasi. That's what these men do. They go after vampires. Evidently, he's found one."

"You don't know that. He's in wolf country. He could have stumbled onto a large pack." She sank back into the chair she hadn't realized she'd vacated.

"It didn't feel like wolves to me."

"Or worse. When the earthquake occurred, it opened a vent to the underground. I think something evil is escaping," Vasilisa continued. "He could need assistance. That's what I'm trained for. Even if he's an expert in vampire fighting, it isn't the same thing as battling demons from the underworld."

She rubbed at her head and started to make a deliberate attempt to disconnect from the man who she was supposedly destined to be with for the rest of her life. She stopped. She would need a way to find him. Perhaps distancing herself just a little bit would ease the ache in her head.

The door opened, allowing a blast of cold air in. The flames rolling over the logs in the fireplace flared into bright, hot tongues of fury. A sudden hush fell over the bar as the newcomers came inside, stomping the snow from their boots and removing their scarves, gloves and hats.

Sorina leaned across the table. "I can't take the chance of being seen. They're certain to come over to talk to you."

Vasilisa knew it was true. She wasn't going to get out of the inn without a conversation with at least one of the government agents. They were looking for members of the monarchy, and she was sitting right there.

"Thanks for coming, Sorina."

"I'll try to help you when you need it," Sorina promised. The lights in the inn flickered and dimmed—just for a moment. Even the flames in the fireplace settled low. Sorina simply vanished. As she did, the tea service in front of Vasilisa became for one, not two. There was no evidence that she had been sitting with anyone, enjoying an evening out.

Vasilisa had gotten used to Sorina's comings and goings over the years. When she didn't want to be seen, she simply faded away. The Carpathian race had their secrets, just as she had her own. She sat back in her seat, rubbing at the painful spot in her head, breathing deep and doing her best to touch the man she was connected to through her mind.

The bridge between them was extremely strong. She had no idea what he looked like or where he was. She knew nothing about him— only that he was hers. She had to work at clearing her mind, something she could usually do very quickly, but the throbbing pain in her head was very distracting—and worrisome. She also kept an eye on the government agents. So far, they hadn't spotted her in the corner of the room. Some of the villagers had deliberately stood in front of her little table, further obscuring her from the view of the outsiders.

She had to hurry and take advantage of the opportunity they were giving her. What could she read about him personally? And what could she see of his surroundings? She knew her land intimately. She'd walked every inch of it, mapped it out in her head, and she never got turned around or lost. That was another gift from her heritage.

He was a vicious fighter. A brilliant strategist. She was, too. They would mesh well there. She liked that they had that in common. She needed to hold on to anything they might share. As a rule, he didn't mingle with human society, avoiding people other than to feed. He was highly intelligent and well versed in magic, capable of outthinking or outsmarting most master vampires, but often he preferred to engage in battle with them. Why?

His brilliant mind alone should have prevented him from making the decision to fight with an enemy when he didn't have to. What was he doing? Why would he put himself in harm's way if he didn't have to? She tried to get an impression of where he was.

"Vasilisa Sidkorolyavolkva?" One of the four strangers stood at the side of her table, staring down at her with hawklike eyes. "I have a few questions to ask you. Do you mind if I join you?"

She didn't care for the way he was looking at her. There was just a little too much male interest. She forced a smile. "I was just leaving, but perhaps I could stay for a few minutes. Not long, though." She glanced toward the bar, where she knew Odessa would be waiting for any kind of signal from her. She indicated the tea set with a small lift of her chin. Odessa hurried through the crowd to retrieve the tea server, never saying a word that part of it was missing.

Around the table, several of the villagers crowded close, cutting off the stranger from his companions as he slipped into the seat Sorina had vacated.

"My name is Nikolay Sokolov and I served with your brother Andros. We were good friends for many years and then lost touch. He told me he lived in a remote village, but honestly, I never considered it was *this* remote." He gave her a quick grin that was mostly teeth. The smile didn't reach his eyes. He waited several heartbeats, but she didn't reply. What was there to say?

So far, she couldn't detect a lie. Nikolay Sokolov had probably served with Andros in the military. They certainly could have been friends. Once Andros was home, it was more than likely they had lost touch.

"There's a rumor that Andros is royalty, that these people follow his rule rather than the government's."

It wasn't a question, but Vasilisa first stared at him with shock on her face and then burst out laughing. "Surely a man as intelligent as you appear to be hasn't fallen for that persistent rumor. Our home, which is on the old palatial grounds, keeps those rumors alive. I must tell my brothers we should burn down the existing house rather than modernize it. Renovations are very costly, so we can only do a little at a time. How utterly ridiculous that you would think they would turn against the government when my brothers served our country with distinction and were honored to do so." She kept her tone light but with just a touch of contempt. She'd perfected that touch over the years.

Nikolay's eyes were sharp. Shrewd. A chill slid down her spine. This man was an adversary worth watching. He was most likely an interrogator. The worst of it was, she could smell treachery. The stink of betrayal. Someone in her village was talking to this man. That meant she would have to ferret out who they were being betrayed by and why.

She didn't like the way his gaze moved over her face and down her body. "I'll let Andros know you're staying here at the inn and would like to visit with him."

"Forgive me for asking a personal question, but I don't see any evidence that you have been claimed by a man as of yet."

Her stomach clenched hard. They were on very dangerous ground. She forced a pleasant smile. "I do have a man," she said simply. "I really must go." Vasilisa stood up decisively, dragging on her gloves and fitting her hat on her head. She pulled her white fur coat more closely around her, making certain the buttons were in place.

"You have no escort?"

"This is my home, Nikolay Sokolov." She inclined her head to show respect to him. He was older, the same age as her brother. "I have no need of an escort, but thank you for your concern." She turned to leave.

"You truly are a beautiful woman." The compliment slipped out almost as if he couldn't help himself and hadn't been expecting it. "Your brother has hidden you away from the world."

She smiled at him. "My brother knows I do not do well away from the forest and mountains. I can't breathe in the cities. Here, he protects me."

"And this man of yours?"

"He is the same." She hoped she spoke the truth. She had no way of knowing whether she did or not. She knew nothing of the man whose soul had been handed down from mother to daughter and guarded so carefully for centuries. Only that he was close now and that he was in trouble.

She lifted a hand, gave Nikolay Sokolov an enigmatic smile and moved into the crowd. They parted to allow her through so she could get to the door. Behind her, they closed ranks, making it nearly impossible for Nikolay Sokolov or his three companions to follow her quickly. By the time they made it outside, she was gone. They couldn't even find her tracks in the snow.

2

Vasilisa raced through the larch forest going up the mountain toward the area she had always known as Drifter's Point. It was a rocky, cavernous, treacherous overhang that dropped steeply into a deep gorge. She was fairly certain the man she had connected with was somewhere near Drifter's Point. She had the impression of that terrain. She ran fast, her feet skimming the snow, making ten- and fifteen-foot leaps to save time.

Urgency was on her now. That whisper of conspiracy. She tasted a hint of betrayal in her mouth as she raced up the mountain. She was connected to all her people through her bloodline. If one fell, she was aware. If one turned, she knew. But which one, that was always the question.

A trap had been set, and she was running straight toward it. Vasilisa swerved off the trail, slowing to consider what to do. She needed to get to her destination, but she had to find those lying in wait for her and dispose of them first. She didn't dare have them at her back.

Removing her boots, she plunged her bare feet into the snow, driving down as far as she could go, seeking a connection with the earth. She felt a disturbance approximately three miles up the mountain, close to the point. She took her time, letting the connection grow. Four men. All four were her kind. Her people.

For a moment, she felt anger flare, hot and bright, the rage that could take hold and destroy all discipline, destroy all thinking, reducing her from intellect to animal in one flash of fire. Her hands hurt, knuckles popping and fingernails burning. Her toenails sizzled in the snow, fiery, scorching, and she knew if she looked at them, they would be bright red.

She had a choice. She could annihilate her enemy—perhaps—or she could stay in control and know for certain she could do it by using her brain. They could simply shoot her if she threw herself at them like an animal, and she would never know whether or not she could have defeated them had she kept her wits about her. With effort, she pushed down the animalistic temper and regained control of herself.

Vasilisa shoved her boots into the larger inside pockets of her coat and once more began the approach to Drifter's Point. This time, she stayed off the accepted path, using the cover of the trees. She called softly to the owls in the area to spy for her. There were several red squirrels in trees near the site where the conspirators waited to ambush her. The squirrels eagerly accepted her orders.

She couldn't call in the wolf pack. That would be too dangerous, considering there were four betrayers waiting, but there was a vicious little wolverine skulking close to the icy stream not too far from where the four men waited somewhat impatiently for her arrival. She touched it. Wolverines were tricky. This one was female. Sometimes they were cooperative; other times, not so much. Mind-to-mind images with animals didn't always work, but she was adept at it, and wolverines were intelligent. This creature had no problem helping her. Vasilisa cautioned her to be careful of any weapons the men might have.

She was within striking distance of the four Lycans now. One betrayer was close. She recognized him and her heart sank. Her twin brothers, Garald and Grigor, had grown up with him, gone to school with him, served with him. They counted him as a friend. In the evenings, they often met with him at the inn to talk and drink and have a good time. She couldn't imagine what would have convinced Alik Bykov to betray her family and their people. She knew her brothers, as tough as they were, would be brokenhearted.

"I thought you said she would be here any minute, Alik," one of the men groused, lying prone in the snow covered in a white snowsuit.

"You need to keep your voice down, Gav Sobol," Alik hissed. "She has very good hearing."

"She's a woman. It isn't like she's going to give us much trouble," a third man said. He was also dressed in snow gear. He had the air of a man in charge and looked bored out of his mind. He sat in the snow with a large knife cradled in his hands.

Alik sent him a pitying look. "Brody Portnov, you know this family is no ordinary family. They have skills. All of them, including Vasilisa. Just because she's a woman, you shouldn't underestimate her. She is very experienced with weapons, and she'll try to fight her way free."

"You say she will come on a mercy run in order to try to save a stranger trapped and hurt in the gorge," said the fourth man. "Why would she have weapons on her? She would bring bandages. Blankets. Aid for him, not weapons." He stood just off the trail, his hands on his weapons.

"She has an affinity with the mountains, Arman Botnik," Alik proclaimed. "She always knows when someone is hurt, and she goes to help them. She'll come this way. It's the only safe way to get down to the gorge. And she'll have weapons on her because no one is safe traveling in this wild place alone."

"I've heard rumors that she is as good as her brothers," Arman admitted, "but I've never seen her in action."

Vasilisa didn't know the other three men at all. They clearly came from another area, outside the territory of the royals. In some ways, she was grateful. It was difficult enough knowing Alik had betrayed them. Having four of her kind that she knew personally would make this battle all the more sorrowful.

A red squirrel raced across the ground, nearly running over the top of Gav Sobol, the man lying in the snow just to the left of the trail. A great gray owl came out of the night like a phantom and swooped low silently, stealthily, huge talons outstretched in an effort to reach its prey. It missed but tore straight into Gav's face, raking his eyes nearly out of his head before the wings beat hard, taking the bird into the air and out of sight into the trees. Gav screamed, dropped his gun, covered his face and rolled over.

At the same time, the red squirrel had backtracked, spinning around as if frightened by the presence of all the men and scurrying straight at Brody Portnov. The squirrel landed in Portnov's lap, looked up at him and then burrowed down between his legs. Portnov tried to shove at the little squirrel, first with his hand, and then he stabbed at it with the knife. The squirrel retaliated by biting down viciously and holding the bite between his legs.

Brody roared with rage, let go of the knife and tried to catch the small animal to tear it away and fling it off of him. Just as he put both hands around it, the wolverine rushed out of the trees straight at him, seemingly intent on claiming the squirrel for a meal. The dripping fangs closed around Brody's upper thigh close to his groin as he flung off the squirrel. The wolverine shook Brody's thigh and then retreated fast, leaving behind blood, a ring of bite marks and Brody swearing in Russian.

Vasilisa came out of the snow, a blur of movement, so fast that even Alik, who was expecting her, was unprepared for her speed. She slit the throat of Arman Botnik as she raced by, not even slowing to watch him fall. As she leapt over Brody Portnov, who was still sitting on the ground, she leaned down and stabbed his jugular. Her next step took her to Gav Sobol. He was lying faceup, still covering his eyes. She cut his throat and then was standing in front of Alik, looking beautiful. Serene. Without a single drop of blood on her. She had disposed of three armed men in less than three seconds.

"Alik. Lovely to see you. Our people have been informed that you have betrayed us. There is nowhere for you to go." Vasilisa watched him closely for any movement. He would be very dangerous. He knew she was going to kill him. He would never get off the mountain alive. Never. Every member of their people would be looking for him for the rest of his life. That included those who had left to live in other countries. They had hunters who were sent after rogues. Betrayers were far worse than rogues.

"You were so fast. I didn't even see you move."

She didn't respond to his comment. What could she say to that? She had been that fast. He would still think he could kill her.

"You don't have to tell me why you would do such a thing, but I would like to know. It seems so out of character for you. You have a mother. A sister. The disgrace and humiliation will be terrible for them to bear, unless, of course, they were in on this and encouraged you to plot against us."

Again, she was very careful to watch him closely. Every minute movement. His expression. His eyes. His mouth. There was a small wrinkle around his mouth when she mentioned his mother and sister. He hadn't liked that at all. His eyes had darkened. She waited, knowing sometimes words were too much. Silence could win battles.

"Oil." He mumbled the word. "It was the oil."

Her eyebrow went up. "The oil? You thought if you told the government about it, they would give you a piece of the profits? Seriously, Alik? You have to know better than that. The government takes. They don't give. They would employ many of you, but under difficult conditions, just like in the past. Too many people die under their watch. The oil field was abandoned after they left. When more was discovered, we took it to the council, and they voted against talking to the government, Alik. Your mother sits on the council. She voted against it."

"She was wrong." He was gearing up to make his move.

"She wasn't."

"We all could have lived in luxury instead of living in this place." He gestured around him and leapt at her.

She was no longer where she had been. She gutted him as she slipped by—a blur, impossible to see. She was that fast because she had secrets of her own. He should have taken into consideration that she'd killed all three of the men he had brought with him, and he hadn't been able to follow along with his eyes because she'd been too fast.

Alik's body shuddered. Both hands came up to hold his entrails in as he went to his knees. "What are you?" he whispered.

Her people had a collective mind. One didn't confess secrets, because secrets crossed mind barriers sometimes. "Royal blood runs in my veins, Alik. You should never have forgotten that fact simply because I'm a woman." Let him put her speed down to that. Let them all put her speed and capabilities down to that.

She leaned down and ended his life, not so much out of compassion for him but out of necessity. Somewhere in the gorge was the bait. Whoever had trapped the stranger there hadn't been betrayers. The man in the gorge was Carpathian, a vampire hunter. He could easily have disposed of most of her kind. Something else had been brought into play, something far more sinister.

She raced up the narrowing pathway to Drifter's Point, her mind trying to fit the government agent she'd encountered at the inn with Alik and the others she'd killed. For some reason, it just didn't compute for her. The oil didn't seem like something a man like Nikolay Solokov would be sent to Siberia to inquire after, especially when he was doing so in a roundabout way.

Once she reached the top of Drifter's Point, where the snow was at its highest peak, she looked down into the steep slopes below. The canyon walls were narrow, nearly straight up and down. Ice formations appeared like sculpted figurines climbing up the snow-covered trees that stuck out of the sides of the canyon walls. Anywhere the rocks shone through the white snow appeared a shiny black, an ominous warning of thick ice, sheets of it.

She leapt over the ridge, barely allowed her foot to touch, skimmed in the snow and lifted again to cover a good thirty feet, then repeated the action until she hit the floor of the gorge. She landed in a silent crouch on both feet and froze, only her eyes moving, searching around her for any sign of movement. She listened to pick up the natural rhythm of the earth.

With her bare feet, she was able to feel the heartbeat, catch the movement of small rodents skittering along the top of the sparse vegetation that had fallen from the few trees that clung to the floor of the narrow gorge. She tapped her chest over her heart until she matched the same beat.

In the distance, she caught the faint sound of air moving through labored lungs. There he was. She had him now. She waited until she was positively certain that this was the man she was connected to. *Her* man. The man whose soul she guarded so carefully. She began to match that labored breathing, allowing her lungs to take on the same ragged gasps struggling for air. Once they were in perfect sync, she began to even the two of them out slowly. He became aware of her instantly.

He went from near unconsciousness to his mind on complete alert. She felt him pushing into her mind, and he was extremely strong. Like a battering ram. A tidal wave.

Be careful, she cautioned. *There are others who might overhear if you aren't cautious. How badly are you injured?*

He didn't withdraw from her, but he remained silent as though thinking whether or not he was going to answer her. *You are?*

She sighed. She should have known he would ask. There was no getting around this. *Vasilisa Sidkorolyavolkva. And you?*

I am called Afanasiv Belan. Or Siv for short. The daughter of the royal wolf, he mused. *Are you aware of what you are to me?*

Vasilisa didn't know if it was because they were speaking telepathically to one another that his voice stroked and caressed like a deep, husky velvet brush. Soft. Gentle. He sounded as if he belonged to the night, just as she did. She only knew it was one of the most sensual experiences of her life.

She wanted to lie to him. She didn't belong to any man. She was her own person and she went her own way. He was the one who needed help, not her. She didn't say any of that. *Yes, of course. I connected to you when you were first injured. Your head.*

Forgive me. Had I known, I would not have allowed you to feel anything. You must leave this place. I will find you once I know you are safe.

Her belly grew hot, and she knew her temper was fighting for supremacy. She hadn't just sauntered down a brick road to get to him. She'd fought a battle and killed men to make certain he was all right. He was laid out like bait in a trap. He *was* bait in a trap. He'd been nearly unconscious when she'd first arrived. A small kernel of doubt seeped in. Hadn't he? He'd come alert awfully fast. Had he been faking?

I do not allow strangers to be accosted on my lands without retaliation. In any case, I believe they are using you as bait to draw me to them. It would be nice to know why.

I wanted the answer to that question. That is why I am lying here on the ground looking pathetic with my head bleeding. They did a poor job of weaving magic to tie me to the earth.

How many? And describe them, please. She ignored his high-handed order to leave. She was born into the house of Korolyavolk—the royal wolf. She *was* royalty, and while she didn't hold that over the head of her people, no stranger was going to tell her what to do on her own land.

You are one of the very modern women who simply ignores anything her partner wants or needs.

She felt him heave a tremendous sigh. It was there in his mind. She might have found humor in the situation, but there was something else she caught a glimmer of—the smallest of scars, although its thickness gave her pause. That scar shouldn't have been there in his mind. It wasn't a barrier. He had those in abundance, hard walls she couldn't penetrate, nor was she attempting to do so. That thick scar wasn't actually in his mind; he'd been thinking of it in some conjunction with him. Sorrow had been instantly overwhelming.

She glimpsed startling shades of color, bright visions he tried to suppress or tone down. She got all of that in that one small glimmer that came through on their extraordinarily narrow connection. He was extremely good at keeping the energy from a telepathic connection from spilling into the air around them.

She went back over the words he had used. *Ignore anything her partner wants or needs.* He had used the word *partner,* a good thing. Why would he need or want her to leave him in a dire situation? *You came with other men? Are you alone, or are they here waiting to help you when this trap is sprung?* That had to be the answer. He had his friends secreted close by, and they had the situation well in hand. He was afraid she would tip off his assailants, and they wouldn't show themselves.

No, I am afraid it is just me that came in this direction. We set out in different directions looking for Dimitri, a friend of ours. He resides here a good portion of the year. We thought it best to find him without calling out. There are vampires in the area. You seem a bit overrun at the moment with enemies.

She thought it sweet that he didn't ask her if she knew Dimitri or where his residence was. Clearly, he didn't want her to have to give up a friend or deceive him.

Yes, I ran into a betrayer and three of his associates on my way to aid you. They are dead, and I'll have to send someone to deal with their bodies.

There are four government agents staying at the inn. I don't trust them at all. They were making inquiries about my brother. One specifically asked me if I had a man.

You told him you did.

He made it a statement.

There was a perverse part of her that wanted to deny it. *I did.*

Thank you, my lady. I would have no problem challenging him to a duel or fighting for the honor and privilege of your hand, but I fear I am far too ancient. The years have not been kind to my soul.

She tried not to allow her heart to accelerate. If she could feel emotions through the earth, he might be able to. He was an ancient. That was bad—really bad. Sorina had spoken briefly to her about ancients and how they sometimes locked themselves away in a hidden monastery somewhere in the Carpathian Mountains. The monastery was covered in clouds and a mysterious fog that kept Carpathians and humans alike from going near it. The ancients entering the monastery were extremely dangerous men, and it would take multiples of their strongest experienced hunters to destroy them should they ever turn. She had paid close attention to the lore of Sorina's culture—it had been fascinating to her. Now, facing the possibility of having an ancient as the man she would spend the rest of her life with was daunting.

She wasn't a coward, and she refused to flinch away from what she had been raised from birth to be. Fate had destined them to be together. She wouldn't run now. They were together for a reason. She had a certain set of skills, as did Afanasiv Belan. Those skills had to somehow mesh together. When they were somewhere safe, they could discuss how.

Why would you want me to leave if you are trapped with no one to aid you?

The trap is set to capture you. They are luring you here. There are vampires, and they have conspired with demons. They are after the other half of my soul. They know you guard it, and they intend to force you to give it up.

How would they force me to do that?

Torturing someone you hold dear is usually where they would start. They might torture me in front of you, but I doubt they would try. I have been subjected to torture many times over the centuries and did not break. You have not had such a pleasure, so they could decide to start on you. There was a distinct edge to his voice and mind when he introduced that possibility.

Vasilisa was caught on a couple of things. He had been tortured numerous times, and he made that sound as if it were nothing. And someone she cared about might be tortured in order for her to give up his soul. Now she did have to work at keeping her body completely in tune with the earth, matching the heartbeat, keeping her breathing even so there was no possible way even a demon created for the sole purpose of reporting movement on the surface of the earth would be able to detect her.

If I didn't come along, what were you going to do?

I hoped to pull the image of you from the one they have prisoner and bring you innocently traveling along to rescue me.

He made it sound like she was going to be walking along the yellow brick road with a picnic basket. It took her a moment to realize he'd deliberately pushed the image into her head to make her smile—not to make her head explode. She needed a better sense of humor. *How do you know about the yellow brick road?*

One of my friends, Dragomir, reads to his daughter quite often. He thinks it is good for all of us to read to children. He claims it makes us sensitive.

He sent her the image of a bull in a china shop destroying shelf after shelf of very fine china. She found herself smiling in spite of the situation. Her smile faded when she realized the vampires and demons had another prisoner.

Who do they have?

He didn't want her to know, obviously, or he would have informed her by now. She tasted fear in her mouth for the first time.

Do not react when I tell you. We will free him. Your brother Garald. The man you called a betrayer delivered him into their hands.

I will be walking along the path and allow them to think they can attack me.

You cannot, lifemate. The one person more dangerous than any other is me. If you were to succumb to their desires and give up the other half of my soul to save your brother, I would be lost. They could command me. There are none here that could defeat me in battle. My friends would try, but I doubt it is possible unless Dimitri, Razvan, Ivory and even Skyler join them. You must not risk such a thing.

Vasilisa bit down hard on her lip. She heard the urgency in his voice and felt it in his mind. He meant every word. *Tell me how to keep your soul safe and how we can save my brother.*

He was silent for so long she was afraid he didn't have any ideas, but then he sighed. *You are not Carpathian. You are not familiar with the ways of our people.* It was a statement.

I have a friend who is Carpathian. We grew up together, so I am not completely ignorant of Carpathian culture.

You have heard of the Carpathian binding ritual.

Vasilisa had known all along that might be the only solution. Her mother had told her the story of how her lifemate might come to her to reclaim his half of their soul. When she had asked Sorina, she had explained the lifemate ritual in great detail. There was only one woman for each man, and he would bind her to him, tying them together when he wove their soul back together again by reciting the sacred binding words. Once said, his soul would be intact—whole once again. There would be no way for the demons or vampires to trap Afanasiv and take his soul.

I have. That would bind us together. You would have no choice but to accept me as your lifemate, Afanasiv Belan, once you said those words to me.

That is correct. And you would have to accept me. We could not stand to be apart from each other.

She moistened her lips. *I wish for you to say the binding words to me for many reasons, not the least of which is to restore your soul to you and to save my brother, but I had thought we would have time to talk about other things first.* She didn't want to be honest. She wanted to save her brother. She wanted to do her duty and save her people. She really did want to restore his soul to him and relieve his terrible suffering, but she had been raised to be honorable. She sensed that he was an honorable man. She refused to be less. *There are important things that you should know about me. Things you have a right to know about me before you take me for a lifemate.*

There was no shame in her voice. She didn't feel shame. She loved who she was and was very proud, but no one could ever know. She kept secrets from her people. From her brothers. From everyone she loved. They wouldn't accept her. She would be banished—or worse. She knew her people needed her, but she would be asking this honorable man to live with her. Worse—eventually he would become like her, and others would hunt him relentlessly if they ever discovered his secrets.

My lady, you humble me. You believe whatever secrets you harbor are worse than what I have acquired in the centuries I have lived and hunted. Before you confess, I must go first. If you refuse to be bound to me, there will be no need for you to give up your secrets.

Right there was one extremely good reason to call him a noble man. He had interrupted her before she could blurt out something that might damn her in his mind. He was willing to tell her his worst sins and let her judge him first. Her heart gave a strange little flutter, the first of its kind. She'd never had such a reaction, and she found her dire situation a strange place for it to happen.

Carpathian hunters lose parts of their blackened souls with the countless kills they make. They end up with that half of their soul in tatters. A lifemate can repair this damage when he finds her and she restores his color and emotions. When the two halves of his soul are once more woven together. But when a Carpathian warrior has lived far past his time—and it can happen, when he has killed too many times—something else begins to take place. Another change happens.

A chill slid down her spine. He was going to confess something that would be really difficult to take—maybe. Perhaps not. She straightened her shoulders and laid her hands palm up on her knees. She was the daughter of the family of the royal wolves. She had special gifts. She'd been trained by her mother from the time she was a toddler and told that she was the lifemate of a Carpathian male, and she was to be prepared to defend him and their children from demons and vampires. She had a destiny. A legacy. There was the prophecy, and so far, the ugly thing was right on the money. Vasilisa was not a woman who would ever back away from a fight. She certainly wouldn't run from her lifemate because he had a few unfortunate character flaws. Hers just might match his.

For centuries we endure the whisper of temptation to kill while we feed so we can once again feel the rush. Just feel. That temptation, at times, is difficult to resist, but honor keeps us from ever giving in. We live the code of our hunters, waiting for our lifemate. Then comes that moment when even the whisper of temptation goes silent, and there is absolutely nothing at all. Nothing. You believe the whisper is the worst, but it isn't. That silence is.

She took air into her lungs—the fresh snow pack that had just fallen in the early morning hours. It was still so pristine in most of the gorge. She was impervious to the ice, not even feeling it against the bare soles of her feet. She breathed for both of them. Vasilisa and Afanasiv.

I realized that where before my soul had become tattered, torn into so many holes it seemed impossible to repair, now there were scars developing on it. Thick, dark scars that I couldn't remove in spite of having knowledge of healing skills. I have good skills with magic and I could not overcome these scars. The more I hunted the vampire and went into battle, the more I seemed to feel something when I fought. Before I planned carefully and would barely have a scratch, but I needed the brutality of the battle. It gave me a strange kind of vicious rush. When I hadn't felt anything in centuries, that euphoria became addicting.

She had seen one of those scars. A glimpse only, but she knew what he was talking about. *Is it possible for me to remove the scars?*

One of my brethren, Sandu, has a lifemate, and she was unable to do so. I try not to allow the weight of those scars to rule me in battle, but it is difficult to overcome that need. I can be more brute than human in those moments.

How is my brother doing?

They worry that they struck him too hard. Your brother and I agreed it would be best that they thought him unconscious, so I have kept him that way.

I can live with the fact that you struggle against becoming more of a brute during battle.

Liking it too much, my lady. Wanting to make the kill. This is against my code of honor.

It isn't if whatever you are doing battle with is evil. I trust you never kill an innocent.

That would not be likely.

Then I can accept your secret, Afanasiv Belan. I hope that you can accept mine. I told you that I have a friend who is Carpathian. We grew up together and have spent time together over many years. We have other friends we occasionally have traveled a great distance to see. Spain, Italy, the border of Algeria.

He was horrified. She could tell he was. She felt his protest, but he didn't voice it.

We often went alone to see our friends, and as two girls, teens and then young women, we got into a bit of trouble. We managed to get out of it, but not always unscathed. Sometimes that required giving her blood. Sometimes, if I was severely wounded, she would have to give me blood. We had no idea that, over the years, by saving each other's life, we would make the other one into something beyond what they already were. Carpathians exist on blood.

The only real difference for her is that now she has the ability to walk into sunlight during the day if she desires. She's faster, stronger, and she can tolerate the sun if she needs to. It is uncomfortable for her, but she can do it if necessary to save her life. And she can tolerate drinking tea. There was the slightest amusement in her voice.

There was a small silence again, and she sobered instantly. He knew of the war that had just barely been avoided between Lycan and Carpathian. No one wanted to speak of it. Certainly, there on the mountain they didn't, not where Dimitri had a residence and where he'd worked so hard to keep the land safe for the wolves.

Dimitri had been at the very heart of that war. He had been taken to a war camp deep in the forests of Russia and hung by silver, allowing the silver to drop into his body, killing him slowly. They had wrapped him in silver so he couldn't call out to his Carpathian brethren and let them know where he was. No one had counted on the bond between him and his lifemate, Skyler. With two of her friends, she had tracked and saved him. Dimitri would forever bear the scars of the silver. The Lycans would forever bear the shame of that underhanded treachery.

Even though she knew every Lycan said aloud that they condemned what the rogues had done to Dimitri, she knew they secretly feared him and wanted nothing to do with him. He had been a longtime resident of their world and had done such good, yet they would shun him—or even side with the rogues over his horrendous treatment.

Afanasiv was an ancient. He understood exactly what she was saying. Her Carpathian friend had exchanged blood too many times with her over the years. They both had become something different. Vasilisa was no longer pure Lycan. Sorina was no longer pure Carpathian. The combination of the two species gave them the best of both worlds, so much so that the advantages were frightening to the Lycans. They sought to eradicate any who were of mixed blood.

She wasn't a pureblood anymore, and she never would be again. If

Afanasiv bound her to him, he would take her blood. Over the years they would exchange blood, and eventually, no matter how careful they were, he would be as she was. And then there was the matter of children. Lifemates for Carpathians were very scarce, and all couples hoped to produce children, especially females to aid their brethren. They hoped that the females would be reborn carrying the soul of a Carpathian hunter who had lived a life of honor. Her child would be of mixed blood.

She waited for his condemnation. Just knowing that their child would bear the consequences of her actions was enough to justify his censure. Still, she refused to bow her head. She hadn't known. Even if she had, they had saved each other's life. The exchanges they'd made had been necessary.

You expect that I will turn away from the woman I have waited centuries for because she is extraordinary? I carved an oath into my back for you. A code of honor so that when I was lost, I would know you were there with me, and I had a reason to hold on in the darkest of times. In that never-ending silence, I had you with me. I would imagine that I would hear you whisper to me to hold on, that you were out in the world waiting for me to find you.

There was such nobility in the way he spoke, although she knew he wouldn't think so. How did she ever deserve such a man? He had spent centuries hunting vampires, defending his people, probably everyone else around him—and searching for her.

Bind us together, lifemate, so we can restore your soul. Once that is done, we can find out exactly what these demons, vampires and whoever else want with us and our people. She was very decisive. They'd had him too long. They'd had her brother too long. As far as she was concerned, they had been on her land far too long.

You have no doubts? Once I do this, my lady, I cannot take it back.

You see into my mind and feel what's in my heart. I have waited for you. I'm nervous, yes, but only because I do not yet know all of you. I do know the most important things. Your heart and soul. Your honor. Those are the traits

I hold in high esteem. We will come to know each other on the journey we take together.

I am honored that you were chosen to be my lifemate.

He was very soft-spoken, his voice like a velvet brush stroking along the walls of her mind, embedding his claim there with each exchange. She wasn't certain he needed ritual words to bind them.

When next he spoke, he did so in his own language, and she felt the power of the words imprinted on him long before his birth.

Te avio päläfertiilam. Éntölam kuulua, avio päläfertiilam. Vasilisa had learned quite a bit of the Carpathian language from Sorina over the years. She interpreted the words as Afanasiv spoke them:

You are my lifemate. I claim you as my lifemate.

Ted kuuluak, kacad, kojed. Élidamet andam. Pesämet andam. Uskolfertiilamet andam.

I belong to you. I offer my life for you. I give you my protection. I give you my allegiance.

Sívamet andam. Sielamet andam. Ainamet andam. Sívamet kuuluak kaik että a ted.

I give you my heart. I give you my soul. I give you my body. I take into my keeping the same that is yours.

Ainaak olenszal sívambin. Te élidet ainaak pide minan. Te avio päläfertiilam. Ainaak sívamet jutta oleny. Ainaak terád vigyázak.

Your life will be cherished by me for all time. Your life will be placed above mine for all time. You are my lifemate. You are bound to me for all eternity. You are always in my care.

She felt the difference as he uttered the powerful ritual words in his soft-spoken way. She would never be the same, but she didn't want to be. Tears burned in her eyes, but she lifted her chin, feeling dazzled and privileged at the knowledge that she was his lifemate—that destiny had chosen her for him. She believed him to be extraordinary.

You have not laid eyes on me, my lady. There was amusement in his voice.

I am about to. Be prepared for the innocent and foolish princess to come looking for her brother and the stranger. My brother is very adept with a sword. I have one I shall be giving him. Make certain he is in good enough shape to join our battle.

He has fought vampires and demons?

My brother has fought anything and everything needed to keep our lands safe. That is what royals do.

S now was a blinding white. Blinding. The gorge had many rocks
coated in thick ice that appeared a true black. Afanasiv had
seen in shades of gray for centuries, and the colors of white and
black dazzled with just the sliver of moon shining on them. Colors were
radiant—vivid—alive and moving behind his eyelids even when he
closed his eyes in order to lessen the impact. But those colors did nothing to prepare him for the sight of his lifemate. Not one little thing.
Vasilisa took his breath away.

In all the centuries of his existence, nothing and no one had ever
affected him the way she did. Every cell in his body was tuned to her.
Every part of his mind. His heart beat with hers. His soul, tattered and
scarred as it was, felt her without reaching. She was just there. She
claimed him. She didn't spend time considering or wondering. She
didn't reject him now that she could see the two halves put together.
She accepted him unconditionally. Siv felt the universe had handed
him a gift beyond any price.

She walked carefully along the narrow trail, not looking as if she
were a helpless young girl alone and lost. She looked alert and ready to
take on the enemy. That was what those hunting her expected, and

that was what she gave them. She was encased in white fur from her neck to her ankles, the slim coat hugging her lithe figure.

It was her eyes that caught him. She didn't shade them from the snow at all, as if the glare didn't bother her in the least. The color was a burning blue, like the hottest flame in a roiling fire or coldest ice of a glacier. It was the color a man could be lost in for the rest of his centuries.

White mist slowly began to swirl around her, creeping up from the floor of the gorge. The vapor appeared natural. He had noticed it first where the frozen waterfall was. The mist came off the ice in abundance, rising toward the night sky in beautiful waves and swirls, drawing the eyes, just like it was doing now as it swirled around Vasilisa.

Siv's mind computed that information quickly. The mist had been there all along, staying close to the floor rather than along the waterfall and tops of icy boulders. The formations the vapor made were what he found interesting. Those loops and whorls had caught his attention as the vapor drifted lazily toward the sky and eventually rose above the gorge. Now, he wondered about them.

Just what magic is your brother capable of?

Perhaps you should have made better use of your time and carried on an actual conversation with him instead of keeping him unconscious.

The note of amusement in her voice did unexpected things to his body. He had to allow the needs to move through him without processing them, just noting and enjoying them while he took in every detail of his lady. She was truly magnificent.

He was too concerned about my relationship to Dimitri. I do not answer questions about my brethren.

He would have been more concerned had you expressed interest in me. One teensy little question would have sparked an entire inquisition.

The moment I set foot on this land, I knew you were here. There was not a single doubt in my mind.

Siv had felt her with every step he took. He'd breathed her into his lungs as if she'd been stamped into every larch tree, every bush and rock. The ground held her imprint deep. She was everywhere.

He did not need to make inquiries about Vasilisa. He didn't want to call attention to the fact that he was hunting her. It was bad enough that they'd made the mistake of asking after Dimitri. They knew he had a home in the area and thought it wouldn't cause a problem asking where his residence was. That hadn't been the case. The people at the inn had been polite but had frozen up immediately, making it clear they weren't going to answer any questions regarding Dimitri or Skyler.

I believe I am being watched.

You are correct, Siv agreed. He nudged her brother, who lay next to him. "Quit faking. Your sister has arrived to rescue you."

Garald sat up with a fake groan. "Vasilisa. Did you bring me a present?"

"Naturally. I never leave home without one for you. I see you have found my man. I trust you put your time to good use and got the interrogation out of the way. Neither of you are really tied down, are you?"

Garald threw back the barbed cuffs that anchored him to the ground. "What do you mean, *your man*? Please tell me you have not been internet dating like the young girls are lately." He glared at Afanasiv, who was unimpressed.

"The idea is to appear a prisoner, Garald," Vasilisa reminded him.

Siv felt the earth beneath him shudder and shrink. Something foul had touched the surface. An abomination. He looked up to catch Vasilisa and her brother share a quick signal as they recognized that the loathsome, vile undead was close, contaminating everything it touched. He knew vampires left behind acid, killing trees and bushes, poisoning the ground and twisting wildlife into deadly mutations. They often created puppets out of humans, giving them a half life, promising to make them immortal but leaving them to feed on the blood and flesh of other humans. They took great delight in their agony and the mayhem they caused.

"The master vampire who has come here calls himself Prince Vitus. He has servants with him. Several of them. Two are of great consequence. Very old and experienced fighters. Rufus prefers to come straight at you, then at the last minute vanishes and comes in from behind. He will appear very handsome with few scars or former injuries. He is vain, and stroking his ego can trap him at times. Mars is all business. He is a bull and wants to be feared. His appearance reflects that. He will intimidate and do his best to confuse you with many tricks. Watch him closely. He'll move constantly, each time coming close and then moving away, using a hypnotic dance to keep you from realizing he is about to attack."

Afanasiv kept his voice low as he imparted the information to the two siblings. The vampires had excellent hearing. He didn't want them to realize they were readying for battle. He continued to act as if the head wound had nearly knocked him out. Garald had once again slumped down in the snow, hiding his freed hands with his body.

Siv could feel the earth shrinking away from the steps of the foul undead as they circled around the two wounded men and Vasilisa. She reacted as if she had just became aware of the danger, head up alertly, eyes flashing, one hand moving inside her coat as she tore open the buttons with the other so she could withdraw what looked like a ceremonial sword. She turned in a full circle, the small sword held above her head.

A scurrying of feet told him he had missed another enemy she had not. He dared to glance at Garald to see if he had known something else was with the vampires. He shook his head, eyes restless. Like Siv, he was looking for other enemies, as well.

"Vitus has several pawns he will sacrifice before he sends in Mars and Rufus. They'll direct the pawns. Vitus will be safe somewhere close by. I'll try to find him. He'll be a blight in the trees or a rock, mirrored in the ice somehow. He is very old and has learned ways to prolong his life that few know. At the first hint that the battle is not going his way, he will attempt to run. I must pursue him if I am at all capable. I cannot allow him to get away. He has destroyed entire villages in his petty need for revenge. He enjoys inflicting horrific pain on humans before he allows them to die. I cannot allow his life to continue."

He knew he was apologizing ahead of time to his lifemate. He didn't want her to judge him too harshly if he left her when he believed she was safe. Naturally, he would want to be with her now that he had found her, but he was a vampire hunter, and he had his duty to carry out. He would have to follow Vitus should he run.

She inclined her head slightly to acknowledge that she heard and understood him. He was connected to her, but he didn't have time to evaluate what she was thinking. The pawns had begun to scramble through the rocks to reach them.

"Fighting a lesser vampire is not easy, although I may have made it sound so," Siv continued. "They are in various stages of development, some barely able to function and some getting very close to emerging into fighting machines. You have to be extremely cautious."

He shouldn't have been so dismissive when he spoke of the pawns. Garald and Vasilisa acted so confident in their fighting abilities, it was easy to feel as if he needn't worry about them, but he wasn't going to take chances losing his lifemate when he'd just found her.

The pawns drew closer, showing themselves against the white backdrop of pristine snow. Most maintained the facade of the Carpathians they once were—tall, handsome men with long dark hair. Eyes were sunken in on some of them. A few had tiny little parasites crawling around their mouths and noses. One had only patches of hair on his head, the bald spots red and raw with a multitude of white parasites wiggling on his scalp.

"Have you seen any of them before?" Vasilisa asked him.

"My lady," he replied as gently as he could. "Had I seen them before, they would not be here now. Why do you still have the sword raised high in the air?"

She had barely glanced at the pawns, and they were drawing

closer. Her attention was riveted on something else—something he couldn't see. He had the vague impression of shadowy figures moving *under* the snow, but he couldn't be certain. It was almost as if he was looking too hard and wanted to find something. But he didn't for one moment dismiss his lifemate's curious concern. He had fought beside his brother Sandu and his lifemate, Adalasia, when she fought demons from the underworld. He had a bad feeling his lady was about to fight that same battle, only she would do so on her own.

"You know they are there," Afanasiv said.

Garald took a deep breath as he surveyed his opponents. "On the right, lover boy, what the hell is that? I thought vampires might be the worst of it, but no, that looks pretty damned revolting."

Even Vasilisa took her concentration off her surroundings for just one moment to glance to the right to see what her brother meant. "Oh. Ugh. Not looking good. I think his head is falling off."

"That is a puppet. A ghoul. Whatever you choose to call it. The vampire takes a human and makes him into a flesh-eating monster. In exchange for his soul, he will do anything the vampire commands, including murder his entire family, his own children, his parents, everyone he's ever known," Siv explained.

Vasilisa turned away from the sight of the puppet as he stumbled and clawed his way up the rocky hill in an effort to keep pace with the pawns.

"He will try to tear the flesh from your bones with his teeth if he gets close despite anything the vampire or the pawns tell him. Puppets have little or no self-control," Siv warned.

"Vasi," Garald whispered, sorrow permeating his voice, driving all cockiness away. "That's Mark. I sent him out to inspect the high meadow right after the quake. He's one of our best trackers. I saw strange tracks I couldn't identify. I would have gone myself, but I was called back by the council."

Vasilisa took a deep, steadying breath before she turned to inspect the puppet staggering up the hillside so determinedly. Siv wanted to step up and put his arms around her, something he'd never done in his life for anyone that he could recall. He could feel the grief coming off both brother and sister in waves.

"You can't allow them to know you know him or care that he is the way he is," he advised, aching for them. For her. He would have to destroy the puppet first, before either of them had a chance to think too much on how this man had gotten the way he was. "He is no longer the man you knew."

Garald started to say something, shook his head and went silent for a moment. "This isn't your fault. Vasilisa, whatever happens, loyalty and love."

"Loyalty and love," she murmured back to him. The ancient sword pointed into the sky, and she called out in her own language. "You cannot hide from the light." The sword blossomed into radiant light, a crystal heat that spread like the sun across the sky, encompassing the floor of the gorge where Siv and Garald feigned being captives. The sudden brightness illuminated the ice sculpture that was the waterfall, as well as the series of dark rocks the falls fell over and the pool of water below.

With Vasilisa's crystal light burning in the sky, the ice sculpture of the falls was magnificent. Nothing but nature could provide such a stunning display of beauty. Siv found it obscene that the swaying pawns, the puppets and the small, strange creatures emerging from beneath the ground at Vasilisa's command could possibly be anywhere in the same vicinity.

The vampires wailed and shrank back, trying to hide from the light. The creatures, seven of them, looked like crosses between small humans and large red or pink salamanders with enormous mouths. They had arms, legs and heads closely resembling those of a salamander, right down to suction cups on their feet and webbing between their toes. Their bodies were longer and shaped more humanoid. They crawled on their bellies toward Vasilisa in little stops and starts. The hideous noises they made sounded either like high-pitched shrieks that hurt the eardrums or excessively low notes that hurt the organs in the body.

Siv turned the sounds down until they were barely heard and then connected with Vasilisa to ensure she had been able to turn the sounds down as well. As a Carpathian and Lycan blend, she certainly was capable. She had done so. She gave him a haughty little chin lift.

Next, he touched her brother. Siv was extremely cautious reaching out to slip into her brother's mind. Garald seemed to be very sensitive to any energy moving around him. The moment it got close to him, Garald blocked it. It seemed to be an automatic response anytime outside energy came near him, which was intriguing.

Few things were new to him. He had seen demons. The hounds of hell. He knew the tricks of the master vampires. He had fought creatures he knew no name for. Garald was undoubtedly Lycan, and he was of a royal bloodline, but what exactly did that mean? Both Vasilisa and Garald possessed something very different in their makeup. He had thought, with Vasilisa, it was the combination of being Carpathian and Lycan, but now he realized it was far more than that.

Are you paying attention to the sickening abominations creeping closer to us?

I am always aware of the close proximity of any vampire, my lady. Have no fear. While you battle the demons, I will take care of the vampires and puppet.

The lesser vampires called out to the puppet to stop, the one Garald had named Mark. Siv could have told all of them that the ghoul was too far gone to hear anything. He wouldn't even recognize his master's voice. He had seen hundreds of them over the centuries, and this one exhibited all the signs of the last stages of decomposition. The skin was rotting and sloughing off his scalp, face and neck. His head was skewed to one side, his neck broken so the head bounced and flopped obscenely with every step.

The high-pitched shrieks and keening continued with every staggering step. Mark's arms were outstretched in front of him, but the skin had split open to reveal another set of raw muscles that were eaten through with the same rot. Worms crawled through the holes in the flesh and dropped to the ground, leaving behind tiny trails of smoke in the snow.

One of the vampires stepped directly in front of Vasilisa, albeit ten feet from her. Siv knew how fast the vampires could move. They had thrown up their arms to cover their faces, but they were moving their feet in a pattern, almost like a dance, swaying in a rhythm in an attempt to hypnotize her.

"Give up his soul to us now, or we will allow the puppet to eat your brother in front of you while he is still alive."

The vampire's voice was harsh, grating on the nerves. Vasilisa barely spared the vampire a glance, looking down her elegant nose at him.

"You are very welcome to try to feed my brother to your disgusting puppet, but I doubt if you are able to do so. A better suggestion, if you want to live, is to move on quickly before you try my patience."

Her voice was so sweet in comparison to the vampire's that it was difficult to adjust to the difference. Even the vampire shook his head as if he had to clear it. He stumbled and nearly went down. All the vampires hesitated in their dancing, swaying pattern as if they had lost their way. Siv realized there were mesmerizing notes of her own embedded in her voice.

Another voice snapped them all back to attention, rapping out a harsh command. "Would you allow a helpless woman with a light sword to defeat you? One woman? The ancient and her brother are bound before you. Eat him then, Mark. He is all yours. They all are. They will make you immortal."

That grating voice came from over Siv's left shoulder, up high and in the distance. It wasn't Vitus. He was far too clever to give his position away. Mars was the bull, wanting to get the fight over. To take it straight to them. He didn't like sitting and waiting for the pawns to wear them down, not when they already had the advantage.

At the urging of Mars, the pawns surged toward Vasilisa. The puppet tried to rush forward as well but stumbled over a loose rock beneath the snow. He fell to his hands and knees. His bones cracked under the weight of his fall, wrists and ankles snapping loudly. That didn't stop him. He dragged himself toward Garald and Siv, leaving long trails of saliva laced with wiggling parasites behind him. The trails had those same strange clouds of smoke rising into the air each place the white worms pressed against the pristine snow.

The salamander devils were creeping closer, using the snow and any other cover in an effort to escape Vasilisa's blinding light. If they came up too fast and didn't have cover, the light struck them, and they emitted a series of low notes that caused a slight tremor in the ground but sounded like a grumble to Siv's ears.

He knew it was possible that earthquakes could be triggered by sound waves. Were these little demonlike creatures trying to create enough sound waves to produce a quake and distract Vasilisa? Undoubtedly, they feared her. The demons would simply keep producing the vibrations until the sound waves affected the finer grains of rock at the interface between the plates.

Siv had no time to answer the questions he had about the demons moving toward Vasilisa. The vampire pawns attacked her, rushing all at once, three taking to the air as hideous mutations of a harpy eagle with enormous talons and beaks. Vasilisa calmly reached into her open coat as she whirled in a circle and withdrew another sword, this one with a long gleaming blade. She tossed it easily so it flew end over end straight past him.

In the quiet of the snow-covered night, the sound of the sword windmilling through the air was unexpectedly loud—an ominous foreboding of coming mayhem. The sword reunited with its original wielder, landing solidly into Garald's fist as he rose from the snow prison where he had been tied down with strands of magic and barbed cuffs on his hands, feet and wrists.

Siv was already in motion, rushing to meet the puppet first, needing to spare his lifemate and her brother the kill of a beloved friend. Still, out of the corner of his eye, he couldn't help but see that Garald had grown in stature. He appeared regal and almost otherworldly, as if he had grown invisible armor around him. He leapt into the air to meet the first vampire, who dove toward Vasilisa with talons aimed at her face.

Siv moved so fast he was a blur, uncaring who actually saw the incredible speed he normally would have taken care to keep hidden. He slammed his fist deep into the rotting back of the puppet as he crawled toward his destination, seeking to reach Vasilisa. Even the hunter's fist tearing through bone, muscle and organ didn't stop him. He howled insanely, but he kept dragging himself toward his goal.

Pity moved through Siv. Pity he didn't want or understand. He had closed himself off to all emotion, falling back on the ways of his life as a hunter of the undead for over two thousand years. Why would he feel pity? Ripping the shriveled and rotted heart from the hapless creature, he glanced up to see his lifemate looking, just for a moment, at her old friend. There were tears in her mind but not in her eyes.

She was surrounded by the undead. By demons. She took time to feel pain for a fallen friend. It was the space of a heartbeat or two, but it could get her killed. Before he could reprimand her, she was facing the first of the salamander demons as it approached, opening its wide mouth to show rows of sharpened, serrated teeth dripping with poisonous venom.

Siv severed the head of the puppet, tossed the heart into the air and called a lightning whip to incinerate both even as he whirled around to leap over the vampire closest to Vasilisa, putting his body between her and the pawn.

Garald smoothly drove his sword into the very heart of the mutation flying at his sister, twisting ruthlessly as if the blade were a skewer. As he landed in a crouch with both feet on the ground, he withdrew the blade, removing the heart. He spun in a circle as he half rose, a small device that appeared much like a mirror in his hand. Small blue flames licked at the snow everywhere his gaze touched, amplified by the strange mirror. He held the tip of the blade with the vampire's heart in the flame.

The vampire screamed as he fell from the air, no longer able to hold the pose as a bird of prey. He landed heavily on the snow-covered ground and tried to crawl to Garald in an effort to retrieve his heart. Garald sliced through his neck with one wicked blow, severing the head from the body and allowing the blue flame to leap to the body and head of the undead.

Two of the lesser vampires flung themselves at Siv in an attempt to overpower him while a third came at him from above. A fourth vampire sent a command beneath his feet to thorny, venomous vines that erupted through the ground in an effort to stab through his leg and ankle to hold him immobile. More vines burst around Vasilisa, rising high to build a cage around her, cutting her off from the two men.

As the two vampires rushed straight at him, their greedy eyes fixed on the open wound on his head, Siv shook droplets of rich, ancient Carpathian blood into the air. All heads turned toward him, including that fourth pawn, the one commanding the vines caging Vasilisa. The vines wavered for just a moment, turning toward him as well, the cage faltering.

Vasilisa paid no attention to the vampires, her brother, Afanasiv or the venomous, thorny vines bursting through the ground forming a towering cage around her. Her entire focus was on the demon creatures dragging themselves into the fray. She was well aware they could burrow beneath the ground and the vines caging her in. The venomous vines seeking to rip open her skin or stab through her to hold her in place came far too close for comfort, but she couldn't take the chance of moving. Any movement could bring a strike.

She kept her light pointed toward the sky, the umbrella of lumi-

nous beams a shield. Any moment, the gathering demons would attack. Timing was everything. She had trained her entire life to defeat
demons, to drive them back to the underworld each time they found a
way through a tear in the earth, a vent, a thinning wall. This was her
job, her purpose. A legacy handed down from mother to daughter
right along with Afanasiv's soul.

She was aware of each of the foul creatures as they came closer.
The earth's heart beat beneath her feet, giving her the information she
needed as they came from every direction, trying to conceal themselves beneath the ground, behind rocks, under the ice, in the trees and
brush. They skittered under the vegetation lying on the ground like
real salamanders might, but they were so much larger, and though they
possessed some ability to do magic, they could not hide from one such
as Vasilisa.

She waited, holding still, needing answers. There was something
amiss here. Humans, Lycans, vampires and demons all acting together
as one, or was this simply a coincidence? She didn't believe so much in
coincidences. With that booming, low-pitched note, the leader in-
duced the others to charge as one. They rushed under the thorny cage
and then scaled its walls, using the thorns dripping with venom as
hand- and footholds to scale up the sides. They didn't seem in the least
concerned with the poison, as if they were immune. That was her
answer.

She went into action before the demons could expand, taking their
true forms. She spun fast, her sword of bright light tipping outward
now toward the cage made of thorny vines with the occupants clinging
to its walls. She called on the heavens above in her soft, angelic voice.
Her musical notes rivaled that of the low booming notes that strove to
displace the finer grains of rock in the interface between the tectonic
plates.

As she spun, the sword aloft in one hand, she released droplets of a
liquid from a vial she held in the other hand. The drops were caught in

the twister she created with her spinning sword. She didn't appear as if she were going that fast because she was the center, the eye, completely calm. The drops expanded to become a deluge of rain, water pounding with force, hurling against the vines and creatures as they tried to reach her.

Siv could hear her soft voice as she continued to speak to the demons. Her tone never changed from that sweet, magical, melodic pitch. "Hear me, demons, sent by the commander of the army of Lilith, queen of the underworld. You cannot have my lifemate. You cannot have my brothers."

She plunged the blade of the ceremonial sword into the icy forest floor. When she did, the vines shivered and shrieked as if she had sliced through them with the cutting edge of the blade. Bright red blood bubbled up everywhere the vines had erupted through the ground. The low humming notes of the salamander creatures turned to shrieks and screams.

"This ground is lost to you. This shape is lost to you. Each form she sent this night is now locked in this consecrated earth." She scattered drops of the liquid from the vial in four directions and then above her head and onto the ground.

On the surrounding trees, malevolent spiders smoldered with smoke and leapt from the trunks, bursting into flame before they hit the snow. Beetles and other insects screeched in distress as they erupted into bright blue flickering flames that leapt into the air and then floated as wispy ashes to lay as black specks on the white surface.

The salamander demons had begun to elongate, stretching from their amphibian forms to something more human. At Vasilisa's sweetly voiced command, they desperately attempted to throw themselves at her with wicked claws extended, with gaping mouths wide, stretched to their fullest extent, serrated teeth dripping with venom. They tried their best to bite her, to sink a venomous-tipped talon into her, but she glided away even within the close confines of the cage of thorny vines.

The rain of liquid fire falling on the demons began to dissolve them. Siv saw that holes began to form straight through the hapless creatures as they wailed and gnashed their teeth. They fell from the sides of the vines onto the snow, where they writhed and sizzled and smoked. The foul stench was sickening even to him. Siv had to cut off his sense of smell immediately. He almost automatically did so for his lifemate, but fortunately at the last moment he refrained.

Bright drops of blood began to appear in the vines as the liquid from the vial hit the thick thorns and branches crawling upward to form a cage around Vasilisa. The liquid droplets also splashed outward to encompass the vines spreading out in an effort to trap Siv. Everywhere those drops hit, the water seemed to spread, crawling up the branches, leaving a trail of blue flames behind.

The vampires closest to Vasilisa had been struck by the droplets of the water from the vial. The moment the drops had touched them, holes had begun to appear in their skin. Black smoke rose. The vampires reaching for Siv and Garald abandoned their plans, writhing and screaming, twisting this way and that.

Garald impaled the one in the air on his sword, removing the heart easily, while Siv took the hearts of two others. All the while, he searched for the one who had created the vines. He wasn't as strong as those in favor with the master, but he nearly was. He knew some magic. Vasilisa had destroyed the demons and consecrated the ground. The vampires would be unable to use it to move through or hide in. If that had been the master vampire's intent, Vasilisa had taken that escape route away.

There were only three pawns left. They had been too far away for any of the drops of water to touch them. The vines collapsed in on themselves as the blue flames became a full burning fire rushing over the branches and thorns. Whatever lay under the earth couldn't surface, and the muffled screams testified that the cleansing fire had gone underground to ferret out the heart of the vines.

Siv saw the middle pawn wince, draw in on himself, as if flinching from the terrible heat of those cleansing flames. He moved with his incredible speed, rushing the vampire, slamming his fist into the chest, driving straight through the wall, fingers digging for the wizened, dead heart. Shocked, the pawn didn't react for a moment, only stood still, his eyes wide, staring without comprehension at the ancient warrior. That moment cost him. Siv extracted the heart, already calling down the whip of lightning to incinerate the still-upright pawn.

He was standing between the two other vampires. They were as shocked as the one he had destroyed. He took their heads, slicing them off so the heads bounced on the white snow, scattering black acid and wiggling parasites everywhere.

As blank eyes stared from the severed heads, he slammed both fists into their chests to extract their hearts. The gurgling noise was disgusting. He ignored the way the acid burned through his flesh as he jerked the hearts from their bodies and tossed them far away from where their bodies would fall. He directed the whip of lightning to incinerate the hearts, the heads and then the bodies. Only then did he bathe his arms in the healing light to rid himself of the acid burns that went all the way to the bone.

Behind you.

Siv was well aware of the vampire creeping up behind him. *Thank you for the warning, my lady.*

It wasn't necessary, I see. There was amusement in her voice.

He loved that little intimate note that seemed to tie them together. They would be friends.

He turned to face Mars as the brute of a vampire confronted him. Mars never bothered to make himself appear handsome in an accepted way. He had been a hulking beast of a Carpathian, with wide shoulders and a deep barrel chest. As a vampire, he had retained both, and he added to the appearance of bulk with illusion. On his face, he often gave himself scars to give the appearance of a warrior experienced in many battles. He always wore a fierce, intimidating expression. Sometimes, like now, he carried a club with a spiked knot on one end that looked to weigh a considerable amount. His legs were solid and ended in wide, flat bare feet with climbing toes and long retractable claws.

Siv gave a short courtly bow. *Remind your brother of what I said of Rufus. He will attempt to kill him and possibly either kill you or acquire you while I am dealing with Mars.*

Have no worries.

How was it possible not to worry when she was his lifemate? He would have to learn to trust her. She had handled the demons without needing him. Still, he would always worry now. He had waited more than a few lifetimes for her.

"I see that you have found a few friends. I never thought you would need to rely on others to fight your battles for you, Mars. You always appeared quite capable yourself." Siv poured flattery into his voice. "Perhaps the years have not been so kind to you." His inflection changed to one of slight pity.

Mars scowled, his heavy dark brows coming together in a straight line. "I have no need of help to defeat you or anyone else, hunter. You know me, then."

"By your reputation. It was very easy to identify you." Again, Siv put a complimentary note in his voice. "Many of the hunters speak of you. They wonder why you choose to serve another who clearly is not your equal."

Mars' chest puffed out just a little farther even as his gaze darted toward the waterfall that was now a spectacular ice sculpture. *Vitus is hidden somewhere in the layers along the waterfall. He is extremely dangerous.*

Rufus had come out of his hiding place to confront Siv as well, but Garald placed himself squarely in front of the vampire, giving him the same courteous half bow Siv had given Mars.

"I greet you, Rufus, you sanctimonious fruitcake of a vampire who is foul and obscene, an abomination walking upon our very lands. I suppose you have come here asking for death, and I have no other choice but to oblige you." He sounded weary.

What part of flattering and pandering to their ego did your brother not comprehend?

That is not his way, Vasilisa informed him, amusement uppermost in her mind. *Have no worries, I will aid him. He is counting on it.*

Mars swayed first one way and then another. He moved toward Siv and then backed away as if restless, staying constantly in motion. Siv kept his eyes on him, but there was a part of him that was watchful of Rufus and also the waterfall sculpture.

If the master vampire, Prince Vitus, thought for one moment his guardians were winning the battle, he would throw his considerable fighting skills behind them. If he thought they were losing, he would take every bit of information he could from the battle so he wouldn't repeat the same mistakes, and he would flee. Master vampires survived by running.

Rufus gave Garald a faint smile. "You Lycans are all alike, so arrogant, believing you are fast. Believing you can jump higher and run faster than any other. What of your friend Mark? Wasn't he your best tracker? You personally sent him out. I saw the memory in his mind." His voice was pleasant as he spoke. So was his smile as he taunted Vasilisa's brother so cruelly.

He rushed Garald with blinding speed, going straight at him. Garald lowered his sword, keeping it chest high to ward off the vampire, but it was impossible to see him. Rufus had vanished, his speed too great.

Triumphantly, the vampire shimmered back into his form directly behind the Lycan. He had defeated countless hunters in just this way for hundreds of years. Pain spread through him, radiating through his chest like a starburst. He tried to look down but couldn't see at first. There was too much brightness, which didn't make sense. There was only the palest sliver of a moon. They had created cloud cover on top of everything else, although the clouds seemed to have deserted them.

The light was a blazing blue and the pain was fierce, as if a flame had gone right through the middle of his chest, tearing a great hole through it. His heart felt on fire. Burning. The stench was atrocious. He blinked rapidly until his vision cleared. First, he saw the woman. She looked beautiful. Serene. Far too calm when he was going to destroy her. Then her brother was beside her.

"You should never have set foot on my lands, vampire. Go to hell, where you belong. This time, you cannot return," Garald announced.

If Rufus squinted against that blue flame, he could make out the sword in his hands.

"You are bound by the laws of Mother Earth and all who serve her," Vasilisa said in her gentle voice. "I command you to the depths of hades, never to return in any form."

Garald swung his sword so fast, the vampire heard the whistle as the blade cut through the air and took his head. Vasilisa's sword had incinerated the vampire's heart right there in his chest. She had been waiting for him at her brother's back.

A fanasiv waited as Mars continued his swaying and constant moving. The "bull" was staying true to his battle form, just as Rufus had. Siv touched his mind, keeping a very delicate connection. The mind of a vampire was disgusting and riddled with obscene, hideous images of the torture and destruction of entire villages, crimes they'd committed in their past and enjoyed remembering.

There was elation, even glee, despite the fact that, or maybe because, Rufus and the pawns had been defeated. Mars took a kind of malicious pleasure in knowing they were gone and Prince Vitus, with his favoritism and continual preening, did not save them. No, it was more than that. Mars was certain he could not be defeated. He was protected, and he would be given his ultimate prize—one he had longed for and believed he had been cheated out of by Dimitri Tirunul. Skyler should have belonged to him. He had nearly had her some years earlier, but she had escaped his trap. A mere human had eluded him, and she would pay for the constant ridicule Prince Vitus and Rufus subjected him to over the last few years.

Skyler? That bit of information alarmed Afanasiv. Skyler and Dimitri kept a residence in Siberia. Not just anywhere in Siberia but in the vast forests that fell under the rule of the royal house of wolves. Dimitri maintained a wolf sanctuary. He fought hard to keep the wolves healthy and their habitat from shrinking. He'd had the foresight to realize humans would begin to cut down the trees and kill the wolves, seeing them as a menace to livestock. From the beginning, he had made it his priority to keep land for the wolves. Whether or not he had known all along that the massive tract of forest fell right in the middle of Lycan territory, it had, which added an additional safety feature for the wolves—but not necessarily for Dimitri or Skyler.

Siv processed the information at high speed, as he did all things. Mars had made a bargain with the head of Lilith's army. He believed himself invincible. There had to be other vampires just like him. Prince Vitus very well could have made the same pact. Vampires lied with every breath they drew, yet they expected the demons from the underworld to keep their word. That made little sense. Siv pulled away from the obscene contact, sickened by every image in Mars' head.

The bull continued his swaying and moving, taunting Siv. "You don't really know who I am, do you?"

Afanasiv shook his head. "The real question should be whether you know who I am. Allow me to introduce myself. You should know my name before you kill me. I am known as Afanasiv Belan to our people. I have lived in a monastery for centuries, but prior to that, and for some time after, I have hunted ones such as you for more centuries than I care to count."

There was a long silence. The wind answered him, blowing hard through the snow. The powerful gusts disturbed the branches in the trees, setting them clicking wildly. Flurries of snow fell from the needles clinging to the branches as the wind whipped through the canopy and brush. He heard the soft whisper of a voice in that wind, cleansing the images tainting his mind that the vampire had put there. His lifemate. Magical. How did she know what to do? How was she able to reach him without connecting and sharing those foul images?

"Afanasiv Belan? The ancient?" Mars asked for confirmation.

The vampire shouldn't have made such a grave mistake. To ask Siv to clarify his identity was the same as admitting he was taken aback by the information. He should have played it cool. Simultaneously, the ice around the waterfall began to crack. At first the sound was a mere crackle here and there. Then the force of it began to roll like thunder, picking up speed as icicles broke off, falling to the ground. Sheets of ice calved off the waterfall, crashing to the jagged ice-covered rocks below.

Siv nodded slowly. Mars seemed mesmerized by the sound of the ice breaking and Siv's nod. Afanasiv burst into action, using his speed as Mars suddenly went into motion, rushing straight at him. Siv used their combined speed to penetrate the solid chest of the vampire, shifting his arm and hand into that of a solid burning spear, incinerating the black acid as he made his entrance.

The vampire screamed and tore at Siv's neck and shoulder with his teeth. He used his claws to tear at Siv's chest to try to get at his heart. Afanasiv shut down all ability to feel pain. One part of him monitored the crumbling ice sculpture that had been the waterfall. Vitus was either fleeing or he was coming to Mars' aid. Siv never stopped the steady extraction of the heart from Mars' body.

There was no hint of sound to warn either the hunter or the vampire, but suddenly Garald was there, his sword catching the blinding blue light of Vasilisa's crystal ceremonial sword as he raised the blade high. The edge came down between the hunter and vampire, flashing blue and black as it cut through the vampire's wrists so the massive claws fell to snow-covered ground, where they tried to dig their way back to their master. The blade never stopped moving, arcing back up toward the vampire's throat to slice right through his neck cleanly.

Mars' head, with vicious teeth still snapping wildly, bounced halfway down the slope, pouring wiggling parasites and black acid onto the pristine white snow. The moment the parasites and acid touched the surface, blue flames erupted, springing from one to the next until the fire had consumed the head, parasites and acid completely. Even the teeth were gone. The hands and talons suffered the same fate.

Siv tossed the withered heart into the air, and the whip of lightning hit it, incinerating it on contact, then the whip followed it down to the body, burning it as well. Afanasiv immediately bathed his arms and chest in the healing energy as he surveyed the waterfall. Vitus was gone. He'd fled, abandoning the others, choosing not to aid them.

Garald held the blade of his sword in the blue flame his sister's ceremonial sword provided. Afanasiv regarded the two of them with his unusual eyes. They were both staring at him openly. He knew his eyes were very different. One moment they could be green. The next blue. Not just any blue. Deep blue. Vivid blue. The same with the green. His hair was blond. Like the other ancients, he kept it long. It was thick and he wore it pulled back away from his face and tied tight at the nape of his neck. The length was knotted with cord every few inches to keep it tidy.

He studied his lifemate. In fact, it was rather impossible to take his eyes off her. He hadn't known what to expect, but he had certainly never dreamed or imagined he would end up with a woman as physically beautiful as Vasilisa. In the Carpathian world, physical beauty meant nothing at all. Age meant nothing. Perhaps all lifemates felt this way. He was certain they must after searching through centuries for their other half. Up close, she was truly gorgeous.

"Lifemate." He whispered the word. It came from his soul. Felt as though it were wrenched from him. Sacred.

She smiled. Her blue eyes soft. "Lifemate," she returned.

Garald groaned. Shook his head. "No. No. Vasi, no, it can't be. You know it's impossible. He's Carpathian. Can't you see he's Carpathian? That's what they call each other when they claim each other's souls. That's an unbreakable bond. You can't be any part of that. You're Lycan and you're of royal blood. Do you have any idea what kind of controversy that would cause? Absolutely not. Say no."

"It's too late, Garald," she murmured, still looking into Siv's eyes.

Garald groaned again and waved his hand between them in an attempt to break their connection. "You two aren't thinking straight. I'm actually trying to help you. This is a physical thing. I get it, Vasi. You're going into heat. It happens. You can't mate with a Carpathian. We'll find you a perfectly respectable Lycan." His voice was soothing when he spoke to his sister.

He turned to the hunter, his tone changing to steel. "I'm sorry, Afanasiv. You're a good fighter. I'm sure in your world you're an admirable man, but you and I both know what happens when our blood mixes. It isn't accepted. You've seen Dimitri. No one accepts him. They pretend to but they don't. We watch over him, but we worry someone will still try to harm him or Skyler."

"I was born with the other half of his soul, Garald," Vasilisa informed her brother very gently. "I have known almost from birth that I was destined for a Carpathian male. Mother knew this and did her best to prepare me for his coming."

Garald continued to shake his head. "Vasi, you are Lycan royalty. Don't you understand what I'm saying to you? This could cause a war. This *will* cause a war."

"Not if you, Grigor and Andros stand with me. In any case, there is no way to stop what is already done."

"I forbid this. You come home, and he must leave this land."

Afanasiv had had enough. "Do not speak to my lifemate in such a tone of disrespect. You must go to Dimitri and Skyler and warn them that there is danger. Mars believed that he was promised Skyler should he defeat me in battle. It is not only possible but probable that others have been promised something similar. I must find Vitus and destroy him. My brethren have run into others on your land. Master vampires with their pawns looking to destroy your people. They too have made pacts with those from the underworld."

"Vasilisa will come with me," Garald commanded.

Afanasiv remained silent, showing no impatience, although he needed to follow Vitus as quickly as possible. This was a matter for his lifemate to settle with her brother. Her decision whether to stay with Garald or go with Siv would set a course for their future.

"Vasilisa speaks for herself, brother," she corrected softly. "I always have. I go with my lifemate. His journey is dangerous and he will have need of me. What's more, I have need to be with him. Our soul is joined together. Where one goes, so must the other. We will return when we have destroyed the master vampire. We need to discover who else is betraying our people and why, because it seems as if the whisper of conspiracy has spread in all directions."

Garald swore under his breath and turned away from them. "You are taking a dangerous path, Vasilisa. One I don't know if we can save you from."

"She will not require you to save her," Afanasiv assured. "I am quite capable of defending my lifemate from any who wish to harm her."

"I am quite capable of defending myself, as you well know, brother," Vasilisa assured him. "Having a lifemate adds to my protection. I also feel that Dimitri and Skyler are in grave danger. He is on our land. Send word to Grigor and Andros that we have a traitor, someone close to us, within the council. We must be very careful. I'll return as soon as possible."

"Three ancients travel with me. They are staying at the inn but may find refuge in other places if they have battled the undead and cannot make it back. Benedek Kovac, Petru Cioban and Nicu Dalca. These men are ancients and very dangerous. They are hunters of the undead, Carpathian, but I cannot stress to you how dangerous they are. Do not challenge them in any way. Keep your young Lycans from them if they are feeling a need to prove themselves. These are not the men to test their mettle on."

Garald did not take offense as Siv feared he might. He gave a short nod, his worried gaze on his sister. "Good hunting," he murmured. "Vasilisa, come home to us."

"Always, brother."

Afanasiv didn't much like the sound of that. He started to shift into a bird and at the last moment stopped himself. His lifemate was quite capable of doing the same, but from the concerns with their union—specifically the mixing of their blood, allowing them both to become so much more than either Carpathian or Lycan—he realized Garald had no idea Vasilisa already was more. He held out his hand to her, his much larger fingers engulfing hers when she took it.

He'd never held hands with a woman in his life—certainly not that he could remember. She felt small and delicate through her gloves. He glanced at her as they walked swiftly away from the black ashes in the snow and her brother, who was quickly moving in the opposite direction. Since they had to slow down anyway, Siv wanted to take the opportunity to catch Vitus' imprint near the falls.

"You are not only extremely intelligent, but you are an accomplished fighter, Vasilisa. I'm honored to be your lifemate."

She glanced at him from under her long lashes, a small smile briefly flirting with her lush lips. "Thank you."

His eyebrow shot up. "I have said something amusing?"

"No, I quite liked your compliment. It's just that most men would have complimented me on my looks. That's all they would have seen. They wouldn't have noticed that I am intelligent, or if they did, it wouldn't have mattered to them. They wouldn't have wanted me to be good at fighting because they would want me to stay at home."

"Lycan women are very good hunters. I recall hearing that one of your most experienced hunters had a female Lycan on his team who was every bit as skilled as her male counterparts."

"Her name is Daciana, and she's an excellent example. She's an elite hunter. Many of the Lycans belonging to the Sacred Circle have decided they don't want the females serving on the elite teams no matter how good they are. The Sacred Circle forbade them to do so. Although many have said they no longer practice those beliefs, they do," she admitted.

"The one thing I have noticed as I have moved through the centuries is if you do not keep up with the times, you eventually become extinct. You cannot hope to survive. I am not going to say I am in any way modern. I am not. In fact, I cannot keep up with technology at all. Computers and the like defeat me completely. Young Josef did his best to try to teach us, but since it is so much easier to just pull the information from other's brains, I admit I saw no use for the device. He tried his best to explain it to us. When he was explaining, it made sense. When I was attempting to learn, it didn't."

Vasilisa smiled up at him. He liked that she was tall. He was a tall man, and he wouldn't have to stoop low to reach her. Still, she was a few inches shorter, and when she looked up at him, as she did now, she made him feel things he couldn't identify. Sensations were strange and new to him. These were good emotions. Powerful ones. He found himself enjoying these new feelings.

He slid his thumb over the back of her hand and then turned her hand so he could feel for the pulse in her wrist. "You didn't flinch once. Demons or vampires. You were prepared."

"I trained from the time I was a toddler—I could barely walk. My mother knew I held your soul and would possibly face vampires. She also knew I would need to know how to face anything that might slip through from the underworld. I must guard one of the gates created in the underworld to hold a beast that is uncontrollable by the demons or by those aboveground."

"There are four gates," he said, confirming his knowledge.

Her head came up, and her eyes went from soft to suspicious. "How would you know this?"

He liked that she was so careful. "I traveled with Sandu, one of my brethren from the monastery, when he journeyed with Adalasia to repair the tears in the earth around the gate she was ensuring stayed closed. We spoke with Liona, a Carpathian woman guarding that gate for centuries. She is Sandu's sister. The reason Adalasia's tarot cards survived all this time is because Liona's blood was spilled on them."

Her eyes had gone soft again, all suspicion gone. "I have met Liona. She is a strong woman, and one I admire greatly. She spoke of Sandu often and couldn't understand why he didn't come to her."

"His memories had been removed by his uncle before he was sent away. He had no idea of Liona's existence." Siv watched the way she moved through the snow, barely skimming over the surface.

"Before we chase after this vampire, and I know you're in a hurry, I need you to do something first."

He stopped immediately. "Of course, my lady. Anything."

For one moment, her eyes met his, and then she looked away quickly. She looked almost shy. He couldn't imagine his lifemate shy. He examined his every interaction with her. The way she took control of the battle with the demons. Her conversation with her brother. Was it just with him? He reached for her, slipped his palm gently around the nape of her neck.

"You are my lifemate, Vasilisa. You have only to ask and it is yours."

She moistened her lips, still not meeting his eyes. He was tempted to lift her chin, but he waited, instinctively knowing she needed to find her own way.

"I have never responded to any man's kiss. I have found kisses to be rather . . . repulsive." Her long lashes lifted, and her startling blue eyes met his once again.

His heart jumped. Skipped a beat. Those eyes of hers did strange things to his chest. He both was amused and felt as though his insides were melting. It was a peculiar and disturbing combination.

"I would very much like you to kiss me. I need to know if this is going to work between us. As my husband, you're going to expect certain things, and I need to know if we have . . ." She broke off, looking uncertain again.

"If we have chemistry," he finished for her. He wanted confirmation that she was looking for that specifically. He knew the power of lifemates and the bond between them. They would have explosive chemistry. Kissing could be dangerous, but he was very willing to oblige her.

Siv didn't wait. He exerted pressure, pulling her closer to him. One hand framed her face. Her skin was unbelievably soft. His thumb slid over her high cheekbone, mapping it out in his mind and then sliding over her aristocratic nose before tilting her chin up. Her long lashes swept down to cover the astonishing blue of her eyes.

Her lips trembled as his thumb outlined their perfection. He leaned down to catch her breath. So sweet. He very gently kissed her lower lip on the corner. Tasted her. Sipped at her. Used his teeth to tug tenderly and then shifted to the other corner to nibble there. His tongue made a little foray over her soft lower lip and then along the seam. He kissed her upper lip gently, with almost no pressure. Moved upward to press a kiss along her very elegant nose and then each eye. Claiming her. Leaving his imprint on her. He moved down her face, along her cheekbone, back to her mouth. Those lips. So soft.

He kissed her gently. Coaxing her response. Breathing for her. His teeth nipping a little harder this time, a little more insistent so that she gasped, parting her lips, letting him in. His tongue swept away the small sting and then stroked a caress over hers. Silky soft. Flames licked up his throat and began to roar in his bloodstream. Their mouths welded together; their tongues, dancing a tango, were as hot as hades.

Vasilisa slid her hands up his chest, and then her arms went around his neck, and she leaned her weight completely into him. He shifted her in his arms so he could get a better angle.

The moment his body felt hers melting into him, he needed clothes gone, needed skin-to-skin contact. It was hard to resist the urgent needs of his body when hers moved not so subtly against him.

Sanity and thinking left and feeling took over. There was a roaring in his head, thunder in his ears and a fierce wildfire burning out of control in his veins, spreading fast and rushing to settle in his groin. The feeling was euphoric. He'd had no idea. As many times throughout the centuries as he'd studied the arts of sexual practices, he hadn't actually participated.

Her lips moved against his like silk. It was as if they'd touched a match to an incendiary device. She had wanted to see if they had chemistry. They detonated together. He had to pull back or lose control altogether. That wouldn't be right. Very reluctantly, he lifted his head, grateful his lifemate chased after him with a little whimper. Definite chemistry. He was fairly certain there wasn't going to be a complaint coming his way.

He smiled down into her upturned face, his thumb sliding gently over her slightly swollen lips. Her blue eyes looked a little dazed.

"What do you think? Good chemistry? We can work on it when we have more time." He bent his head and tenderly brushed a kiss along her lower lip, the one that appeared to be pouting just a little bit. "We'll practice, my lady, and get it right."

She blinked as if coming out of a dream. "You think we need practice?"

He nodded solemnly and stole another kiss. A long, fiery one. When they needed air, he broke off. "Many, many long hours of practice to get it right."

Vasilisa let him take all of her weight for just one moment. "I agree completely. I've always been a perfectionist. We wouldn't want to do anything half-assed, as my brother would say. My mother raised me to do things right."

"As far as I'm concerned, Vasilisa, you are already more than excellent at kissing. I hope you do not find me repulsive in this department."

She shook her head, stepping back. His hands slipped to her arms to steady her. She still wore that dazed expression. He wanted to go back to kissing her, but Vitus was escaping justice. It didn't do any good to have a master vampire on the loose. He could wreak havoc wherever he chose to go. He wouldn't be happy that his followers were destroyed. Vitus was a vampire who believed in retribution. He would do his best to find a way to retaliate against Vasilisa, Garald and Afanasiv.

He would think Afanasiv would have to warn his friends using the common Carpathian pathway—which would include him. The ancients had their own pathway forged long ago. He used it now, reaching for Petru, Nicu and Benedek. *The master vampire calling himself Prince Vitus is running. He is angry and looking for revenge. Do not allow him to use you for that purpose.*

There was a short silence. Petru was the first to respond. He preferred fighting with weapons and was lightning fast with them. He didn't need the weapons; he just enjoyed using them. He was also a master of strategy. Few could outthink him in a battle.

I am engaged with a master vampire, his underlings and several demons just east of you, Siv. They were in the process of attacking a number of households. The strange thing is he has one of the members of the house of royalty with him, not as a prisoner. This man betrayed his countrymen.

Vasilisa froze in place. "He is mistaken. That cannot be true. It is an impossibility for any of us to turn traitor."

Afanasiv frowned. *Is it possible this vampire is a master of illusion and has created an image of one of the members of the house?*

It is impossible to fool me. You know that. This man, this Andros, is the real thing. A part of his brain is fighting against what he does, but he is cooperating with the vampires and demons, Petru assured him.

Siv reached out to wrap his arm around Vasilisa. At first, she stiffened and attempted to step away from him.

"Lifemate. We take this journey together. Whatever comes our way. We both know it will be a difficult one, and we face danger. Many battles. Adalasia read the cards for me. I asked her if you existed in this century. She told me we would face many battles, and we would have to surround ourselves with those we trusted in order to survive."

"I trust my brothers."

"Then we free him from whatever has a hold on him, but we do it together, Vasilisa. That is how we must go forward from now on." He looked straight into her eyes, needing her to understand that point. He meant it. It mattered little that his voice was low. Soft. He meant every word. He was an ancient doing his best to fit into a modern world, but this was a command. She didn't yet realize that with his claim, they were woven together. One couldn't do without the other.

Vasilisa lifted her chin. For a moment, a blue flame burned in warning in the depths of her eyes as she regarded him steadily. They stared at each other. He could feel the turmoil raging in her. This was her beloved brother Petru had accused. The ancients didn't know him. They knew nothing of her family, of the pact that existed in the house of royalty there. Her mind raced so fast, she didn't believe he could follow her stream of thought.

"I have an oath to you scarred on my back. It has been there for centuries, Vasilisa. It has been there to remind me when I lived in a gray void of nothing for centuries to stay strong for you. Only you. I am not your enemy. I live with honor to serve you."

That halted the tumultuous rioting going on in her head. Siv was honestly amazed at how fast her brain worked. She took a deep breath. "I'm sorry. I don't know why I suddenly wanted to take my fear and anger out on you. Even on your friend for giving us such bad news. He isn't the one responsible. But I'm telling you, this cannot be true. Our family cannot betray our people. It is an impossibility. The way our DNA is programmed, we cannot possibly betray the ones we serve."

Afanasiv considered what she was telling him. How could that be countered? What measures could a vampire take to overcome what had been built in to protect Vasilisa's people? The answer was, it would be extremely difficult. It would take centuries, and the vampire would have to be wholly focused on that task alone. No vampire would be able to keep his mind on that single chore for the time it would take. Who, then? Vasilisa was following his thought process.

"You are assuming your friend . . ."

"Petru," he supplied.

"Yes, Petru is correct and my brother is helping this vampire."

"And the demons from the underworld." Afanasiv was thoughtful. "I have had some dealings with demons, Vasilisa. I will admit, part of my memories are gone from the time I spent in their company. I have not tried very hard to resurrect them, as I know that torture was involved. Demons are malicious and vengeful creatures. I carry scars from the time they had me in the underworld with them. I do know that I thought it would be impossible to trick one as ancient and as knowledgeable as me, but I have been there."

Her blue eyes still held those blue flames, but the fire had calmed a bit, burning low. "Did they manage to use you in some way? Enslave you so that you did their bidding?"

There was a challenge in her voice, in the tilt of her chin. She wanted to see if he would put himself above her family. Did he believe himself better than the Lycans? Was there truly a prejudice in him against her and her brothers because they were wolf and he was Carpathian, and that made him superior?

"I have told you, my lady, I do not remember all of what transpired. I chose to forget most of my time spent with demons. Before you decide the convenience of such a thing, the memories are still there, waiting to be accessed. We can retrieve those memories after we ensure my other friends are well and advise them of what is happening. I do not care for the fact that Vitus was most likely after your brother Garald. There was a traitor waiting for him. The puppet was a particular friend of his, was he not?"

She again looked anxious. "My older brother Andros has been seeing a woman, Lada. He's been seeing her quite a bit recently. He goes to her home and stays for a week or two at a time. She has a little girl, and he wants the child to really get to know him. Lada has a little place on the outskirts of the village up in the eastern slopes, close to where Dimitri's sanctuary starts."

Afanasiv immediately got a bad feeling in the pit of his stomach. "When was the last time you heard from him?"

"I feel sick. Andros is the one closest to Dimitri. He would have spoken with him. If for any reason he couldn't get to him, he would have checked in right away to tell us. That was why I wasn't very concerned about Dimitri." Vasilisa pressed her hand over her stomach. "What do these vampires want with my brothers?"

"The vampires seek to control you through your brothers. They believe you will turn over my soul to them. As for the demons, they want something else altogether from your family. I do not know what that is. The answer may be in my memories."

"I feel as though my world is suddenly falling apart." She took the hat from her head and swept a hand over her hair. She had it up in order to accommodate her hat, so he couldn't see the silky mass other than that it was sable in color and very thick.

"Let me reach out to Nicu. He sought out Dimitri. Nicu always runs with the wolves. He's the most feral of all of us, and the wild ones respond to him. Dimitri and Nicu have been fast friends for centuries. He knows Zev, your Lycan elite hunter. Zev is lifemate to Branislava Dragonseeker. Like you, she comes from one of our most revered families and is related to Skyler. They have come to visit her just to see that she is settling in after all the chaos that happened to her. Skyler had died and was brought back up the tree of life by her lifemate, Dimitri. He had never fully relinquished her spirit, and somehow, she hung on, even with all her wounds, waiting for him. Theirs is an amazing story that all Carpathians talk about. Gabriel and Francesca, the Carpathian couple who adopted her when she was human, were devastated when they thought she had been killed. She is a very special woman to our people."

Afanasiv was trying to comfort her. If several of his people and those she knew to be hunters of rogue Lycans were converging on her lands, she would be able to build an army to fight whatever or whoever was threatening her people. He was connected to her, mind to mind, without intruding too far, and he saw immediately that she recognized the name Zev Hunter. He would have been astonished had she not.

Zev was considered an elite rogue Lycan hunter, sent out after any Lycan who refused to follow the rules of Lycan society. Zev didn't return until he had finished his mission. Those on his team were considered elite, just as he was. Zev had now come under suspicion by the Lycan council since he had chosen to become the lifemate to Branislava of the Dragonseekers. The mixed bloods were not tolerated in the Lycan world. They were considered killers, and the Lycans thought they should all be exterminated. The Carpathians considered them guardians.

Afanasiv knew there were arguments for both sides, depending on one's experience with them. He knew many of the Lycans on the council had tried to bring more understanding among their people. The resurgence of the popularity of the Sacred Circle among the villagers had made the acceptance more difficult.

Just knowing Zev was close had Vasilisa settling even more. "We have to hurry, Siv. Find out about Grigor."

Nicu, have you encountered a master vampire in league with demons from the underworld? Is there a member of the royal house with them?

Yes. Fighting them off as we speak. The voice was clipped.

Do you need aid?

Dimitri and Skyler have come to my aid. With them are Fen and Tatijana.

Do not allow anything to happen to the royal if you can help it. He is under some kind of influence.

That is evident.

"I just spoke with Nicu, my lady. He said it was very evident that the royal was under some kind of influence. He is not acting on his own. That means Andros is not, either. It also means Garald was a target. Whatever trick was used on the other two, it was unable to be used on him."

Vasilisa wrung her hands together. "That is the point, Afanasiv. No trick should be able to work on my brothers—or me. Something isn't right. This is truly frightening. They're strong. They hear lies. They can feel threats coming at them. Energy in the air, good or bad, even the slightest risk can be felt."

"Yet they managed to ensnare two of your brothers and one of your strongest trackers. Andros, by all accounts, is fighting against whatever was done to him, as is Grigor. We need to find out as fast as possible what they have done to entrap your brothers."

"We must go to Andros, then. He is strongest."

In principle, that sounded like the right path, but Afanasiv wasn't so certain. He didn't want to act so quickly that they missed what was right in front of them. They had asked Garald to go find Dimitri and warn him of the possible danger to Skyler. Nicu was already with Dimitri. Garald's brother Grigor was there as well, a pawn to be used by the demons and a master vampire to lure his twin to the same fate.

Vitus had heard every word. He knew Garald and Andros had been sent to the same place. It would be such a blow to his ego to have another master vampire succeed in capturing both royal brothers and binding them to the underworld. He would lose all status with Lilith, if that was what this was all about.

"I believe we have to intercept Garald and protect him from Vitus. Vitus will be wholly focused on acquiring him," Afanasiv said, giving his opinion. "Vitus was here to acquire him. Or you. I believe he wanted Garald for the underworld. He wanted you for himself, and that was only because he believed you held the other half of my soul. These are only guesses."

Once again, her gaze was steady on his. "How would he know that?"

"That is a question I have not an answer for, my lady."

She indicated the broken ice sculpture. "Can you track this master vampire?"

"I can."

"Let us follow him, and while we do so, I think it would be a good idea to inspect these memories that are missing."

He wasn't so certain, but he did think it was necessary.

PART TWO

THE HANGED MAN

5

V asilisa couldn't understand how Andros or Grigor could have been entrapped by vampires or demons. It had always been deemed impossible for anyone of their bloodline, yet she was connected to Afanasiv's mind when he spoke with his brethren, and there was no doubt that each of them had believed it was the truth.

Her lifemate. She let herself taste the words—feel them in her heart as she followed his lead. They took the shape of owls and used the birds' silent wings to follow the master vampire as it raced through the night toward the easternmost corner of the thick forest.

There were few brave enough to have homes near those high ridges and deep gorges. The snow was deep and food was scarce. The village Andros' woman came from was very old-school. They adhered to the old ways of the Lycans and believed in the very oldest of the versions of the Sacred Circle. That was a belief still practiced by many of the older Lycans, although it had been proven corrupted by a dark mage. Most modern Lycans refused to continue following the old customs— at least in public. Those in the outlying village near the eastern border practiced openly. They made no bones about viewing the mixing of blood as sacrilege.

Allow your mind to calm, my lady, Afanasiv said gently. *There is little we can do until we know the facts. Before all else, we must ensure your brother Garald's safety. The best way to do that is to stop Vitus from reaching him. Vitus will have more than one plan. He has not survived this long without having something else up his sleeve. He is not counting solely on his demon allies.*

Vasilisa thought that over. He was right. As a rule, she was not one to panic. She did so only because these were her brothers, and she wanted them out of the hands of the demons. She had studied the underworld from the time she was very young. She knew how twisted and depraved the creatures were. The tortures they could conceive and delighted in had been so disturbing, when she'd first been studying them, she'd had nightmares for years.

There was nothing she could do for either of her brothers at the moment if they were already in the hands of the demons. She had to make certain Garald didn't fall. She wasn't making a very good showing for her lifemate.

You're right, Afanasiv. I'm sorry. As a rule, I am careful to look at every angle. It makes no sense that my brothers were able to be captured and used. I know what demons can do, and there is a part of me in total panic.

Vasilisa, you must be kinder to yourself. Anyone would want to rescue their siblings from the hands of these demons or a vampire. The vampires will find that the underworld will not give them exactly what they bargained for. That is always the way with these creatures.

She noticed he streaked through the night sky without hesitation, following some unknown trail only visible to him. She would never have been able to find the vampire. Her brother, on the other hand, she could have found. They had an unbreakable bond. Blood called to blood, even hers, so different now. She had found that the Carpathian blood hid itself deep within the Lycan blood when her brothers reached for her, so they never suspected she was different.

Afanasiv had confidence born of experience. He wasn't cocky or a braggart, and she liked that about him. He didn't treat her as if she were less than him. She liked that, too. She settled into his mind, trying to track the vampire with him, determined to learn from him, just as she felt he was willing to learn from her.

At first, she couldn't see what Afanasiv was following. She tried to see with her eyesight and then with her other senses. Her acute hearing. Her sense of smell. She was used to relying on physical senses because hers were developed. After a time, she realized Afanasiv wasn't using any of his physical senses. He was using the owl's senses but also relying on a psychic trail, a kind of foul footprint left behind in the sky by the vampire.

It was automatic for her lifemate to track the vampire the way he was. He didn't think about it; he just did it, the same way she tracked prey when she was hunting on her land. He had provided the information for her there in his mind; she just hadn't utilized it.

I have never noticed that sticky mark in the sky before. It's no more than a smudge. How did you ever see it and associate it with a vampire? She often hunted with Sorina, a Carpathian one had to consider quite old, although she appeared very young. They had defeated vampires together out of necessity. They hadn't deliberately sought them out. Never once had she noticed the little dark smudges that looked almost like the beginning of a cloud forming. Not even that. The mark was faint in the night sky.

When you follow a master vampire, you have to look for anything that is consistent, no matter how small. That little piece of dust in the sky was a comet in his wake. I do not know how often I missed it to begin with, but once I did notice it, I would instantly recognize it and lock onto it. The trail does fade over time, but it is as if the touch of the vampire has fouled the air itself, and it takes time to heal.

Vasilisa studied the tiny smudges that could barely be seen against the dark background. Now that she knew they were there, she saw them, but she wasn't certain she would ever have spotted them in the first place. There were a few places where there were two rows of them. She indicated them.

Why do they appear like that?

He doubles back to see if he is followed, Afanasiv explained. *He does it often. He has spies in the trees telling him there are wolves in the forest. He suspects those wolves are Carpathian hunters or the wolf pack that runs with Dimitri and Skyler, or Ivory and Razvan. Both are known to hunt vampires with their wolves.*

Do you think they are doing so now?

Not Dimitri and Skyler, Afanasiv said. *They are east of here, according to Nicu and Petru. I have no idea if Ivory and Razvan are in the area. These are most likely actual wolves, but they are slowing him down. I worry for the wolf pack, but their presence keeps Garald from harm for the moment and allows us to gain on Vitus.*

As he spoke, fiery balls descended from the sky, streaking toward the wolf pack as they steadily weaved in and out of the trees moving to surround a herd of deer. Without thinking, Vasilisa countered, turning the fiery balls to ice so that when they hit the snow-covered ground, they were no more than a flurry of unexpected hail.

I'm sorry, she gasped the apology, but she wasn't really sorry. These animals were part of her custodial duty. Aside from that, she felt a kinship with them.

No need. I would have done the same thing. You were faster. Go after Garald. I will engage with Vitus.

She wanted to protest, but he was already streaking after the vampire, hurling fiery spears at the dark figure to keep him from attacking the wolves—or her. He clearly didn't want the master vampire to have the slightest inkling she was anywhere in the vicinity. Vasilisa didn't waste time arguing. She gave the vampire and her lifemate a wide berth, using the cover of the night that enfolded her as Sorina had taught her. She circled around the larch forest below, feeling a little as if she were abandoning her lifemate.

Once she felt she was in the clear, she put on a burst of speed, abandoning the body of the owl to assume that of the Brazilian free-tailed bat. She added a headwind to give another boost to the already hundred-mile-an-hour speed the tiny creature could achieve with its aerodynamic body and longer-than-average wings. This was another form learned from Sorina.

In the freezing cold of Siberia, especially there, high in the region where Vasilisa and her family lived with the feral wolves and the independent and fierce people, many of these creatures wouldn't survive for long. The small amount of time she used their forms as she pumped warm blood through their bodies did them no harm.

She caught up with her brother very quickly, long before he reached Dimitri and Skyler, where they would have been working in their wolf sanctuary. He hadn't yet come upon the other vampires or demons, and remained unaware that he was in possible jeopardy—or that his brothers were.

Garald skimmed over the top of the snow in the way of the royal family, barely touching the surface. He was light on his feet and he leapt long distances, covering anywhere from ten to thirty feet at a time. When he landed, he did so lightly and in perfect balance, continuing his run without breaking stride. He was beautiful to watch, and she stayed in the sky for just a brief moment longer than necessary to admire him.

He turned his head to his left just as she spotted the "rabbits" crossing the snow using webbed feet. They appeared to be white as they converged on Garald, looking for all the world like the wolves she'd just seen hunting the deer in the forest. They came at him from all directions, attempting to surround him. The creatures blended in with the snow as long as they stayed low to the ground, but when they popped their heads up in an attempt to see where their prey was, they appeared to be a dark blight on the land. They were fast, disappearing in a flash, but the movement caught Garald's eyes. He was too good a huntsman not to notice.

She dove fast, streaking down from the sky to land beside her brother, going back-to-back with him. "Demons," she said.

"I got that. How many?" He didn't question that she had practically fallen from the sky on top of him. That would come later.

"Looks like nine. I counted fast, though. They're all aboveground. I locked the ground so they can't come at us that way. They can't go back, either. We have to find how they came through, Garald." She was going to have to tell him about Andros and Grigor. Just not now. She needed his full attention on this fight.

"Where's your man?" Her brother's tone was just a little bit too sarcastic for her liking.

"Fighting the master vampire. He was on his way here to join with the demons to get to you. You were the target all along."

Garald looked at her over his shoulder. "How do you know?"

"Let's take care of these demons and I'll tell you. Afanasiv will be here when he defeats Vitus." She wouldn't consider that there was any other outcome. The sky flashed bloodred and then darkened in the distance. She knew the battle raged. A part of her refused to disconnect from her lifemate, although she knew she should. He wanted her to. He didn't force her. He didn't order her. That was so like him, giving her the opportunity to make up her own mind.

The "rabbits" drew closer, coming in from every direction. Garald lifted his sword. Vasilisa lifted hers. Her breathing was slow and even. She waited, feeling the energy all around them. The creatures were feeling a collective triumph as they had succeeded in surrounding Garald. They hadn't yet lifted their heads to see that Vasilisa had joined the fight.

Demons were cunning and very adept at guile and deceit. They could charm and persuade. They were rarely if ever sincere. She turned that over and over in her mind, making a note to discuss it with Afanasiv. She liked that she had a sounding board now.

The dark blights appeared, lifting their heads almost as one. She noted that they seemed to rise up at the same time, like a puppet on a string. Was someone else out there actually creating an illusion? She frowned. No, they felt too real. These were actual demons, but they were under another's bidding.

Two seemed to be dragging something behind them in the snow.

A body? Her stomach lurched. These demons were after her brother. Whoever that writhing, still-alive person was, it had to be someone close to Garald.

"Garald." She kept her voice very low. "Have you been seeing someone you haven't told us about?" Silently, she sent up a prayer to the universe that he hadn't been. The universe had been so cruel, particularly to their family. Having royal blood seemed to guarantee only one thing—when you loved, you did so with all your heart, and your heart was brutally shredded to pieces.

"Why?"

Just that abrupt question was her answer. "You cannot react to anything you see or hear. Demons are deceivers, and they are doing their best to acquire you. They are dragging something behind them. I believe this is someone who matters to you. Don't look or indicate in any way that you see them."

Garald swore under his breath. "Vasi," he finally said. "She is young. Very young. I should never have even looked at her. Her parents brought her to one of the dinners we held. After, as always, there was a dance. I stood in the ballroom in the shadows the way I do, and I couldn't take my eyes off her, she was so bright. My heart felt lighter than it had in years. I'm fifteen years older than she is. I might have looked the part of the playboy, but I didn't want the curse of our family to fall on a woman I loved."

There was so much despair in his voice. So much sorrow. Vasilisa felt that sorrow weighing her down. Andros and Grigor were in the same way, she was certain of it. The women they had chosen had to have been used against them. The enemy, using the women they were involved with, had trapped her brothers.

The demons thought they would capture Vasilisa using Afanasiv. The vampire had other ideas for her. She wondered what would have happened if she and Afanasiv hadn't defeated them so quickly. Would the demons have destroyed the master vampire? It seemed he wasn't so easily defeated, or Afanasiv would be with them.

"She is not lost to us yet, Garald," Vasilisa assured him.

"She is lost to me. She is young, as I said, and any kind of violence would be abhorrent to her. For me to be responsible for her torture would end our relationship before it ever began."

Was there a sob in his voice? Please don't let her have heard a sob. Maybe it was in his heart. All the royals were connected by their blood. They could cut one another off so the others didn't feel emotion or hear thoughts, but in unguarded times, anything could slip through.

"I'm sorry, Vasi. I love her. I've never loved a woman other than you and Mom. She completely took over my heart. I didn't share with anyone, not even Grigor. I was afraid if I said how I felt about her aloud, something terrible would happen. I didn't even tell her."

Again, she closed her eyes briefly. Her fingers gripped her sword just a little tighter, and then slowly she loosened them.

She felt a burst of dark, almost sadistic joy hastily cut off. *I will be with you shortly.*

Vasilisa had the impression of an intense battle taking place on the ground. Afanasiv was no longer in the sky, and there was more than one opponent. He was experiencing an almost euphoric rush of brutal excitement as he fought the master vampire and his servants. She hadn't expected that of him, and for a moment, she was thrown by the knowledge that he was completely different than she had thought him. That tiny glimpse of him showed an animalistic side that savored viciousness.

The demons came within fifteen feet of them and abruptly halted. As if they were in a synchronized ballet, they all stood straight and tall, easy to see now against the white backdrop. They were strange mutations of mountain hare. They looked human, standing tall, nearly all men, but with their bodies covered in thick bluish-white fur. Their ears were long like the rabbits', white and tipped black. They had the faces of human males, but the noses were those of rabbits. They wiggled them often, which Vasilisa found a little distracting.

The demon facing Garald didn't deign to acknowledge Vasilisa. None of them did. They stared only at him. "We have brought you a gift." The one talking had sharp serrated teeth in his mouth. She presumed the others had those same sharp teeth. "Would you like to see it?"

"Don't answer him yet, Garald," Vasilisa whispered. "Do you see that they don't seem to notice me? I don't think they even realize I'm here. These demons are programmed by someone we don't yet see, and they don't really see us that well. They see what they expect, which is only you. It would be interesting to see what he says if you don't answer him."

Silence hung in the air. The wind blew through the trees, and snow fell from the branches when they shook and trembled, showering them with a blend of snow and ice.

"Vasi." Garald's voice shuddered nearly as much as the branches. "That's Taisiya. I recognize her hair. Her hair always reminded me of a mink, that deep rich brown."

"She's alive, Garald," she pointed out again. "Right now, that's all that matters. We're going to take her back from them and heal her. She's Lycan. She's strong. You keep their attention on you. They haven't seen me. I'll move around them and try to find who is actually orchestrating everything. Don't touch her or allow her to touch you. Something happened with Andros and Grigor. I don't have time to go into that now, but we can't afford for the demons to trap you as well."

"Hurry, Vasi," Garald pleaded.

Vasilisa put her sword away and instantly shimmered into transparency and then completely disappeared. She circled around her brother, making certain to stay above the ground. She moved slowly enough that she didn't displace any snow. It was very difficult not to look at the young Lycan woman lying trussed up like a game hen with small, deliberate cuts all over her body. Signs of suffering and strain were on her face, seen at just a quick glance. She had her head tucked down and was trying to avoid Garald's gaze, but the demon closest to her prodded her with the sharp nails on his enormous paws.

Vasilisa studied each of the demons. It stood to reason that one of them might be the driving force behind all the rest, although she thought that the demon would have noticed her. She took her time, not wanting to miss anything important. None of them seemed different from the other. They stood straight and tall, acting in that strange synchronized motion as if they had been trained to perform on a stage.

It is possible they have been. Or they are being directed by someone who has been a performer. Someone close to your family. Someone who knows your brothers and you.

That voice was calm and steady. Even soothing. But the moment he spoke, anger exploded in her. The emotion was unexpected, but it was profound. Harsh. Beyond her capacity to feel. She realized she had tapped into her brothers—all of them. It was common for the siblings to share intense emotions, but she hadn't thought they could hear her lifemate when he was trying to help her sort through possible answers. Not only was that wrong of her, but it was dangerous. She closed her mind to her brothers.

I'm sorry, Afanasiv. I had no idea I was sharing with my brothers.

You are worried for them. It is only natural. Afanasiv excused her.

But two of them are compromised. Whatever is said between us might possibly be heard by our enemy.

Was he getting closer? She had never had trouble solving problems or working alone, but she knew this journey wasn't hers alone. She had read the tarot cards handed down for hundreds of years from mother to daughter that very evening, and she knew she would never be alone again. There was unexpected relief in knowing that. She understood her brothers' anger and fear. They didn't want to be alone.

You believe the person directing this abomination is someone who is or was close to my family? Someone who knows all of us intimately?

They would have to, wouldn't they? They trapped your brothers. They know the very thing that would get to them.

How would they know about me? I have never discussed guarding your soul with anyone, not even Sorina until this evening. She hadn't. That secret had been a sacred charge. Even as she tried to dismiss his more-than-valid inquiry, her mind began to go through a list of suspects. At the same time, she began to search her surroundings—the sky, forest and landscape—to see where the conductor might be hiding.

All vampires know Carpathian males have a lifemate and that lifemate is the guardian of the other half of their soul. I was taken into the underworld and subjected to torture. I could not have told them about you because I did not know who you were. Someone from your line had to have known. Perhaps someone who has passed. Someone female whom your mother might have confided in.

Dread began to gather in Vasilisa's stomach. Hard knots formed. Someone in her family, not a family friend. Her mother would never have confided in a friend. She would have kept their legacy a secret from everyone, just as she had drilled into her daughter to do. Vasilisa couldn't imagine a scenario in which her mother would have broken her word unless there were dire circumstances. What would those be?

She would have to think she was dying and unable to pass my soul to her daughter. She would want to entrust it to someone she thought would pass it to her child. Did she have a difficult birth with you? You were her last. What were the circumstances of your birth?

"Garald, you must answer, or I will think you do not want this wretched woman," the demon intoned.

"Why would you bring me a gift? What have I done to deserve it? I know nothing is given freely." Garald was careful in his choice of wording. He didn't accept or reject the offering, and he was also cognizant of using a droning tone so that there was a distinct lack of inflection of interest.

The demon waved his hand at the woman trussed up and bleeding from dozens of places. She shivered continuously. When he did, all of the demons waved their hands as if they were all on the same wavelength. The arms rose and fell together in perfect synchronization. Where had she seen such a thing?

Sívamet, you know who this is. I see the knowledge in your mind. You reject the answer.

The betrayal hurt. Her own flesh and blood. Why would she do such a thing? Olga? Her aunt? Her mother's sister? She had always been loving and kind. They had been close, all of them, her brothers protective of her. Why would she turn on them? She shook her head, rejecting the idea, ashamed she'd even considered her as a suspect. There was no possible way Olga would be in league with demons.

Afanasiv didn't try to convince her. He remained silent when she wanted him to argue with her so she would have an excuse to lash out at him—at someone. Betrayal at such a level was soul destroying. Her brothers had always defended and loved Olga. They would do anything for her. All of them treated her as a second mother, particularly after their parents had been murdered.

"Come close and see what we bring to you. She is special. A woman you like."

The demon chanted, a low droning sound. It couldn't penetrate the shield she'd put on the earth, so there was no way those low notes could produce tremors and shake open cracks that would allow more demons to escape.

"What is your price for this hapless woman you have dragged here?" Garald repeated, using his same careless droning tone. He sounded almost bored.

"A small one. A very small price."

"You see," Garald said. "Always you act as if you are doing a favor, yet you are not. Your price is never small. I do not recognize this woman. She looks old and haggard. I think she is one of your many illusions. The times you have managed to escape the underworld, you delight in playing tricks. I have no time for playing games with you at the moment."

There was a small silence, as if the conductor didn't quite know how to react to Garald's statement. She was proud of him for acting so disinterested. She knew it was difficult. She felt the strain on him, the heartache. He hadn't looked at the bundle of misery. He'd looked over the top of it and at the surrounding snow, but not actually at the woman.

Vasilisa floated close to her brother. "I am going to check Taisiya for damage, to see if she will survive what they have done to her. Then we will take her back. We have to know if they have made it so they intend to kill her if we make a show of aggression."

Garald moved his body subtly so that when his nod came it seemed natural, as if he were merely changing his position slightly.

Vasilisa hovered over the woman again, this time assessing her injuries. She had been tortured. There was no doubt about it. What was the purpose? Just so Garald would come to her rescue? Just to get him to cooperate with them? Taisiya had something clutched in her fist. Vasilisa could see she was trying to open her fingers to release the object but couldn't get them to open. Each time she made the attempt, a fresh flood of silent tears would roll down her face, but she persisted. Along with those tears, drops of blood ran down her clenched palm to her wrist and forearm to drip into the snow.

Frowning, Vasilisa floated closer until she was nearly lying on top of Taisiya. That close, she could see the needle and syringe in her fist and fingers sewn to them. Taisiya was desperate enough to use one finger to try to pull at the stitches and pop them loose one by one. It was clear she was doing her best to hide what she was doing, not from the demons towering over her, but she kept looking at trees in the forest. Vasilisa followed her gaze.

Afanasiv. I think I see the demon controlling the others. Taisiya keeps looking fearfully toward one tree in particular. There appears to be a blight growing on it. There wasn't one before. I know every tree in the forest. That large outgrowth wasn't there before.

Do not engage, she instantly commanded her brother without thinking. Then, in a softer tone, she told him the reason. *She is doing her best to warn you of something. We must have time to figure this out.*

He took a step forward and then forced himself to stop when

Taisiya shook her head and waved him off with her hand. It was more of a fist wave, but he caught that slight movement. They were trained to catch the slightest nuance of an enemy, so he would no doubt see the tiny hand shaking to warn him off.

Garald's body shook with the effort to keep from hurling himself at his enemies. He did his best to look indifferent, shaking his head and looking at the woman with disdain. "I have never seen this wretched creature before, or if I have, it was brief, and I do not remember. Why would you bother me when you can see I have business to attend to this night?"

The demon threw back his head and laughed. As he did, so did all the demons with him. He took a step closer to Garald, and again as he moved, so did the other demons, the circle narrowing around Vasilisa's brother.

The miserable bundle that was Taisiya was nearly within reach of Garald. Vasilisa could see her clearly. She became frantic, ripping desperately at the stitches holding the needle and syringe in place, moaning and crying out occasionally and then muffling the sound in order to keep Garald or the demons from looking at her. More blood ran onto the snow in bigger droplets. The red clashed with the white of the snow, making it impossible not to see, and yet the demons' focus wasn't on her. It remained on Garald and his every movement.

Vasilisa didn't like the eagerness on the demons' faces, the way their mouths gaped open to show their serrated teeth as if they might leap upon Garald and tear him to shreds. Their eyes had gone bright and shiny, glowing red in the night. Garald was surrounded by them. He had to feel their anticipation, the rising excitement in them, and yet he didn't break a sweat. He appeared relaxed, his sword loose and even nonthreatening. He looked bored and unafraid, as if the demons were beneath his notice.

"Do you not wish to save this woman? We could kill her for you," the head demon offered.

Garald's answering laugh was harsh. "And then I would owe you a favor. I am not a young lad to be tricked by such foolishness. What is it you want from me? Tell me or be gone."

The demon closest to Taisiya drove his foot with those terrible toenails into her side. At the same time, the demons all chanted three words over and over. *Voz'mi yego krov'.* They repeated the chant incessantly, swelling in volume. Taisiya screamed, writhing as if she were having a seizure.

"Run, Garald." She managed to get the warning out before her throat closed and she went into a fit of coughing as she lunged toward him, stabbing with the needle.

Automatically making herself into a thin, pancake-like figure, Vasilisa inserted her body between her brother and the young girl who fought so hard to save him. The needle appeared to lodge in Vasilisa's artery under her arm and instantly drew blood into the cleverly concealed tube in the girl's fist. Taisiya's fist dropped away, and she was rolled toward the demon, who ripped the syringe and tube of blood from her.

At once, a howl of joy went up from the demons, and they began to dance and sway in a circle around Garald. Vasilisa was certain it was to distract him. Taisiya lay at his feet in the snow, broken and bleeding. That would be a distraction as well.

Did she injure you or your brother?

Neither. I inserted a thin coating of armor and made it appear as if she drew blood into the tube. Garald will see to her while we track whoever is going to take the blood back to the source of all of this.

Nice plan, my lady. There was pride in his voice.

In their family, even though they tapped into one another's emotions, she had never been praised for her fighting abilities or her looks or anything else. She hadn't had a sense that her parents were particularly proud of anything she did. Andros disapproved of her most of the time because she didn't adhere to his commands. Grigor and Garald spoiled her but, like Andros, wanted her to settle and produce babies.

They didn't understand why she wouldn't do as Andros insisted. Having her lifemate praise her and mean it might seem a small thing to others, but it meant a lot to her.

"Garald, I will hunt the traitor, you take care of the demons."

Her brother was just waiting for the go-ahead. His sword glinted with a blue light in the slim silver of the crescent-shaped moon. That blue flame was necessary to kill anything from the underworld. The demons rushed to meet his attack. Others tried to murder Taisiya, but Garald stood over her, his lethal sword swinging, the blade beheading the demons so that unnatural black blood stained the snow alongside Taisiya's crimson-colored blood.

Vasilisa had to leave her brother to his fate and chase the one demonic creature racing across the snow-covered surface to bring the prize to his mistress. She became aware that once again she was sending out mindless prayers to the universe that the betrayer was not her aunt Olga. It would be so devastating. She and her siblings had so much heartache and trauma already in their lives, so many betrayals. She didn't want this one for them, either.

Andros had grown cold and withdrawn. He'd built a cage around his heart. It felt as if icicles, sharp and lethal, guarded that cage, which had no lock and key. As the years went by and more pressure was put on his shoulders, more icicles filled the cage and gathered on the outside of it.

Grigor and Garald hadn't fared much better. Too much responsibility was put on their shoulders too fast. She knew because it was the same with her. Sometimes it felt as if she would break under the tasks of helping so many people, of running herself thin to help the elderly and keep the young from dark, dangerous roads.

Now she followed the demon as he rushed across the snow into the heavier woods. He wove in and out of the brush, heedless of the low rocks and broken branches weighed down with snow that had cracked and given way under the assault from the freezing temperatures. The demon stumbled and picked himself up, slowing down again and again until she wanted to shake him.

Patience, sívamet. This is a waiting game. You have endless patience as a rule. Why are you so eager to begin this hunt?

That was a good question when she really didn't want to see to whom the demon was bringing the blood. She moistened her lips. They were speaking mind to mind on a chosen path between lifemates, but she didn't want to chance any energy spillage. There were too many Lycans around and far too many vampires.

I don't honestly know. I don't want to see if it is true that this is my aunt Olga. She is my mother's sister. We all love her. My mother adored her. Aunt Olga trained in ballet, and when she injured her foot and could no longer perform, she wrote plays and choreographed many of the dance and singing routines. I don't want the traitor to be her. It wouldn't make any sense. Why would she ever choose to do something like that?

There are many reasons for betrayal, Vasilisa. It is better to step back and wait for information than to speculate. You cannot change what already is. If your aunt has been working with the demons, she has been doing so for a long time. How they were able to trap your brothers wasn't something they discovered overnight.

That much was true. She did her best to follow his example. He was somewhere close, acting as her guardian, giving her the lead position. That was another thing she really liked about him. He was an ancient Carpathian. Everything she'd heard about Carpathian males had prepared her for an arrogant, overprotective, demanding man she would have to learn all kinds of compromising for.

Afanasiv was—unexpected. He did seem to view her as a full partner. She wrapped herself in that knowledge as she followed the demon's path through the woods.

Does the vampire seem like he's more of a problem? Do you think Olga senses us? She has royal blood in her veins. It could be she feels me closing in on her. She wanted—no, needed—the reassurance of someone to discuss the worst possibilities with.

You would know before she did, Vasi. You are more. You always were more, but now with both Carpathian and Lycan blood in you, there will be little escaping you. You are on full alert. She will not be able to elude you. Have faith in your abilities.

His calmness and absolute belief in her brought tears to her eyes. She had to dash them away. He was wonderful. She didn't want to fall in love with him. That wasn't in her plan, not with the royal curse hanging over her head. All of them knew better.

Look at poor Garald right now. He had started off innocently enough, determined to stay away from a young woman he knew better than to see. He was thirty-four years old, and they each had the weight of their kingdom pressing down on their shoulders. Crushing them. Garald stayed in the shadows. When he came out, he acted the playboy at the parties and had one-night stands with many, many women, but he didn't ever have relationships. That wasn't part of the agenda. It couldn't be, and they all knew that.

The demon held out his hands eagerly toward the very tree Vasilisa had pointed out to Afanasiv earlier. The demon had made a full circle around the outlying forest and had returned to the place where he had started, yet just inside the woods.

Vasilisa took her eyes from the blight on the tree to hastily look down to ensure her brother was in good condition. Demon heads rolled in every direction, spilling dark contents across the snow. Garald strode to each of the bodies crumpled like paper dolls and stabbed down with the point of the sword, then swirled around to set the body on fire. The flames leapt from body to body and then head to head. A foul, noxious odor permeated the night air. Only when the last demon had burned to ashes did he turn his attention to the woman bound so tightly. At once, his body language changed completely. He looked impossibly gentle, tender even, as he began to remove the ropes binding her, murmuring to her soothingly.

Vasilisa turned her attention back to the one demon left alive, the one staring up at the tree, holding his offering as if it were the most precious thing in the world. Her heart began to beat faster as the bark seemed to part, like curtains being pushed to either side. A rope ladder dropped from a seat bench, and then an elegant leg clad in black stretch trousers appeared. Then the backside and hips as the woman began to descend.

Vasilisa would know her anywhere.

She is?

My aunt Olga.

6

Afanasiv cursed under his breath in several languages. He would have spared his lifemate this heart-wrenching moment if he could have. He wanted to take her into his arms and surround her with his strength. Or put her somewhere safe. Command her to sleep until this nightmare for her family was over. He knew she was not a woman who would stand for such a solution.

The best he could do was move close to her as they hovered in the air watching the woman as she stepped onto the snow-covered ground. Olga turned from the ladder to face the demon. There was no fear in her expression as she looked at the creature with his wide grinning mouth and teeth that seemed to have grown even longer in the time it took to get to his mistress. She snapped her fingers, and the demon placed the vial of blood into the bag she held out to him.

She sealed the bag and began to turn away.

"Mistress. Wait. You promised me a reward. My heart's desire."

She turned back to him. Afanasiv again wanted to spare his life-mate. He edged just a little in front of her, but didn't entirely take her field of vision. He knew if he did, she would immediately fight to see what her aunt was doing. Olga had turned back with a cruel, evil look he had seen many times throughout the centuries. It was a look of pure maliciousness. This woman was corrupt right through to her soul.

"You want your precious reward? Your heart's desire? You worked so hard for it, torturing those young women for me. Enslaving my nephews. But you missed with Vasilisa, didn't you? Do you think I should reward your screwup, Hattie? My niece is very dangerous. If she ever finds her Carpathian lover, she would be doubly so. She was the ultimate prize to me."

The demon dropped to his knees. "Please, mistress," he whined.

"Perhaps it wasn't your fault. She is very astute and difficult to trick. Her downfall will be her brothers. She has always been too sentimental. I will get her that way." She beckoned to the demon. "Crawl to me, Hattie, and you shall get everything coming to you."

The demon immediately dropped all the way to his hands and knees and crawled through the snow to his mistress. She reached into her very chic jacket and pulled out a dagger with a spiral blade and a wicked point on the end. It looked suspiciously like the ones Afanasiv had seen in the caves the dark mages had practiced their arts in. She plunged the blade into the back of the demon's neck, severing the spine.

The demon's mouth gaped open wide in a silent scream. Olga twisted the spiral dagger out of the demon's neck and plunged it into the middle of his spine. There was a cruel smile on her face as the dark blood bubbled and sprayed up like a fountain. Three more times she repeated the malicious action. She appeared to be in a state of animated bloodlust.

Afanasiv couldn't help turning Vasilisa's head into his chest and using his superior strength and his larger hands to keep her locked there. *It is not necessary to witness any more of her evil depravity.*

I need to determine if she is under a spell.

Afanasiv studied the cruel woman. He could distance himself from her actions, when he knew Vasilisa couldn't. This was her beloved aunt.

Olga was no longer that person. Who knew how long ago she had succumbed to her baser desires and sought out a master of the dark arts to help her achieve her goals? She had sold her soul to the devil. She served him—or his wife—now. There was a conspiracy against the royal house of wolves, and Olga was a major part of that conspiracy.

Olga shoved the body of the demon away from her with one foot. "You fool. I need blood from *all* of them. Vasilisa cannot escape us. As long as she is out there, no one is safe."

Olga waved her hands in the air in a complicated pattern, chanting as she did so. The blood disappeared from her face and clothing where it had splattered over her. Afanasiv recognized the pattern. It was an old one the high mage Xavier had used often when he sacrificed animals or humans on his altar and the blood splashed over his robes. Siv had seen this in the minds of young mages who had practiced under Xavier but deserted when the Carpathian race realized he was trying to wipe them out.

Xavier is dead and no doubt is in the underworld, gnashing his teeth and desperately thinking of ways to return. Xavier was killed by Ivory and Razvan while Natalya and Vikirnoff guarded their backs. Xavier is one of triplets. His brother, Xaviero, has also been defeated and sent to the underworld by powerful Carpathian women.

I have heard of Xaviero. He tried to start a war between Carpathians and Lycans, and very nearly succeeded, she acknowledged.

Skyler was one of the women to defeat him. Ivory was also one of the four. The other two were Branislava and her twin sister, Tatijana. Three of the four women come from the legendary line of Dragonseekers. Razvan also comes from that lineage. They have powerful ties to the land. It is said that no Dragonseeker has ever turned vampire.

Vasilisa rubbed the heel of her hand along her forehead and down to her temple. She didn't ask Afanasiv to remove her headache, but then, maybe she was unaware that he could. *These two mages are no doubt in the underworld. They can wreak havoc from there?*

Demons do, why not mages? Wouldn't you enlist anyone who could forward your cause? Lilith would believe she could control them, just as she believes she can control the beast enclosed behind the gates. He is a prisoner for a reason. Afanasiv rubbed the back of his neck. *We didn't expect living so long to affect us so adversely. Once our soul is in tatters, scars begin to develop. They cannot be healed, even by our lifemate. If we find her, that is the miracle, but she cannot remove the stain on our souls. Those remain to remind us we crossed a line. Each time I go into battle or take blood to sustain my life, my soul is at risk.*

Vasilisa once again reacted to his confession in an unexpected manner. Instead of pulling away from him in utter disgust and horror, she leaned her body into his and wrapped her arms around him. *You have fought with honor your entire existence, Afanasiv. I do not think you would succumb to temptation now, when you have a lifemate. You aren't going to give in to temptation while you are taking blood to sustain your life.*

She was amazing. No condemnation at all. He searched her mind to see if any was hidden from him, but there was nothing but compassion and admiration. He shook his head as he placed his fingers on her temples and briefly chanted a plea to the universal gods to remove her headache. He wasn't a master healer, but he could get the smaller jobs done.

Xaviero had a son who not only watched him and recorded every dark spell but also did the same with his uncle Xavier. When I say recorded, he had a good memory, and he would write the spell in his book when he could. Unfortunately, as you know, sometimes you forget a small important detail unless you have a photographic memory. Even that can be unreliable when under stress.

Great. Now there's four of them. I presume he's just as bad as his father and uncles.

Afanasiv nodded slowly, keeping his gaze fixed on their prey. Olga was busy ensuring there wasn't a drop of blood on her anywhere to be seen.

Yes, Barnabas is a cruel man and yet appears to be civilized and young. He often chooses to play the part of a college professor. Once he invades the woman's life, she is lost unless she seeks help and someone powerful enough can drive him away.

Could he be behind this? Could he have tricked my aunt?

Anything is possible, my lady. He kept his voice as gentle as possible.

You said "triplets." That means they have another brother, but you didn't mention him. Is he dead, as well?

Xayvion. As far as I am aware, he still lives. He was with his brother Xaviero when the trap was set once your people were attacked. He begged his brother to flee with him, but Xaviero refused. Xayvion is able to continue with the original plan if he wishes to do so, which is to wipe out your species and mine, and conquer the human race so the mages rule.

I am grateful Xaviero didn't even come close to wiping out our species. Fortunately, we have council members who worked it out with your prince.

Abruptly, he changed the subject. *Did your aunt Olga die? It is possible her form is being used as a different kind of puppet, one we have not seen before.*

No, she is alive, or at least she was. She plans all the balls and events the royal family holds. We would never think of them, and the family really needs to entertain, not just sneak around fighting off enemies no one ever sees or knows about. My parents and then Aunt Olga always said it was important that we made certain to create good times for our people and share those good times with them.

Did she marry? Was she in love with someone who possibly died, and she couldn't stand the thought of waiting for him?

No. She never married. She took lovers, especially during the . . . um . . . heat cycle. But she never said if she fell for a man. Or a woman, for that matter. Vasilisa rubbed her face against his shoulder, unaware she looked to him for comfort. *This is going to really hurt my brothers. They loved her so much.*

You loved her so much, sívamet, but this is not the woman you loved.

She is a replica of her, yes, but that is only the outside shell you see. Inside, she is not your beloved aunt. Think of her as an illusion.

Vasilisa lifted her head and nodded. One hand came up to his jaw, her fingers feathering lightly along the hard edge. *You managed to say the right thing. Thank you.*

I have no doubt that you would have figured that out sooner or later, but I'll take credit, as I'm certain I will make many mistakes.

Olga abruptly turned away from the demon she had killed and walked briskly through the snow toward a little-used path through the trees. Brush parted for her and closed behind her, cutting off sight should any try to follow her. Vasilisa and Afanasiv took to the air, careful not to display too much energy or allow it to leak out around them.

Lycans were very sensitive to energy, particularly to Carpathians' low-key energy. They were one of the few creatures that could sense the presence of a Carpathian hunter in the vicinity. Vasilisa was used to hiding her presence from her fellow Lycans. The change in her had taken place slowly. She had time to practice the things she needed to before she was fully *Sange rau*, which was what Lycans called the mixed blood of Carpathians and Lycans. They were rogues, killers. They destroyed entire villages in a single night, leaving no one alive. It took hunters banding together and suffering tremendous losses to bring a single *Sange rau* down. That was not the same thing as what Carpathians thought mixed bloods were. To them, they were guardians of all, unless they had already turned vampire, and then they were referred to as the *Sange rau*.

When Vasilisa had first become aware that she was changing, that she was growing into something *more*, she had been terrified. Her natural inclination was to go to her brothers and confess, ask for their advice. She'd brought up the subject tentatively, and all three of her siblings had instantly voiced their opinions in loud, negative ways. She changed her mind about telling them when they spoke with such vehemence against the *Sange rau*.

Alone and frightened, Vasilisa waited to see if she suddenly developed murderous tendencies. When it didn't happen, she wondered if women fared better than men. But there was Dimitri. He was *Sange rau*. The Carpathian community called them "guardians of all" in their own language. She didn't think it made much difference what they were called. Only that some were murderers and some were protectors, just as Lycans and Carpathians could be both.

Olga continued to hurry through the forest on the now perfectly closed path of thick brush. Vasilisa and Afanasiv couldn't afford to lose their prey, so they moved through the air above her about fifteen feet behind. Afanasiv shielded both of them from Olga and any others who might be watching. He did so automatically, not because Vasilisa was a woman or because he thought her not up to the task.

Why do you ask if Olga had one man in particular?

It was possible she wanted to bring him back from the dead. No one goes willingly to the underworld. She is there now by her choice, but to voluntarily go to serve, you have to make that choice. Justice, the one held behind the gate, is a scarred Carpathian. He willingly sacrificed himself and his soul in order for his family to live. There was a young Carpathian child taken. She had no choice but to stay until recently, when she was offered a way out. She chose to stay so Justice wouldn't be alone. As far as I know, Justice is still holding out from serving those ruling the underworld. The child is fully grown now. I believe she is holding out as well.

He fell silent for the first time, saddened by the story of the two Carpathians lost to them. Justice, like all the ancients who had lived in the monastery high in the Carpathian Mountains, bore the scars of his sins on his soul.

Afanasiv didn't look at his lifemate. Had he been wrong to claim her? To tie her to him? He hadn't imparted the actual concern he had when giving her the explanation. If anything, he'd downplayed the danger.

My aunt is strong-willed. Once she gets something in her head, she would need to follow it through. She wouldn't change her mind.

We will see who Olga meets. There was no point in speculating. Soon they would have an answer. If he managed to kill whomever Olga was reporting to, would that end the hold she had on Vasilisa's brothers? Or could it do irreparable harm to them? He turned that thought over and over in his mind. He doubted if Olga had the kind of power needed to bring her nephews to such a state—serving a master and fighting it every step of the way. Someone more powerful than she had created the illusion for her, but Olga thought she was the one with the control over her nephews. It would be a terrible blow to her ego if she found out.

Olga suddenly stopped her forward momentum, snapping to attention like a soldier. Afanasiv half expected her to salute. An eerily familiar, not-so-welcoming voice greeted her.

"Idiot woman. What have you brought to me?"

"The blood of Garald, as you have instructed," Olga replied shakily. "The demon servant did not get Vasilisa's blood. We had her in the trap you devised, but she escaped with her lifemate."

Silence stretched out, long and uncomfortable. Olga's hands went to her throat as if she were choking. She tried to talk but no sound emerged. On her neck, great purple and blue depressions marred the smooth perfection of her skin. Her face went from beautiful to ugly, lines carved deep. Her eyes began to bug out of her head. She went to her knees, tears running down her face.

Vasilisa started a forward movement, but Afanasiv's arm around her waist effectively stopped her. The instant Vasilisa moved, those hands left Olga's throat, and a transparent figure dressed in a long robe shimmered into view. He stood behind Olga, a ceremonial knife to her throat, one hand in her hair, tipping her head back.

Olga shrieked. "Xavier. No."

"Vasilisa. How kind of you to join us. Put down your weapons if you want your aunt to live. I am not a patient man. Your lifemate can testify to that fact."

"And I'm not without intelligence, Xavier. My aunt went to you willingly and sold out my brothers and me, as well as our people, for some selfish reason of her own. If you kill her, it will spare me having to do so. Get on with it."

Afanasiv was proud of Vasilisa. She didn't give away where she was. Xavier couldn't detect her, how close or how far from him she was. There was no energy spilling from or around her. He was helping with that, but still, she could have done it on her own. She had extremely good skills. The more he was with her, the more he admired her. How hard it must have been to say her aunt meant nothing to her and to go ahead and kill her, but she spoke in a disinterested, almost bored tone.

Afanasiv watched the mage carefully and saw that he was loosening his hold on his victim and bending closer to whisper to her. Leaving Vasilisa, Afanasiv floated closer to hear what the mage's orders to her were, and then he invaded Olga's mind. She might be Lycan, but he was ancient Carpathian, and few could stop him when he was determined.

She wanted the power of the royal family to be hers alone. She wanted to rule and have the people bow down to her. She felt she didn't get the respect she deserved. Those feelings had started when a young lover had rejected her, wanting to go to Vasilisa without the stain of taking what Olga offered him first. Afanasiv shared those memories with his lifemate as they unfolded.

Olga let out a terrified wail and then pleaded for her life as the mage loosened his hold enough to allow her to talk. "He forced me, Vasilisa. *Forced me.* Do you think I would betray my beloved nephews? Or you? Our people? Why would I do such a thing?"

Olga was a superb actress. Her voice trembled. She sounded and looked tragically frightened and remorseful. Siv had no idea whether or not Vasilisa would hesitate even though she knew her aunt was lying.

You are a fighter of demons. Xavier does not belong in this realm. How do we return him to the underworld and seal him there? He sought to keep his lifemate focused on the reality of their situation. He could send demons back to the underworld, but sealing them there was beyond his capabilities. Demons were a specialized field, and his partner certainly had an expertise in that particular realm.

He is mage, and therefore his spells are very difficult to figure out. I have to know them to counter them.

The spells are reinforced by Lilith in the underworld. I can see a tether attached to him, Afanasiv told her.

That's all to the good. The tether will draw him back if I succeed.

If she needed the spell that had brought Xavier to her territory, then he would get it for her. *Stall for time. Draw him out. Flattery generally works on his kind.*

"Who forced you, Aunt Olga? Who could possibly force you to do anything? You've always been the strongest among us."

Invading the mind of a Lycan was extremely hazardous, but invading the mind of a high mage was suicidal. He was going to attempt it anyway. If Vasilisa could send Xavier back and seal him in the underworld, that would be one less enemy they faced. And Xavier was a dangerous opponent.

I don't think it's a good idea to attempt getting into his mind, Afanasiv.

Call me Siv. And maybe not, but you need the information. Stay connected to me but in the background. That way, you can pull me out if needed, and you can see the spell firsthand without me repeating it. It will require you to keep talking to Olga and Xavier simultaneously.

I won't have any trouble unless Xavier becomes aware of you.

Afanasiv doubted if anyone had ever had the audacity to slip inside the high mage's mind. He did so slowly, barely using any energy. It was a quiet invasion, only the slightest disturbance, a small bite of cold that had the mage shaking his head while Afanasiv quickly adjusted the temperature.

He began to sift through the mage's memories as fast as possible, going through them at an alarming rate of speed. He needed to find the moment when Xavier had first entered the human world again and where the portal was located. He saw the rituals the demons carried out under the lashes of their mistress, Lilith. She'd taught them the low humming notes that would cause a shift in the earth's plates. In turn, cracks would form, large enough to release her spies.

She promised Xavier she would send him back to the Carpathian Mountains with Xaviero if he proved worthy by collecting the blood of the royals for her. She wanted them under her control. She would send him to the surface in a limited capacity in order to achieve his goal. If he failed her, he would know torment for thousands of years.

Xavier had no intention of failing. He immediately recruited Barnabas, Xaverio's son, as well as the third triplet, Xayvion, to aid him. Barnabas was a ladies' man, and he set out to seduce Olga, taking the image of a slightly older Lycan, a member of the Sacred Circle. He intrigued Olga, took her down a dark path sexually and began to whisper to her about how she should have been the one to rule, not the others. He kept her from sleeping, all the while taking her blood and reinforcing their dark bond with sex.

Then Barnabas gave his proposal to Olga, that if she would aid Xavier in collecting the blood of the royals, she would have her heart's desire given to her. By that time, she had become twisted and cruel, enjoying the suffering of others while she took her pleasure. The thought of usurping the younger royals and stealing their birthright out from under them left her giddy with pleasure. She agreed immediately.

Afanasiv watched as Xavier called for a staff with a crystal in the exact center of it and a round globe at the top. Lesser demons sent by Lilith gathered around him to do his bidding. He had already chosen the one he wanted for his sacrifice. A female. Young. He had what he referred to as the horn of a unicorn, a long dagger that spiraled from hilt to point. His sacrifice was tied to the altar and he was in his robes.

He began the opening spell, chanting aloud, his hands held high over the female demon. The dagger was clutched between his two palms. He shifted his hands to the left and right, drove the point upward toward the sky and then downward toward the earth. He made a circle with it and then plunged it into the heart of the woman, swirling it deeper and deeper into her chest in a counterclockwise manner.

> *By below, by above, by west, east, south and north,*
> *I am free of the restraints of death.*
> *I walk the earth unfettered by any other than my mistress.*
> *I do her bidding and serve only her until she releases me.*

As he spoke, he withdrew the dagger from the demon and ran his snakelike tongue around the blade before handing it to the closest demon.

> *Drink your sister's blood and be sealed to me.*
> *Each of you will do my bidding and*
> *Any that I appoint to serve me.*

The demon did as Xavier had, using his tongue to take the blood from the spiral blade. He passed the dagger to the next demon in line, who took it with a grimace but followed suit.

Afanasiv watched carefully as Xavier scooped blood from the huge hole he had made in the female demon's chest. He dropped the blood onto the ground and began to move his hands in a complicated pattern.

> *Earth accept the blood of this strong one*
> *That I may walk once more on your soil*
> *Or burrow beneath it should I have need to do so.*

He scooped blood from the cavity he had made in the woman's chest and flung it into the air over the demons and himself. Once again, he lifted his hands and formed complicated patterns as he chanted.

Sky, take the blood of this strong one
Allow me to ride in your clouds
Unseen by others, unknown to others.

He scooped more blood and rotated in a counterclockwise manner, flinging the blood west, east, south and north. His hands came up stained with the blood of his victim. The blood was on his robes and in his beard. He began another set of complicated patterns.

Lastly, he opened the crystal ball at the top of his staff and scooped up blood directly from the victim's chest to fill the chamber. When he had enough, he closed the crystal ball. He took the heart he had removed and placed it carefully in the eye of the staff, then closed and locked that chamber as well.

Stepping away from the altar, he walked out to the surrounding forest, a pleased smile on his face. "I will return Xaviero with the blood of the royals. We both will walk out of here free."

Afanasiv could make out Xaviero sitting in the shadows, rocking back and forth as if in terrible pain. Xavier strode boldly up to a tree that looked decidedly familiar. It was one close to the inn where Afanasiv and his brethren were staying. This tree was slightly different. The trunk and branches were twisted and darker in appearance.

Xavier tapped the staff to the earth's floor three times and then raised it toward the sky three times. He walked in a circle counterclockwise, not around the tree but in front of it.

I call on all that is unholy to aid me this night
I seek revenge on those who would put me in such a plight
Come forth out of your hiding places
Shed light on my enemies' faces
I must walk above to achieve my goal
Open for me a large portal.

In front of Xavier, a tear in the fabric in the walls between the underworld and aboveground appeared. It looked to Afanasiv like a giant archway. Xavier stroked his beard and then started forward. Before he could step through, another voice stopped him.

"You will remember who you serve, Xavier. If you fail to keep your staff with you, my army will reacquire you immediately. If you fail to answer when I call, you will die immediately. Do not believe that because you are aboveground that you can escape me. That would be very foolish thinking."

"I understand fully, mistress." Xavier bowed low and then turned back to the portal. With great confidence, he stepped through.

"You had better," the voice followed him. "If you lose your staff, you will come straight back to me."

As Afanasiv was gathering the information for Vasilisa, she was stalling Xavier and doing her best to keep his attention centered on her.

"How did they force you, Aunt? You have always been the strongest among us. When there was no one to aid my dying mother, you fought off the attackers and kept them from violating her body. You did that with no one to aid you." Vasilisa didn't have to reach for admiration and love, it was right there whenever she pulled up the memory of Olga desperately trying to save her sister's life.

Olga nodded her head. "Yes. I did try so hard to keep her alive, but there were so many wounds, Vasi, so many." For once, there seemed to be genuine sorrow—or maybe Vasilisa just wanted there to be. "Before she died, Bronya told me how extraordinary you are and how I must guard you at all times and continue teaching you to fight. I was to encourage you in learning all sorts of defensive and offensive techniques. She told me you hold the soul of a Carpathian and must guard it at all times. That it was a sacred trust, and no matter what, you had to be up to the task."

Olga's expression turned crafty the moment she mentioned the soul of the Carpathian. "Maybe you can barter with that soul. It's only half, in any case. Maybe the mage would take that in return for our lives."

"Why would I want half a soul when I already have two whole ones right here?" Xavier snarled, but there was no way for him to contain the look of pure glee. The blood in the crystal ball swirled around like mad. Suddenly, the heart began to beat a fast rhythm.

Afanasiv found the overly loud beat distracting. The rapid heartbeat thundered in his ears and roared out a challenge as he backed out of Xavier carefully.

Olga pleaded with the mage. "Don't kill me, please. Take the soul of the Carpathian instead. Vasi, give it to him now."

Xavier pretended to consider that. He shook his head a couple of times, looked off into the forest as if contemplating, frowned and then sighed. "Oh, all right, then. Hand it over to me now, and I won't kill this worthless being."

"What would you want with half a soul?" Vasilisa asked.

"Vasi," Olga wailed. "Don't make him mad. He agreed to our bargain."

"*Your* bargain. I didn't make the bargain with him," Vasilisa pointed out in that same confident, quiet way she had. She continued to look at both of them, yet they couldn't make her out. The snow around her was blinding white, as was the coat she wore. The white hat covered the dark hair she had fixed on top of her head. One moment she appeared there, and the next she was somewhere else. "I need to know why he wants this soul before I turn over my legacy to him."

Olga screamed as the knife pierced the delicate skin of her neck and blood began dripping down onto the material of her blouse and jacket. She shuddered and shook, opened her mouth again, and no sound emerged.

"I tire of the sound of your voice. This conversation is between Vasilisa and me. You stay out of it." Xavier waved his hand and mumbled a curse as he did so. "I cannot abide high-pitched shrieking."

Vasilisa sighed. "I will admit, her steady high-pitched shrieks were getting to me, as well. It makes it hard to think when someone is continually screaming in the background."

"You can't imagine how many times I warned her I would take away her ability to speak if she kept it up. I warned her several times to just have a clear, concise way of speaking."

"She always *used* to have a clear way of speaking. I never noticed that she screeched like that."

Afanasiv thought it brilliant the way Vasilisa was subtly playing to the mage's ego and aligning herself with him.

Olga's reaction was to fight harder, until Xavier pressed the blade tighter against her skin in warning.

"She's seventy, you know. That isn't much in age to someone like you, or even in the Lycan world. We have tremendous longevity, but sadly Aunt Olga's eyesight began to fade a bit. She was considered an up-and-coming star in the dance world, and that became closed to her." Vasilisa poured sympathy into her voice. "She was always brilliant onstage. She'd taken the world by storm. Then accidents began to happen. Small ones at first. Then much bigger ones, until finally her ankle and foot were shattered when a beam came down on her left leg during a performance."

Xavier petted Olga's head soothingly, as if he cared for her. Olga settled under his continuous stroking, much like a dog might when her master indulged her. "How sad for Olga."

"It was, really. There was an investigation, but the findings didn't help Olga recover or ever dance again. Another girl wanted to be the prima ballerina, and her parents had arranged for the accidents. They were punished, but there was an outpouring of sympathy for the girl. She claimed she knew nothing of what her parents had planned. She cried so prettily in front of the cameras and managed to convince the world she was innocent."

"But she wasn't, was she?" Xavier coaxed. His voice intoned sympathy, but his facial expression couldn't hide his glee.

Vasilisa pretended not to see. "No, she was guilty, and was such a good friend of Aunt Olga's. She visited Olga in the hospital every day. Cried with her. Brought her news of the ballet. Talked over whether she should accept the position of prima ballerina when they offered it to her. Aunt Olga encouraged her because she was certain she was her friend."

"Ah, yes, friendship. I have no doubt when Olga found out her friend betrayed her, it was a dreadful time for her. And yet, when Barnabas came to her, she still believed in forming strong attachments. She didn't learn her lesson, did she? Given such a painful one, I have to conclude she has a stubborn streak, or she is so desperate for someone to care about her that she will debase herself for the chance to serve them if they show her a little affection, false though it be."

Vasilisa's stomach lurched. Instantly, Afanasiv surrounded her with warmth. *I am here with you. We have only a few more minutes to get through. Once we have the entire pattern, we can bind Xavier to the underworld for all time.*

Afanasiv felt her reluctance to expose her aunt's private life any further. He couldn't blame her, but he worked without emotions. Vasilisa didn't compartmentalize her emotions in the way that he did. He hadn't felt anything for centuries. It was easy for him to slip back into hunting mode and become the ancient warrior tracking vampires when he had no emotions.

Vasilisa felt everything. These people were her family. Her friends. People she looked after and loved. No death or betrayal was going to be easy on her. She wouldn't be able to push her feelings aside.

"Her friend's name was Inessa," Xavier said. "Isn't that so, Olga?" He used her hair to make her nod her head up and down. "She was quite beautiful. Still is, even with that scar on her face. I wonder how it got there? Your nephews investigated further, as I recall, when you told me the story. They weren't satisfied and believed Inessa lied. You didn't hear her lies because you were given pain pills at first, and later, you didn't want to believe she was guilty. You would rather be lied to than face the truth of betrayal. Do you see how weak and pathetic that makes you?"

Vasilisa nearly took a step forward. By doing so, she would have given away her position. Afanasiv stopped her. *You have his entire pattern. He cannot flee to the underworld if he is in possession of his staff. I can shatter both the crystal and the eye with lightning. You will have to reverse his spell in order to send him back and seal him to the underworld for all time. As for Olga, she may get away while we deal with Xavier.*

Let her. I can track her. We need to know every portal where the demons are slipping through.

Afanasiv didn't like how weary she sounded. He needed to hold her, not go chasing after vampires as he had for two thousand years. He hadn't realized her care would become his top priority rather than the hunt and battle of the undead.

Let's get this done, my lady.

In the distance, he built a storm. They could hear the roll of thunder as it moved rapidly toward them. Lightning lit up the sky for a moment. Xavier laughed and raised his staff high, as if seeking power.

"I never saw Aunt Olga in that light," Vasilisa admitted. "I thought of her as powerful to carry on after my brothers exposed Inessa to the world for betraying her."

"But even then, Inessa turned the tables on her and made her look weak, didn't she? She refused to bow down. She kept her head high and sneered at how pathetic Olga was. Even then, some of the Lycans agreed with her."

When the storm was just over the ridge, still a distance from them, Afanasiv directed two forks to streak across the sky, aiming straight for the crystal ball holding the swirling blood and the heart in the center of the staff. Both hit with deadly accuracy, shattering the crystal and incinerating the heart and blood instantly. Blue flames raced up the staff, burning so hot that, howling, Xavier had no choice but to drop the twisted wooden pole into the snow. Still those flames leapt higher, consuming the staff as it lay on the icy ground.

Olga crawled backward on her knees as the knife slid away from her. Both hands went up to her throat as she clawed at it, trying to regain her ability to speak.

Vasilisa stayed in the midst of the swirling snow, columns shooting up to veil what she was doing as she countered the patterns Xavier had used to provide a portal for himself and his demons to come through.

Xavier dropped to his knees and began to throw snow on the blue flames burning the thick knots and spirals that made up his staff. The more he piled on the snow, the higher the flames leapt. The fire crackled and popped and threw a strange light into the sky. Xavier's beard began to smoke. His long robes smoldered. He paid no attention as he wailed and then abruptly rose and looked around for the pieces of broken crystal.

The chambers had shattered and were lost in the sea of snow now dotted with blackened ash. Xavier held up his hands and began to chant, trying to find a way to bring his staff back to one piece. Afanasiv knew the mage had no hope to restore the heart or blood of the demon that had helped to carry him aboveground. The blue flame was Vasilisa's, one she used to fight demons from the underground. Technically, Xavier was just that—a demon. He might be a mage, but he was also a demon sent by Lilith to do her work above the underworld.

Vasilisa worked fast, moving backward through the spell that had brought Xavier through the portal as the high mage concentrated on attempting to command the pieces of crystal glass to him. Xavier's beard and clothes began to pull toward the right, along with the wind. Afanasiv subtly changed the direction of the storm toward the portal, where it had been constructed outside the inn.

The robes flapped around the mage and began to drag him backward. His gray hair pulled him along with his beard. Stunned, finally realizing what was happening, he shook his head and let out a scream of protest. "Lilith, no. Give me more time."

Vasilisa reached for Afanasiv's hand as the high mage was carried away from them, spinning through the trees toward the portal, where he slipped through as it collapsed behind him.

"No, take me with you," Olga implored. Without Xavier, his spells were broken, and she had her voice once more. "You promised me. They won't accept me here. You promised me." She stumbled to her feet and looked around fearfully.

7

Snow fell in light flurries as silence once again settled over the forest. Afanasiv wrapped his arm around Vasilisa. She didn't want him to. She was terrified she would break down weeping uncontrollably, and he would see what a hot mess destiny had stuck him with. At the same time, she wanted to lean into him, press her face against his chest and, just for a few moments, let him comfort her.

"I think I would much prefer the latter." Afanasiv's large palm cupped the back of her skull to hold her against his broad chest. "Holding you is always going to be my first choice, Vasilisa. I know you're strong. You never have to pretend with me."

"I don't feel very strong right now. I don't understand what happened to my aunt. If she was having problems or doubts, why wouldn't she come to her family? Why wouldn't she first talk to us? Didn't we deserve her trust and loyalty after all the years of loving her?"

"Jealousy is an ugly flaw, and it can destroy people from the inside out. It can eat away at relationships, erode them slowly, *sívamet*. I have seen this happen many times in my life over these centuries. Your aunt was jealous and perhaps didn't recognize it at first because she had her dancing. Once that was taken from her, she felt lost. She didn't know who she was anymore."

Vasilisa could understand what he was saying. Olga loved dancing. She lived to dance. She would often take out her ballet shoes and talk to Vasilisa about dancing on the stage and how magical it was. A light would shine in her eyes, and her entire face would light up. She seemed to go somewhere else. Vasilisa loved to see her so enthralled, but then Olga would look so sad when she put her slippers away that it made Vasilisa's heart ache. She would wrap her arms around her aunt's neck and kiss her face all over to try to make her feel better.

"It was so sad to see her when she would reminisce about dancing on the stage. And that horrible Inessa woman, who betrayed their friendship the way she did, made it all the worse for her."

"Inessa certainly didn't help, but I think by that time, Olga had already started down the path of destruction. Barnabas, no doubt, had already come into her life. This conspiracy against your family started some time ago, Vasilisa. It is well thought out and planned. It is their bad luck that you and I were destined to become lifemates. Clearly, they had no idea that you are such an excellent demon slayer."

Vasilisa sighed and lifted her head. "We should check on Garald and then track Olga. I'm sure she is heading toward the portal the demons are slipping through. We need to find it. Then we have to find a way to get my other two brothers back out from under the demons' commands."

She was going to have to rest soon. Vasilisa knew that the kinds of spells she was working with, fighting against those in the underworld, were particularly draining. Afanasiv was shoring her up, but even his vast strength couldn't last forever.

Without a word, Afanasiv lifted her into his arms and carried her close to his chest as he whisked her through the snow to the shelter her brother had taken Taisiya to. The small shedlike building was one the shepherds often occupied. It had a good wood heater and was always kept supplied. Garald already had the woodstove glowing hot, and he was attending to Taisiya's many wounds. The cuts appeared to be mostly superficial, but a few were deeper lacerations that had to be closed with stitches. They covered her entire body.

Garald looked up as they entered.

Taisiya covered her face with her hands. "Don't look at me," she implored.

"Little sister," Afanasiv said. "You suffered each of those wounds protecting Garald. Protecting the royals. Those are badges of your courage. They speak well of who you are and why Garald thinks you are an extraordinary woman."

"That is so," Vasilisa agreed. "I have soothing ointment to cover the wounds after my brother finishes. It will help to heal each injury much faster and leave no permanent scar."

"If I hadn't looked at you in the first place, this never would have happened," Garald snapped, his eyes glittering a deep blue. "I was wrong to ever seek you out. I'm sorry, Taisiya. I let myself believe for one moment that I could find happiness with you. That I could protect you from enemies. They surround us all the time, chipping away at us. And then there's the family curse." He flicked his gaze to Afanasiv. "I'll bet my sister didn't mention the family curse."

"Garald, I know it hurts to see Taisiya this way, but—"

Garald cut his sister off. "You think it hurts to see her this way? It *kills* me to see her this way. It *destroys* me. I did this to her just by looking at her. Just by showing in public that I cared about her."

"Don't say that, Garald," Taisiya pleaded. "That means you take away my free will. My choices. I would never have willingly done this for anyone other than you, because you are my choice. Always my choice. From the moment I saw you there in the shadows all alone. Those demons tried to break me. That hideous woman tried. They said things about you, but I wouldn't believe them because I believed in you. Don't take that away from me."

Garald's answer was to bring both of her bruised hands to his mouth. He kissed them gently and then turned her wrists up to be kissed equally as tenderly. "I could never leave you, Taisiya. Ignore the crap coming out of my mouth. I'm venting."

"What hideous woman?" Vasilisa asked. "If you don't want to re-peat what you suffered out loud—and who could blame you?—please allow the three of us to link together, and we can look at the images in your mind and see who did this to you. We will not view anything else. On that I give you my word."

The last thing I want to do is stumble onto her fantasies about my brother.

Taisiya's eyebrows drew together in a delicate frown. "You can do that?"

Garald kissed her knuckles and nodded. "It's a gift handed down to royals. We have various other things we can do. I tried to tell you we're not always what we seem. Our life isn't royal balls, it's mostly serving our people. I didn't want you to come into it with rose-colored glasses."

"It's just that if you can read my thoughts . . ." She trailed off.

He grinned at her. "You can't lie to me. I meant what I said when I told you there would never be other men in your life."

"Or women in yours," she added.

"We're loyal."

"Time, Garald," Vasilisa reminded him as gently as possible while still showing urgency.

"We're going to look at your memories of what happened very quickly," Garald explained. "I'm right here. I'll be with you."

The moment Taisiya nodded, Vasilisa and Afanasiv slipped into her mind, taking Garald with them. They sifted backward until they came to the moment when Olga knocked on the door of Taisiya's par-ents' home. She introduced herself, although they knew who she was and were delighted that she had come to visit them. She took her time, basking in their admiration of her clothes and gracious ways. She told them she wanted to "borrow" their sweet daughter for a few days in order to better introduce her to the life of a royal. There were certain protocols Taisiya needed to learn, and Olga would guide and teach her as she had Vasilisa. She would act as a chaperone, as well, to make certain Garald was always a gentleman.

Taisiya's parents readily agreed, pleased and flattered that Olga had taken an interest in their daughter. When she was told to pack clothes, Olga waved that away and said she would see that Taisiya had suitable clothing for the court she was going to. No one seemed to notice her evil smirk. Once she had delivered Taisiya to the underworld, using the portal provided by the wizard, the poor girl was subjected to torture, hundreds of knife cuts and all sorts of threats. They wanted her to voluntarily collect blood from Garald.

Olga told her he visited other girls nightly, had several women at the same time and laughed at her innocence. Taisiya refused to believe her. In the end, she went silent, and the demons, angry with her, trussed her up like a turkey and stitched the syringe and tube into her hand while Xavier cast a spell demanding she get blood from Garald. Olga danced with the demons like a madwoman, laughing with glee before following the demons and high mage out of the portal and back to the surface.

"So, it was my aunt who delivered you into the hands of the high mage," Garald said. "Everyone thought him gone, but all this time, he's been plotting revenge." He passed his hand over his face as if that would remove a veil for him. "And Aunt Olga? Why such treachery against me?"

"Not just you, Garald. She is responsible for what has been done to Andros and Grigor as well. They have become marionettes under the rule of the dark queen. Andros is fighting it every step of the way. I have not yet seen Grigor, but battles have taken place where both siblings have traveled."

Garald half rose, looked at the young woman under his care and slowly sank back down. "Are you certain of this information, Vasi?"

"Yes, it is the truth. Afanasiv and I will go to them after we find the portal the demons are coming through. We need to close that."

Garald shook his head. "That's unacceptable. You go after our brothers first. What if you seal them down there, and we can never bring them back?"

"I'm careful in how I word everything, Garald." She was so tired. She didn't want to argue with her brother and waste time.

"Did you read the tarot cards?" he demanded.

"I always read them first thing every evening," she admitted. "It's how I start my day. Today was no different. I got the hanged man repeatedly, but he was upright. The tree is rooted in the underworld. When the hanged man is upright, that is a signal to suspend action, or at least give more time to reflect in order not to make a mistake. I'm not making any mistakes when it comes to Andros and Grigor. Everything in me urges me to rush in and get them out, but I've lived my life with those cards as my guide, and I'm not going to start implementing change now."

Garald put both hands over his face. "I feel as if our entire world is crumbling, Vasi, and I'm doing nothing to stop it."

"Take me home," Taisiya suggested. "My parents can care for me, and you'll be free to go with your sister."

Vasilisa shook her head before Garald could answer. "He can't do that. The moment you're with your parents, the demons will once again strike at him through you. They'll kill your parents and take you back with them to the underworld. Garald will have no choice but to follow you there."

Even as she uttered the words, the realization came to her. "We know Andros was seeing a woman in the eastern section—a young widow named Lada. She hadn't been married long when her husband was killed taking down trees. She was already pregnant with his child. Andros didn't give me the information; the rumor mill did."

Garald nodded. "Andros did mention her a time or two."

"Who was Grigor seeing? You would know. Don't pretend otherwise. This is important."

Garald sighed. "Karine, a friend of Taisiya. You know that ability Grigor has of seeing everything at once. He was standing there talking to me, and then he was gone, weaving his way through the crowd straight toward her. Later, when I asked about her, he said she sparkled, had this weird glow from the inside out. They danced together all night. He wasn't nearly as cautious as I was, but then he was always more adventurous."

"That's how they got the others to do their bidding," Vasilisa said. "Olga must have lured Lada and Karine away from the safety of their homes and families by saying she wanted to teach them royal protocol. They were taken to the underworld and tortured, made to think Andros and Grigor no longer cared for them, and then tricked into taking their blood."

"Or," Afanasiv corrected gently, "they did hold out in the way Taisiya did, and your brothers followed them into the underworld. Both are courageous men. I doubt they would back down if they knew their women had been taken."

"They wouldn't," Garald agreed. "They're both like me. I would follow Taisiya and take her back."

"Even if it was a fool's mission, and you knew you would be trading your life for a very slim chance?" Afanasiv pressed.

Garald thought it over and then nodded. "Yes."

"I believe, *sívamet*, you figured out how your brothers were lured into the underworld and forced to work with demons and vampires."

"I don't understand how Olga is involved," Garald said.

"This is not our aunt. If she comes here knocking on the door and looks as sweet as a little lamb, take her head off with your sword the instant she opens her mouth. I've got to go. Taisiya, we'll meet again under better circumstances. Do whatever my brother says in order to get better."

She turned her blue eyes, sparkling with mischief, on her brother. "Do *not* compromise that girl unless you intend to marry her immediately."

Garald pointed to the door. "Worry about yourself. And get out. Love and loyalty."

"Love and loyalty," Vasilisa answered, blew him a kiss, waved at Taisiya and stepped out of the shepherd's cabin.

Afanasiv followed her out and closed the door behind him. He remained a few moments longer in order to throw a quick spell of protection around the small cabin, over it and under it, making it nearly impossible for any enemy to get to the couple inside.

Vasilisa's heart contracted. It was a small thing, but it meant a lot to her that he would take the time to think of watching out for her brother and Taisiya. Those small kindnesses were ingrained in him, whether he knew it or not. They were part of what made him who he was.

"Where to, my lady?" He gave her a small courtly bow.

He was a big man, and the bow should have seemed ridiculous, but he was so graceful, every movement fluid, he appeared almost princely.

"I think tracking Olga to the original portal would be the smartest move. There was an earthquake not too long ago, and almost at once, we began to have strange occurrences. My brothers and I became certain the quake had opened a passage to the underworld. Now that I've seen those demons and realize they were programmed to use those low notes to displace rock and move plates, I'm sure that I'm correct and Lilith is behind the earthquake."

Afanasiv scooped her up, cradling her close to his chest.

"I really am good at flying."

"I'm sure you are. You seem to be good at everything you do; however, in this instance, as I'm not tired and you are, this makes sense. You can conserve your energy while we hunt for your aunt. We'll be able to track her from the sky. I can cover the distance fast once we have a direction. You pay attention to the ground and any signs that you might see of Olga's passing. I'll be moving fast," he warned.

"My eyes can keep up." Unless she fell asleep. He was warm and she felt safe with him, an odd thing when her entire world seemed to be imploding.

He laughed softly in her ear. She didn't know why his breath against her ear or that low laughter seemed so incredibly intimate, but it did. Just like that, she became aware of him as a man and her as a woman. She burrowed closer to him, sliding her arms around his neck but keeping her gaze on the ground.

I suppose the snow has covered her tracks, Afanasiv ventured.

I can track her. Vasilisa gave a little sniff of disdain for Olga's chances of escaping her. *She thinks she is so much smarter because she has a few demons for friends, and they've talked to her about how much slyer and more cunning she is than we are because we trust her. I am the most loyal of friends, as are my brothers. But we make bitter, relentless enemies. She betrayed her family. She delivered her nephews to the underworld. For all I know, she may have tortured and killed their women. She will not elude me.*

He might as well know some of her worst traits before they got too far into their relationship. She wasn't an easy person to be around. She spoke right up and gave her opinion, even when it wasn't asked for. She considered herself an equal with any man in the room. She wouldn't back down if she believed she was right. She was Lycan through and through, and she would hunt an enemy and never stop until she found and eradicated them.

You are exactly the woman for me, Afanasiv said without reservation.

She heard the pride in his voice. She wasn't used to a man like him. He made her want—more. Want a real relationship. Want physical intimacy. She wanted so much more than that, if she was admitting the truth to herself and to him. He was in her mind. He could read her thoughts.

I grew up in a wonderful family. My parents were good to us, but . . .
She hesitated, feeling disloyal. *They didn't always stay in step with one another. Or they felt out of step to me. My mother kept this secret from my father. Her legacy of protecting your soul and then handing it to me when it was time for her to have children. She had sons first and finally me. She passed your soul to me and told me from the time I was little that I had a sacred trust that had to be fulfilled, but that no one else could know, not even Papa.*

Afanasiv remained silent, allowing her to choose her words, never hurrying her. Never impatient with her. He flew low over the ground, shielding them from any eyes, but true to his word, he flew very fast.

I think Papa knew she kept secrets from him, and after a while, it took a toll on their marriage. She told me often that she loved my father. Really loved him, and I believe she did, but how could she?

She was not my lifemate, sívamet. Once she was of a certain age and realized she was merely the guardian of my soul, she was free to love whomever she chose to give her heart to. In that way, she would have children, or at least a daughter to continue the legacy. I have heard of such things but had no idea I would ever be a part of it. Your legacy of demon fighting was also something your mother kept from your father?

Vasilisa nodded her head and then rubbed her cheek against his chest even as her gaze followed her aunt's stumbling tracks in the snow. *Slow down just a bit, Afanasiv. I think we're closing in on her.*

Through the snow-shrouded world, Vasilisa caught occasional glimpses of a tall, slender figure wearing trousers and a very fashionable matching jacket that in no way would keep anyone warm. As she peered down, Afanasiv took them directly over that pitiful-looking woman. It was, indeed, her aunt.

Olga appeared much older than Vasilisa had ever seen her look. Her hair was disheveled and falling in strands around her face. From her position above, Vasilisa could see that small patches of her scalp were bare. Olga reached up and tore at her hair, ripping some out by the roots. She was ruining her own hair and didn't seem to notice the damage she was doing.

Olga alternated between muttering curses, promising revenge and sobbing. She fell in the new knee-deep snow and pounded on it with her fists before managing to extricate herself. Snow clung to her clothes, forming little balls that hung off her and made it more difficult to walk. Still, Olga persisted.

Why doesn't she shift? She's Lycan. If she took her wolf form, she could run over the surface much more easily. This makes no sense. Vasilisa tried to puzzle it out. Olga was intelligent. In their world, Lycans were respected, and they ruled the territory. Should someone come along, they wouldn't know the difference between the shifter and the real animal.

She might not even remember she is Lycan, my lady.

His voice, so tender. Wrapping her up in a velvet heat to comfort her when sorrow threatened to overwhelm her.

She was once our beloved aunt. When our parents were murdered, she fought off the intruders. The boys helped and so did I. There were so many of them. Eventually, when it appeared as if we were going to be overrun by the enemy, she demanded we enter the safe room. When we said we wouldn't go without her, she insisted. She backed us up right into it.

Vasilisa rubbed at her temples. The headache that had been there earlier had come roaring back with a vengeance. *We could hear and see everything through the audio and video our father had set up. She fought them off. I don't know how many she killed to keep them off us, but she took up a position in the narrow hallway leading to the safe room and forced them to come to her the only way they could.*

Afanasiv brushed kisses on top of her head, his lips lingering in her hair. *Always remember her that way. That is your true aunt, not this shell of a puppet. Your aunt died a long time ago, and it is proper to mourn her. When this is over, that is what we will do for her. I can assure you, sívamet, your aunt is no longer alive.*

She knew he was right. She had to come to terms with the idea that her beloved aunt was truly dead. If she thought of this woman as a puppet, her body an illusion rather than the same woman, that would be a huge help when she had to deal with her.

Thank you, Afanasiv. Seriously, I don't know how I would get through this without you.

I have no doubt that you would find your way, but I am grateful we are facing this together. She has stopped and is looking around her for landmarks.

Vasilisa didn't want her aunt to be lost. Lycans didn't lose their way, but if her aunt couldn't remember being Lycan, then she might not have a navigation system, either. That would mean they wouldn't find the crack in the earth the demons had opened in order to slip through.

She will find it, Vasilisa. She is guided now by her connection to the underworld. She won't be able to stop herself. She will keep going until she finds it.

She's going to freeze to death if she's out in this snow much longer, she countered.

Do you see the snow melt beneath her steps? That makes it harder for her to walk. She doesn't realize it yet. She may never realize that the way she is using the heating system given to her by her demon friends, she is not making it easier for herself.

Vasilisa's brows drew together as she watched much more closely the way Olga placed each foot in the snow. Earlier, she had been skimming lightly over the surface, but now she was sinking with each step. There was a curious glow coming from her body, down low around her ankles, almost as if she had a battery pack she was switching on and off.

Olga left the safety of the trees and stepped cautiously out into a small clearing. She kept looking around her as if she expected trouble.

Do you feel that? The warning in the air? Afanasiv asked. *Olga does. She is being watched by half a dozen sets of eyes.*

Are we safe? Should we be up in the trees and still? Vasilisa was anxious, but mostly because she was doing her best to connect with Olga. She wanted to know if she could and how far that connection would go. All the way into the underworld? Was that a possibility?

Those are real wolves, Vasilisa, Afanasiv reminded her. *If she is to live, she had better use that portal immediately.*

I can send the wolves away.

Once again, his hand came up to the back of her head, fingers starting a slow massage on her scalp designed to ease the tension out of her. As massages went, this one worked. She found herself relaxing into him.

There is no need. She is moving fast to the other side of the clearing and that deep but narrow gorge right there. That seems to be her destination.

Vasilisa clutched his arm, suddenly excited. *Look down into the gorge, Siv. There's a crack that runs along the far wall from the top to the bottom in a zigzag pattern. That's it. That's where they're coming in.*

The opening was difficult to see. Hidden in the dirt, brush and rocks that jutted out from the wall of the gorge, the fracture looked as if it were just a darker stripe among so many. The snow hadn't yet covered it because of the overhang from above.

Olga slid down from the top of the gorge on the opposite side, traveling at breakneck speed along what had clearly been used as a chute by many before. The slide was slick and packed down, much like an alligator slide that had been in existence for a number of years. At the bottom, Olga shot off the slide and onto the floor of the gorge. Rocks buried in the dirt and snow were everywhere, making it a particularly hard landing. Olga didn't seem to care. She picked herself up and began to make her way to that dark, narrow opening in the wall.

Is it possible for us to enter the underworld undetected? Would we be able to enter using Olga somehow? Or just go in ourselves?

Vasilisa wasn't certain she wanted him to answer her in the affirmative. The idea was terrifying, but if they could get in, they might discover her brothers and the women used to lure them there.

For the first time, Afanasiv hesitated. She felt the hesitation keenly.

It is possible but extremely dangerous. I told you I was held for some time before I was able to escape. They can smell human flesh, and they go into a frenzy. One mistake and it would be over for you. Or me. Or both of us.

I'm not talking about taking our physical bodies, Siv. Deliberately she used a more intimate nickname for him. *I'm suggesting we shed our bodies in the way Carpathians do and travel with Olga.*

I understood your plan, Vasi, he countered, amusement in his voice. *What do you plan on doing with our physical bodies while we travel? They would freeze to death in the snow. Or someone might run across them and move them, believing we were really dead. The other worry would be that Olga would be punished or, worse, beheaded. Where would that leave us?*

She hadn't considered those things, and they were legitimate worries. *Do you have any ideas, Siv?*

His nod was slow in coming. *I think we should allow Olga to return on her own. We know where the demons are coming and going. This, to me, is the right time to slow everything down so we don't make a wrong decision. I have memories in my head I seem to have misplaced. Whether it was done on purpose or not, I can't tell you. I do know I sometimes get alarming images rising up out of nowhere, and I am aware I'm accessing those memories.*

These are memories from when you were imprisoned in the underworld?

Now she wanted—no, needed—to comfort him. Once again, she slid her arms around his neck and pressed her body tightly against his. *Afanasiv, we don't have to look at those memories if they upset you. We can find another way.*

I am your lifemate, Vasilisa. I provide whatever you need. Right now, you need to find a way to recover your brothers. We have no choice but to use every scrap of information available to us. He indicated the gorge with a jerk of his chin. *There she goes. Are you able to follow the pattern she is using to open the fracture so she can use it?*

Already he was taking them closer, giving Vasilisa every opportunity to study the specific spell her aunt was using so she could copy it when she needed to.

Olga looked as if she were climbing up the side of the wall, and then she slung one leg over the top of the fault and pulled herself up. She hesitated. The interior suddenly glowed orange and red. When it did, Olga leapt down out of sight.

Vasilisa let out her breath. "That was unexpected. Do you think she jumped into a furnace of flames?"

"No, I believe that was a signal to allow her entrance. She was waiting for that before she entered fully."

"Great. How are we going to get in?" Vasilisa asked.

He grinned at her and put her down. "First, before anything else, we're going to explore those memories I have stored away. I wanted to forget them for whatever reason. If I did something terrible, I ask for forgiveness ahead of time."

She bit down on her lip and regarded him steadily with what she hoped was a stern expression. "What kind of terrible thing are we talking here? It would make a difference."

His eyebrow shot up. "I might have killed a few people."

She shrugged and waved that away. "I'm certain they were deserving of it. What else?"

"I started with the worst," he admitted. "I don't know where to go from there."

"Apparently, you aren't nearly the badass you think you are. There's a shepherd's cabin just over the ridge. We could go there and sort through your memories if you'd like."

For an answer, he scooped her up and held her close to his chest again. She liked being there too much to protest.

"What indiscretion were you thinking you might find, Vasilisa, that could be unforgivable?"

She felt heat rise into her face. She refused to meet his eyes. "It was a silly game we were playing. I was teasing you."

"Perhaps a little silly and maybe a game, but the question held some kind of significance for you. What was it?"

She set her teeth and wished she was like some of the other Lycan women who would never succumb to a man's request, no matter how reasonable he sounded. They had formed their own society in opposition to the Sacred Circle, refusing to be shut out of the things they'd fought so hard to achieve. No one wanted to be relegated to child care and cooking for a man while he could do anything he wanted to do and had complete control in everything said or done.

"There is nothing wrong with staying home to take care of a child or cooking for your spouse, which, I assure you, you will never have to do. At least the cooking part. And I'm the type of man who believes if I father a child, I want to be there every moment of his or her life. The wonder of just thinking about such a miracle is amazing to me."

"You would stay home to take care of a child?" She did her best to keep sarcasm out of her voice, but really? Afanasiv was born a predator. She didn't see him shrugging off that part of himself so easily.

"Absolutely, I would. I don't do anything by halves, Vasilisa. When I become a father, I intend to be the best father I can be. I understand the need for women and children better than most. I treasure my lifemate and will certainly treasure any children we have together."

She believed him. She believed he would stay home with the children if she didn't care to. He'd probably homeschool them, as well, and they'd rock every assignment.

Vasilisa found herself smiling. "To the right, just follow that little worn path. The shepherd's cabin is there."

Afanasiv set her down right at the door. Like the one Garald and Taisiya occupied, this cabin was well stocked with supplies for anyone in need. Wood was neatly stacked in one corner of the room close to the woodstove. The single cot that stretched along the wall closest to the stove had several neatly folded blankets stacked on the mattress. Canned goods were stored on crude shelves over a sink. Two metal plates and forks and knives were arranged on another shelf.

It was a familiar sight. Over the centuries, Afanasiv had seen many cabins, some not so fancy and others on wealthy ranches, but they were all there for the same reason—to aid the shepherd or cowboy in bad weather.

They settled quickly in the warmth once Afanasiv got the fire going. He simply waved his hand, and the logs burned brightly, flames rolling over them to heat the interior fast.

Vasilisa sank down onto the cot, leaving the chair for Afanasiv. She pressed her back to the wall as she watched his face carefully. By others' standards, he would never be considered a handsome man, but he was wholly masculine and, to her, utterly attractive. He always appeared calm when, right now, she was a mass of nerves.

"Relax, *sívamet*, I am no longer in the underworld. I'm safe here with you. They cannot call me back."

"You don't know that."

"I know." He was firm about it. "I'm going to drop my shields now. You may find some shocking battle tactics, but ignore them. We have to consider the time. If dawn reaches us, we will have to go to ground and try this on the next rising."

She hadn't thought about the position of the moon or sun. Sorina was always chastising her, reminding her to be cognizant of when the sun rose and fell.

Vasilisa nodded and shed her body. She was becoming more adept at doing so. It was a matter of letting go of one's ego and becoming a healing light or attempting to discover what was wrong without any truly selfish motive. Afanasiv did the same. The two of them traveled through his mind, Vasilisa not really knowing what she was searching for, but certain she would know if she stumbled across memories of demons.

Here. She had no idea how much time had passed before Siv called out to her. *These are the memories I lost, or a better way of putting it is "misplaced."*

Vasilisa was so elated, she almost missed the uneasiness in Afanasiv's voice. *Let me look while you keep watch,* she suggested, not wanting him to have to relive the experience.

Afanasiv had followed one of his brethren to the underworld, determined to find him and bring him back. All along, it had been Afanasiv they wanted, not his fellow Carpathian. They were interested in two things: his unusual eyes, with the colors that swirled from blue to green and back again, and the birthmark he had carried for centuries that never faded—a small warriorlike symbol of the dragon. The dragon appeared to be etched into his skin, yet when the demons went looking for it, it faded away, hiding from them.

He was tortured in brutal, violent ways that no one should ever have to endure. Vasilisa, at times, found herself weeping for him, praying his body wouldn't stand up to the abuse and he would die, but then she realized he had overcome what the demons had done to him. He was alive. He had escaped. She watched every detail of his escape carefully so that if there was a need, she would know the way out. Only then did she return to her body.

"You are Dragonseeker. Why not use that name, an old and well-respected name?" She made certain there was no judgment in her before she spoke, although it made no sense to use a surname no one would recognize.

"A distant relative, no more. You saw what the demons did. They were in a frenzy to get me to betray my lifemate and code of honor. No Dragonseeker has ever turned vampire. I was not about to be the first. There is so much hatred toward the Dragonseeker lineage."

"Is there any wonder, Siv?" She watched his face closely. Perhaps he really wasn't putting it all together. "Skyler is Dragonseeker. Tatijana is Dragonseeker. Razvan is Dragonseeker. Branislava is Dragonseeker. Natalya is Dragonseeker. Every name is someone who played a part in defeating one of the high mages. Getting just one Dragonseeker to turn would destroy the legend."

"I did not give up my lifemate in a moment of madness?"

"How could you when you had no idea if she was in the world?" Vasilisa countered. This time she went to him to comfort him. Wrapping him in her arms, she lay her cheek against his heart. "You're only guilty of holding out against the demons in the underworld, and that isn't a crime."

8

Y ou must stay aboveground and guard my body," Afanasiv announced. "I will travel into the underworld and find your brothers and their women. If the women relinquished their souls, they will be left there. If not, I will try to find a way to protect them while they are there or bring them out with me. Regardless, I will get your brothers out if at all possible." He wasn't going to add that if they had also surrendered their souls, they would not be coming home to her.

He caught her head in both hands to still it. "Stop shaking your head, woman. You know it will be much easier for me to simply look after myself. I cannot be divided when I go into the underworld after your brothers and their women. In any case, you didn't look too closely at the reality of what went on when I was down there. What those scars on my soul mean."

"It doesn't matter what they mean."

"It does, Vasilisa. Everything matters in the underworld. Carpathians can become demons, beasts without thought or reason when they go into battle. They live for the need of violence, to feel the rush when, finally, we can feel something—anything, even as primitive and brutal as a fight to the death."

"Why would having those scars matter?"

"You are innocent. You may think you aren't, but you are. I have done things in these long centuries of living that you cannot conceive of. Those scars provided me safe passage out of the underworld. The guards that had been put in place recognized me as one of their own. You would not be so lucky."

"You think I would be detected even without a physical body?"

He nodded. "I'm sorry, Vasilisa, but I know you will. You give off a certain energy. It feels pure. There is no hiding that, and in the underworld, your innocence would stick out like a sore thumb."

"I take it you're not speaking of sexual innocence."

He couldn't help smiling at her. That question alone proved he was right about her. She killed when she had to because enemies invaded their land. She didn't live for the hunt or find joy in it the way he did. There might be the momentary Lycan rush during a full moon, but she lived her life in a civilized manner. She wasn't feral. She wasn't a woman to actively look for a fight. She only went on a hunt when it was necessary. She didn't look at herself the way he viewed her: elegant, beautiful, extraordinary.

"No, my lady, I am not. In any case, I will need you here to guard my physical body with the same ferocious spirit with which you guarded my soul. Should they become aware my spirit is separated from my body, they will send everyone they have seeking this form. You will need every instinct to keep me safe." He meant every word.

"Whatever plan Lilith has devised, she's determined to carry it out, and to do so means she needs a Dragonseeker under her control."

His woman suddenly lost her look of certainty and appeared unsure. "Maybe this isn't a good idea. Reach out to your brethren and see what is taking place. How soon can they help you?"

He reached for her, drawing her away from the wall and into his arms. He lifted her onto his lap, needing her to feel safe. Dropping his chin into the mass of her glossy hair, he rubbed gently, allowing the bristles along his jaw to become trapped in all that silk.

"Stay connected to me," he advised. He wasn't going to sugarcoat it or keep anything from her. If there was bad news, she would see it firsthand.

Vasilisa gripped his forearm as if that gave her added strength. He felt her move in his mind, a gentle presence, but there all the same, firm and anchored, believing in him.

Petru, I have need to know what is happening where you are. What news of Andros? Are there demons close to you? How many? Vampires? Are you injured?

The fighting was fierce. We were able to kill most of the master vampire's pawns and his second in command. He got away. Benedek is chasing after the master vampire now. He broke off from the demons, who have ducked into a vent, taking the royal with them. He fought them, but they pulled him down into the underworld. There were so many Lycans wounded here on the surface, and I didn't dare follow them into that hellhole, so I remained here to mark the vent and heal as many as possible.

Thank you for the information, Petru.

"There is more than one fracture," Vasilisa whispered, grabbing at the one topic that didn't include her brother or her people.

"That stands to reason, *sívamet*." Afanasiv pressed kisses from the top of her head to her temple in an effort to soothe her. "I would imagine once Lilith knew the exact notes for her demons to create the quakes, she would do so in remote places no one would think to look, as well as the strategic ones for battles."

"You're right, Siv. She's been planning this for a very long time."

"She's patient. She didn't get far when she first tested her abilities against Adalasia and Sandu when defenses were crumbling around the gate Adalasia and Leona guard. Lilith didn't give up; she simply switched to another gate and another plan," he said.

"You sound as if you admire her."

Over her head, Afanasiv had to smile at the little bite in her voice. "There is much about her to admire. Always study your enemy, Vasilisa. She's a brilliant strategist. If we can figure out why she wants control of your brothers, we can shut her down so much faster. She had to have worked for years to develop something that would work against whatever is in your DNA that prevents a royal from being compromised."

"How was she able to start in the first place? For any experiment, you have to have a starting point."

"Your aunt. Lilith somehow connected with Barnabas, most likely through his father, Xaviero, and Xavier. Barnabas seduced your aunt and eventually got her to voluntarily give up her soul to Lilith. Once she was enslaved, taking her blood would have been easy enough. She would do anything Lilith required of her. For that matter, she would have given her blood to Barnabas should he have asked for it."

"I always thought Aunt Olga was so strong."

"Everyone has a breaking point, my lady. Or a something or someone they value so much they would do anything for them or give anything to keep them safe."

"Even you?"

"I have you. Before I would have said no. But now there is you." He was honest.

She was silent, staring at the wall with her head resting against his chest. "If the demons ever succeed in taking me, Afanasiv, and they are torturing me in front of you to make you do something horrible to the world, what would you do?"

"Forgive me, *sívamet*, but I am far too dangerous to unleash on the world in the control of Lilith or anyone like her. If I knew with all certainty that there was no hope of escape, I would have no choice but to take both our lives simultaneously. First, I would tell you how much you mean to me and what a miracle you are. In my mind, I would make love to you and transport us to another world as we left the one of pain and torment behind." Uneasiness rippled through him, a kind of dread, and he shut his mind to what their conversation was dredging up.

"A woman could so easily fall in love with you, Afanasiv," she murmured.

"That is my hope, Vasilisa, because every moment I spend in your company, I find I want more time with you." He brushed more kisses in her hair.

"Please contact your other friend and find out what happened with Grigor."

Afanasiv reached out immediately. *Nicu, how does the battle go? Did you manage to destroy the master vampire? What of the demons and Grigor, Vasilisa's brother?*

It was a terrible battle. The vampires and demons and even the royal seemed intent on taking Skyler captive. No matter how many we killed, more kept coming. There is a vent close, but I have been unable to take the time to find it. The demons fled, and Dimitri and I are still fighting the vampires.

Did the demons take the royal with them?

Yes. Skyler was injured, and Ivory and Razvan took her with them. They will guard her, along with both packs of wolves. With them are Branislava and Tatijana Dragonseeker. Zev and Fen are with us.

Afanasiv didn't like the fact that so many Dragonseekers were gathered in one place. That place might be undisclosed to everyone else, but Lilith could have ways of knowing exactly where it was.

"Are you able to read the land and who is on it? Where every individual is if you seek them?" Afanasiv asked Vasilisa. "If someone attempts to hide from you, would you be able to find them?"

"Eventually, but our territory is quite large, and it would take a long time."

"If you knew the general vicinity and could narrow it down?" he persisted.

She nodded. "Yes, we are able to do that. It isn't easy, though, Afanasiv."

His uneasiness grew into alarm. *Nicu, I think the vampires are a distraction to keep you away from the real target. Get back to Skyler and the other women. They want a Dragonseeker. Or they want to kill them all. I don't know which it is, but they are definitely after a Dragonseeker, and you have three women and a male in one place. The royal can guide them to that place without prior knowledge of it.*

"Please tell them not to kill my brother. I know that may be difficult, but if at all possible . . ." Vasilisa pleaded.

I know the royal appears as if he is completely compromised, but he is under some kind of spell or manipulation. If possible, spare his life and take him prisoner so we can aid him.

We will do our best, Nicu answered.

"That is all anyone can promise, Vasilisa," Siv said, nuzzling the top of her head. "When it comes to a battle, things tend to happen very fast."

"I understand."

"I have got to go." He stood up with his lifemate in his arms, and he set her firmly on the floor of the little cabin. "I'll get back as soon I can."

"I'm going to stay connected to you for as long as possible."

He shook his head. "Vasilisa, the underworld is no place for you. If you see your brothers being tortured or acting in a way that would be upsetting to you, you could easily give us away. You didn't see everything that happened to me during my time in the underworld because you deliberately skipped over the worst of what they did to me. They will be doing those things to your brothers in an effort to break them completely. Lilith knows a part of your siblings is fighting against her control. She will punish them for that."

She lifted her chin. "I'm stronger than you think. If my brothers have to suffer, as I'm certain they will, why should I be spared? If I can aid you in any way, even by my presence, I want to be able to do so."

Afanasiv considered what she was asking. He would feel the same. He wanted to protect her, but she was another pair of eyes. She also was very steady as a rule, and a woman. Lilith tended to use women as the captains of her armies. She might spot something important before he could.

"Never make a sound, *sívamet*. If you must retreat, do it slowly and quietly. Only a very small part of you can be with me. The rest of you must guard this cabin at all times. Put up your strongest safeguards. Sorina did teach you how to do this?" He made it a question.

"Yes, since I was fairly young and we played together. I didn't know at the time that was what she was doing, but she was. After we realized we were both changing into something different, she really worked at teaching me how to safeguard any place I was sleeping."

"Let's do this, then, lifemate." He framed her face with both hands and looked into her vivid blue eyes. She had beautiful eyes. Eyes a man could drown in. He brushed kisses gently over both eyes, the tip of her elegant nose and then the corners of her mouth. "I'll add my safeguards to yours," he murmured against her soft lips. "The weaves will be in my mind for you to follow."

He ran the pad of his thumb over the curve of her bottom lip, etching the feel and texture of it into his soul for all time. Then he took her mouth. Gentle. Coaxing. Tender. Promising. Tasting her as she opened for him. The rush started. The heat. The flames. The fire. He wasn't certain if he was the match or she was. They came together in a fiery explosion that was never-ending. He didn't want it to end. It was the most feeling he'd ever experienced. Overwhelming. Good. Paradise. His brain turned off, so there was no real ability to think. He had Vasilisa and the way she made every nerve ending in his body come alive. Hot blood rushed through his veins and thundered in his ears, roared in his groin, pooling to make urgent demands.

He didn't know who pulled back first, but suddenly he felt very much bereft, his mouth just scant inches from hers. "I know I was supposed to go somewhere and do something very important, but that's gone up in flames."

Her laughter was low, her blue eyes soft. Her fingers traced his bottom lip gently. "I believe you were about to go off on a rescue mission to retrieve my brothers from the depths of hell. Something easy like that."

He nodded and captured her hands. "Be safe, Vasilisa. Don't take any chances. Anyone coming to the cabin—anyone at all—related to you, looking like one of your friends, could easily be someone compromised."

She nodded her head. "I'm well aware. I won't allow anyone in, no matter the circumstances."

"They can get inventive. Wolves devouring someone right outside your door."

"They could try that, but I control the wolves. If they didn't obey me, I would know immediately that it was a setup. Go before the sun is up."

"Seal the fault after me. Leave one tiny space my spirit will come through that only you know of. Do not share with me."

Afanasiv saw the uneasiness on her face. "You cannot. We need to take precautions. A part of you will be with me, so you'll know if you will need to escape quickly. This is a dangerous place. I cannot emphasize that enough. I have demons in me; you do not."

Vasilisa nodded. "Go then. Hurry back to me."

He turned away from her, one of the most difficult things he'd ever had to do. He knew what it was like in the underworld. It hadn't been easy escaping. He'd been there with his physical body. This time he was only taking his spirit. That gave him both advantages and disadvantages. He lay down on the cot, stretching out to full length, and—without allowing further thought on the subject—shed his physical body.

Vasilisa touched his mind. Afanasiv felt her entrance, that sweet feminine brush along the walls of his brain. So light. Not tentative. She was never that. She knew what she wanted, and she acted with confidence most of the time. She generally filled every empty, lonely space with her energy, making him feel whole and complete. Right now, she found a very small space, barely there, and fit her spirit inside it.

He moved fast. He knew exactly where the fault line was, and he hastened to it. Vasilisa would be exposed, alone out in the wild while she sealed the long fissure and then set the safeguards for the cabin. Afanasiv wanted to quickly disappear into the underworld so she wasn't exposed aboveground for too long.

He didn't wait or hesitate. A single spirit, one already possessing demon properties, would slip past the guardians easily—and he did. The fetid odors didn't get to him the way they had his physical body when he'd been there before. He could separate the smells of blood and sweat and agony, even fear and terror. There were levels of all of those things and scents to each that could easily debilitate one.

In his spirit form, he was wide open to the suffering and agony of those held in the underworld. He felt anguish and fear bombarding him from every direction. The hopelessness of those in torment and misery was debilitating. Worse, those sounds and feelings, amplified by his ability to feel emotions, triggered pieces of his memories to come alive to taunt him. His lifemate hadn't gone back far enough. There had been more than one visit to the underworld, and there had been many reasons to shut, lock and barricade the doors to those memories.

He knew where the prisoners were kept, at least the ones that Lilith took an interest in. These prisoners weren't the lucky ones that were kept in cages and mostly forgotten. These were men and women and sometimes even children she had tortured for her own pleasure or because they committed some infraction against her. He hurried past several sentries, down a long corridor, until he could hear the moans and despairing cries of the captives locked in their cells.

He stopped his forward progress near the cell of a young woman dressed in torn clothing. Her dress had once been a beautiful gown, one she might have worn to a party, but it was in tatters and smeared with blood in some places, and in others, the blood was thicker and much more of a bright crimson. She rocked herself back and forth in an effort to self-soothe or run away from the pain she obviously felt.

"Karine, you must look at me," a male voice commanded.

The girl shook her head. "Don't talk to me. You're an illusion. I refuse to do one single thing you want me to do. I will not believe Grigor would turn on his people. I will not believe he would go back on his word to me. Beat me to death. Kill me right now. I will not do what you want me to do. I will not say what you want me to say."

Afanasiv liked her at once. She was a spunky little thing. He even saw the glow that Grigor had told his twin brother about. She did shine from the inside out.

"I am only here because I thought I would be able to rescue you from this terrible place," Grigor explained. "My aunt Olga seems to have betrayed our family."

Karine's gaze leapt to Grigor's face. For the first time, she looked as if she had hope. "Grigor? Is that really you? You came to this awful place to rescue me?"

"It wasn't one of my better ideas," he conceded. He looked around him. "They're watching us and recording everything we say and do."

"What do they want?"

"I don't know yet. But something from my family. I think my older brother is here as well. I didn't see him, but I swore I heard him at one point. If they have him, they have a tiger by the tail and don't yet know it."

"Is there a way out of here?" Karine asked.

"If there is, we'll find it," Grigor assured her.

Afanasiv was watching his face. His expression said he didn't believe that for a moment. He moved away from the two cells and hurried past several unoccupied cages. Rounding a corner, he came to a long cage that had a few more amenities in it than the one Karine was in. This one had a chair and what looked like a mattress rather than a cot. There was a privacy curtain around the bucket where one relieved themselves—far more than what Karine had.

Although the cell looked as if it were housing an important prisoner who was treated like a princess, the woman lying on the bed looked to be in far worse condition than Karine had. She moaned continuously. The moaning wasn't an affectation, either. She was clearly in a great deal of pain. Outside her cell, a very worried demon with cloven hooves and even a set of horns paced with another demon.

"Lilith will kill us if she dies," the one with the horns announced. "You have to do something. Can you get Gaia here? Maybe she can save her."

"She was really mad at us the last time. She said if we ever hurt anyone like that again, she would let Lilith skin us alive," the other demon whispered, looking around her.

Afanasiv gave his lifemate the information as quietly as possible, just by thinking of it. *Gaia was a Carpathian child stolen from her family when she was about ten. Already she was showing promise of speaking with animals and taming beasts. Xavier traded her to Lilith in exchange for parasites he needed in his experiments to cause our women to miscarry. Gaia was taken to the underworld and raised by Lilith.*

Although Vasilisa didn't make a sound, he felt her question. Why would Lilith need a small child to talk to beasts for her?

Behind the four gates—each positioned north, south, east and west—is caged the biggest beast of all. He was a Carpathian male who had lived too long in the world. He had served his people with honor but had not gone quietly into the next realm when it was his time, nor had he succumbed to the temptation of losing his honor. Like me, he remained in the world for centuries, and the scars began to develop, marking him a beast. A demon. He became too experienced in battle to ever have hunters take him down. He is a legend in the Carpathian world, but he does exist. Should he ever escape, he would wreak havoc such as the world has never seen. Lilith hoped Gaia could control him. Through Gaia, Lilith would control him. His name is Justice and he is very real.

Afanasiv detested the fact that Justice had lived such an honorable life and that his ending had come to this—existing in the underworld. Kept behind four gates made of safeguarded wood. Even his last act as

a Carpathian had been to sacrifice for his family. He fought the demons back, giving Sandu, his parents and sister the time to run out of
the underworld and close the portal behind them. Justice had always
been a man of honor. Now he was a raving beast who, by all accounts,
had moments of clarity, but they were few and far between.

*Gaia is grown now, and although she'd had an opportunity to escape
the underworld, she refused, choosing to stay with Justice to try to keep him
as sane as possible. She isn't his lifemate, but they formed a friendship of
sorts, and she fears if she leaves her post, he will be completely lost. Her
brother recently went to see her in order to try to persuade her to leave, but
she still refused.*

Afanasiv felt a little sorry for Gaia's brother, Tiberiu. He knew
Tiberiu had searched for his little sister for centuries. It had to have
been painful to finally find her only to lose her again to the underworld. On the other hand, Tiberiu was an ancient Carpathian male
and didn't have emotions. He had a sense of duty. Leaving his sister
went against that sense of duty more than anything else.

"We've got to do something," the demon with horns snapped. "Gaia
can heal her. Otherwise, we're both dead. And Lilith won't let us die
easily."

The smaller demon threw her hands into the air and then hurried
off. The demon with horns unlocked the cell with a giant key that was
on a chain around her neck.

"Lada. We have a healer coming to look at you," she crooned. Only
her voice was very low-pitched, and it came out more like growls instead of the reassuring way she was trying to speak. "She'll fix you
right up, and you won't hurt anymore."

Lada didn't answer or acknowledge her. She turned her head away
and gave a piteous cry just at that small movement. Afanasiv didn't want
to risk getting too close to the demon with horns. He had no idea how
sensitive she was, but he needed to see how bad Lada's injuries were.

Afanasiv also wanted to know where Andros was. Grigor had been
put in a cell directly across from Karine, which made sense if Lilith

wanted to spy on them and listen in on their conversations. Why wouldn't she do the same with Andros and Lada? Did she already know about Lada's condition?

Afanasiv drifted closer to the woman, taking the long way around the cell to avoid the demon altogether. He positioned himself first at Lada's head. He was used to inspecting from the inside out, and he did so, slipping into her body to see what damage they'd done to her. The lacerations with the knives weren't the worst of her injuries. Her internal organs had taken a beating. Someone had systematically struck her repeatedly. She was leaking blood from her liver and spleen. Afanasiv returned to the surface to look down at Lada's swollen face. He didn't quite understand why they would do such a thing to her if their intent was to show Andros visible wounds—unless they beat her in front of him or somehow coerced him do it.

Very agitated, the demon with the horns paced up and down in Lada's cell. "You shouldn't resist and taunt me so much. I get angry and can't stop myself. The mistress knows this, and yet she keeps sending me to you. I think you're a test to see if I can hold my temper, but you won't cooperate. I get terrible punishments if you don't do as mistress wants."

She kept muttering, her tone between guttural and growling. At times it was difficult to decipher. The demon wasn't remorseful for hurting Lada so much as fearful that she'd gone too far, and Lada might be too injured and might not be able to do the things her mistress demanded. In that case, the demon was going to be punished.

Where was Andros in all this? Had he witnessed Lada being beaten by this demon? Did they subject him to such a torture? For a man like Andros, that would be far worse than if they had flayed the skin from his back. He'd finally found a woman he believed he was in love with, and she was lured to the underworld by his aunt because of her ties to him.

Afanasiv found it was far easier to carry on his work without emotion. Feelings got in the way and threatened to shake his centuries-old discipline. He found himself fighting down a berserker's rage. The demon in him was rising to take these women from the ones that had harmed them so cruelly. He hastily reverted back to the way of the Carpathian hunter, shutting out all emotion so he could process everything and make the best decisions based on logic.

The other, smaller demon returned with a young woman in tow. Clearly, the woman was Carpathian. This was Tiberiu's sister. She was tall with long dark hair. She walked with easy strides, going straight to the bed where Lada lay so restless in her pain.

"Why would you do this to a prisoner and then call me to heal her?" She hissed as she laid one hand gently on Lada's abdomen. "Do you think I'll be a part of your insanity? Hurting a victim and then making them well so you can hurt them all over again?"

Afanasiv could see that Gaia hurt just looking at Lada. She had to have seen a great deal of terrible things having grown up in the underworld, but it hadn't destroyed her natural empathy. In spite of what she'd said to the demon, her palm was lightly skimming over Lada's body, assessing the damage.

"Mistress sent succubi to Andros many times to seduce him, but he resisted. She was very angry. So she sent one looking like Lada, but Andros knew the difference. That made mistress very, very upset." The smaller demon did the talking while the demon with horns sulked and stayed a good distance from Gaia.

Afanasiv would have known if the demons had tried to pawn someone else off as Vasilisa. Even knowing her for such a short time, he would have known. Lilith could duplicate looks but not the entirety, the whole of what she was. Her scent. Her taste. The expressions flickering across her face. Her laughter. The way she could light up a room. Even worn down, maybe especially in that state, he would know. As did Andros.

The demon continued, shaking her head. "Lilith told us to get Lada to cooperate, or else. She said we were useless to her if we couldn't get Lada to listen to reason. She had only one simple task, and then she could go home."

"What was her task?" Gaia asked.

"She was to tell Andros she didn't love him. That she never did and she wanted to give him back his ring. She was to throw his ring at him and walk away. Lilith thought he would break down, and in that vulnerable moment, she would be able to gain complete control of him."

"Why does Lilith want to control Andros?"

The little demon shook her head but then looked around and stepped closer to Gaia. "The royals have different blood—maybe they can control the beast." She whispered the message to the Carpathian woman. "The mistress must have all of the royals' blood mixed together. The blood Olga gave to the mage this night was not the blood of a royal. Grigor tricked them somehow. They had to throw out the entire experiment because the false blood tainted the royals' blood."

"Lilith is making war on these poor women and all the places above just in the hope of controlling the beast? That's what this is all about?"

The little demon nodded frantically. "She's in a really foul mood. If you don't save us, she'll kill us, Gaia."

Gaia nodded her head. "Most likely she will. The thing is, Molly, it would be a service to you if I let her. You're always partnered with Patsy, who loses her temper and does everything wrong. She hurts you. She hurts whoever she's supposed to be guarding, and she hurts herself. If I keep bailing you out, she'll keep doing it."

Patsy snorted and stomped her cloven feet, then dragged them backward as if she were about to charge. She even put her head down in a threatening manner, pointing her sharp horns at Gaia, who rolled her eyes and put her hand up without looking at the horned demon. Patsy froze in place.

"See what I mean, Molly? She has no self-control. This just turns into a vicious cycle. Where is Lada's man? The royal? Where are they keeping him?"

Molly moved even closer to Gaia. "They took him to the bad place, Gaia. The really bad place." She shook her head. "He won't come out of there alive."

Gaia closed her eyes and bowed her head. "No, most likely he won't. I'll heal this woman for you this one time, but only this one time. If this happens again, I'm not going to help either of you."

The bad place. The underworld was one big bad place. Afanasiv had shoved all memories of being in this world into a compartment and slammed the door closed, then nailed it shut. He hadn't wanted to ever remember the experience. Now, it was necessary. His memories were returning bit by bit, in spite of his determination not to let them escape. He had been in the place Andros was. He had to find his way there and make certain Andros knew how to get out.

He moved away from the prisoner's cell, making his way down another long passageway lit with glowing purple candles set in sconces up high on the walls. Occasionally, he passed a guard with wicked-looking swords or spears standing at attention in front of narrow staircases leading to chambers below. Afanasiv remembered each of those chambers and what took place in them all too vividly. He placed a shield in his mind to keep his lifemate from seeing too many of the memories welling up.

For the first time, he felt Vasilisa protest. She feared leaving Lada in the condition she was in. He sent her waves of reassurance. Gaia was quite capable of taking care of Lada, and they needed her healed and on her feet, ready to make a run for it when Grigor and Andros could get them out. Afanasiv had to plant the escape route in Andros' mind. Afanasiv would have to provide the distractions so the prisoners could escape. That meant, at some point, he would have to allow Andros to know he was there.

They control him, Vasilisa cautioned. *This might not be such a good idea. We should wait and think this through. Have a concrete plan.*

It is necessary to give him hope before it is too late for him. You should make your way back to the surface. The things that take place here are not for you to witness.

I will stay with you, Siv. She made that as firm and resolute as possible.

Afanasiv loved that his lady had so much courage. She would need all of it when they descended into that ring of fire. He continued moving down the corridor. When he'd passed the sixth guard, he slowed his progress. The seventh descending stairway appeared unguarded, but he knew better. Two demons waited on either side of the entrance for any unsuspecting wretch who tried to escape and managed to get that far.

Afanasiv had discovered the guards the hard way. He still had the scars of their long spears when they simultaneously stuck the razor-sharp blades into his sides and tried to lift him. Just remembering the pain could have made him shudder and pause before attempting to get past the hidden demons, but he had already pushed all emotion aside and felt nothing as he made his approach. He was spirit only. They might feel a slight breeze as he slipped past, but beyond that, they would see and hear nothing.

Very quiet, he cautioned. Without waiting for Vasilisa's assurance, he moved into the narrow opening. The guards stank of death and horror. They were flesh eaters, and when gladiators fought to the death in the arenas, they would leap out of the bleachers and tear apart the fallen to feast on them.

He knew Vasilisa saw the images in his mind. He needed her to know what kinds of horror her brother would be facing in the rings below. Lilith was really not happy with Andros to sentence him down here. The heat was stifling even to his spirit. The demon in him reached for the joys of the various arenas. He had battled in all of them—and had been the victor. Being the victor meant he lived. It also meant he had to live with the things he had done in order to survive.

Warmth spread through him. Not the terrible heat of the under-world, but a gentle healing warmth that spread to every cell in his brain and created a shield. His lady. Looking out for him. Letting him know he wasn't alone in this hellhole. He didn't have to face the torture or the memories alone. She was right there with him, and she didn't intend to go away. He hadn't known love or what it meant, but he was certain it was something very close to what he was experiencing with her.

The sound of those screaming in pain reached them as his spirit descended into the lowest rung, where the arenas of torture and death were. Immediately, he saw Andros with a long bullwhip in his hand. The whip appeared to be red-hot, sizzling with life—with burning flames. Each time he expertly brought the fire and flames down on the back of a demon, removing the skin and cauterizing the wound at the same time, those in the stands howled with glee.

Andros wore an expression of joyful cruelty, as if the demon side of him had taken over completely. Over the speakers played pounding music that sounded harsh and demanding. The music swelled in volume. Rappers began to demand the heads of the demons Andros had flayed with his fire whip. Soon the entire stadium was yelling for Andros to gut the demons and cut off their heads.

Afanasiv detested that he'd agreed to allow Vasilisa to come with him. Suddenly, the audience went silent as a young woman shuffled out. She wore the same tattered dress that Lada had been wearing. Her long hair hung down her back in a thick braid, and her arms were bare. She looked young—too young to be a widow with a child. Too young and beat up to be subjected to brutality for the demons' entertainment, and yet Lada was there.

She stumbled into the center of the bloody ring, a sword and shield in her hands, although it appeared she had no idea what to do with them. Demons sat or lay on the ground, moaning and growling threats. She didn't spare them so much as a glance. Once she spotted Andros, she didn't look anywhere else. She had eyes only for him.

Another gate lifted and Grigor strode into the ring. He also carried a sword and shield. He looked worse for wear, but the bruises and knots on his skin didn't appear to slow him down in the least. He went straight into the middle of the arena, stopping Lada's forward stumbling.

Another gate opened and Karine was shoved in. She nearly fell but managed to stagger and recover. She looked around her, covered her mouth with the hand holding the shield, and then her gaze found Grigor. She gave an inarticulate cry and hurried across the floor of the arena toward Grigor. She didn't seem to notice the fallen demons until one caught her ankle and tripped her.

Karine went down with a little choked cry. That cry galvanized the two royal brothers into action, both running toward Karine. Andros was closer and reached her first, his sword swinging in a giant arc. Lada followed him, shaking her head. Imploring him to stop.

The crowd erupted in a roar of approval.

PART THREE

WHEEL OF FORTUNE

ragonseeker. Afanasiv had skipped right over that information almost without acknowledging it. Vasilisa paced back and forth in the small confines of the cabin. He retained all the information he thought important in order to bring her brothers and their women out of the underworld. What he hadn't done was pay attention to the fact that he was Dragonseeker. That blood ran in his veins. Why hadn't they just taken his blood while they had him down in that disgusting, vile place? She should have asked that question.

If Lilith managed to get Dragonseeker blood, what could she do with it? Was it valuable to her? Or was only the physical person valuable to her? With so many Dragonseekers in one place, there had to be a reason. Something had drawn them all there at the same time. Vasilisa didn't believe in coincidence, certainly not to that extent.

She was aware of the stories that came out of the Carpathian Mountains. How Xavier had murdered Mihai and took his lifemate, Rhiannon, prisoner. Rhiannon was Dragonseeker. She had given birth to three children, Soren, Tatijana and Branislava. Xavier then murdered Rhiannon and kept his children as his blood slaves. He imprisoned Tatijana and Branislava behind an ice wall in the form of dragons. Soren took a mage as a wife and had children, Razvan and Natalya.

Vasilisa stopped at the window to stare out at the snow coming down. She'd never had a problem being alone, yet she had a feeling of impending doom. The cabin seemed far too small, and she could barely breathe all of a sudden. Her lungs fought for air, and the room was too hot. She tapped on the windowsill, a small drumming beat that matched her accelerating heart.

Staring out the window, she caught glimpses of wolves as they came out of the surrounding forest. They were healthy animals, big and in their prime. They had silvery coats that made them difficult to see in the snow, but she had excellent eyesight and could see through the snow flurries, spotting them easily. They slunk across the small clearing, coming straight at the shepherd's cabin as if drawn by the light she had in the window.

She had a kinship with the wolves and dominion over them. She didn't fear them and would have thought it unusual if they threatened her in any manner. The moment they caught her scent, they would pay tribute and back off.

Dragonseeker. What would Lilith need with a Dragonseeker? Could it really be so simple as wanting one of them to turn so the legend could be refuted? Vasilisa shook her head. That didn't add up. Not with the trouble Lilith was going to. She'd lost a few of her demons and nearly lost one of her mages. By all accounts she wasn't happy.

Vasilisa found it a little disorienting to be in two places at one time, but most of her remained firmly behind in the cabin, guarding Afanasiv's physical body. He lay as if dead, and several times she went to him and fussed over him, pushing back his unruly hair with the pads of her fingers. She tried to absorb him through her hands. She couldn't believe how connected she was to him just because they shared the intimacy of each other's mind.

The wolves surrounded the cabin and one leapt up, giant paws on the window, peering in with amber eyes. She stared him down. She was alpha whether they liked it or not. The wolf held her gaze for a moment and then dropped down into the snow-packed earth once more. He sat back on his haunches and lifted his nose into the air. He began to howl. The other wolves followed suit in a tribute to their queen.

At once, a short distance away, came answering howls. Even farther away, she heard more wolves take up the song. Then, from an even greater distance, more wolves joined the chorus. She envisioned Ivory and Razvan's wolves joining in. She'd heard Skyler and Dimitri had their own pack traveling exclusively with them, a gift from Ivory and Razvan. If that were so, it was quite a gift and a huge responsibility.

The singing died away, and the wolves began to fade into the snow, intent on hunting. She watched them go with a feeling of sadness. For a moment she had been comforted. She had felt isolated for years, never recognizing how lonely she'd been until she was with Afanasiv. He'd been in her mind, filling all those places she hadn't realized were lonely.

Dragonseeker. Her brain returned to the puzzle. The wheel of fortune card had come up. First had been the chariot, then the hanged man and then the wheel of fortune. She had pressed forward, forgetting she was deep in the midst of enemies. She needed to regroup and think things through.

What did the wheel of fortune mean? First, the wheel continued to turn. That gave one hope. No matter if she was in her darkest hour, the wheel reminded her that it would keep spinning. Time never stood still. The worst luck turned positive after a short interval. The best luck would also be gone just as quickly. One could always count on the wheel turning season after season.

She continued to stare out the window, a part of her staying with Afanasiv, alarmed at the condition of Karine but grateful Grigor wasn't nearly as hurt as she expected him to be. She tapped her fingers on the windowsill, finding a rhythmic beat. The snow was letting up again, and now it fell in small flurries to the tune of her fingers. She'd covered Afanasiv's body with a blanket to keep him warm. The cabin still felt overheated to her in spite of the outside temperature.

Her lifemate's spirit traveled away from Grigor around a corner and stopped abruptly when he discovered Lada. Her fingers stopped moving as she observed Lada's appalling condition. Where was Andros? Why wasn't he in the cell across from Lada's as Grigor had been across from Karine?

Movement beneath the trees caught her eye. It was stealthy, as if the creature, a lone wolf perhaps, didn't want to be seen. Immediately, she turned her full attention to the spot where she was certain there had been a beast lurking and watching the cabin. She automatically blurred her image and added a thin layer of covering to the window, a dull gray to blend in with the snow and fog that was building along the ground. If the creature wanted to see her, it would have to come close in order to peer through one of the windows.

She waited quietly, turning inward, once again paying close attention to Afanasiv and what he was doing. She knew just the short conversation about his hidden memories had opened up a floodgate of recollections for him. He remembered how to maneuver through the labyrinth that was the underworld down below.

He was watching a Carpathian woman scold a couple of demons. The woman was clearly accepted in the underworld. This, then, was Gaia—the woman who had been traded as a child by Xavier for a bucketful of parasites. Lilith had wanted the girl to help her control the beast locked behind the gates. It looked as if she still retained her natural goodness. How that could be when she was raised in such a terrible place, Vasilisa couldn't understand.

Vasilisa monitored Afanasiv, knowing that traveling in the underworld would affect him adversely. He wasn't aware of it because he shed his emotions and went forth as a Carpathian hunter might—or he embraced the demon in him. His one fear was that the demon grow-ing inside him would take him over the longer he was in the under-world. The terrible scars he bore called to the battle lust inside him, to a berserker's rage. She had insisted on going with him, just a small part of her spirit, because she feared he would need her to guide him back.

Something brushed against the cabin wall. It sounded like the slide of fur, and then someone tried the door. The sound seemed overly loud in the silence of the night. Vasilisa backed up three steps, taking her almost dead center into the cabin, where she could more easily monitor all the windows and the door.

Silence followed the testing of the doorknob, and then there was a loud knock. "Open up. It's freezing out here."

Vasilisa recognized the voice of Odessa Balakin, one of the owners of the inn. Vasilisa kept her eyes closed so that she couldn't see the older woman as the innkeeper moved around the cabin, peering in the windows and pounding on them, becoming more agitated as she did so.

"Vasi, is that you in there? Open up, dear. I have to restock the cabin on my way back to the inn. I've been making the rounds, and this is the last stop."

It was true the innkeepers did stock the shepherds' cabins. It made sense to do so in a familiar route, leaving this particular cabin for last. It was the closest to their home, and they would finish and go directly to their home after they were done.

Finally, Vasilisa approached the door, leaned against it and called out. "I'm sorry, Odessa, but I can't allow you in tonight. I'll see to stocking the cabin myself."

There was a long silence. Vasilisa counted slowly in her mind, over and over, willing Odessa to be the real woman and not some crazy illusion that Lilith had conjured up in an attempt to acquire Vasilisa or Afanasiv. So far, in the underworld, it didn't appear as if anyone suspected he was there.

"Is something wrong, Vasi? With those government men coming in, I told Kendal something was wrong, and we had to be close in case you and your brothers needed help."

"Everything is fine, but I can't let you in. I need for you to just go home as fast as possible tonight, Odessa. I swear, I'll restock the cabin for you. Just get home where it's safe."

"I can leave the supplies right here by the door. You can bring them in anytime at your convenience," Odessa suggested.

"Thank you, that's kind of you," Vasilisa said. She wasn't about to open the door even after Odessa left, in case it was a trap. She had to wait it out inside the cabin for Afanasiv to return, just as she promised him she would.

There was movement at the front door on the tiny porch. "I'm putting the supplies just under the rocker," Odessa said helpfully.

Vasilisa didn't answer. She didn't want to encourage Odessa to stay. She found herself holding her breath as the movement on the porch increased, and she heard the creak of the rocking chair.

"Kendal is meeting me here. He dropped the supplies off on the other side of the circle. That way, it goes much faster. We're not so young anymore." Odessa laughed as if she had made a fine joke.

In the distance, a wolf let out a howl. Listening to the mournful notes, alarm spread. Those were the warnings for the pack. The alpha considered her part of the pack, and that particular warning was for her. Something was moving toward the cabin. It had flashed past the pack as they hunted deer to keep them alive.

Vasilisa dared to look out the window toward the forest. "Odessa, don't wait for Kendal, you have to leave now," she ordered, pouring a compulsion into her voice.

"Yes, yes, I have to go now, Vasi. See you tomorrow. Be safe."

"Be safe," Vasilisa whispered back.

She watched as the older woman left the porch and began to make her way toward the forest where the shortcut to the inn was. As she made it to the first trees, a man emerged, and she stopped to chat with him. Relief made Vasilisa sag against the wood seat built into the window as she watched Kendal embrace his wife.

She was about to turn away when Kendal abruptly took hold of Odessa's hair and yanked her head back to put a knife to her throat. Vasilisa's heart clenched painfully in her chest as Kendal dragged Odessa back toward the cabin, leaving two long grooves in the snow where Odessa tried to dig her heels in to stop him. By the time they reached the cabin, there was blood trickling down Odessa's throat from the sharp blade Kendal held against it.

Vasilisa took a deep breath and stepped back from the window. Once again, she went to the small cot where Afanasiv's physical body lay totally vulnerable. She ran her palm over his chest, over his heart, and back up to his strong jaw.

"This is going to be rough, lifemate. I need to feel you just for a moment before I make this decision." She already knew there was no decision to make. She just had to find the necessary courage to do the right thing. Odessa was a lifelong friend. One she treasured.

She ignored the pounding on the door. No matter how much Kendal hammered on the door or windows, the safeguards would hold, and he couldn't get in. With one hand on Afanasiv's chest, she turned inward to see more fully where her lifemate journeyed in the underworld.

Afanasiv's spirit was moving along a dark corridor lit by purple sconces. The strange lighting cast ominous shadows along the floor and along the walls. If she looked at the shadows, men and women appeared to be consumed in fiery flames or reaching out of the flames, imploring anyone who could see them for help.

Vasilisa could sense Afanasiv's reluctance to take her with him down into the lower parts of the underworld. They had a brief discussion over it, but she held fast, believing she should stay with him, even that small part of her. The further he descended into that horrible place, the thicker those scars on his soul seemed to be, and the more they surfaced, threatening to take him over. She wasn't going to allow that to happen.

For a brief moment, she felt very alone and overwhelmed. She had to figure out a way to save Odessa, as well as her lifemate, her brothers and their women. Kendal used his fist to hammer on the door, the sound loud, almost booming in the quiet of the night. Sparks flew out from under his skin as he landed each massive fist, so he spewed curses as he hit the door. The sparks floated up into the air, currents taking them aloft until they began to dance in the sky just over Kendal's head.

He gave up on knocking and went to the largest window, the one facing the forest. With one powerful blow, he attempted to smash through the glass. Sparks of all colors raced skyward as tiny blue flames engulfed his fist. He howled and pulled his injured hand back to him.

"Open up, Vasilisa, or I'll slit Odessa's throat."

He growled more than he spoke, but she understood everything he said quite clearly. How could she not? Taking a deep breath, she sent another small sliver of her spirit outside. She utilized the sparks of color above Kendal's head to assess the situation. This was definitely *not* Kendal from the inn. That made her feel a lot better. Lilith hadn't corrupted the innkeeper and turned him into one of her puppets. This was a demon masquerading as Kendal. It was no wonder he was treating Odessa with so little care.

Could she lure the demon back to the porch, get Odessa into the cabin and shut him out? The risk was too much to take. Her brain discarded the idea. Kendal dragged Odessa away from the window once more toward the porch. She watched as Odessa struggled, twisting this way and that, her feet dragging in the snow as Kendal forced her to cooperate with him.

Vasilisa hovered above the demon, positioning herself to strike, leaving just enough of her spirit to fight off an attack inside the cabin should Kendal manage to breach the defenses. Now, being torn in three directions, she was disoriented and feeling slightly sick. There was no way she could kill the demon before he would retaliate against Odessa.

She looked closer at Odessa. She fought and struggled, but there was something off about the way she was going about it. Vasilisa wasn't certain what it was exactly, but in her fear for her friend, she had accepted what and who she was seeing at face value. That was the number one cardinal rule you didn't break in dealing with demons. That had been drilled into her since she was three years of age.

Slow down. Have patience. If demon Kendal killed his hostage, he wouldn't have any leverage. He could stand outside the cabin and pound away until every appendage he had was burnt to a crisp. It wouldn't matter. She wasn't opening the door.

Vasilisa narrowed her gaze on Odessa. If she was a replica of the innkeeper, it was a very detailed one. Her heart sank, but she persevered, studying Odessa in great detail. Her legs were stretched out in front of her as Kendal dragged her to the front porch and up the stairs. They flopped around and thrashed, as if she were fighting him, but in reality, it was more as if she were a rag doll, and her legs followed the body being propelled forward. At times, her feet appeared to be on backward. Kendal dragged Odessa over a rock hidden beneath the surface of snow, and Odessa snapped a reprimand in a harsh, guttural tone.

Vasilisa let her breath out slowly. Odessa was a demon as well. This wasn't the innkeeper but a substitute. Lilith hadn't had time to capture the two and put her plan into motion. These two demons had been caught aboveground when Vasilisa had sealed the earth, so they couldn't return to the underworld. Lilith must have commanded them to bring Vasilisa to her—or she wanted Vasilisa dead.

The demon began to drag Odessa up the three stairs to once again gain the porch so he could break down the door. This time, when he placed his feet on the stairs, the embers dancing in the darkened sky above his head began to whirl around to the beat of her fingers on the windowsill. Her spirit directed them from above the two demons, moving the sparks together inside the fast-spinning cones.

The demon stopped when he heard crackling fire. Looking up, he could see what amounted to a roaring wildfire already out of control, but this one had telltale blue flames. He dropped the knife from Odessa's throat and tried to run, leaping off the stairs and, with a hoarse cry, turning in midair to face the raging fire. Odessa shot to her feet and dove away from the cabin in the opposite direction from Kendal. That didn't stop the deadly fire from finding either demon.

Inside the cabin, Vasilisa opened her arms wide, directing the blue flames to drop down over the demons and consume them. Staggering, nearly drained completely of all energy, she almost fell over backward. She had to hang on to the chairs and then stumbled her way to the bed to lie down beside Afanasiv.

It was the bad luck of the hapless demons that she'd been taught to wield blue flames—a demon killer—since she was a child. She'd started out controlling it on her palm. Making the flames spring to life and then dance. She had many scorched curtains and covers. Twice she'd set her room on fire. Bronya, her mother, had been so patient with her, laughing and turning Vasilisa's frustration into laughter, as well.

Bronya had regaled Vasilisa with the many times she'd set things on fire, including her father's best shirt as he was escorting her mother to a play. She'd hurled the blue flame out the window, not realizing her parents weren't in the carriage yet. The flame had landed on the back of his shirt and raced up the material as hungry as could possibly be.

Fortunately, her mother was facing Bronya's window and saw the blue flame streaking like a comet out of the sky, and she dealt with it, getting her husband to change his shirt without any fuss. Her mother was very skilled in that area.

Vasilisa lay for a long while, savoring the memories. They were good memories, ones she treasured. Thinking of anything her mother had told her about her life—especially now, when the wheel of fortune seemed to be upside down for her—gave her a necessary boost of confidence.

When she felt strong enough, she made her way to the window again. Looking out over the snow, only ashes drifted away on the wind. She went back to the small cot and sat beside Afanasiv.

"Tell me, lifemate. Do you have a plan for getting my siblings out of that vile place? Is there even a remote possibility of doing so? Is Andros already too far gone?"

Now that she was once again intact, all but that small part of her spirit with Afanasiv, she paid strict attention to details around her lifemate where he was in the underworld. Before he'd descended to the lower chambers, Afanasiv had attempted to have her stay behind again. She'd refused. If her brothers were there, she was going. Truthfully, she didn't want to risk losing her lifemate, and she felt the risk was very real.

She was horrified at what she saw in the arena. Worse, the moment they'd gotten to those corridors, she'd felt the berserker, the demon, in Afanasiv rise and threaten to take over. She was not going to let what happened to Justice happen to Afanasiv. He wasn't sacrificing his life so her family could live.

The royal family had a duty to their people, and that included sacrifice. It was expected of them to lay down their lives for their people. They understood that premise, and everything they did, they did with that in mind. Afanasiv had been raised to be a protector, a guardian, but this was Lycan territory, not Carpathian. He wasn't going to die for all of them only to be reborn as a demon, not when he'd lived so honorably for several thousand years.

She'd remained very quiet at his demand as they were forced to go past the two demons guarding the staircase leading to the arena, where Afanasiv was certain Andros had been taken. She'd felt the demons' hunger as they slipped through. It was raw and edged with violence. One stared straight at them as if he could see the spirit moving through the darkness. She'd fought with her heart, keeping it slow and steady, matching Afanasiv's.

It was possible she really was going to endanger everyone. The demon guard looked horribly suspicious, his gaze following them down the spiral stairs. She didn't make the mistake of looking at him directly.

The sights sickened her. The demons in the curving stands were clearly cannibals, just waiting for the chance to tear into the losers of the contest. Andros used a bullwhip as if he'd been born with it in his hands. The bullwhip glowed red and orange, appearing on fire as he lashed the skin off a demon's back. The demon had lost his own bullwhip and was using a flimsy shield and spear to try to ward Andros off. The crowd had come to their feet, demanding blood and death. They wanted Andros to separate the head from the body.

Andros is half-crazed right now, she whispered. *Afanasiv, Grigor, Lada and Karine are in terrible danger.*

It was so difficult to see her beloved brother with such a cruel look on his face. The demon had taken over, and he was enjoying what he was doing.

No, there is still a part of him holding out. Trying to think his way out of all of this. Do you royals have a way of communicating no one else knows? Something he would recognize came only from you. Your aunt wouldn't know it. Only you, Andros, Grigor and Garald would know.

Naturally they did. They were siblings, growing up in a world of secrecy. They'd developed all kinds of code. All kinds of ways to communicate the rest of the world knew nothing of.

Yes, but how will we get him out from under the control of Lilith?

Don't say her name here. Try not to think it. She can be called very easily.

It was the first time there was an edge of nerves to Afanasiv's demeanor. He hesitated, and then came an admission. *Gaia can remove the evil one's control. It is not an easy task. She will have to start with Andros first because his is the strongest. He has been worked on the most.*

For one terrible moment, Vasilisa nearly jerked away from him.

Afanasiv must have anticipated her childish reaction because he surrounded her with his warmth.

You know her, Vasilisa accused. *You acted as if you didn't, but you know her. She has been in your mind.*

She is part of the things I wished to forget. She aided me in escaping, and I . . . left her here in this vile place. It was her wish, but no Carpathian male worth anything leaves behind a female in such a situation. I buried the memory of her deep so I could continue. It was only when I saw her and watched her hands moving as she chanted the healing chant that I began to remember her again and the shame of leaving her here.

Vasilisa detested that she found herself upset that the Carpathian woman had been in Afanasiv's mind. It was an intimacy only she should ever share with her lifemate. The closeness she felt with him was due to getting to know him through the thoughts and images of the past he allowed her to see. He had the same access to her mind. They might not have yet shared their bodies with each other, but she had never felt so close to another human being. She didn't want another woman to feel that same way.

Carpathians have a mutual path we can communicate with one another on. I didn't use it to talk to Petru or Nicu because the vampires would hear. The ancients who have been in the monastery all use a different pathway, so I used that one. Gaia needed blood. Once we exchanged a small amount, she could talk to me and I to her. She helped me escape at great cost to herself.

Was there a reprimand in there? She was looking pretty pathetic to him if she was jealous. She started to explain but then just stopped questioning him. They could hash everything out later.

So, Gaia comes to help. What are we doing?

You let your brothers know you are going to get them out of here. That someone is coming to help them get out from under the evil one. They can't give it away that anything is different. Can you handle that?

I will have to leave your mind and . . .

No. That is forbidden. We stay together. You direct me and we'll go there.

That was a resounding no. He meant that, and she wasn't going to be able to just sneak off and implement her plans if his didn't work.

Fine, then, Afanasiv, but I'm warning you right now, you are not staying behind for any reason at all. You will not be left here like that poor beast living behind gates and being poked at by perfectly horrid demons. You will be coming home with me. So if you're planning anything else, you remember you're the one who gave the order that we stay together.

She was quite happy to turn his decree right back on him. Had she had her physical body, she would have smirked at him.

Gaia arrived, moving with her usual grace. Those watching from the stands were up on their feet, calling for Andros to cut off the head of the fallen demon, and they roared as the demon grabbed Lada's ankle and tripped her, bringing her down. Everyone ran to help her. Grigor wrapped one arm around Karine and practically lifted her. Swinging the long blade of his sword back and forth in front of him, he ran toward Lada. He cut a wide path, sending several demons away bleeding, with intestines spilling out.

Andros swung his sword first before anyone could get to him. Lada didn't make a sound. She didn't move. She just looked up at Andros with love in her eyes and waited for the sword to take her life and free both of them. The blade separated the demon's head from his neck. The head went rolling across the bare floor straight for Gaia. She casually stepped over it.

Now, sívamet, tell both your brothers you are here to free them. They cannot give away by any means that you are close. Gaia is giving aid no matter what it appears.

Vasilisa stared at Andros for a few moments, taking in every detail of his appearance. She had only her imagination for everything else, but he had given her quite a bit of details about his life. She built a picture of him at church in a suit, looking very fine. He liked to race cars. She found herself at the track with him often, one of her many concessions. As a rule, she would never go to something she didn't care for, but in her fantasies, she was willing to do anything to be with her big brother. They had especially liked silly knock-knock jokes. They made up their own and relayed information to each other that way.

> *Knock knock, brothers dear*
> *Sister Vasi is oh so near*
> *Found the path, found the way*
> *Don't want either of you here to stay*
> *Gaia will help, so heed her word as well as mine*
> *We want out of this hellhole and now is time.*

Andros stiffened, but to his credit, he simply reached down and helped Lada to her feet. She winced and bent slightly to relieve pressure on the extensive injuries to her body.

"Who beat you like this?" Andros demanded, ignoring Gaia, who stood with her hands on her hips very close to Lada.

Lada swayed and almost went down. Gaia caught her around the waist at the same time Andros did. Gaia leaned toward Andros and whispered into his ear. "I have to take your blood and give you mine in order to talk you through the labyrinth and get you out of here."

"Do it," Andros snapped curtly, bending closer.

He brought Lada right up to his side. To those in the arena, the three looked as if they were trying to keep Lada on her feet. She began to struggle wildly, her arms flailing and her body jerking from side to side.

Gaia was fast, taking the blood from Andros' neck and then using her teeth on her wrist and offering the bright red drops to him. Without hesitation he took her blood. The struggling Lada, with her arms flopping wildly, helped to cover what was really taking place.

Grigor and Karine crowded close. The moment Gaia pulled away from Andros, she offered her wrist to Grigor, keeping her hand low, hiding it between their bodies. He also took the blood without hesitation.

Vasilisa was proud of her brothers for not questioning or hesitating when she used the old nursery rhyme they would often say back and forth to one another as children in a secret code. They were very young and thought they were so clever.

"Where's Patsy?" Andros demanded loudly. "You always brag you can take the sword away or get my whip from me with your sword. I challenge you this night, Patsy."

What does he think he's doing? Vasilisa whispered to Afanasiv.

He is providing the distraction for the others to get across the arena. Your brother is very courageous.

He must go with them. If he becomes trapped, they'll tear him apart and eat him alive. Look at those demons. They're actually salivating.

Vasilisa didn't want to see those terrible demons in the stands sur-rounding her brothers and their women. Some of the demons were drooling. Long ropes of saliva poured from the sides of their mouths and hung in white slobbery fluid. They paid no mind to the strings of slobber, yelling out encouragement to Patsy as she came striding out, horns lowered, her cloven feet stomping hard on the concrete.

Patsy ignored the fallen bodies of her fellow demons. She even stepped on some, driving down with her hooves into their gutted bellies as they lay writhing and moaning. Each time she did, a cheer went up from the crowd. Patsy raised her shield toward the crowd and pointed her sword at Andros, snarling and blowing steam from her flared nos-trils.

Gaia pointed to the far side of the arena where the door led to the hidden staircase rising to the corridor and leading to the upper cham-bers. She wrapped her arm around Lada. Karine positioned herself on the other side of Lada, and they began to stumble across the arena floor to get out of the way of the big spectacle. Grigor walked back-ward, sword in hand, watching his brother, who stood confidently in the center of the arena, simply waiting while Patsy made her grand entrance.

Andros, Afanasiv said, using the link Gaia provided. *You cannot allow Patsy to get between you and the others. Each time she starts to circle around you, drop back and cut her off. When she charges you directly, make certain not to use a circular defense. Always know where you are in relationship to the others.*

Vasilisa's heart began to pound. There were so many demons. How could her brothers possibly escape, especially with Lada in such terrible condition? *Maybe this is a bad idea. The evil one might be so angry at them for attempting to escape that she might just kill them all outright.*

This is no place to live, my lady. You see what she's doing to your brothers. You don't want them to become fully demon. Gaia is working on healing Grigor right now while Andros is making his opening moves. Once she has gotten rid of the evil one's ability to control Grigor, then she will start on Andros, he soothed.

Vasilisa touched her brother Grigor. She could see the thick scars in his mind already dissolving. Gaia was fast at erasing them.

Can she get rid of your scars?

Your brothers' scarring is new. It is also different from mine. They didn't acquire it through a fault of their own. They didn't kill over and over as I did. They chose to save the life of a loved one. Their scars are scars of sacrifice.

Instantly, Vasilisa was outraged. *And your scars are not? You didn't get them in the defense of your people? Of all people? Mine? Human? That is some bullshit right there, Siv.*

In spite of the gravity of the situation, she felt his amusement wrapped up in a deeper, growing, very genuine affection for her. That felt—good. Authentic. She didn't want him to be with her because she had guarded his soul and they were destined. She wanted him to be with her because of who she was—the real, flawed, imperfect Vasilisa.

A flood of warmth spread through her as he surrounded her with his strength and approval. *Perfection is in the eye of the beholder, and it is supposed to be flawed so the devil doesn't look too closely at it.*

Vasilisa would have thrown her arms around him and kissed him if she had a body right then. The crack of a whip snapped her attention back to Andros. He had backed halfway across the arena toward Gaia, Grigor and the two women.

Did Gaia check to see if the evil one still had any control over Karine and Lada? she asked, worried. She still didn't understand how the escape was going to work.

Yes. When she was healing them. That was the first thing she did.

Vasilisa was just a little annoyed that she hadn't been in the loop on that.

I tried to fill you in, but you had shut me out. We will talk about that later.

There was an ominous ring to the way he put that, even though he'd used that low, compelling tone that felt like he was brushing velvet over her skin. She had shut off the connection between the two of them automatically, worried that if things went wrong, he would not be able to help her brothers. She checked in with him to ensure things were going according to plan, but she hadn't told him what had transpired on her end—at least not yet.

Gaia was now up against the door, Lada with her. Lada seemed to be standing better, although Karine had her arm around her, so it was difficult to tell for certain. Grigor stood in front of the group, making it even more difficult to tell what was happening.

Why aren't they going? Andros can't keep engaging with Patsy. What if he slips and goes down?

Patsy charged him more than once. She was massive, as big as any bull and fast on her feet. She utilized her size and strength, sometimes on four legs and others on two. She wielded her sword expertly. On the other hand, Andros snapped the fire whip with equal or superior expertise, so much so that furious betting was taking place in the stands. He scored over and over, the sizzling-hot orange-red flames streaking out to flay flesh from Patsy's massive body. Patsy stumbled when the whip wrapped around her neck several times and Andros yanked hard, taking his prisoner to her knees. He dragged her toward him as he went backward, all the while continuing to wrap the fire whip around Patsy's body.

Now, Vasi, the crystal flames. Turn the fire whip to a demon killer, Andros ordered.

She didn't see how that was going to do anything but incite the demons to riot and possibly rush her brother and the others. She sent the blue flames licking along his whip, and Andros sent more coils around Patsy.

Smoke burst from her hide, and holes began to appear through her. She howled and stomped as he pulled the whip tighter and tighter around her neck and down her arms so that she was forced to drop her sword and shield. Flames licked up from her hooves to her horns, blue-hot, leaping high, spreading fast, jumping to the bodies on the arena floor and to the columns holding the structure in place.

The demons in the stands suddenly began humming low, and cracks appeared in the arena floor as the ground shook over and over. The greedy blue flames seemed to take on a life of their own, rushing over the crowds in the stands, finding the living demons and consuming them as they tried to run.

Gaia opened the door to the stairs. Instead of sending them up, she pointed to a very narrow door leading down. "Go that way. Hurry. I'll be right behind you. Go, Grigor. Take the lead."

Andros came behind them, coiling the fire whip around his arm. Afanasiv barely made it through the door before it slammed closed behind them. Gaia turned and safeguarded the door, blocking it from opening on either side.

A fanasiv had taken this route with Gaia once before. Back then, so long ago, it had been just him running for his life. He had been severely wounded, drained of blood, so much so that Gaia hadn't been able to replace what he'd lost. She had done her best to get him to safety, and he had been grateful, but she had insisted she stay behind. No matter what he said or did, Gaia refused to go with him.

Lada was in much better shape than she appeared, thanks to Gaia's healing efforts. Once Gaia caught up with them, she led the way, with Grigor following right behind her. The two Lycan women were in the middle, with Andros bringing up the rear. Afanasiv stayed close to Gaia. He knew where the threats would come from. If Lilith had added any new traps in her house of horrors, he wanted to be able to find them before any of the others.

Pay close attention to the walls, floor and ceiling, Vasi, he cautioned. *Note the slightest change. Anything that might indicate a difference. An insect. A smear of dirt where it shouldn't be. The walls and floor are hostile. The ceiling could suddenly come down.*

He gave the same warning to her brothers. He wanted as many

pairs of eyes looking as possible. He didn't include Karine and Lada simply because the two women were exhausted, and both had injuries. They needed to conserve strength for running in case of an immediate threat—and there was bound to be at least one.

Because he was in spirit form, he could travel at will along the walls and ceiling, inspecting quickly for anything out of the ordinary ahead of Gaia. Their group moved fast, but Afanasiv was adept at using his vision swiftly.

Broken spider web, Gaia, he reported.

Gaia held up her hand and instantly everyone stopped. Afanasiv moved slowly along the wall, located the spider in a crevice and studied it carefully. The arachnid appeared real enough, but he wasn't convinced. The urge to make a run for it was strong, but Afanasiv wasn't going to take any chances. He moved very carefully between the spider's anchor line and radius thread to get behind the web to see inside the crack behind the spider. A sharp awareness vibrated through Afanasiv's spirit.

Vasilisa. Do you see this? There must be hundreds of them. The evil one has an army waiting for any who try to escape her. He included Gaia and her brothers in the loop.

Are there more on the other side, or is this the entire nest? Vasilisa asked.

Afanasiv backed out slowly, taking great care not to disturb the web. *No one move or make a sound until we deal with this.*

He examined the opposite wall thoroughly. He couldn't find any evidence of hidden spiders on that wall, in the ceiling or on the floor. Unfortunately, the inspection took time they didn't have. Chaos reigned above them in the form of fire and earthquakes, but once things settled, Lilith would demand to know where her prisoners were. She would suspect they would go out the same way Afanasiv had gone, and she'd take extra precautions to have her demons waiting for them on the other end.

When we get back to the crevice, Vasilisa will burn out the demons while they're in their spider form. The moment the blue flames start, you move forward, but keep watch. The evil one won't have stopped with just this one trap, Afanasiv said.

Once again, he started moving very carefully through the spider-web. The radius threads were very close together, and it was difficult, even as a spirit, to slip through without the slight breeze disturbing the silk in passing.

Andros spoke to him for the first time. *Who are you?*

I am Afanasiv, Vasilisa's lifemate. He answered the royal honestly. *Most call me Siv.*

Andros technically ruled the Lycan world, although the royals claimed it was only the small territory in Siberia that acknowledged them. Afanasiv knew better. Dimitri had studied the Lycan ways for centuries, and when Afanasiv and his brethren had asked questions, Dimitri had answered. He was protective of his wolves and their Lycan guardians but saw little harm in explaining the culture and history of the Lycan world. Afanasiv thought it extraordinary of Dimitri after the torture the Lycans had put him through that he remained loyal to them.

You have made your claim on my sister and sealed her to you? Andros' voice was very mild, but there were notes of both censure and authority in it that said he was a royal and didn't like that he hadn't been consulted.

Afanasiv wasn't about to get into any discussions about how one asked permission from a king for his sister's hand in marriage. They were already married in the eyes of his people. His soul was sealed to hers. Hopefully Vasilisa understood fully that they were mated for eternity. He was certain she understood the claiming ritual. He'd explained carefully that once he wove their souls back together, nothing could break them apart.

I have. She is my wife.

He made it through the silken web to the shadowy crevice where the demon spider and its army lay in wait. *You will have to get all of them in one shot, my lady. Close off both ends, but the general is the one who will communicate with the evil one. That must not happen.*

Afanasiv conveyed absolute confidence in her. He honestly wasn't certain if it was possible to do what he was asking of her, but if anyone could do it, he was sure it was Vasilisa. He felt her studying the army of spiders.

Move back about six inches, Siv.

He did so. The moment he did, the blue flames poured out of nowhere, leaping at the general first in a concentrated burst, devouring him completely, then sweeping left and right and back again. The long sweeps were very controlled and took in the entire army of demon spiders, burning row after row. The stench was foul. Gaia automatically cleared the air of any trace of the noxious odor before it could overpower her charges. When the last of the spider army had been destroyed, Afanasiv rejoined Gaia to lead the way.

Keep watch on the walls and ceiling. Place your feet carefully, Gaia reminded them. *Stay as quiet as possible.*

As they hurried down the corridor, it began to narrow. Afanasiv knew instantly this wasn't right. His shoulders would have scraped the walls on either side had he been in his physical form.

What is this place, Gaia?

She would expect us to follow the route I took you on, Siv. I cast an illusion that we went that way, but I am taking us on an alternate course. It is a maze down here. This track loops around the arena and begins a steep climb to a portal that is closed. Mostly closed. I have seen cracks in it. I think, with help, Vasilisa can open it for you.

Afanasiv sighed. That didn't sound as if she intended to leave with them. *Why do you persist in staying?*

Gaia was silent as she hurried as fast as possible while still studying the walls and flooring before her. *If I were to leave, who would come to the aid of those the evil one targets? And who would ensure the beast held captive behind the four gates remains a beast and doesn't fully commit to the demon in him? I will stay until I feel there is a better solution.*

Afanasiv knew from his past experience with her that Gaia wasn't going to budge. *This beast, Justice, is not your lifemate.*

No, he is not. Her response was clipped. In all his dealings with her, Gaia was always calm, gentle and sweet. She sounded irritated, as if she knew her lifemate might be looking for her and was having none of it.

It is possible your lifemate cannot find you where you are. He took a stab at finding out if she was hiding from her lifemate.

That could be the point. Perhaps he shouldn't have overlooked me so dismissively when he had the chance those years ago.

The corridor turned even narrower. The ceiling above was dirt, as were the walls and floor. The air was musty and it was much harder to breathe. Automatically, he provided better air for the Lycans.

Gaia, you were taken as a child and brought to the evil one by Xavier. You have been down here since.

Have I? I know every escape route. Do you think I can't come and go as I please? she countered. *In any case, we should drop the subject, as I need to concentrate on this next passage.*

Gaia hadn't been raised by Carpathians. She was totally independent of them. In some ways, she ran wild and free. Lilith most likely didn't pay that much attention to her.

Who raised you, Gaia?

She was silent for a long time, her head going back and forth between the walls before she stepped forward into the next section. *Mostly, it was Justice. Some of the demons would poke at him with sharp sticks and throw fiery rocks at him. They had these really long spears, and they'd jab him with them. I was really little, but I didn't like it, so I would throw rocks at the demons to try to make them leave him alone. They would chase me and say they were going to eat me. I had hiding places I could fold myself into that they couldn't, but one day I wasn't fast enough. I ducked into Justice's pen to keep from getting eaten. As it was, they scraped the skin off my legs.* She gave a delicate shudder at the memory.

Afanasiv had his own memories of the cannibals. He could well understand a child living with the nightmares of a terrifying band of demons pursuing her, yelling that they were going to eat her. She would probably have a difficult time getting over that trauma.

Justice caught me up before they could drag me out from under the gate, and he protected me. After that, I stayed with him most of the time. None of the demons dared to come inside his territory. He was too fast. He was deadly. And he was my friend. She said the last defiantly, as though she thought he would ridicule her.

I'm thankful you had him, Afanasiv said sincerely. *He is a legend in our world. His sacrifices for his family and his people are incomparable. Clearly, he has passed that same code of honor on to you.*

Gaia suddenly held up her hand, and everyone halted instantly. *Siv, take a look at this and tell me what it is.*

Afanasiv quickly moved ahead to look at the spot where Gaia indicated. The passageway was extremely narrow and angled up toward the surface. The dirt walls had crumbled away in places, leaving little stacks of debris on the ground. Above their heads, roots hung from the ceiling. Rust-colored water dripped down one wall, falling from one of the many shoots hanging from above them. As he neared the dangling roots, the smell hit him. It wasn't water. This was blood, leaking from some chamber above them.

Not just any blood, Siv. That's Dragonseeker blood. It's been tainted. Compromised in some way, Vasilisa told him. *Have there been other Dragonseekers that the evil one has had down here?*

Not to my knowledge. He switched to the path that included Gaia. *What room is directly above us?*

That is the only "cold" room down here. The freezers are kept there. It's a huge room. Xavier and his brother require a great deal of blood for their experiments. It is kept there frozen.

It appears as if the freezers had a meltdown, Afanasiv pointed out.

Must have been that earthquake. Gaia sounded complacent. *Those demons shouldn't have been practicing those low notes the evil one wanted them to perfect.*

Afanasiv took the lead. He started ascending up the steep slope, very conscious of each step the Lycans would take behind him. It was nearly a blackout in the passage. Very little light seeped in. He had an advantage in that he didn't need his physical vision to see. Gaia didn't either. The Lycans had good night vision as a rule, but this wasn't about night vision. This was a false darkness.

Off on the right side and low to the ground was a pinpoint of light running about a foot long. Directly above that was a similar pinpoint of light running about a foot long. A door built into the wall and camouflaged with dirt and rock.

Let me take a look before any of you move. He didn't wait for a protest; he slipped under that crack to find himself in a wide area dug out to resemble a room of sorts.

Three demons sat in chairs sipping at homemade brew and chomping on old bones. They each held playing cards in their hands. The cards were smeared with grease and dirt. Old blood stained them, but the demons didn't seem to notice. They tipped their chairs back and continued with their conversation.

"She won't stop until everyone is dead," purple shirt groused. "I've never seen her so driven before. Lucifer shouldn't have laughed at her."

Polka-dot shirt nodded solemnly. "He's going to find himself with a spear through his heart if he doesn't watch out."

"And she's got those creepy mages working for her," pink shirt added. "She's taking over down here, and no one's noticed, least of all him."

"Because he doesn't think she's a threat to him," purple shirt said. "Why does she want that Skyler girl so much? The mage wants her as well. What is it with everyone and the girl? Maybe we should get in on that and get to her first." He threw two cards on the table and added two new ones to his hand.

"She'd skin us alive," polka-dot said. "Are you crazy? She's done that before, you know."

Pink shirt tilted her head. "Why does she want that girl?"

Polka-dot shirt sighed. "Quit cheating. You can't just take new cards whenever you want them. You didn't hear this from me. It's who her mother was. Her father is Dragonseeker, right? Razvan is really her birth father. And he's Dragonseeker. But her mother . . ."

"Human," pink shirt said with a little sniff of disdain. "They don't even taste all that good."

"Do you want me to tell you or not?" polka-dot demanded.

Afanasiv wanted to know. He thought a gag might be appropriate to put over pink shirt's mouth. He waited.

"Her mother came from a big-deal mage family. I heard the whispers after Xavier was sent here. The mother also had some big affinity to Mother Earth and all that mumbo-jumbo crap Lilith likes to talk about. You know how she is about being one with the earth. She could heal the earth and had all kinds of power over it."

Purple shirt snorted. "Bullshit. No one can do half the things Lilith says they can."

"She believes it, and that means it's real to her. So we'd better believe it, as well." Polka-dot gave a casual shrug and stabbed an overripe peach with his knife and lifted it to his mouth. The juice ran down his arm and dripped onto the table. "Seems that this particular woman, Skyler, has all these superpowers because of her blood. See, she's Dragonseeker, but she's also got this Mother Earth thing going on, too. Everyone thinks her mother was strictly human, but she wasn't. She was mage, and her family was even more powerful than Xavier's." He grinned, revealing three gold teeth and a mouthful of peach.

Pink shirt rolled her eyes. "That's not telling us anything. Why wouldn't all Carpathians know Skyler was mage? What's the big deal?

They all seem to be one with the earth. Even Gaia is. She can do all sorts of things with dirt."

"Sheesh, how the hell would I know what that means," polka-dot asked. "I don't care one way or another. I'm just telling you what I've overheard. I don't think Skyler even knows why her mother is such a big deal."

Purple shirt threw his cards down right in the middle of the peach juice. "I hate being cooped up in here. I should be out there finding this bitch Skyler. There's no reason for me to be pulling this kind of duty when I have seniority."

"Think of it as a vacation. We can eat and drink for a few days and rest. Just do nothing. We know no one's coming our way. If they did, the spiders are going to take care of them. We'd hear screams by now," polka-dot shirt assured them. He stood up abruptly. "Speaking of screams." His grin turned obscenely evil. "I think I'll go pass the time with the new widow and her daughters. She didn't like me eating her husband, but it did make her cooperative. Does anyone want to go with me? I explained to her about buying protection from those pesky demons, and she agreed she needed it now that her husband was gone."

Purple shirt stood up so fast his chair fell over. "I'll go with you."

"Wait a minute," pink shirt said. "That's not fair. I want to go, but someone has to be here just in case." She stood up. "We should draw cards for the chance."

"I'm not drawing cards against you," purple shirt said.

Vasilisa, is it possible to target all three of them as they stand? Afanasiv asked.

Her response was to shower them from above and spray them from all sides with the blue crystalline flames. While Afanasiv had been listening to the conversation to gather information, she had been setting up for a battle. The moment he gave the go-ahead, she was ready, engulfing the three demons in pure flames.

The instant the three demons were incinerated, Afanasiv gave the order for Gaia to move the group forward. She did so quickly, and Afanasiv joined her. The passageway led upward steeply. It was a crude underground corridor, hastily hacked out of the dirt with few supports. At times, they had to find their way over large piles of dirt, where the sides of the tunnel had collapsed and the mounds of soil slid onto the narrow floor.

The door to the portal is just up ahead, Gaia informed them. *Afanasiv, you will have to check to see if there are going to be enemies waiting. It's possible she ordered them to guard every portal to this side.*

Thank you for your aid, Gaia. He wasn't about to waste time on arguing with her to accompany them.

Afanasiv's spirit slid under the door, taking the small piece of Vasilisa's spirt with him as he entered the world. The sun hadn't yet come up, but he would be racing the clock. There were five demons on either side of the portal and another five facing it. Fifteen in all.

I cannot use the demon killer flames on them, Vasilisa admitted. *It takes so much energy to wield the flame, and I am unable to produce enough.*

Afanasiv could hear the exhaustion in her voice. *There is no need, my lady. This can be done another way. You rest, you have done much this rising.*

He sent word to Gaia and the others. *I will have to retrieve my physical body in order to keep these demons under control while you escape with your women. It will only take a few minutes.*

He didn't wait for an answer. He raced the sun, streaking across the sky to the small cabin where his lifemate protected his body.

I should tell you, there was a little bit of trouble at the cabin, Vasilisa confessed. *In all the excitement of rescuing my brothers, I forgot to mention it. I was going to tell you right away, but you wanted to make sure . . .*

What kind of trouble? he demanded.

A couple of demons showed up and performed a little act. They tried to make me think one was my friend, the owner of the inn, and when I re-

fused to let her in, she said she was leaving a basket of things to restock the cabin.

I do not care in the least about baskets, sívamet, and you know that very well. Get on with it.

I did not open the door, so stop acting like you think I did.

I did not say I thought you opened the door. His tone was milder. *I dislike leaving you alone. It is my nature to protect my lifemate. Hearing that you had trouble is upsetting to me. I apologize if I sounded gruff. I knew you didn't open the door simply because we are here together, and we rescued your brothers and their women. I am not running about looking to find where they have taken my lifemate.*

Vasilisa sighed. She didn't want to tell him she'd been fooled by Odessa. In her defense, she knew the cabin was due to be restocked. It was on the to-do list posted on the wall at the inn and again in her office at home. Her aunt, when she visited, could have easily seen the schedule, and so could anyone visiting the inn.

Why do you keep this information from me now?

They were approaching the cabin. The dead bodies of the demons were nothing but ashes lying in the snow not far from the cabin steps. Afanasiv was an elite hunter. He would be able to read exactly what took place without her having to confess a thing. He was asking her out of courtesy.

I'd prefer to show you the images, Siv. I don't come off looking very intelligent. I took Odessa at face value instead of paying closer attention and really watching her every move.

Afanasiv was silent as he studied the replay Vasilisa had stored in the memories of her encounter with the demons. *I would say you did very well, considering restocking the cabin was already expected. Not certain where you want to go from here, my lady.*

He moved swiftly over the ashes and began unraveling the safe-guards surrounding the cabin. Once inside the cabin, his spirit traveled straight to his body. He'd been away from his physical body far too long, and he needed to allow himself time to reorient himself. Unfortunately, Gaia couldn't handle fifteen demons on her own. Andros and Grigor would fight to the death, but they wouldn't win against demons without the proper tools. Afanasiv didn't know how experienced they were in fighting demons. He wasn't going to take chances with his lifemate's brothers.

"You want to sit this one out, *sívamet*? I would be grateful." He didn't make it a command. His woman didn't react well to commands. She had to make her own choices. He was coming to understand that his need to protect her was bound to be in a constant war with his need to make her happy.

She came across the room to stand in front of the cot where he sat. Her hands framed his face, crystal-blue eyes looking down into his. "You know I cannot. These are demons we face. I am the most experienced out of the royals at demon killing. I can open the portals and consecrate the ground, closing it off so they cannot escape from the underworld. You know I am needed. I was taught from birth that this is my destiny, my role. You are a hunter of the vampire. I am a hunter of the demon. Just as what you are is embedded deep, so is my legacy embedded deep within me. I will get my energy back quickly."

He had known what her answer would be. Still, a part of him had hoped. "We have to get back now, Vasilisa. Who knows how many Lilith can muster quickly? Once she realizes which way her prisoners have gone, she will send as many of her demons as she can to retrieve them. The sun is rising, and I will have to go to ground. She is aware of that, as well—that you will have little help during the daylight hours."

Vasilisa stepped back to give him room to stand. "I suspect she is wrong about that, Afanasiv."

He arched an eyebrow at her in inquiry.

"Tell me you are not capable of walking in sunlight if you have to," she challenged.

"Why do you think that I can?" His tone was curious.

"I just have this feeling," she countered. "You cannot lie to your lifemate. Can you be out in sunlight?"

His impossibly long lashes swept down and then up again, lending him a softer look as he gave her a slightly mischievous grin. Her heart did a funny little somersault and sped up. "Can't everyone?" He took her hand and led her back outside. At once he dropped her hand and launched himself into the air, shifting into the body of an owl, wings straining to gain altitude fast.

"Show-off," she muttered, but found she was laughing. How could she not when being with Afanasiv was fun, even under these circumstances? There was no leaping into the air and shifting for her, although she was tempted to try it. Lycans were capable of tremendous vertical leaps. She was going to practice the minute she had time. She would not be outdone by him.

His laughter was low and played along her spine, scattering goose bumps over her skin. She stood on the railing of the porch, took a little hop as she shifted, holding the image of the owl in her mind as feathers broke out over her body.

She noted the male turned in a circle above her, waiting for her to complete her metamorphosis before he rushed off to aid her siblings. Clearly, she was his first concern. While she did want him to save her brothers, she couldn't help the thrill that ran through her bloodstream at the idea that he would put her first. In her life, no one, not even her parents, had ever done that.

Once in the air, the two owls flew fast together to the small portal where her brothers waited with their women and Gaia. When that door was opened, it would alert the commander of the demons, and those demons lounging would come to full attention and do their best to kill the escapees.

There are five demons on either side of the door. They are armed with swords and eager to use them. The main five are straight in front of the door about thirty yards out. These demons have seen plenty of combat, and the commander is one of that group. I will take on those. Grigor, you will have to fight off the ones to the left of the door, and, Andros, you the ones to the right. Gaia, the sun is already in the sky. If you are feeling the effects, you must go to ground before it is too late for you, Afanasiv warned the Carpathian woman.

She sent an image of her laughter to him. I live among demons and Lycans. Where do you think I get blood to survive? I am mixed blood. I have been for a very long time. If it is necessary, I can walk in the sunlight. It will never be my preference.

Afanasiv turned that over in his mind. Carpathians often hypothesized about what it would be like to walk in the daylight. Which kinds of activities they would choose to do if they were given only a few hours to be awake during the day. He loved the night. There was such beauty in the sky, in the moon and stars. He loved the night storms that poured water from the skies, while thunder roared and lightning forked with loud cracks.

He built one now in the not-too-distant sky and let the wind bring it to them. "You wanted a storm, I give you one." He gave her a sweeping bow, and she realized how quickly he had shed the bird image and was already sauntering into the sight of the demons.

The demons were caught completely off guard. They expected their prey to come out of the portal, not walk up to them with his sleeves rolled up, revealing muscular arms and more tattoos.

I will have need of your blue flames soon, my lady, so continue to rest. Please stay hidden as long as possible. If they suspect you deliver the killing flame, they will do anything to get to you.

"Good morning, gentlemen," Afanasiv greeted them. He faced the five most dangerous demons, but with his body angled slightly sideways, he could keep an eye on the two other teams. "I was a great distance from here and heard you calling my name. You summoned me, so here I am." Once again, Afanasiv bowed.

The leader shuffled forward, his hand on the sword at his side. "You need to leave. No one summoned you."

Afanasiv looked disappointed. He scratched his head and looked all around him. "Are you certain?" He took several steps closer to the captain of the demons. "Let me see the list of names you have. Surely I'm at the top."

All the demons' attention was riveted on Afanasiv. *Now, Gaia, get them out. Hurry, I can only hold them so long. Vasi, stay with me.*

"There is no list, you fool. If you don't want to die this day, leave now," the demon thundered.

"Of course there's a list," Afanasiv insisted. "Lilith always makes lists. She was very angry when I escaped. I know she put me at the top of the list, and if I get away again, she'll put your head on the chopping block." He pointed to a smooth boulder. "I can sit right over there while you consult with her. But I warn you, I'm not going to wait long."

"You must be insane to come here and just turn yourself in. I'll have one of my men escort you below, if that's what you want."

"You misunderstand me," Afanasiv said with a small smile that showed his white teeth. "I have come to challenge you. You must defeat me in combat in order to take me in."

The captain heaved a sigh. "Just who are you?"

"I am Afanasiv Belan Dragonseeker." He dropped the name casually.

There was an eerie silence filled only by the capricious wind. The breeze picked up the powdery snow from the ground and tossed it into the air in thin spinning columns all around them. In spite of the sun struggling to make a debut, dark clouds rolled overhead, looking for all the world like a witch's cauldron with a roiling brew. Inside the clouds, lightning forked, briefly lighting the sky with crackling energy. Thunder boomed directly overhead, shaking the ground.

The commander gripped his sword tighter and glanced both left and right to ensure his soldiers were close behind him. "I believe our mistress is eager for your return," he admitted.

As he spoke, he rushed forward with the blade of his sword held low but pointed slightly up, as if to gut Afanasiv. Afanasiv waited until the last moment before his own sword appeared in his hand, and he parried the thrust with a decidedly hard blow. The force of it spun the commander around and sent shock waves up his arm. At the same time, as the demon was sent spinning, the blade of Afanasiv's sword severed his head. Before anyone could fully comprehend what had happened, blue flames swarmed over the head and body, incinerating both almost instantaneously.

Lada is having a difficult time walking, Siv, Gaia reported. *Andros will have to carry her. Grigor is away with Karine. There is one demon to your left nearest the portal who keeps sniffing the air and turning back toward us. You will need a bigger distraction. I'll cover their tracks in the snow if you can divert attention without getting killed.*

Afanasiv held his arms straight out, sword gone, deliberately looking only at the four men who stood in front of him, as if he'd forgotten completely about those behind him. "I'm sorry about your commander. He wasn't as good with his sword as he thought he was. Lilith has a very large reward out for me. If you want a prize like that one, you have to earn it."

He spoke softly so the demons would have to strain to hear what he said. That drew those behind him out from around the portal leading from the underworld to aboveground. He felt their movements, their heady triumph as they closed ranks behind him in a loose semicircle.

Afanasiv. Vasilisa sounded distressed. *Let me help you.*

It will be fine, sívamet. Just be ready with your blue fire. He kept his tone calm and reassuring. She didn't know him that well yet. He was an ancient, well versed in battle. He wasn't showing off; he was stalling, giving Andros time to get his lady to safety. What Siv was doing might be considered a calculated risk, but he was certain he would have no trouble fighting off the demons as they attacked him—*if* his woman stayed put and he didn't have to worry about her.

A hum began, that low note started by one of the demons off to his right. That demon was dressed in a blue-colored shirt, and he had black spiked hair with blue tips. His thick horns were sharp tips, and the broad forehead indicated it was bony and extremely strong. Because he started the hum and the others followed suit, it stood to reason he was next in charge.

They spoke to one another in their demon language, but Afanasiv had spent time in the underworld, and he had no problem picking up languages. On the signal, they were all to attack at once. That wasn't a surprise, either. It was a common enough tactic the demons used when falling on their prey before they tore it to pieces with their sharp, serrated teeth.

"Really, gentlemen, you're going to cheat? Where is the honor in that? Oh, I forgot. You're demons. There is no honor in demons. That means I don't have to fight fair, either."

The sword once more leapt into his hand as the demons crowded even closer to him. He spun in a smooth circle, the razor-sharp blade slicing through bellies as he completed the circle before the demons were even aware he had moved. The second spin, he went low, taking legs out from under them, his speed blurring his image. On the third spin, the demons became aware of the fact that most had to hold their bellies to keep their intestines from spilling out. Then their legs were suddenly not attached just above the knees, and black blood poured onto the snow. That terrible blade of Afanasiv's was going for necks this time, severing heads as he spun.

Some of the demons tried to retaliate, holding up their swords in an effort to block the blade coming at them. The force and speed of Afanasiv's attack made it nearly impossible to stop. Swords went flying and arms went numb. He was using the strength given to him by so many years of hunting the undead. So many centuries of battling with vampires had honed him into a fighting machine. He knew the majority of the tricks from every conceivable enemy he faced.

Your charges are away, Gaia reported. *Good luck to all of you.*

Thank you for your aid, Afanasiv said.

Vasilisa echoed his thanks. *Perhaps sometime in the not-so-distant future, Gaia, we will be able to sit down and have a nice evening talk together.*

Sometime, Gaia agreed.

The few demons—and there were only three of them left able to walk or wield a sword—backed away from him and tried to run for the portal. Vasilisa was there ahead of them, sealing it off from those below as well as from those above. There couldn't be a crack or crevice open that the demons might take advantage of. She was thorough, even as she sent the blue flames to incinerate the fallen demons. Very carefully, she consecrated the ground, making certain the demons could no longer use it for coming or going.

The three demons trapped on the surface turned to face Afanasiv, spreading out to give themselves room to fight him. They talked over their strategy using their language to do so.

"I hate to break it to you," Afanasiv said, "but I know your language. That isn't going to work on me. Just come at me one at a time."

The three rushed him.

"Or not," he said, once again moving with blurring speed.

Afanasiv felt the berserker's rush of excitement rising. No matter how hard he tried to push it down, it came storming back more powerful than ever. The thick scars on his soul called out to the demon in him, declaring he had waited far too long in this world, and sooner or later he would have to pay the consequences. He didn't like his lifemate seeing him as one of the demons—and she would. He might be smooth wielding the sword, but he was still just as cruelly cunning. He dispatched the last three demons and waited for Vasilisa's blue flame to incinerate them so they wouldn't rise again.

Afanasiv and Vasilisa went back to the first portal so she could make certain that it was closed for all time and sealed both above and below. He held out his hand to her and nodded in the direction of the palace. "Shall we?"

There was the slightest of hesitations. Vasilisa put her hand in his. "Yes."

11

Afanasiv allowed his lifemate a full day and night of rest before waking her to take her back to the palace, where he knew her brothers had expected her to be. He didn't much care what they expected or how angry they were, as long as they kept their anger centered on him and didn't allow it to spill over to their sister. More than anything, he wanted to be alone with her so they could work out the kinks of being a new couple, but he understood her better than she knew.

Vasilisa was uncomfortable with the idea of a physical relationship with him until she felt wholly accepted by him. The lifemate bond made it especially difficult to prove to his woman that he wanted her for herself and not just because fate had decreed that they be together. He wasn't going to complicate things further by forcing her to accept him when she wasn't ready.

"Andros can come across as very arrogant and rude," Vasilisa whispered as they ascended the steps leading to the back part of the palace. "Please have patience with him."

He looked down at the top of her head. "Do you believe I am an unreasonable man?"

Her long lashes lifted, and for a moment, he caught a glimpse of her blue eyes looking back at him with a certain amount of anxiety. "I wouldn't use the word *unreasonable*," she said diplomatically. "It's just that Andros is the ruling authority here. His word is law and no one questions him. You're every bit as dominant. It wouldn't do for the two of you to get into any kind of a heated exchange. I've been handling my siblings my entire life. It might be a good idea to allow me to talk to him first."

"Do you mean I should hide behind my lifemate's skirts?" He kept all inflection from his voice, not allowing her to see how much the idea of Vasilisa talking to her brothers before he did really upset him. He didn't forbid it, but it wasn't happening, no matter how well she knew her brothers. Let them rage. They would deal with him, not her.

"I didn't mean that at all," she denied. "You're twisting my words. I want them to like and accept you, Afanasiv. That's important to me. I love my brothers. The last thing I want is a huge rift that could have been avoided if we were careful."

"I will listen to all your brothers have to say," he promised. "But I will not allow them to talk down to you or make you feel guilty or bad in any way. You have done nothing wrong. Without you, your siblings would be dishonored, their women most likely dead, and they would be pawns or worse for Lilith."

"I don't know about that," she hedged, slowing as they came to the back entrance to the kitchen. "You were the one who did most of it. Don't think I'm not aware how difficult it was on you. I know I would never have found a way to get them out of there."

"You would have," he insisted. "I know that you saved them, Vasilisa. Hopefully, they are grateful to you. Once we speak with your brothers, we must find my friends and Dimitri and Skyler. It is best we know what we are facing and why."

"It has something to do with the power of the Dragonseeker lineage," Vasilisa guessed. "I find it strange that so many of you have gathered in one place. Isn't that unusual?"

"It is," he confirmed. "As a rule, Ivory and Razvan keep to themselves. They gifted Dimitri and Skyler with wolf pups and are helping them learn how to hunt with them. Fen, Dimitri's blood brother, has not yet been able to be far from him since your people sentenced Dimitri to death by silver. Tatijana is his lifemate, so naturally, she travels with him. Zev is Lycan and returns often to his homeland, and his lifemate, Branislava, accompanies him. That covers everyone."

"With the exception of you," Vasilisa pointed out.

He didn't want to talk about being Dragonseeker or what that meant. He had buried all those memories deep. Not just the ones of being in Lilith's house of horrors but the ones from his childhood. Centuries upon centuries earlier. His mind shut down the moment he started to crack open that door. There were things better left alone. He found he was gripping Vasilisa's hand just that little bit too hard.

"I'm sorry, *sívamet*." He used the pad of his thumb to rub over the spots where his fingers gripped her too tight. "Did I hurt you?"

"No, I would have protested," she assured him. She turned her hand over to thread her fingers through his. "Andros is a particularly good friend of Dimitri's. He was terribly upset when he heard what was done to him, and he reached out right away. Things have been strange here since then. It's difficult to know who is a friend and who isn't anymore."

"We discovered that a mage was hard at work undermining the Lycans in order to drive a wedge between them and start a war with the Carpathians. Who's to say it isn't happening a second time?" Afanasiv asked.

He opened the door and stepped back to allow her to enter first. They were using the back kitchen entrance on purpose, hoping most of those working at the palace wouldn't see them enter. The cook and food preps turned as the cold draft hit them, smiles of greeting slowly fading as they took in Afanasiv holding hands with Vasilisa.

"Miss Vasi," the cook greeted her. "His highness is expecting you. He said to ask you to meet him in the formal dining room if I were to see you."

"Thank you, Clareese."

The cook nodded, staring at Afanasiv. He allowed Vasilisa to tug him around the three big center aisles, where the food was chopped up to prepare for the banquets often held on the grounds.

He went through the kitchen double doors into the wide hallway, listening to the storm of whispers that followed them as soon as they left.

"Did you see him? They were holding hands. He isn't from around here." A pause. A few giggles. "He's gorgeous. All man." More pauses. Then one voice. "He doesn't look like one of us. He looks more Carpathian than Lycan. She can't be with a Carpathian. You know what will happen."

"Hush, Randy. Don't talk that way," Clareese chastised. "We don't abide that kind of thinking here. You signed an agreement when you came to work here."

"I'm just saying what everyone else is thinking. I'm a member of the Sacred Circle and I'm proud of it. I don't know who else is, but if you are, you should stand with me on this. One of the royals can't possibly be with a Carpathian. That would be sacrilege."

"Stop, Randy," Clareese implored. "If you continue, I'll have to report you to Andros. You'll be sacked, and I know you need this job for your family."

"If you dare to report me for saying and doing what's right, you'll receive a midnight visit from those upholding the laws of the Circle, Clareese, and you'll be punished."

Before Clareese could say a word, there was a stunned hush in the kitchen. Vasilisa halted abruptly. Afanasiv felt the ripple of unease that swept through the entire palace.

"How dare you threaten anyone in my employ," a low-carrying voice snarled. Andros spoke with all the authority of a ruling king. "Do you think I don't know what goes on in my own house? It's your family that will be receiving a visit quite soon, and I'll be expecting answers. If I hear one lie, your farm will be forfeit, and you will be driven from these lands for all time. I cannot abide traitors, and my patience has grown even thinner knowing many of those pretending to follow the old ways are really in league with Lilith and her demons."

A collective gasp went up from those in the kitchen.

"Go, Randy, before I challenge you to a fight to the death. Tell your parents I will be seeing them very soon. If they wish to leave our territory and give up your farm, they should do so before my arrival."

Randy sputtered and tried to backtrack on the things he'd said, but there was no real way for him to do so. There was another silence and then a door slammed.

"Clareese? Are you all right?"

"Yes, sir. I'm fine. I just wasn't expecting him to threaten me like that. It's been years since the Sacred Circle went around threatening people if they didn't comply with their standards. I thought that group was outlawed."

"They're making a comeback. They meet in secret," Andros said. "What they don't understand is that the land itself speaks to us. There aren't any secrets from us. I am fully aware who has gone back to the old ways and just how treacherous they have become."

Afanasiv halted in the great hallway to look down at his lifemate. The *land* spoke to his woman? Mother Earth spoke to him. He had Dragonseeker blood running in his veins. He might not claim it to the outside world, but there was no denying he was fully Dragonseeker.

Vasilisa looked up at him with her crystalline blue eyes. "What is it?"

"Your brother referred to the 'old ways.' He acted as if those in the Sacred Circle were committing treason against your family."

"Not just our family, Afanasiv, but our people, as well. Those that fall within our charge, such as the wildlife. Dimitri is a part of our land. He came to us long before I was born and is a legend here, yet suddenly he is treated with mistrust and suspicion after all he has done for us. He has relentlessly hunted vampires at great cost to himself. He has acquired permits for the land to keep it wild and free, something none of us would have thought of. Where did the mistrust come from? The underground Sacred Circle. We should have shut it down immediately when the movement began to grow again."

Afanasiv waited for an explanation of why they didn't.

Vasilisa sighed. "These people are our friends. We grew up with them. Most of those adhering to the stricter laws of the Circle were older. The younger, modern Lycans seemed to ignore or just be amused by their archaic beliefs."

Afanasiv brushed the pad of his thumb along the back of her hand. "I have the feeling your brother is angry enough that he will do just that, drive those from his territory who insist on staying with those beliefs." He couldn't help framing the side of her face with his hand. Her skin was even softer than it looked. "You do realize that when he forces them to leave their homes, they will hate him and want revenge."

"We are used to being hated—and hunted. I am concerned about the government agents staying at the inn. They inquired specifically about Andros, and they also mentioned him ruling over the land. That would be considered treason. If a member of the Sacred Circle had evidence that Andros was the king here, or we were considered a ruling family, that would be enough for his arrest and imprisonment."

Afanasiv heard the note of worry in her voice, and that set alarms going off. "Surely you are able to jam the cell phones or any kind of device from recording when you are speaking."

"We can, although we sometimes forget, even though it is a safety rule. We get so comfortable with people, believing they are our friends. I'm especially guilty of that. I tend to take people at face value rather than intrude on their thoughts."

Afanasiv resisted the urge to give her a lecture on personal safety. She was well aware that had she scanned her aunt a few times, she might have saved them all a tremendous amount of pain and suffering. He didn't need to point that out to her. His woman was soft inside. She might be a fierce warrior, more than capable of standing with him in any fight, but she was soft and compassionate. He filed that away. He needed to protect that part of her—even from herself.

Andros came up behind them. "I wish to see you in the formal dining room, Vasi," he said. His tone was cold enough to match the outside temperature. "*Both* of you."

Afanasiv was not a man to take orders from anyone. He had shut himself off from all contact with humans or Lycans for two hundred years simply because he didn't trust himself, not because he was sentenced to go there. He imposed strict controls and discipline in order to keep those around him safe.

The tone Andros used was offensive to him. The way he stalked past them and continued down the wide hallway to yank open one of the double doors and slam it closed behind him was more than offensive. It was a deliberate insult. Afanasiv felt his teeth slide into place. The familiar well of white-hot adrenaline rushed through his veins.

He found it odd and a little disconcerting to have to tame emotions after not feeling anything for century after century. Right at that moment, he wanted to tear the king limb from limb for his audacity to treat a Carpathian warrior who had saved his life with such disrespect.

"My brother is an arrogant ass," Vasilisa said. "We don't have to go in and hear his lecture if you'd rather not."

Afanasiv's gaze moved over her upturned face, dwelling on her high cheekbones, her aristocratic nose, her large blue eyes framed with dark lashes to match her dark hair and that generous mouth that tilted so invitingly at the corners. A slow smile started somewhere inside him and built until it actually reached his lips. A genuine smile.

"You're afraid I might challenge him to a duel."

Her lashes fluttered. "You are a bit old-fashioned and he was *very* insulting."

He was grateful she acknowledged that her brother was disrespectful. He arched an eyebrow. "Old-fashioned? I assure you, my brethren believe I am very forward-thinking."

Outside the palace walls, wolves began to howl. First one and then a chorus of others answering. Afanasiv scowled. Vasilisa burst into laughter.

"Even the wolves can hear that white lie. I believe your friend is close."

Afanasiv nodded his head. "There is a bond between us. Those of us who believed we owed it to our lifemates to survive as long as possible but were too dangerous to continue hunting and killing vampires went to the monastery. We took an oath, had it carved into our skin, an oath sworn to our lifemates. When the emptiness became too severe, we chanted together to remind one another of that oath of honor. We passed two hundred years in the monastery ensuring that we stayed true to our lifemates and our code."

"And he is close now because . . ." she trailed off.

"He felt my annoyance with your brother. Carpathian hunters do not feel emotions until they find their lifemates. Nicu felt mine, and because I am unused to emotions, mine were uncontrolled and very raw. He feared I could become a danger to others, so he hastily made the journey to ensure he was near should I have need of him."

Vasilisa frowned, her brows drawing together. He had the unexpected desire to rub his thumb over her lips and then her eyebrows. He did just that.

"My understanding is that once you claim your lifemate, you can't turn vampire. You're perfectly safe. Did I get that part wrong? It was explained very hastily to me, so maybe I didn't understand it fully. You tied us together and your soul is intact, right?"

Afanasiv felt he was treading on quicksand. He didn't want to have this conversation with her, not now when her brother was waiting to chastise her for her choices. "My soul is whole and safe, Vasilisa. It was guarded by your family and handed down mother to daughter until my lifemate was born. I owe the women in your family a debt I will never be able to repay."

Her little frown began to come back, but the door to the formal dining room opened. This time it was her brother Garald who called out to them. "Vasi, Afanasiv, quit making eyes at each other and come on in before Andros wears a hole in the granite." There was amusement in his voice, but even with that, Afanasiv caught that little note of concern.

Afanasiv took the opportunity to avoid talking about claiming and what that might mean in terms of making Vasilisa wholly his and keeping him safe. He took her hand again, enveloping hers in his much larger one to go straight into the dining room.

It was enormous, a banquet hall more than an actual formal dining room. A hundred guests could easily be accommodated, far more than that number. The floors gleamed a beautiful black and white, with thin bands of gold running through the marble tiles. Beautiful chandeliers hung overhead, dripping teardrop crystals that glittered with color. The tables gleamed a brilliant cherrywood. The walls were marble as well, as if the tiles had run from floor to high ceiling, causing the room to seem even larger. The gold streaks appeared to widen as they reached higher toward the chandeliers. The overall effect was breathtaking.

Andros Sidkorolyavolkvo paced the length of the entire banquet hall, and yet that didn't seem enough space to contain his ire. He turned his head slowly to look his sister up and down and then really look Afanasiv over. He took in every aspect with those same eyes Vasilisa had, seeing far beyond the outer shell to the person inside.

Afanasiv paid him back in kind, standing unflinching under the intense scrutiny as he assessed the man who ruled the Lycans. Andros wasn't simply regarded as the authority there in Siberia but was the authority over all Lycans. They had a council, and for the most part, decisions were made at that level. But when disputes erupted that couldn't be fixed by the council, the matter was presented to Andros. His word was absolute law in the Lycan world.

Afanasiv knew the royals were never spoken of outside the Lycan people. They were protected by being kept a secret. Lycans were very good at secrecy. If Afanasiv was worried that members of the Sacred Circle would turn on the royals, Andros had to be worried as well. Having his sister be a lifemate to a Carpathian had to be just one more headache for him.

Andros paced back up the room until he was standing directly in front of them. "Just how far has this courtship gone?" he demanded.

Afanasiv was torn between amusement and irritation. He was an ancient Carpathian, which meant he had a couple of thousand years on Andros. Being taken to task as if he were a teenage boy was absurd— and insulting. He just stared at Andros with a blank expression on his face, allowing the man to vent his frustration and anger at the situation.

"Courtship?" Vasilisa echoed, looking up at Afanasiv. "I'm not certain what you mean by 'courtship,' Andros."

"Where did you meet? How long have you been seeing each other? How far has this relationship gone? I don't think that's too difficult to understand." Andros stepped directly in front of his sister, hands on his hips, pouring sarcasm into his voice.

"If you're going to talk to her, do so with respect. If you can't manage that, speak only to me," Afanasiv said, his tone low. Mild. Anyone who knew him would have heeded that warning.

"I'll speak to my sister any way I wish or think is warranted," Andros declared.

"You could continue being an arrogant rude ass, but you won't be speaking to her because you'll find yourself without a voice," Afanasiv said. "I don't give warnings more than once. She's my lifemate, which means, in Carpathian terms, she is my wife. No one, family or not, speaks to her with disrespect. Especially when she is the one who not only saved your ass, but she saved your brother and your women. At the very least, you could have thanked her."

There was a long silence. Andros stared at Afanasiv for quite a while before turning back to Vasilisa. "He's right in that you saved us,

Vasi. So did he. We owe you both far more than we can ever repay. Lada would not have lived through another round of torture. I would have done almost anything to spare her."

He turned away from them and shoved both hands through his hair several times until it was completely disheveled. His hair was dark sable, now interspersed with shimmering silver. "Vasi, you know we already have problems with quite a few of the population believing that a mixed blood between Lycan and Carpathian can't be tolerated. That's not even factoring in the Sacred Circle making a comeback. That's the general population."

Vasilisa lifted her chin. "It's too late, Andros. I think you know that. It was too late years ago."

"Sorina." Andros said the name in disgust. "I should have put a stop to that friendship, especially when I knew you were off hunting things better left alone."

"Why didn't you?" Afanasiv asked. He genuinely wanted to know why Andros had allowed his sister to hunt the undead. "What she was doing was extremely dangerous."

"I know that now. I didn't at the time." Again, Andros ran his hands through his hair in agitation. "I should have been paying more attention to her, but I was serving my time in the military and trying to take care of my duties here. It didn't occur to me that my baby sister would decide to hunt vampires and demons while I was looking the other way. By the time I realized what she was doing, she was already very good at it and didn't listen to anything I said."

"I listened, Andros," Vasilisa objected. "There was so much work to be done, and I needed to do my share."

"When you say you are lifemates, and Vasi is your wife, does that mean you claimed her with the ritual binding words without my consent?" Andros suddenly demanded.

"We are lifemates. She is my wife, and she was claimed properly with the ritual binding words. The only consent I needed was Vasilisa's." Technically, he hadn't needed her consent. The ritual binding words were imprinted on him before birth. When he found his life-mate, he was bound by their laws to say them to her.

"I am the head of her household. It is my consent you needed, and I did not give it."

"Oh, for heaven's sake, Andros." Grigor threw his arms out to encompass his sister and Afanasiv. "I think it's a little too late to chastise them. It isn't going to do you much good to try to play king to some man who is a few hundred years old, either. He'll laugh at you."

"Thousand," Afanasiv corrected. "I am one of the ancients from the monastery. Have no fears that your sister is in good hands. I am quite capable of protecting her."

Grigor exchanged a long look with his twin. "Thousand years. There you have it."

"And since we owe both Vasi and Siv our lives, I suppose we could be a little grateful instead of wanting to sentence him to the firing squad." Garald sounded amused.

"Is that so?" Andros whirled around and faced his brothers. "Do you have any idea what's going on here? The Sacred Circle has been slowly making a comeback, infiltrating our people and turning them against one another. Forcing them to choose sides. Vasilisa is *Sange rau*. Your sister. For all I know, so is . . ." Andros gestured toward Afanasiv with disgust.

Afanasiv remained silent. Andros did have a problem. He understood that. All the railing at Vasilisa wouldn't solve it. Being upset and angry at Afanasiv wouldn't stop it.

"Dimitri has been our friend for years, and yet he is slowly being ostracized by the very people he has helped to protect over the years. Why? Because he is also *Sange rau*. For all I know, all of them are, including Zev Hunter and his lifemate," Andros continued.

"And Lada?" Grigor asked. "She is from the region where the most fanatical Sacred Circle believers come from. Is she also a believer in the Sacred Circle?"

Andros looked tired. "Unfortunately, her parents both hold positions of power in the church and preach all the time the basic tenets of the old ways. Lada chose to go against them, and they threw her out of their home and refused to speak to her. She married very young for protection. The man she married was a member of the church and one her parents had chosen for her. He courted and married her without telling her he was a member of the church and that her parents had put him up to it."

Andros sank into a chair and regarded his siblings and Afanasiv with his brilliant blue eyes. "They told her they would rather see her dead than marry outside the church."

"There is no chance that she is actually a member and is playing you?" Garald asked.

Andros looked as if he might leap out of the chair and strangle his brother. "I'm still quite capable of hearing lies. Our aunt trapped Lada and I just about lost my mind. In my arrogance as a royal, I thought I could rescue her from the underworld. Apparently, Olga had managed to find a way to compromise all of us."

"Not all," Grigor denied, indicating Vasilisa. "She managed to stay out of Olga's hands, and when she realized what she was up to, she warned Garald before he could be compromised."

Andros studied his sister. "How did you see through Olga? How is it that you realized she was with the demons when I didn't?"

"I didn't want to see," she admitted, her voice trembling. "Afanasiv helped me at one of the darkest hours when we followed the demon with the vial of blood back to his mistress, back to our aunt Olga. She was evil and cruel. So far gone there was no saving her. I could see that. I wanted to be wrong, but I could see she had been working for Lilith for a very long time."

Afanasiv wrapped his arm around Vasilisa, pulling her beneath his shoulder, sheltering her against his much larger body. She felt ice-cold in spite of the warm clothes she was wearing. Carpathians regulated their body temperatures naturally. It was possible she didn't have that skill down quite yet, so he did it for her. She wore white trousers, a matching long-sleeved blouse and vest, and a white, very feminine tailored jacket. She seemed to favor the color white right down to her boots lined in white fur.

"How did I not see that she was in trouble?" Andros asked them. "You and Sorina fighting vampires and you becoming *Sange rau*. The Sacred Circle getting a foothold and hurting our people, threatening them if they didn't join. Aunt Olga hurting Lada the way she did. Lada has been through so much already, with the way her parents treated her and then her first husband. I was being so careful with her, waiting to present her to our people as my choice. I didn't ask her to marry me when I should have because I was afraid some nutcase would target her. Isn't that laughable? I don't have a chance in hell with the only woman I'll ever love."

"She wears your ring," Vasilisa pointed out.

"Not a formal engagement ring." Andros covered his face. "As the ruling king, I pretty much screwed up everything."

"Andros." Vasilisa went to her knees beside him. "Why would you even think such a thing? You've brought prosperity to our people. Look at their homes. Their farms. You turned everything around. Life was hard here. No laughter or hope. You made a difference."

"Have I, Vasi? Then why are our people suddenly turning against us? What could have caused our aunt to betray our family the way she did? I asked Lada to marry me and she turned me down. I don't blame her. She went through hell because of me. She was *in* hell because of me. She'll carry the scars on her body and think of me every day of her life and how I failed her."

Afanasiv had a difficult time believing Lada wasn't in love with Andros. "Would you mind if I spoke with your woman? This seems out of character for her. When I saw her before Gaia was called, she very much seemed to be in love with you. As for her scars, I am certain I can remove them if that is her desire."

Andros looked up with his hands over his face but fingers spread wide. "Why do you think she loves me? Did she say she did? She's never said it to me."

"Take me to her," Afanasiv ordered, forgetting he was speaking to royalty and his brother-in-law.

"I'll give my consent to the marriage if you can get her to say yes to marrying me," Andros promised.

"We're already married," Afanasiv said, exasperated. "I care nothing for your consent. Vasilisa is my wife. My woman. My partner. And you already have consented."

"I have?"

"Yes. Because you love your sister and she deserves to be happy. Anything less than full consent would be petty and beneath you."

Andros scowled at him. "I can see I'm always going to have problems with you."

"Only if you make Vasilisa unhappy. Take us to see Lada. I believe the outcome will be what you have wanted all along."

You want to make certain she doesn't belong to the Sacred Circle, Vasilisa said.

I am certain this woman is in love with your brother. It doesn't add up that she would turn down his proposal of marriage. She had to know he was going to ask her. There is a reason, my lady, and I fear it has something to do with her parents and their fanaticism.

It will break his heart. He is drowning under the weight of his responsibilities.

Then we will work faster to get to the bottom of whatever is happening here. Afanasiv was certain Lada had some part in the drama being played out in the middle of the royals' territory. He wanted to question her without Andros present.

"It will be best if you allow Vasilisa and me to speak with your woman without you there so she is free to say what she feels," Afanasiv said as they followed Andros out one of the five doors of the great banquet hall and down another corridor.

Andros threw a wary look over his shoulder but didn't stop walking. The palace was spacious and had a multitude of rooms. It was also a little drafty. Afanasiv took in the various entry and exit points, everywhere there could be a vulnerable place that the palace could be penetrated easily if under attack. As fast as he assessed the problem, he found a solution to fix it. His mind worked that way and did so at a rapid rate of speed. He was aware of Vasilisa following his thought process, keeping up with him every step of the way.

I never considered that the atrium might be a way for our enemies to infiltrate the palace. The glass is bulletproof. The material on the roof and sides is reinforced with every protection I could think of. Even if they used C-4, those wards should hold.

Perhaps, but there is no harm in adding to your protections.

"Stop talking telepathically," Andros snapped. "The buzzing in my head is adding to my headache. If you have something to say, just say it."

"We were discussing how better to defend the palace against an attack," Afanasiv said. He lengthened his strides until he walked beside Andros. The man was holding his pain in, refusing to allow it to spill out where his sister or Afanasiv could feel it. This wasn't just an ordinary headache.

"Wait, Andros," Afanasiv ordered. "Let me examine you. Gaia made certain Lilith no longer had you under her control—she did that with each of you—but Lilith may have been able to plant something else in you."

Andros halted immediately. He pressed both hands to his head. "I feel like my skull is too tight, and any minute, my wolf is going to emerge and go rogue. I feel him raging. Snarling. He isn't like that and yet I can't seem to control him."

"Lilith managed to get your blood, Andros," Afanasiv pointed out. "I need to examine you. I must have your consent."

"Yes, just do whatever you need to, but fast. My wolf is very agitated. Every time I look at Vasi or think of her, my wolf becomes enraged."

Afanasiv didn't wait. *Nicu, I have need of you. I do not think Vasilisa is safe. I believe her brother Grigor, Lada and Karine will target her. Grigor most likely will come at her as a wolf. I am searching Andros now in the hope of finding what was placed in him that has been activated to create such hatred for my lifemate.*

"I have asked that my brethren join us. If there is something in you, Andros, there could also be something in your brother and the women, all targeting Vasilisa. My lady, Nicu is closest, right outside. Please allow him in to guard you. Once he is inside, I will see to your brother." He didn't give her an option, forestalling any argument by simply stating he would wait to help Andros until she was protected.

Vasilisa went to the nearest exit and opened the door. Nicu strode in. He was a tall man, all muscle, sleek and powerful. His facial features appeared angular. A scar curved from his left temple to the corner of his eye. His eyes were gray. He had long black hair he kept braided with leather cords. He appeared every bit as dangerous as the feral wolves who howled for his return.

He nodded to Afanasiv and leaned his tall frame against the wall behind Vasilisa, chewing on a toothpick. Afanasiv shed his physical body and all ego to become a white-hot healing spirit entering Andros. He moved through the royal's body, examining the bloodstream first, then the vital organs, bone marrow, and lastly, he traveled to the brain.

All along, Afanasiv feared whatever had been planted within Andros must be in his brain. That would make the shadow very difficult to find. Not impossible, but difficult.

Siv. Vasilisa spoke quietly, making certain her telepathic connection to him didn't spill over so her brother wasn't bothered. *Lilith was trying to acquire me this entire time. I have the blood of the royals in me, too. Why would she wire all of my relatives to murder me if she believed she was going to have me under her control? I don't think these orders came from her. Do you?*

He didn't want to speculate, not with Vasilisa. She was too intelligent and asked all the right questions. *I doubt that Lilith programmed your brothers to kill you.* He agreed with her because one never lied to his lifemate.

There it was. A tiny angular dot clinging to a spot under one of the folds in the frontal lobe. *This is the work of a mage. There is a small sliver of him here.* Afanasiv looped in Nicu.

Xavier cannot travel to this realm. He is sealed in the underworld, Vasilisa objected. *I was very thorough, Siv. He cannot cross into this plane.*

He is one of three—a triplet. One of his brothers, Xaviero, is in the underworld, as well. If he put a sliver of himself in each of those returning to the surface, he would have eyes everywhere eventually. The fact that he decided to turn your family against you is most likely an order from Xavier and Olga. They both are very vengeful.

Nicu took charge, no longer leaning lazily against the wall beside the door. "When Siv drives the sliver from your brother, it will seek a host. I must destroy it before it manages to do that. Vasilisa, you must stay hidden and far from this abomination. I have to bring in a lightning fork to destroy it. That means opening the door and possibly allowing it to escape if I'm not fast enough."

"I can open the door without being detected," Vasilisa offered. She shimmered for a moment, became transparent, hovering above the door so Nicu could see for himself where she intended to be.

Nicu sized her up and then nodded curtly. *The storm is overhead, Siv. We are ready.*

Afanasiv immediately turned his white-hot spirit on the sliver, blasting it with pure light. The sliver shuddered, the edges curling, smoke rising as it raced away from the light. Afanasiv was faster, pursuing the tiny piece of Xaviero as it raced to desert Andros' body in the hope of finding a new host.

"Now," Nicu commanded Vasilisa.

She yanked open the door, and Nicu called down the jagged spear of lightning, aiming at the dark sliver as it slithered so quickly across the marble tile, racing toward the door and freedom. Lightning sizzled and cracked, the bolt of pure energy slamming into the tiny sliver so precisely the spear pinned the dark shadow dead center.

At once, a foul stench permeated the hallway. On the far wall, a figure in a long robe appeared in shadow form, his head thrown back in agony. He extended a long arm, bony fingers outstretched as if he might be able to grab Vasilisa before he was consumed by the flames licking at his feet and legs. The robe went up in a fiery display, and then he was gone in a flash-fire of orange and red.

Andros stared at the smoke and ash and then looked up at Afanasiv. "That thing was in my head? In my brain? It was telling me to kill my sister?"

Afanasiv nodded. "I fear your brother Grigor has one in his brain, as well. It is possible Lada and Karine are hosts to these slivers. If so, Xaviero has spread himself thin. Each piece lost diminishes him. They seem small, but they add up."

"We should check Grigor first," Andros said. "He can be very dangerous."

"So can I when it comes to my lifemate's safety," Afanasiv warned.

Vasilisa was excited to meet Skyler, Dimitri's wife, but she wished she could do so under different circumstances. Skyler looked so young it was shocking. She had pale, almost flawless skin other than a small crescent-shaped scar above her temple. She had dove-gray eyes that were sometimes shockingly blue or green if one studied her long enough. Vasilisa recognized the same strange phenomenon in her that appeared in Afanasiv. Their eyes changed color depending on their mood or the circumstances. She realized it was a Dragonseeker trait.

Skyler seemed far too young to be the heroine in the stories whispered about her. How she saved Dimitri's life by sneaking into Lycan territory with two of her young friends. They pretended to be studying wolves in the wild while they were really mounting a rescue operation. Her laughter was contagious, and the soft look of love that came over her face every time she looked at Dimitri was enough to convince Vasilisa that she was genuinely in love with him.

Dimitri's house was built into the mountainside, very difficult to find. One could walk up on it and never even see it. The interior was well lit despite being inside the mountain. It was also cool without being cold. He had managed to regulate the temperature to be perfect for each visitor.

Dimitri and Skyler were comfortable with their houseguests—Ivory and Razvan, Fen and Tatijana, and Zev and Branislava. The four couples clearly enjoyed one another's company often. Once again, Vasilisa put together who was Dragonseeker. Skyler, Razvan, Branislava and Tatijana all were Dragonseeker. She was there with Afanasiv, who was also Dragonseeker. That made five Dragonseekers all in one place. It was impossible to believe that was a coincidence.

What was it, aside from having Dragonseeker blood, that all of these people had in common? Vasilisa let the conversation flow around her while she tried to puzzle it out. They had similar characteristics. Loyalty. Endurance. Perseverance.

She glanced up at Afanasiv. He was very quiet, seemingly not paying any attention to anyone, yet she knew that wasn't the case at all. He was very aware of everyone and everything. He held her hand, fingers loosely threaded through hers, but he wasn't looking at her. She knew he was in her mind, reading her thoughts, but even that wasn't enough to pull him from whatever dark place he'd gone to.

They had been summoned to the house of Dimitri and she had been so excited to go, but Afanasiv had been reluctant. He had turned to her, shaking his head. "We shouldn't go, Vasi. We need to talk. My forgotten memories are coming back, and none of them are good. In fact, there was every reason to forget them. If we go, there might be need to disclose them, and you should hear them before anyone else."

She should have listened to him, but the call continued, and she had wanted to meet Ivory and Razvan and especially Skyler. She had been wrong to ignore Afanasiv's reluctance. Now he sat quietly, turning inward, going somewhere dark she couldn't follow, but it scared her.

The man Afanasiv had introduced as Petru flicked his gaze a few times toward her lifemate. Every now and then, he would glance at the one called Benedek or Nicu as if they were having a private conversation. If they were, she knew they were talking about Afanasiv and were as concerned as she was.

Ivory and Razvan noticed that Afanasiv didn't join in the conversation, not even when it turned to the slivers of Xaviero and how he had chased them out of Vasilisa's two brothers and their women. At first, Lada had objected to being examined again, but when Andros explained about the mage being able to spy on everyone, she allowed Afanasiv to shove Xaviero's sliver out of her. Afterward, she wanted to be alone, refusing even to talk to Vasilisa.

Andros had looked so tired and discouraged that she had wanted to go shake some sense into Lada. It wasn't Andros' fault that Olga had targeted her. Andros had practically sacrificed his honor for her. There was nothing she could do, so she'd left with Afanasiv to go to Dimitri's to see if they had any ideas on why Lilith or the mages were being so persistent or who was behind the Sacred Circle making a comeback that was undermining the royals.

Afanasiv said little to her as they made the approach to Dimitri's home. She knew he liked Dimitri, so it made little sense to her that he distanced himself from her and from a man he both respected and liked. Before she could question him, his brethren had joined them, and then they were at Dimitri's home, and she was caught up in the spell and myth of Skyler and Dimitri.

Now, she slid closer to him protectively, feeling guilty that she hadn't listened to him. Ivory and Razvan studied him with the eyes of warriors. Shrewd. Assessing. Both seemed to see things beyond skin and bone, and Vasilisa didn't want anything exposed that Afanasiv didn't wish to reveal. It was no one's business but his that he had spent time in captivity in the underworld.

The room was suddenly too small, and she found it difficult to breathe. She glanced once more at her lifemate. She was feeling his emotions, not her own. She ran her thumb over the side of his hand, wishing she knew how to comfort him. He was always the one to surround her with his warmth when she needed it the most.

We can leave this place, Siv. I am with you no matter what happens around us.

She needed to be less impetuous and consider what her lifemate needed rather than jump into something because of what she wanted. Part of her had wanted to postpone any serious conversations. She thought the two of them would enjoy the company. She liked Dimitri, and she did want to meet the legendary Skyler, who seemed to be able to connect with the earth as well as any Lycan—maybe better.

That brought her up short. Skyler did connect with Mother Earth. What of the others? She thought Afanasiv did because of her. Because of the Lycan in her. What if it was his Dragonseeker blood? Dragons sought caves and gems, things of the earth. They burrowed in tunnels beneath the ground.

Not in here, beloved. We will talk when we are alone.

That startled her, but she didn't make the mistake of looking at Afanasiv. He might be struggling with something dark in his past, but he wasn't running, and neither would she. He didn't intend to shut her out, either.

"The name Belan is unique in the world of Carpathians, not one I have heard," Razvan stated. "How did you come to use this name?"

It was a question that, on the surface, seemed only curious. Given that Afanasiv was Dragonseeker and didn't acknowledge to anyone that he was, the question seemed ominous.

Afanasiv shrugged his wide shoulders as if it didn't bother him one way or the other to provide the information. "In the old days, it was necessary to provide a new name every so many years as we moved around. There was a human family who did me a great service at much cost to themselves. Out of respect for them, I took their name when I had need to shed my own. It just so happened that I moved often after that, and there was no need to continually make new identities. I remain Afanasiv Belan."

Vasilisa didn't look up to see his expression. She knew what he would look like. That lazy, almost bored expression he could get. Dismissive, as if the subject was a little on the ridiculous side.

"But you are Dragonseeker." Ivory made the statement as fact.

There was instant silence in the room. Dimitri looked up, snapping his head around to face Afanasiv. Petru and Benedek lost their masks of indifference, giving way to shock. Nicu simply nodded as if he had suspected—or known all along. Fen and the female Dragonseekers went quiet, each studying Afanasiv much more closely.

"I am," Afanasiv admitted.

Vasilisa let her breath out. She hadn't realized she'd been holding it until that moment. Now her lungs felt raw and burning, aching with the need for air. Aching for him, Afanasiv. *Beloved. Let us leave this place.* Again, she tried to tell him she would go anywhere with him. She didn't need to be in the good graces of everyone. She needed to stay long enough to ensure that her people were safe from the government agents and that she had sealed the portals so the demons remained in the underworld.

It is too late.

"Your eyes and coloring give you away," Razvan said.

Ivory shook her head. "It is your absolute stillness. I find it unsettling that so many Dragonseekers are in one place. That cannot be a coincidence."

"My woman just said the same thing to me, voicing her concern." Afanasiv offered nothing else. He simply sat there, waiting for the others to draw their conclusions. Idly, he began to thread his fingers through hers and then bring her hand to his chest, press her open palm over his heart so she heard the combined music of their heartbeats.

Vasilisa found herself uncomfortable with the way Ivory and Razvan continued to study Afanasiv. It wasn't as if they were rude and just stared at him. It was more as if when they did look at him, they could strip away every shield and see inside where he had memories he hadn't yet dealt with. She felt so protective of her lifemate, she wanted to stand in front of him and be his shield.

They try, but they cannot, he assured her. *Thank you for caring, my lady.*

"You are Dragonseeker?" Dimitri asked. "In all the time I have known you, Siv, you never mentioned this to me."

"I do not speak of it," Afanasiv admitted. "Dragonseeker is a revered name and one that is often spoken aloud with awe and respect. I do not deserve those accolades. I have not earned them. Perhaps, if I do, I will change my mind and use the name I was given at birth."

Razvan frowned over his steepled fingers. "I do not recall ever hearing that you dishonored the name of Dragonseeker. I, on the other hand, have often been accused of doing so. Dragonseeker is a lineage. It is a birthright. The blood runs in your veins. You cannot falsely claim it."

Afanasiv didn't respond to Razvan's observation. He sat quietly, his features without expression, but beneath that serene, calm exterior, Vasilisa knew there was a feral, dangerous predator far too close to the surface feeling trapped. She did her best to soothe him when she didn't know why he was feeling the way he was.

Let's leave this place, she suggested again.

He shook his head. "If taken, we can change the composition of our blood so it is useless to those in the underworld. Lilith and the high mage struck a deal some centuries back with the idea that they would both benefit. Xavier wanted to be immortal. Lilith was determined to rule without interference."

Afanasiv fell silent even though the expectation in the room was very high. Vasilisa knew what it would cost him to continue. Those memories that had been misfiled on purpose.

You were taken to the underworld more than once, she guessed.

I was there three times. I was never taken. I found my way all three times. His tone was abrupt. *The memory you accessed was the last time I was there, not the first.*

Her heart jumped and then began to pound. She hastily stifled the sound. He immediately soothed her, sending her warmth and comfort. *It was many centuries ago, my lady, and I survived. My parents did not. I fear my soul did not, either.*

Vasilisa allowed her lashes to veil her eyes. Just for a moment she leaned against him, needing his strength. Such a simple, matter-of-fact statement. *I survived. My parents did not. I fear my soul did not.* That said nothing and yet said everything. It was no wonder he didn't want to resurrect those lost memories. He wanted them to stay lost.

The memories were painful, and he knew it. He must have deemed it necessary to tell the others or they would already be gone, somewhere the two of them could be alone together. Anywhere not where they were. Vasilisa could only surround him with her growing affection, admiration and warmth. He had warned her, and she hadn't listened to him. This was on her.

He sacrificed a tremendous amount for others, and he wasn't even aware of it. He didn't view emotional damage as sacrifices. He simply did whatever he had to in order to get the job done. Whenever she felt she couldn't admire him more, he did something else, something new to gain her respect.

"I saw evidence of Xavier consulting with demons on many occasions," Razvan said, that frown still on his face as he contemplated the information Afanasiv gave to them. "He was always obsessed with blood, mine in particular and that of my children and aunts. They are Dragonseeker, as well. Like you said, the composition was changed to make it useless for him to experiment with. There were times the blood changed on its own without my aid. I was too far gone, weak and did not know what was happening to me."

Afanasiv suddenly leaned forward. "The obsession with Dragonseeker started centuries before Xavier became part of it. My mother was trapped by Lilith and her demons and taken to the underworld. My father and I followed to bring her back." For the first time, there was emotion in his voice, and it was difficult to hear. Loathing filled the room, but not for Lilith and the demons. It was for himself.

Knots formed in Vasilisa's belly. The others in the room had no way of knowing that Afanasiv's revulsion centered around his actions, not those of the demons. She dreaded what he was going to tell them. All along, there had been a warning, a red flag telling her things were best left alone. This was going to affect her—affect them. Whatever he was about to reveal was going to be a blow that had the potential of tearing them apart—at least Afanasiv believed that was so. His crime was so terrible that he had changed his name and refused to use Dragonseeker.

Don't. She implored him. *I don't want to lose you, Afanasiv. Whatever this is, we can deal with it first alone. Don't do this.*

His fingers tightened around hers, and he looked down at her. His eyes were cobalt blue. Sad. The weight of his sorrow pressed down on her until she wanted to weep a river for both of them. *I have no choice, sívamet. If I do not give them the truth, let them know, they have no chance of figuring out what Lilith is after. Xavier and his brother are a nuisance, but it is Lilith who is threatening our lineage. She has to be stopped.*

What of us?

You have the right to know what I did. I should have told you before I claimed you. That was wrong of me. Another sin to add to so many.

Vasilisa attempted to pull her hand away. She wanted to curl up into herself and escape the scrutiny of Ivory and Razvan. She wanted to go outside and allow her wolf the freedom to run as far and as fast as she could. Anything but stay and listen to Afanasiv confess to those in the room things she knew were going to be terrible for her to hear.

Let go of me please.

I cannot. I need your courage to do this, Vasilisa. Stay with me.

You have no idea what you're asking of me.

I do know. And yet I still ask.

His thumb slid along the back of her hand. His gaze never left hers. She was drowning in him. Surrendering to his will. Weak with the need to help him when she really needed to help herself. She stopped trying to pull away and nodded.

Thank you, lifemate. You are beloved, whether you agree to stay with me after this or not.

He continued to look at her for another long minute, as if memorizing her. "We found a portal and made our way down through the labyrinth. I was very young and had not quite lost all emotion. The depravity and tortures sickened me, and yet I still had the arrogance of youth. Lilith had taken my mother, believing a female weaker than a male and that she could control her, but it wasn't so. My mother was extremely strong. Lilith had her tortured. The things done to her were unimaginable."

Tiny beads of blood dotted his forehead and trickled down his face. They caught glimpses of flesh being torn from a body and demons gathering around a woman they could barely make out to abuse her flesh in the worst ways possible.

"We had to bargain for her. For every hour of bargaining, the tortures worsened. Lilith agreed to give her to my father if I stayed with her for a specific period of time as her lover. She wanted my blood and a child. If she wasn't with child by the end of that time, I could leave but had to return at least one more time to try again. My father and I went over the contract word for word. It would be binding. I wasn't about to give her a child, and she couldn't have our blood. We knew she wasn't going to allow my mother to go with our father. He would have minutes to take them away from there. But we had to make certain I didn't sign anything I wouldn't be able to live with. In the end, we signed the contract. She brought up my mother, but she was already dying. I lost both of them."

Vasilisa couldn't conceive of the horror of watching both parents die with the woman who had them tortured and murdered waiting to be serviced. She could feel the absolute loathing and repugnance he felt. He wasn't emotionless at that point. He had still retained some of his feelings. He must have wanted to kill Lilith, to kill all of them.

"The bodies were of no use to them and vanished immediately. Lilith acted outraged that my mother was in such a bad way and berated the demons who brought her to us. She kept trying to tell me how sorry she was. She evidently didn't—and still doesn't—realize we can hear lies."

Afanasiv's voice was so low Vasilisa felt she had to strain to hear him speak. She realized she not only could hear him, she also caught images of the empty spot where there was only a dark crimson pool left behind where his parents had been. Fire glowed around him. Not the flames of a purifying fire, but muddy flames that threw off a bloody coppery shadow.

Lilith sidled up to Afanasiv and attempted to run her fingers down his arm in a show of sympathy as she smiled up at him. "Come with me. I'll make you feel so much better."

"I told her we had rituals when warriors had fallen, and I had to attend to them. That gave me two days of reprieve before I had to fulfill my part of the contract." Afanasiv's voice had gone back to strictly expressionless.

Vasilisa let his statement actually sink in. The contract he signed to get his mother back included him being Lilith's lover. Giving her blood. Giving her a child. *His* child. Afanasiv's child. The child that should be theirs.

There was a strange roaring in her ears. He'd been lovers with Lilith. What else could he have done? But a child? His mother would never have agreed to such a contract. Thoughts rushed through her mind fast, and she couldn't slow them down. Her emotions were all over the place. Anger. Sorrow. The need to cry.

"How long were you in the underworld before you were allowed to leave?" Razvan asked.

"There is no keeping time," Afanasiv said, rubbing his temples. "At least not now. My memories were lost to me. I put them away so I did not have to look at the things I did. The words of the contract were such that I could make use of my Carpathian illusions, and I did so. Lilith believed them, and that was what mattered to me. Later, I wondered where the honor was in what I did, but she murdered my parents, so at the time, I cared little whether she got her side of the bargain or not."

Wait. What was he saying? What did he mean? Vasilisa struggled to understand. Carpathian illusion? His honor in what he did?

"I knew there would be no child, and she couldn't pretend because she would want me to come back. I insisted she allow me to leave. I told her I would return and when I would return. She struggled with allowing me to leave, but the contract had been signed by both of us. The repercussions to her would have been severe."

"Then you went back because it was a matter of honor," Razvan said.

Afanasiv inclined his head. "Yes. I knew getting away would be much more difficult. I had studied their ways and kept maps in my head of the labyrinth, but it changed constantly, so I couldn't always rely on the layout down below. The one thing that was useful was information on the demons. I was able to catalogue the powers each had. Strength and weaknesses and what each could do. Some were extremely foul and others not so bad. There is a hierarchy. I was able to learn that and how to appeal to the ones who would take bribes. I learned everything I could the first time I was there because I knew that the second time, I would have to find my own way out."

"I can't believe you put yourself into their hands a second time," Ivory said. "That took such courage."

"Or stupidity. Lilith was wild. She would go back and forth between acting as a lover might and being so angry and hostile, believing I was deceiving her in some way. I was, but she couldn't catch me at it. She wanted a child and she wasn't getting pregnant. She wanted my blood and yet the Dragonseeker blood eluded her. She would send me to be tortured and then show up weeks later begging for forgiveness, wanting to take care of me, promising it wouldn't happen again. It did because Lilith wanted her way and wasn't getting it."

"In the time you spent there, did you have any inkling of why Dragonseeker blood was so important to her?" Dimitri asked.

Vasilisa had the uncharacteristic urge to yell at him. Why was he calmly asking that question when Afanasiv was telling them he had been tortured? That he'd been subjected to the whims of Lilith repeatedly for who knew how long? Months? Years? Time meant nothing in the underworld.

"I tried to talk to her about it. She changed her answer often. There were a few times she would talk about Mother Earth and how she paid homage to her, started covens and yet was never accepted as her child. She talked about cousins she had who were so good that Mother Earth accepted them, but not her. But she got her revenge. She slept with the lifemate of her cousin, and he was so corrupt he tried to murder his own lifemate. He killed her mother and nearly managed to kill the unborn baby sister as well. Lilith was so delighted by that. She danced around the room singing. Then she flew into a rage because she wasn't accepted by Mother Earth as her child, and nothing she said made sense after that."

Those in the room exchanged long looks as they puzzled out what that meant. Who Lilith was talking about.

"Lilith could be talking about Arabejila. Her lifemate, Mitro, murdered her mother, who was pregnant with Arabejila's sister. Dax saved the baby's life. He and Arabejila hunted Mitro, and eventually they were able to defeat him," Razvan said. He looked at Skyler. "You met this child, Arabejila's sister, when you were very young. I have caught glimpses of her in your mind."

Skyler made a little face and turned toward Dimitri, as if he could access the memory for her. "I'm sorry, I have no recollection."

"She healed your mother's injuries. There were so many." There was regret in Razvan's voice. "Eventually, your mother was taken prisoner by the high mage. He detested her because of her lineage—one that was far more powerful than his. That was why he kept her so weak and drained. "He was certain he knew she was mage, but she kept up the facade of being human to protect you from him. She didn't want him to know you had any power at all. Once he had you, he would never have let you go. She thought as a human and behaved as one for your protection."

"Now Lilith has several Dragonseekers right here, all together," Benedek said. "Clearly Skyler is a child of the earth, as well. Who else would be considered a child of the earth?"

"Tatijana and Branislava are," Ivory said. "Razvan is."

Benedek turned his attention to Afanasiv. "There are five Dragonseekers in this room together, Siv. Four of the five have admitted to being children of the earth mother. Are you?"

Afanasiv sighed and nodded his head. "Sadly, I must answer in the affirmative."

There was a stunned silence. His brethren exchanged a puzzled look. Vasilisa managed to pull her hand away from his. He hadn't told her. She had been so certain he tracked and read the ground so easily through his connection to her, but he had his own connection. He didn't need her at all. She'd never felt so distant or off center in her life. She thought they were so well suited, but suddenly everything she thought she knew about him was wrong.

She folded her hands carefully in her lap and tried to make herself as small as possible. She didn't need anyone noticing her. If she wasn't sitting next to him, she would have been able to disappear. She was good at it, blending in with her surroundings until she faded away and everyone forgot she'd been present in the first place. She wanted time alone to think about what had been said and what it all meant.

"Why sadly?" Skyler asked. "It is a great honor to be given such a gift."

Afanasiv inclined his head. "Yes, it is an honor, and one I felt I didn't deserve. I did manage to escape, but there was no skin on my bones, and I am not altogether certain I was entirely sane. Lilith was furious that she didn't get the child she wanted. She punished me by making me watch over and over the tortures my mother went through while I was being tortured. I could take the physical torture, but strangely, when I shouldn't have been able to feel anything, it was the mental torture that got to me."

"Why do you persist in blaming yourself for not upholding your honor?"

"Where was the honor in what I did?" Afanasiv asked. "Was it honorable to trade deceit for the life of my mother? Was it honorable to deceive Lilith simply because she is an enemy? Was it honorable to return and spend the entire time deceiving her and plotting my escape?"

"Afanasiv, do you think it would have been better to allow her to torture your mother and then your father to death in front of you?" Ivory asked. "I think you ask too much of yourself. Clearly you have a personal code of honor. All of your brethren have one. The Dragonseekers have one."

"That is true," Afanasiv agreed. "There is honesty included in that code."

Skyler smiled at Afanasiv as she leaned toward him. "But then you were strictly honest, weren't you? You and your father went over the contract very carefully before you signed it. Lilith wrote it up. She's the one who was dishonest, deliberately deviating from it in order to try to persuade you to give her what she wanted. You stuck to the exact wording of the contract. There was no dishonesty."

"I had no intentions of ever giving her what she wanted," he pointed out.

"You couldn't give her what she wanted," Dimitri said. "Your father knew that and so did you. Lilith wrote out a contract, and you negotiated until you were able to put in writing something that would work for you. During that time, your mother was being hideously tortured. Lilith wasn't being fair even then. She deliberately did her best to distract you. She was the one without honor. If you ask me, Siv, you were down there so long and she tortured you so much that you became disoriented and started questioning yourself and your integrity because she was questioning it."

Afanasiv rubbed his temples again. Vasilisa could feel pain pounding through his head. It manifested itself in a strange rhythm, a knocking, as if someone were trying to invade his mind, but his shields were too strong to allow them in. Still, they persisted, trying to wear him down. Had they been alone, she might have tried to help him, but not in a roomful of people she didn't know. Not when she felt too shocked and numb to be able to sort through everything she had heard.

After the blow of knowing her aunt had betrayed them and knowing many of the people they had spent their lives helping were turning on them, this felt like one too many hits. Vasilisa wanted to be alone. As soon as she could, she was going to excuse herself, go back to the palace and lock herself in her room for a long time. First, she would let her wolf run so she would be numb and exhausted.

"Dimitri speaks the truth, Afanasiv," Petru said. "You did not break the code of honor."

Nicu nodded. "There was no breaking the code."

Benedek agreed. "Absolutely, there was no breaking the code. You upheld the code of honor better than most could have done, Afanasiv."

Razvan and Ivory nodded their heads. "Without a doubt."

"You will have to worry about one thing for certain, I fear," Dimitri said. "Lilith is possessive and vengeful. She doesn't like to be thwarted. You have something to lose now, where before she couldn't get to you. Now you have a cherished lifemate. You and Vasilisa prevented her from getting the royal blood. Specifically, Vasilisa's blood. Why do you think hers was the most important of all?"

That should have scared Vasilisa, but it didn't. Vasilisa wasn't the ultimate goal. She was a means for Lilith to get to Afanasiv. She wasn't the true prize.

"Why would she need to be a daughter of Mother Earth when she commands the underworld?" she asked. "The two aren't compatible. The underworld is all about twisting and mutating nature, and Mother Earth is all about growing and nurturing."

"Lilith doesn't exactly command the underworld," Afanasiv countered. "Lucifer does. He allows Lilith her little rebellions because it amuses him. If she goes too far, he reins her in very fast. She doesn't like being under his thumb, but she knows better than to try to take over. She isn't powerful enough."

"Does she think having Dragonseeker blood would give her more power?" Razvan asked Ivory. "Would it?"

Ivory frowned as she considered the possibility. "It would aid her. Being a daughter of the earth would certainly give her far more power and aid her in ways she probably hasn't even considered. A combination of the two, the blood and becoming accepted by the earth, might give her what she needs."

"If she could also control the beast behind the gate, if she had all three powers," Vasilisa mused aloud, "she might be able to wrest complete control from Lucifer."

"I don't understand what that means," Ivory said. "What gate? What beast?"

Vasilisa had never made such a mistake before in her life. Not to her brothers and not to anyone else. The color rose under her skin. She shook her head. "It is nothing. You're right about her trying to find a way to take the power from Lucifer."

"That's a big gamble. If she failed, she would be punished for a thousand years or more," Ivory said.

Vasilisa was grateful Ivory didn't insist on an explanation. She shouldn't have engaged, just stayed out of the conversation altogether. The things Afanasiv had disclosed had thrown her. She just needed time. Inwardly, she shored up her defenses and kept chanting that mantra over and over in her head.

"She has Xavier and Xaviero with her. Two high mages with enough spells to cover just about anything she would need. Who could counter that combination? She just has to keep them happy and on her side," Razvan said.

"Xavier wanted the blood of the royals," Nicu said. "He has some scheme up his sleeve as usual. I would venture to say that it is Barnabas who's planting subversive ideas in the Sacred Circle's collective consciousness. He is known for persuading people with his voice. If he is here, we will have to find him and remove him. No matter what you do, he will continue to turn your people against you and your brothers." He spoke to Vasilisa directly.

She nodded her head. There was a gentle flow, a probing, as Afanasiv started to say something to her, but she had deliberately raised her shields, barricading her mind against him. She was unsure of her thoughts and didn't want to say, do or even think something she couldn't take back.

Afanasiv looked at her quickly, his eyes going a deep green, then golden with only a few flecks of green. He had a focused stare now. Alert. Predatory. The stare of a great jungle cat before it brought down its prey. She felt the wolf in her respond, come close to the surface to protect her. Her heart responded to the dangerous interaction between them. She couldn't stay in Dimitri's house surrounded by Afanasiv's brethren. She had no allies here. They were all his. Her wolf would be torn to pieces if she tried to fight her way out.

She stood up, a smile plastered on her face, portraying a look of serenity and feminine sweetness. She had perfected that look over the years, practicing until she knew she could fool the entire council if necessary. The council was made up of the elder Lycans who were very good at spotting lies or misdirection any of the royals might give. Because they kept the land clear of vampires and demons but didn't want to reveal the gifts they had to anyone, they often had to be very careful what they said to the council.

"Dimitri, Skyler, I love your home. Thank you for inviting me. Forgive me, but I find myself exhausted and need sleep. It was lovely meeting everyone, and I hope to see all of you soon. Afanasiv, please feel free to stay and visit with everyone. I'm going to allow my wolf to run, and then I'll be heading back to my room."

Afanasiv stood as well. She was tall and used to looking a man in the eye. He was taller, and she felt as if he loomed over her.

"I will go with you. Given that I believe Dimitri is correct in that

Vasilisa was torn between laughing and crying. So much for being alone. She would have been safe regardless of these men guarding her or not.

"Thank you." There was nothing else she could do other than throw a tantrum, and she wasn't that woman. She needed to let her wolf out and run mindlessly until she was so exhausted she didn't care about anything. The entire wolf pack was waiting for her. She wasn't going to keep them waiting one moment longer.

Lilith will have a special hatred for you, and you're already a target, think it best if we always stay close to each other." He gestured towar the door.

There was no arguing with him in front of the others. He wasn giving her a choice. She had to be gracious and keep her sweet smil plastered on her face. Keep her heart beating exactly the same rhythm Make certain that her hands didn't tremble. Most of the time, thos things were automatic. Now she had to think of each separate piece t make certain no one noticed she was agitated.

Before she could exit the house, Nicu stepped in front of her, hold ing up his hand. "Allow me to make certain there is nothing harmfu waiting, Vasilisa." He didn't wait for her to agree. He went out th door, leaving it open so she could see him as he went down the ston steps into the white world. At once, shadows came out of the trees t join him. The wolves were large, with healthy winter pelts of thicl silvery fur, so they blended in with the snow and ice.

The wolves continually circled Nicu and pushed against him, lift ing their heads to look him directly in the eyes. He knelt down in th snow and took the alpha's head in his hands. It was obvious to Vasilis that the two were communicating. She had heard that animals fel under Nicu Dalca's spell, but witnessing it was much like watching a miracle.

After ensuring that he had touched each wolf, Nicu turned his attention to the trees. Vasilisa looked up as well, and was startled to see that the branches held a multitude of birds, mostly owls but other night birds, too. Several opened their wings and fluttered them or called down to him using various haunting notes.

Nicu turned to her and beckoned. "It is safe for you to run with the wolves if you choose to do so, Vasilisa. I will run with you to ensure your safety."

"As will your lifemate," Afanasiv stated firmly.

"We will be with you, as well," Petru said.

Benedek nodded. "Have no fears. You will be perfectly safe."

PART FOUR

Vasilisa slowly laid the tarot cards out on the small table in front of her the way she did every evening on rising. This was her third time, and no matter how many times she shuffled the cards, the same three came up. The death card was front and center in the upright position. She stared at it for a long time and then, with a little shake of her head, started to scoop up the cards.

"Wait." Afanasiv had come up behind her. He indicated the cards. "What does that mean? Adalasia read the cards for us. They looked very different from these."

Vasilisa picked up the cards, an idea suddenly coming to her. "Mine were designed exclusively for me. Adalasia's were designed exclusively for her. Her ancestor's mother had to have drawn her cards for them just as mine did."

She cleansed the deck and then indicated for him to sit across from her at the little table. She hadn't said much of anything to him the night before. Her wolf had run free over the powdery snow in the middle of the pack, the ancients running with her as wolves. She left behind every care, every sorrow, experiencing only the joy and freedom of being wild. By the time the sun showed signs of coming up, the ancient Carpathians had turned the pack toward the palace, allowing

her to stumble into her room and black out the windows with her
heavy drapery.

Vasilisa didn't say one word to Afanasiv before falling into bed. He
didn't seem to mind. If she expected a fight, or a scene with him, she
wasn't getting one. He just tucked blankets around her, cleansing her
body first so she felt refreshed. He bent over her, brushing her forehead
with his lips, not asking for anything in return. He didn't even try to
push into her mind again, not since discovering her shields had been
put in place as barricades to prevent him from reading her thoughts.

When she woke, the sun had already set, and she knew Afanasiv
was up, consulting with his brethren. Her mind instantly wanted to
tune itself to his. There was an emptiness inside her that continuously
reached for him. She felt off-balance without him. That was annoying
to her. She wasn't a woman who needed a man, yet she felt she had to
touch him to reassure herself he was alive and well. Silly, when she
knew exactly where he was.

Vasilisa had showered and dressed with care. During the time she
performed her regular routine, she had to fight to keep from reaching
out to Afanasiv. Now, with the cards in her hands, she expected the
need to lessen, but it only increased. Sitting across the small table from
him, she could smell his fresh scent. What was it that appealed to her?
Besides everything?

"Take the cards, Siv. Shuffle them and choose three cards."

There was no hesitation on his part. He took the deck, wrapping
his large hands around the cards. Instantly, the cards reacted to his
power. Wind rushed through her sitting room as if they were outside
and exposed on the highest peak. The shriek was loud and ominous
as the gusts hurled through the room at breakneck speed, subsided and
then struck again and again.

Siv didn't move, not even when twin columns of water burst from
the cards in his hands and twisted through the room in a maniacal
dance. Only his eyes reacted, changing color from blue to green to a
brilliant turquoise. His breathing never changed. His muscles never

tensed. He didn't fight the power of the cards. He simply didn't react at all, just kept his hands cupped around them, holding them away from Vasilisa so all reaction was pointing toward him, not her.

Eventually, the wind died down, then faded away completely. The water elements retreated back into the cards. Siv began to shuffle as if nothing amiss had taken place at all. His hands were sure on the cards. She couldn't help noticing how easily he manipulated them. Now that the goddess accepted him, the cards cooperated with him.

"Choose any three cards and lay the deck aside."

His eyes on her, Afanasiv did as she requested. It was difficult to look away from him. His gaze was too green, too blue, swirling with turbulence, completely at odds with his calm demeanor.

"Lay the cards faceup for me."

He did so, still looking at her rather than the cards. She looked down and her breath caught in her throat. He had been given the exact same cards that she had. She was being resistant to what she knew was her destiny. She had been so on board with everything, and then she felt so out of sync with him.

Vasilisa looked down at the cards and sighed. "It seems we share the same fate."

"Did you believe otherwise, my lady?"

There was no mockery in his tone. Nothing to suggest that he was amused by the situation. He just watched her intently. "There is the death card again. You had it. Now I have it. What does it mean?"

She studied the card and the frightening image of the wolf staring back at her. "I know many people are afraid of this card simply because it is named death, but in reality, it is a card of change or transition. It signals that it is time to put the past behind you so you can seize your future with both hands."

"As the others were telling me to do last rising," he said. "Is that what you mean? That I should let go of my doubts that I have had about my honor and be more open to using my birthright?"

She nodded slowly. "I believe it does mean something of that nature, Siv. Sometimes you have to let go of the past so you can accept your future. Close a door so a new door opens, that sort of thing. Or it can mean a literal transition. A transformation of sorts. A death of one version of yourself in order for the new version to have life."

"If you got the same card, how does this pertain to both of us together?"

"Ordinarily, I do readings for individuals, so it wouldn't, but I'll admit I was asking the cards to read for both of us earlier. I believe our fate is tied together. Often this card signals the end of a relationship, not the beginning of one."

She watched him closely for a reaction. He was without an expression. None. Completely unreadable. Her heart ached. She had been traumatized by the events that had occurred, but so had he. Reliving those memories that had been buried so deep couldn't have been easy for him. She hadn't offered him solace of any kind. She'd been more compassionate and understanding of Andros than of Siv. Why? What was wrong with her that she wanted to pick a fight with him and try to challenge the terms of their relationship?

The moment she thought about getting out of their bond, she wanted to cling to him. The thought of losing him was terrifying, and yet she wasn't opening herself up to him. It was as if she had a block in front of her that stopped her from even discussing what she was upset about.

Afanasiv sat back in the chair, his long legs sprawled out in front of him. "How would you go about ending our relationship, Vasilisa?"

She blinked at him. His tone was so mild. His voice was low. Almost gentle. He looked lazy—until she looked into his eyes. There was nothing lazy about his eyes. The color had gone almost pure amber with green flecks. There was nothing human about his eyes.

She shook her head. "I have no intention of ending our relationship, Afanasiv. If you wish to do so, you'll have to be the one to find a way to do it. You asked about the death card, and I'm telling you the possible meanings." She kept belligerence out of her voice. If he could act cool, so could she.

"It seems we are in for a bit of a transitional period with the death card, and we both are going to have to embrace change if we want to get through it smoothly."

She avoided his gaze by scooping up the cards.

"Do the swords mean anything significant? It seemed as if there were a lot of swords for only three cards and one of them being the death card."

"We're in for a fight, but we knew that."

He nodded. "Before we decide where to start, we need to straighten our problems out. I'm sorry I didn't tell you about my time in the underworld and what had happened. I didn't because I didn't have all my memories. They returned in pieces. When they did come back, it was too late, and I knew I was going to have to disclose what had happened in front of you."

"You asked me to wait and not visit Dimitri and Skyler. I didn't listen to you. That's on me." She stared down at the cards for a moment, shuffling them because the cards brought her solace—just the familiar feel of them in her hands. "How could you know that Lilith wouldn't get pregnant? What did you mean?"

"I never touched her. I never had any intention of touching her. I gave her that illusion. Even had I touched her, I can control whether or not I release potent sperm or she releases a viable egg. That doesn't matter, though, because at no time did I ever put my hands on her. A few times she was suspicious because she didn't get pregnant and she set up cameras. I had to put the illusion on the video, then find the camera in front of her, watch it with her and throw a fit and delete it."

"If she ever found out . . ."

He shrugged. "She had me tortured often, Vasilisa. For weeks or months. Sometimes it was for so long I swear she forgot about me."

He drummed his fingers on the table. The rhythm seemed familiar.

She watched as he rubbed at his temples. "There was one important thing that happened that I didn't tell the others. I will tell only you. My mother's condition was deteriorating daily. The longer we took to negotiate, the more she was tortured. My father was certain Lilith had no intention of releasing her—or him. He told me that when the time came, if my mother were to die, he would go into the thrall."

She had heard of the thrall but wasn't entirely certain what it meant, so she arched an eyebrow at him.

"It's a kind of madness, an insanity. That is when many honorable Carpathian hunters are lost. No Dragonseeker has ever turned vampire. My father didn't want to be the first, but he was in the underworld, where he had seen the woman he loved viciously and brutally tortured over time. He worried his mind would fragment and he would become exactly what Lilith was driving him toward being. We planned out what to do in the event my mother died, just as we planned the wording of the contract. We went over it step by step a hundred times and then again even more so our responses would be muscle memory and not emotional."

Vasilisa narrowed her eyes, watching Afanasiv as he pushed his forehead into the heel of his hand. There were smears of blood from tiny beads of sweat left behind. He didn't seem to notice. She didn't move when she wanted to get up and comfort him. She was afraid that if she moved, he would stop speaking. She sat very still, observing him carefully. Something was off, and she needed to figure out what it was. She had seen this the night before. The tapping was part of it, that rhythm. She couldn't allow herself to be too immersed in what he was saying and not see all the signs of his distress both in the underworld and here in the present day.

"Lilith brought the contract and pens for us to sign. She was particularly elated, almost high, very flushed, her eyes overbright, and she kept telling us to read the contract, that she was certain we would be happy with the terms. She ordered two of the demons to get my mother and bring her to the arena immediately. It bothered us that we were to meet her in the arena rather than in one of the rooms. It was very hot, more so than usual, and it was difficult to breathe the air down there."

Vasilisa took the chance of looking around the arena to note as much detail as possible in his memory. There were drums beating, a rhythm that was pervasive, and demons sat in the stands humming a deep low note to accompany the drum. Low embers lit the arena in various places, and they would suddenly flare up in a dark red fan of flames and then subside again. When the flames were at their height, Vasilisa saw distorted faces with teeth and claws and red glowing eyes. They disappeared into the darkness as the flames settled.

"I smelled the cannibals. She had them hidden in the darkness, waiting until the negotiations were over so they could rush out and tear at my parents when she took me out of there. We had known all along that was the plan. She sometimes would douse the air with drugs, and it was difficult to tell reality from fantasy at first. I learned, but it took time—time my parents didn't have."

That persistent drumbeat was giving her a headache. It felt as if someone were trying to get inside her head, but she knew she was feeling his physical pain. The knocking persisted determinedly. She refused to allow her heart rate to increase. She sat across from him, breathing evenly, watching both places, present and past, just as obstinate as Lilith, maybe even more so.

You can't have him, she whispered in her mind. She could afford to have that conversation with herself. Her shields were up, and no one, not even her lifemate, had penetrated them. If she wanted to tell Lilith to go to hell, she could. There might be some irony in that.

"She kept dancing around, trying to keep us distracted. When the demons brought my mother, it was clear she was already dying. Lilith pretended great sympathy. She berated the demons who brought her. My father went over to my mother and carried her to where we were reading the contract. It was the only spot where there was any light, a single sconce with a weak candle flickering."

Vasilisa's heart went out to Afanasiv. She saw the condition his mother was in with the skin torn from her body. There was little left of her. Still, she looked at her husband and son with love in her eyes.

"My father whispered to her, told her he loved her, told her the plan. She looked at me, and I could see she didn't want me to stay there. She tried to shake her head, but she was too weak even for that. I knelt beside her, the contract in my hand—the only way I had to keep Lilith from having the cannibals rush them—and told her I loved her."

There was emotion in his voice. So much it shook her. Tore her up inside. Vasilisa refused to give in to emotion. She needed to make sure that she didn't miss anything significant in either the past or present.

"She drew her last breath and I signed the document. The moment I signed, I felt the difference. A hush fell over the arena."

What he said was true, other than the drumbeat. That continued. It didn't pause for a single moment. Vasilisa felt the expectation in the arena. The mad triumph of Lilith. The sorrow pouring off Afanasiv. His father had gathered his mother into his arms, cradling her on his lap. He threw back his head and roared his anguish to the world. As he did, Afanasiv slammed his fist into his father's chest and extracted his heart. He turned and threw it straight into the nearest flames.

The heart was pure and the flames were not. The fire leapt and spread, rushing throughout the arena in an ever-widening circle, burning through rows of demons, burning white-hot and pure until it reached Afanasiv's parents. The flames caught them up and incinerated them, taking them in seconds so there was nothing left, not even ashes.

Red blood tears tracked down Afanasiv's face. He looked at his lifemate. "That is what really happened to my father and mother that night. He never would have turned. Never."

"No, he wouldn't have, Siv," she agreed, because she was certain he wouldn't have. "But he knew those cannibals would have eaten him alive, and Lilith would have made you watch. You spared him watching his beloved wife being eaten after all the tortures they'd subjected her to. Your father managed to slay demons, most likely many of the ones who had tortured his wife. You spared him horrendous suffering. This was his plan, and you carried it out at great cost to yourself. You did what a loving son was asked to do without hesitation. It's what you always do, Afanasiv. You sacrifice yourself over and over for others. Has she ever tried to convince you there is a child?"

He nodded. His gaze never left hers. "I know there isn't, so when she pulls that one on me, I can breathe easy."

"How does she contact you? You no longer go to the underworld. How is she able to get to you?"

He frowned and rubbed at his temples. "She would become a woman preyed upon by vampires. She'd be in a village that was set upon by a master vampire with lesser vampires or a puppet. She would look completely different, and I would have no way of knowing who she was until I got close enough to her. The battle was always fierce, and I would sustain many injuries before I reached her. Everyone else was dead, so getting one person alive from the village seemed a victory. Then I would get close and know that it was Lilith and that she had orchestrated the entire event. All those people in the village dead just so she could try to persuade me she had nothing to do with my mother's torture. Or mine, even."

"When was the last time she did this?"

"It has been well over two hundred years. Maybe more. I have been in the monastery. She could not find me there."

"You sleep in the ground every night, and the soil heals you. It welcomes you, right?"

He nodded, puzzled, pressing his fingers against his temples, trying to figure out where she was going with her inquiry.

"You are Dragonseeker and also a child of Mother Earth. Did it occur to you to ask for healing from the constant headaches you have?"

He pulled his hands from his temples. "I don't have headaches." He looked puzzled. "Do I?"

"You have a headache because Lilith is trying to make entry into your mind. It's the drumbeat from that night. You have a trigger, and it starts to play in your head, re-creating that scene over and over so she can call you back to her."

Afanasiv sat back in the chair, his strangely colored eyes drifting over her face. "I do not allow myself to think of those memories. I told you they were lost to me until I forced myself to remember them in order to ensure your people—and you—were safe."

"There is such a thing as the subconscious, Afanasiv," she pointed out as gently as she could. He never lost his calm exterior, but she could see that the headache was becoming worse. "You do revisit that terrible nightmare and you get headaches. You've had them ever since your parents died, but because you lost all emotion and you don't feel or recognize pain, you never acknowledged that you had headaches. You don't acknowledge that you feel them, so you don't see that they're triggered by something outside of yourself."

Afanasiv was suddenly out of his chair and flowing across the room, his power filling the space until the walls expanded and contracted as if they couldn't possibly hold him in.

"Why did you cut yourself off from me?"

Vasilisa hadn't expected him to ask her point-blank. He had his back to her, but he suddenly turned to face her, his strange eyes staring directly into hers, piercing every shield she had so that she felt stripped bare and vulnerable.

"You are still holding yourself away from me."

Twice she opened her mouth to answer him, and twice she swallowed down what she was going to say. What could she say? That he was the only person she truly feared? That he made her weak? That she was obsessed with him? She'd always been her own person and went her own way, and suddenly she couldn't think without wanting him right beside her. She wasn't that kind of woman. She feared she was losing herself. And then hearing that he'd been lovers with Lilith . . . She'd grabbed at that as an excuse to run from him. Only she couldn't run far, because all she could think about was him.

All she wanted was him. She *ached* for him, but the truth was, she didn't respond to men. She didn't respond to women. Even during the full moon, when the heat was on the Lycans and they were all crazy for sex, she could *pretend*, but she didn't feel anything. Until Afanasiv had kissed her. She touched her lips. She thought about that kiss way too much. She felt his kiss deep, melting her where she was nothing but a solid glacier of ice. Still, she was terrified she wouldn't respond, and he would be disappointed in her. She couldn't bear to see disappointment on his face.

His eyes narrowed and then focused completely on her like a laser beam. He took a step toward her. For some reason, he looked huge to her. Afanasiv was a big man with broad shoulders and a thick chest. He had muscles on his muscles, and they rippled whenever he moved. He was hot. Gorgeous. And somehow he got to her. She felt threatened on a level she'd never felt before. Her entire body went into some kind of excited frenzy. Every single cell was aware of him.

She stood up and backed through the archway into her makeup chamber, which only seemed to invite him to stalk after her. The makeup chamber was smaller than her sitting room and had floor-to-ceiling mirrors on all four walls. There was a marble sink and a long counter and a makeup table with rows of lights. The bench was padded in a soft lavender. Even the ceiling was a mirror so she could view her hair from above.

Afanasiv looked enormous as he entered her very feminine space and closed the door behind him. She looked in the mirrors and saw him surrounding her. Her heart accelerated, and for no reason at all, her panties were suddenly very damp.

"Take your hair down."

His voice was very low, a soft velvet, but there was no doubt that it was a command he was giving her. She'd spent time putting her hair up. It wasn't that easy to tame it; she had a lot of hair. She hesitated, sure she wasn't going to give in, but she wanted to. Her blood pounded through her veins, hot and wild, finding her clit and keeping a beat there. Her hands went to the pins in her hair, and she pulled them out one by one until the thick dark mass snaked down her back, falling free like a waterfall.

Afanasiv stepped into her, his large hand reaching for a handful of her hair, rubbing the strands between his fingers and thumb. "It's softer than silk. So beautiful. When you're lying naked waiting for me, I want to see your hair fanned out on the bed."

He murmured it as he wrapped a length around his fist and dragged her closer. Leaning down, with his tongue, he flicked the spot where her pulse beat so frantically in her neck. His teeth grazed her skin gently, back and forth, and then his lips brushed kisses over the sting.

Pleasure shot through her, so intense an actual moan escaped before she could stop it. Her entire body trembled, and goose bumps rose on her skin. His palm cupped her chin, lifting her face to his. His lips brushed hers with exquisite gentleness. She leaned into him, unable to help herself. She had to taste him again. Heat rushed through her as his tongue slid along hers, and a million champagne bubbles seemed to explode in her mouth.

He groaned as he deepened the kiss, a sound that made her breasts feel swollen and achy. Her panties were soaked now, and she could barely think straight. He lifted his head, his eyes nearly a dark gold with lust burning over her. He'd never looked at her like that, and it made her feel weaker than ever. She curled her fingers in his shirt to keep upright, her breath coming in ragged pants.

"You're still determined to keep me out of your head. Why? I wonder." He released the fistful of hair and ran the pad of his thumb down the curve of her face. "What are you so afraid of, my lady?"

She should just tell him the truth. Get it over with. Taking a deep breath, she dropped her shields. *I don't respond properly to sex. There's something wrong with me, and you are going to be very disappointed.* It shamed her to admit it to him. She could be his partner in all things, but he would learn she was no more than a tease when it came to sex.

"You are my lifemate, Vasilisa. Sworn to my care and happiness."

Those golden eyes darkened even more with undeniable lust. Her nipples hardened, feeling like twin points of fire rubbing against her bra.

"Turn around. Look at the mirror. I want you to follow my every command."

Vasilisa couldn't resist that mesmerizing voice. She wanted to do whatever he said. She had sworn to his care and happiness. She might not be able to be fulfilled, but she could see to his sexual needs. At least that would make her feel like she was worth something. In any case, just the way he was demanding she obey him aroused her for some strange reason. She stared at herself in the mirror. Her skin was flushed and her eyes were bright, almost dazed.

"Remove your robe."

Her breath hitched. Her eyes met his in the mirror. She wore only her thong underwear and bra beneath her white robe. He was fully dressed. He didn't command her again, but his eyes did. She found herself wanting to show him her body. Wanting him to see her breasts and hips. She had curves and she liked having them.

She opened the sash and let her robe pool on the floor at her feet, watching him in the mirror the entire time, needing to see his expression. His cock was very large in his trousers, bulging against the material. His golden gaze drifted possessively over her, taking in her curves as if he owned her body, making her feel almost dizzy with excitement.

Afanasiv's large hands cupped the cheeks of her bottom and began to knead them. His thumbs spread her cheeks apart as he massaged and kneaded, taking his time, as though memorizing the shape and feel of them. She was nearly sobbing with need, her body coiling tighter and tighter, and she didn't have any understanding why. He paid no attention as she thrust back into his hands, exploring as one might a new toy, his expression serious and yet filled with that same dark lust that aroused her beyond anything she'd imagined.

Then he was on one knee, gripping her soaked panties and ripping them from her body with a quick jerk. The fabric tore easily. The sound not only made her jump, but fresh liquid teased her entrance, inviting him closer. She heard herself whisper his name in a plea. For what? She didn't know. Only that her body felt on fire, and that tight spring inside her continued to coil past all sanity.

His hands moved up the outsides of her legs from her calves to her thighs. They were big and calloused and felt sensual on her skin. He pushed her legs farther apart and then kissed his way up her inner thighs, stopping just short of where she needed him to touch her.

She could see him in the mirror, that blond hair sliding over her skin, and she did sob his name, begging him this time. He stood up slowly, trailing his palm up her body, his fingers skimming up to her breasts. Again, his mouth went to the frantically beating pulse in her neck as he undid her bra and tossed it aside, spilling her aching breasts into the cool night air.

"Look at you, *sívamet*. So beautiful."

He picked her up and placed her on the marble counter, his hands lifting her breasts as his mouth descended. She expected him to be rough. He barely touched her. He circled her tight nipple with just the tip of his tongue, featherlight, a slow easy burn that felt as if he were igniting a wildfire that had paused. Was on the brink. His finger moved on the other nipple, creating the same slow sensation. It was heaven. It was hell.

Vasilisa dared to look in the mirror. In *all* the mirrors. She'd never seen anything so sexy as looking at herself entirely naked with Afanasiv fully clothed. Her body was flushed, shaking with need. She could see liquid glistening between her legs as she rocked her hips urgently. Hot blood pounded in her clit. In her nipples. Still, that slow burn persisted until she thought she'd go mad. Without warning, he flicked her left nipple hard and bit down on her right one. She nearly exploded. So close. So close. She felt the tidal wave rush at her and then slide away before she captured it.

"Siv." She gasped his name in desperation.

He murmured something against her breasts, rubbing his face over the curves, between them, and on the sides, so that the bristles on his jaw scraped the soft flesh. It was erotic and added to the burn that kept building and building inside of her. Whatever he said in his own language was murmured low and guttural, as if he were swearing to himself, and she found that also added to her heightened state of arousal.

Seeing him surrounding her in the mirrors, the monster bulging in his trousers, made her want to drop to her knees in front of him and worship his body the way he seemed to be worshiping hers.

He suddenly pressed a hand to her belly so she had to recline back on her elbows on the marble counter. He took each foot, kissed the sole and placed it carefully up by her bottom.

"What are you doing?" She could barely get the question out, she was shaking so much.

He leaned forward and pressed a kiss to her belly button. "I'm going to devour you. Eat you until you remember who your lifemate is and you promise me you will never shut me out again."

"But, Siv . . ." She wanted to protest, but she knew it wasn't going to do any good. His eyes were pure gold. Turbulent. Relentless.

He spread his legs wider, his thighs twin columns of pure muscle as he loomed over her. Looping her legs over his arms, he spread her wider, leaving her exposed and vulnerable.

"Look at you, so wet for me. I think you liked everything I did to you."

She didn't have time to assure him one way or the other. He lifted her body to his waiting mouth almost casually. She watched in the mirror, watched the harshly sensual expression on his face, the way the lines deepened, the way the gold smoldered and nearly burst into flames in his eyes.

Then he licked up the side of her thigh and over her throbbing clit. His tongue began that slow circle he'd done to her nipples, the one that drove her out of her mind. She tried to ride his mouth, but he held her firmly, easily, with his superior strength. His breath was hot, a steady stream that inflamed her even more. Then he licked her with a flat tongue and she nearly convulsed.

He licked her again, slow and easy, a cat savoring a bowl of cream. He made a sound, half groan, half snarl, and his lazy facade began to disappear. He went from laid-back cat to raging jungle cat devouring its meal after a long starvation. He made sounds of hot, desperate hunger, feasting on her, his mouth pulling the liquid from her as if it were his own personal aphrodisiac. All the while, his arms and hands held her perfectly still, allowing him to control all movement.

She was desperate to thrust against his mouth. At least to get him to rub her clit harder. To do something. To do more. She was losing her mind. A little sob burst from her as she looked into the mirrors again, watching as his blond head was buried between her thighs. It was so sensual. Unbelievably so. His tongue stabbed deep over and over, drawing out more and more nectar.

He lowered her bottom to the cool marble as he stepped even closer, growling something indistinguishable when she cried out. His finger penetrated her entrance even as he flicked her clit. The tension that had coiled deep suddenly ignited like the hottest storm imaginable. Flames rushed through her veins. A wildfire flashed through her, burning out of control. The rolling fury consumed her, taking her over completely until she couldn't see anything but the white-hot flashes behind her eyes or feel anything but the intense pleasure rolling through her.

She heard herself sobbing his name. Then he was kissing her and she could taste herself on his tongue. On his skin. She should have been embarrassed, but she was too overcome with the shocking realization that her body had responded with total arousal to everything Afanasiv had done to it.

"Shall I start again, or do you understand that my lifemate does not close her mind to me?" Afanasiv asked. He hadn't released her. He still held her pinned on the marble counter.

She blinked up at him, trying to decide if she could live through another lesson. In any case, it wasn't fair. She hadn't relieved the tension in his body.

"I understand that I shouldn't close my mind to you." She did her best to sound meek, but she was feeling elated just knowing that her body actually worked like it was supposed to.

"As long as you are sharing your mind with me, there is no way for anyone else to get inside where they don't belong." He gently released her legs and reached for a washcloth.

Vasilisa struggled to get her breathing under control. She skimmed her fingers down the front of his trousers. "I might not be the most experienced, but I do want to take care of your every need, Afanasiv."

"And you will," he said. "You doubted yourself as a woman, my lady. As my partner. That was hurtful to you when you thought it was possible that I had another lover at some time. I never want you to feel a lack of confidence in any area. If you do, you must come to me."

He was very gentle as he washed between her legs. Once he had cleaned her carefully, he swept his hand over her body and her hair was back exactly as it had been. She was once again wearing her underclothes and robe. He was clean and refreshed.

He leaned down and framed her face with his large hands, his peculiar eyes looking down into hers. Now the color was blue like the sea, but with green swirling through it. So like a Dragonseeker. His thumbs moved gently over her jaw, tracing the bones. He bent down and took her mouth. Gentle. Rough. Hot. Claiming her all over again with just his mouth and tongue. When he lifted his head, the pads of his fingers slid along the bottom curve of her lips.

"You're so amazing, Vasilisa. I never want you to feel as you did. You can never be less than any other woman. Never that. You didn't respond to other men because you are my lifemate. I don't respond to other women because you are my lifemate. My body responds only to you. I find only you attractive. It will always be that way."

Could that be the truth? She definitely found him *very* attractive.

"Why don't you want me to . . . ?" She gestured toward the front of his trousers again.

"You do not yet know me or trust me completely, and you need that to feel wholly comfortable with me before you can be intimate."

Color rose under her skin. "I think what just took place might be considered very intimate, Siv."

His smile was slow in coming, but when it did, it was so sexy it took her breath. "That was just a very small sample of the pleasures I intend to show you. You deserve to be courted, *sívamet*. I think this was a very good start, and we will continue to build from here."

She certainly didn't want to slip backward. She was all for going forward.

"This trigger you believe I have that brings on the headaches. Have you a suspicion what it is? A drum seems too obvious, and how often am I around a drum?"

Vasilisa was still having trouble thinking clearly. How could he go from being so sensual to taking care of business in what seemed like minutes? Maybe it wasn't minutes. Maybe time had gone by and then he'd kissed her. He had kissed her. She'd lost her mind again when he'd kissed her.

She laughed. "It isn't a drum. It's tapping. The birds tapping their beaks on the tree trunks or on a windowsill. It's easy enough to send a bird out to repeat the tapping, isn't it?"

14

Conspiracy had a distinct smell to it. Add in treachery and fanaticism, and there was a stench. Afanasiv, Petru, Nicu and Benedek had been alive far too long not to recognize the never-ending cycle of extremism. There was also the underlying edge of dark magic tainting the land as they entered the easternmost corner of the territory. The strain was very faint, but it was there, a particularly ugly weave dedicated to turning friend against friend and family members against family. The weave was ancient but very powerful, taking the best of nature and turning it back on itself.

The ancients had gone in unseen, taking the form of clouds, knowing that if there were trouble, this place was the most likely center of it. Lada's parents and their friends held leases to the largest farms. They held regular meetings for those belonging to the Sacred Circle, those holding to the old ways.

The plan called for Vasilisa to visit Lada. It would be natural for her, as a royal, to check up on Lada after her ordeal. In fact, it would be unseemly if no one visited her. It sounded like a solid plan when Vasilisa laid it out to everyone. Now, looking down at the tracks in the snow and seeing the jagged crack that split the earth at the back of the Belov property, Afanasiv wasn't as happy with the plan as he had been.

Someone had tried to cover the fissure by heaping snow around it so no one could see the fracture that allowed passage to and from the underworld.

Vasilisa wasn't traveling alone. Dimitri's lifemate had volunteered to accompany her on the visit. Where Skyler went, Dimitri wasn't far behind. He traveled with the ancients, drifting with the low-lying clouds, inspecting the land below them.

The forest wasn't as healthy as it should have been. The trees showed signs of strain. On close examination, Afanasiv couldn't find evidence of the undead, but there were other toxic chemicals at work slowly poisoning the trees and bushes. He could hear them crying out for aid.

All those living or working on the Belov farm, all those visiting, would most likely be Lycan. Lycans guarded the forest and everything in it. How could they not hear the cries for help? How could they not see the healthy plants being choked to death by some outside source leaking into the soil?

I like none of this, he sent on the path used by the ancients. Dimitri was part of the path and could easily hear what he had to say.

Something is very wrong here, Nicu agreed.

I have seen this blight creeping close to the preserve, Dimitri said. *We did not allow it to gain a foothold. The moment we spotted it, we wiped it out.*

What is it, and where did it come from? Afanasiv asked. His radar was going off, telling him not only that something was very wrong but that there was danger here. He didn't like that he wasn't with his lifemate.

We suspect that this is something a mage has introduced into the soil. When we tapped into the mycelium system belowground, Dimitri said, *that was the best explanation for what was happening.*

Afanasiv knew the mycelium system was often a name given to the vast rootlike structure that connected the trees and plants, aiding in communication to ensure the health of the forest. *Why would a mage want to poison the plants and trees?* He was no longer drifting but was moving with purpose toward the farmhouse where Vasilisa would be arriving any moment to pay Lada a visit. Dimitri circled around toward the back of the large sprawling structure.

They hadn't worried too much about the fact that Skyler would be considered *Sange rau*—an abomination—by the Sacred Circle members. Ordinarily, they would never be rude in front of a member of the royal family. If they refused to allow Skyler entrance to their home, that would go a long way to telling the ancients and royals just how strong a foothold the fanatics had.

Afanasiv believed Vasilisa would be able to handle any inquiries Lada's parents might have regarding Skyler. She was adept at structuring answers and conversations so there was never a lie if anyone was good at hearing them the way Carpathians were.

Slow down, my lady, Afanasiv advised. *I want to see what is taking place inside before you go in. This place feels wrong to me. It is heavy with darkness.*

Dimitri added his opinion as well. *It feels oily to me, mage oily. He's here somewhere.*

Not Xavier, Afanasiv said. *Vasilisa sealed him in the underworld. He cannot escape. Even should he try to send slivers of himself, they would not get through. This is someone else.*

Petru joined the conversation. *Perhaps his brother Xaviero, or Barnabas. He is far worse than his father or uncles.*

I have had no dealings with Barnabas, although I have heard of him. Word was sent to our prince, Mikhail, Dimitri acknowledged.

Afanasiv was at the actual farmhouse, moving with the slight breeze he had created with his brethren. The structure was made of logs that fit snugly into one another. The verandah was long and narrow, with a sloped roof matching the one above it so the snow could slide off easily. He didn't make the mistake of expending energy, not if a high mage was close. He cautioned the others to be very careful, as well. He moved in close, though, allowing his senses to flare out as he scanned the interior of the large home.

Although there were few vehicles to give away the fact that several people were inside, in one room, six people sat in a row of chairs facing a group of nine others. All were adults. He recognized Lada standing alone between the nine and the six. It felt as if she were in a courtroom being judged.

He had not taken blood from Lada, nor had he given her blood, so there was no bond between them. *Vasilisa, did you give blood to Lada?* He was extremely cautious now, ensuring that when he reached out to his lifemate, there was no spilling of energy that could be picked up by the mage he was certain was in the farmhouse.

There was nothing to show that a mage of great power was present, but the impression was there. It was nothing more than the feel of darkness—of gloom—hanging over the farmhouse. The weave of dark magic, an ugly pall he felt when he approached the eastern section of the royals' territory.

Yes, several times, Vasilisa answered.

Is it possible for you to touch her mind without her being aware? Without any other being aware, even if someone else occupies her mind?

It would be a daring thing to do, even for an ancient. Afanasiv felt the immediate rejection of his plan by his brethren, all but Dimitri. Dimitri's lifemate traveled with Vasilisa. If the mage had spies anywhere close to the farmhouse, they would have spotted the two women by now and reported to their master. Skyler couldn't just disappear without a reason. Afanasiv intended to enter the farmhouse with Vasilisa through Lada. They would be able to ascertain what was going on and how safe it would be to continue with their plan.

Vasilisa didn't answer right away. She thought it over carefully. *I have never entered another's mind when it is occupied by an enemy, my lord, but I am willing to try.*

This mage is extremely powerful, sívamet. I would not want you to have to go up against him without any preparation. Afanasiv was careful in how he worded what he said. He didn't want in any way to diminish her in front of the others or to make her feel as if he thought she couldn't do it.

I have a delicate touch and have never been detected. I will try if you think it is necessary.

She wasn't bragging. Vasilisa didn't seem to have an ego when it came to being a warrior. If she said she had a delicate touch, she did.

His brethren gave a collective protest, although it was faint, ensuring that no energy was spilling out where the mage, if he was in the farmhouse, would feel any disruption in the air.

I will be with you, Vasilisa. Do not allow Lada to feel you. No matter what is taking place in that house, you cannot reach out to her or aid her in any way. Is that clear? Afanasiv used his compelling voice. A commanding one. Ordinarily, he would never use his gift on his lifemate in front of others, but her life could very well be at stake.

She didn't answer him right away, and his heart dropped. He would call the entire operation off before he would allow her anywhere near the people inside the farmhouse if she refused to follow his lead on this.

Very clear, lifemate.

Was that sarcasm? No one, not even a master vampire, was resistant to his voice when he compelled obedience. He merged with Vasilisa and settled quietly, waiting for her to seek out Lada. She and Skyler delayed approaching the farmhouse by stopping to examine several bushes that looked to be very unhealthy. That would be something expected of a royal. The care of the forest and all surrounding property was in their hands.

Vasilisa had no problem gaining access to the inside of the farmhouse. No one had thought to safeguard it against any creature other than vampires. She slipped under the slightly open window, a crack only, that revealed they were in the study, where the occupants of the house were gathered.

Lada wept continuously, shaking her head. Her denials were so loud in her mind, Vasilisa and Afanasiv had to turn the volume down.

"You had one assignment, Lada," an older man in a long black robe said. "One. Your parents assured us that you would be able to carry out this small task for us. In return, we would ensure you and your daughter would once again be together."

Lada pressed a hand to her mouth as if she could choke back the sob that slipped out around her fingers anyway.

"Enough of this, Vovo." A tall man, younger than the others sitting in the six chairs facing Lada, stood. He was very good-looking, his features chiseled and sharp. His eyes were a slash of silver in color and appeared quite stormy. His hair was also very silver and thick, like the winter pelt of the wolf. He shoved his chair out of the way with calm movements and walked around the row of five judges left sitting. He placed his hands behind his back as he paced across the room with slow, deliberate strides and then walked right up to Lada to stare into her eyes.

Afanasiv held his breath. Just that stare held immense power. Barnabas projected a gentle, caring man. He appeared almost sorrowful, his eyes drooping with pain and empathy for Lada. "My dear, this inquisition must be so terrible for you. Everyone, including your parents, shouting questions at you. No one allowing you to finish a sentence. Threats against you and your daughter." He half turned as though to censure Vovo.

He removed a handkerchief from his pocket and stepped closer to Lada, one arm very gently wrapping around her waist while the other dabbed at her tears with the cloth.

"There's no need for these tears. We can come to an understanding without all this shouting. Someone needs to stand for you. I thought your parents would do so."

Again, he turned, this time toward the three rows of three chairs set up facing the six judges. He gave the couple in the front row a long look of condemnation. The woman who bore a small resemblance to Lada squirmed. The man with a receding hairline shook his head.

"You have too soft of a heart, Nikita," Lada's father said, addressing Barnabas by the name they knew him by. "She was to deliver the royal to us. Trap Andros, get him to ask her to marry him. How could she have failed when she was so prepared? She was coached in everything he liked. Still, she failed. It's a humiliation on our house. A terrible burden for our family to bear."

"Perhaps the fault lies with the royal and not with your daughter," Barnabas protested, dabbing at the tears running unchecked down Lada's face. "Andros is a playboy. He very well could have seduced this lovely girl and then deliberately insulted your house by leaving her after everyone knew he had used her so ruthlessly. Men like that feel so entitled. They go off with their friends and laugh over their conquests, never thinking about the way they wreck lives."

Lada flinched under the commentary Barnabas had supposedly defended her with. He'd painted her as a naïve woman Andros had taken advantage of. All the while he continued to dab her face with that cloth.

Afanasiv realized the handkerchief contained some kind of drug. Each time Barnabas placed it around Lada's nose, she would shake her head and weep softly.

"He didn't ask you to marry him after all the preparation your parents gave you?" Barnabas asked sadly. He couched it as a question.

Afanasiv felt Vasilisa hold her breath. Lada couldn't lie to the mage. Her senses had to be confused by the drug he was subjecting her to via the cloth. Lada shook her head adamantly, but she didn't utter a single word.

A soft knock on the door had Lada's father snapping out a quick inquiry. A servant partially opened the door. "Miss Vasilisa and a friend of hers, Skyler, wife to Dimitri, are here to see Lada," she announced.

"Ask them to wait in the sitting room," Lada's father said.

Barnabas smiled at Lada. "This is such good news for you, dear. Vasilisa will certainly be able to tell us whether or not her brother is a playboy and was just playing with your affections. If she backs up your story, surely everyone here will apologize for not believing you."

"Nikita," Vovo said. "She brings with her a *Sange rau*. We all know Dimitri is *Sange rau*. His wife must be."

"Not necessarily. It will be interesting to find out, though, won't it?" Barnabas looked pleased with himself.

"She could not have done the things that it is rumored she did if she was not *Sange rau*," another judge objected. He was also older and very stern looking.

"Artyom," Barnabas said, "it has been the experience of everyone who has crossed paths with the *Sange rau* that they are killers. They do not come calmly to visit in farmhouses. But we have an opportunity to see for ourselves."

"We cannot all go into the sitting room. Vasilisa will know immediately that something isn't right," Lada's mother said. She glared at her daughter. "Stop that incessant crying, Lada. You're lucky Nikita has stood for you yet again."

"Go wash your face, Lada," Barnabas said, stroking his hand down her arm. "Do you need me to help you, or will you be able to face Andros' sister without me sitting right beside you? Was she nasty to you? Did she look down her nose at you?"

Lada frowned and shook her head. "No, no, she isn't like that at all. She isn't like the others . . ." She trailed off as if she didn't know what she was saying.

Her mother took her arm and led her out of the room.

Barnabas turned to the other judges. "We have a very rare opportunity here. It sounds to me as if Vasilisa is not like the rest of her family. I am looking forward to meeting her. It will be extremely interesting to question her friend. I ask that no one be rude and embarrass the Belov family. They have been gracious enough to allow us to use their home for our meetings."

Lada's father led the way into the sitting room, with Barnabas walking beside him. Vasilisa and Skyler stood at the far end of the room, where Lada's mother had sectioned off a large corner she'd turned into an atrium. It was a small greenhouse, but she grew a few exotic plants that seemed to do quite well.

Vasilisa and Skyler turned around as the two men entered the room. Behind Barnabas and Lada's father came Vovo and Artyom.

"Vasilisa, how good of you to come," Stepan Belov greeted her. "You've brought a friend. Welcome, welcome."

"Yes, this is Skyler, Dimitri's wife. Skyler, Stepan Belov and Dimitri have known each other for years. Have we come at a bad time? You have company."

"No time is a bad time for you to come, Vasilisa," Stepan beamed at her. "This is my dear friend Nikita. You know everyone else. Sit, sit. Lada will be in soon with her mother."

Barnabas went right up to Vasilisa and held out both hands to her. "Wonderful to meet you. I've heard nothing but good things about you."

Vasilisa placed both hands in the mage's. His fingers closed around hers and he drew her to him, kissing her first on one cheek and then the other. Afanasiv studied their enemy up close. As the mage leaned in to kiss Vasilisa, he blew softly onto her left cheek as his lips brushed her skin.

He planted a marker under my skin. Vasilisa sounded matter-of-fact. Calm. Outwardly, she looked serene and sweet, as if she didn't have a clue what the mage had done.

Afanasiv was very aware that the mage had marked his lifemate. He felt close to panic, so much so that Dimitri demanded to know what happened.

Siv, I can deal with his marker. He doesn't have a clue what I am. He has taken me at face value. He holds the belief that women are inferior and have no power. He looked Skyler over and dismissed her without even touching her. How could he not feel her power? She is part mage. Surely he would at least feel that in her.

Afanasiv wasn't buying that a mage as powerful as Barnabas would dismiss Skyler. She was a target, a huge prize for the mages to be able to drag down to the underworld. He was uneasy that a portal was so close.

He knows who Skyler is, he assured Vasilisa. *Be on the lookout for treachery. Be careful of anything you are offered to eat or drink. And they will offer it if for no other reason than to prove that Skyler is* Sange rau. *Although, to be honest, he will not allow anyone to do that, not if he wants a chance to take her to the underworld. He must be elated with her being so close to the portal.*

"Please sit down." Stepan waved toward the very comfortable upholstered chairs. "I see you were admiring Polina's little project. The temperature must always be kept constant, or those flowers won't survive."

"The flowers are so beautiful. Some I've never seen before," Vasilisa said. *This thing under my skin is wiggling. I have to get it out.*

Let me take a look at it. Afanasiv moved right up against his lifemate, so close he could inhale and take her into his lungs if he had them. He was only molecules. The sitting room window was cracked open, the tiny slit allowing fresh air to circulate in the room. For what purpose? He was certain Barnabas was aware of the breach of safety. He had to have either allowed it or orchestrated it.

"Yes, the flowers are exotic and would never survive our extreme cold," Stepan advised her, pride in his voice. "Polina had to study each of the exotics and learn what they needed to thrive. It took a great deal of time and effort."

I will take on the safety issues while you see to the tracker the mage put under the royal's skin, Benedek instructed.

He is up to something, Petru reported. *There is activity at the portal. A five-man team of demons awaits at the entrance.*

Afanasiv considered what that meant. *Describe them to me.*

As he waited for Petru to give him the description, he moved to the left side of his lifemate to study her cheek. She had gorgeous skin. Almost luminous. Her complexion was smooth and very pale, almost alabaster, as she rarely saw the sun. Her long, feathery eyelashes and mass of sable hair appeared even darker, contrasting with the tone of her skin. Then there was the color of her eyes. They could go a deep royal blue, like now, or a light, almost crystalline blue that seemed to pierce one's soul.

"Was this a joint project? The various shelves made from rock and wood are beautiful and really seem to showcase each species of flower," Skyler said. "I especially love the ones that are grouped around the little waterfall. Those rocks look so natural."

Stepan's chest expanded. "Polina must take the credit for all the work with the flowers. She is the one who manages to get them to thrive. She tells me what environment she needs, and I provide it for her. That is very little to contribute." He spoke modestly, but the underlying tone was definitely a brag.

Both women immediately exclaimed over the rock shelving and wooden settings.

The demons are fierce in appearance, with massive bodies in that they are dense. Each has four horns, two on the front of their skulls and two larger ones in the back, but up on top of their heads. The horns have very wicked points.

Afanasiv feared he knew the five demons already, before Petru was finished describing them. In the hierarchy of demons, these five were at the top for a very good reason. They rarely failed when a prisoner fled. They were sent after escapees Lilith wanted back at any cost. If they couldn't return them, she wanted the prisoners killed and the bodies brought to her. That was the usual state of any escapee she set the team on.

Their heads are very large and look heavy, the jaws extended in order to accommodate their teeth. They have more teeth than can fit into their mouth, so no lips, just curved, spiked teeth that look as if they can do a lot of damage. The forehead clearly has a bony plate between the horns. Lots of hair.

Afanasiv studied the tiny flaw that was under his lifemate's skin. It showed itself the way a blackhead might appear, although this moved in tiny increments. At first, he could barely tell that the thing was attempting a migration. When it moved, Vasilisa would put her hand to her cheek and rub or scratch over the spot with a long fingernail. Each time she did, Barnabas's gaze would jump to her, his eyes almost glowing. The tiny creature would stop moving, and Vasilisa would drop her hand and continue the conversation as if nothing had happened.

These demons are taller than some I've seen. Deep chests, strong arms, big thighs. They have claws, but their hands work, just that they have fingernails that look more like a cat's hooked claws. I think they're venomous, Petru continued.

Afanasiv knew they were. *That is one of Lilith's most lethal teams right there. They are considered elite even in the underworld. If any other demon comes upon one, they step aside for them instantly. If they don't, the elite will kill them without a second thought. They are venomous. Behind all those teeth is a long tongue. It looks like a snake when it unfolds and it drips venom. It's spotted purple and will strike just as if it were a snake. Their bite is poisonous. Their claws are. Even their horns are, if they gore you.*

Lovely, Petru said. *How do you kill them?*

Under their arms, in the armpit, and if they open their mouth to use their tongue, you can fire into the back of their throat. The eyes. If you notice, they wear protective eye gear. It's for a reason. They have body armor, so it is pretty difficult anywhere else, but their eyes are very vulnerable if you can strip away the eye gear. Their eyes bulge in the sunlight. Or any light if you shine it directly at them. The protective shield over the lens of their eyes doesn't help them much, Afanasiv explained.

Vasilisa leaned toward Stepan, her gaze going toward the door as if expecting Lada and Polina to appear at any moment. She lowered her voice. "I want to apologize personally for the way Lada was treated. She's wonderful, absolutely wonderful, and I would consider it a privilege to have her as a family member."

Her voice rang with honesty. With sincerity. Why? Because every single word she said was the absolute truth.

Stepan placed his hand over his heart. "Thank you for that, Vasilisa. I appreciate you coming here to tell us this."

"I think of Lada as a friend. I don't want to lose her friendship. I also wanted her to meet Skyler. When I was a little girl, Polina would always tell me it was my lady friends who would be important to me when I grew up. I'm finding she is right."

Again, Stepan beamed. "Polina still teaches the young ladies. Some listen, some don't."

This thing under my skin feels as if it has a thousand feet, Siv. I want to tear it out.

Patience. I'm going after it in a minute.

Vasilisa had once more covered the tiny creature with her fingertips and then scratched at it. Barnabas turned his attention to her, frowning, and the little dot subsided. Afanasiv was right up against it and felt the energy pushed in the direction of the creature. The mage was communicating with it, giving it orders.

"But what of your husband?" Barnabas asked Skyler. "Where does he fit into your women's circle? Do you rely on him?"

Skyler sent the mage a beautiful smile. "My husband always comes first in everything I say or do, but I always enjoy my female friends. It gives me a different perspective when I talk to them. Also, they share so many viewpoints on how to manage things I didn't know how to do. They give me advice, I guess, is what I'm trying to say."

Barnabas steepled his fingers, his strange eyes going glittery as they rested on Skyler. "You look very young to be married."

"I get that quite a bit," Skyler admitted with a small shrug of her shoulders.

Polina and Lada entered the room, Polina with a wide, welcoming smile on her face and Lada looking very subdued. Vasilisa rose, immediately going to Lada and Polina, hugging them warmly and introducing Skyler. Polina stiffened just the slightest bit, but held on to her smile, tossing a quick look at Barnabas, who gave her a stern flick of his fingers toward her kitchen.

Once they were seated, Polina ordered tea and scones for her visitors, and the maid brought them in immediately. Polina waved her out and poured the tea herself, serving her visitors first, then Barnabas and Stepan, along with Vovo and Artyom.

"I've never been able to make scones," Skyler said. "Is this your own recipe?" she asked Polina.

"Indeed." Polina inclined her head, watching Skyler closely.

Vasilisa took a sip of tea, breaking down the compound quickly to test for drugs. *The tea is just tea, Skyler.*

Skyler took a sip of the tea. "Black currant. This is delicious." She tested a small bite of the scone. *The scone has nothing wrong with it and does taste delicious.*

"This is amazing. Vasilisa, seriously, I've never tasted a scone like this before." Skyler switched her gaze to Polina. "My mother lives in Paris, and when I visit with her, we often go to little cafés for our alone time. We like to sit and people-watch while we're having tea and pastries. Your scones rival anything I've ever had there." She looked and sounded perfectly honest and sincere.

Polina appeared both proud and confused. She looked to Barnabas for guidance, as if now that Skyler had eaten actual food and drunk tea, that meant she couldn't be the dreaded *Sange rau* they all had been so certain she was, and Polina didn't know quite what to say or do.

"Did you really save your husband from death by silver?" Polina blurted out.

"Polina," Stepan said, chastising her.

She turned red, but it was obvious to Vasilisa that it was a question everyone in the room wanted answered.

"Forgive me," Polina said, ducking her head.

"No, really, I don't mind." Skyler took another sip of tea. "I get that question quite a bit. I wasn't alone. Everyone kind of forgets that. I think it makes for a great story that I was all by myself and did all these amazing things when, really, I had friends who were amazing."

Her voice rang with sincerity because she believed what she was telling them.

Afanasiv had seen enough of the little creature Barnabas had placed beneath Vasilisa's skin. The intent was to migrate upward toward her brain, where it would allow its master to give Vasilisa commands.

When I tell you, my lady, I want you to smack your cheek as you would an insect biting you. Cover your cheek with your palm. I will destroy the creature at the same time. He felt her instant relief.

Please hurry. It feels the way the demons feel to me. Not just dark mage but demon. He is using a combination.

Afanasiv heard the warning in her voice. She was concerned he might not recognize the hybrid. It wasn't the first time he had seen such a thing. *I spent much time in the underworld, sívamet. This mage is not giving us his best work because he doesn't think he has to. I want him to think that as long as possible.*

"Tell me, Vasilisa," Barnabas said. "We were having this discussion at one of our meetings regarding the youth of today and how far their morals have fallen. What are your views on having children out of wedlock? Your personal views and the views of the royal family."

Vasilisa exchanged a frown with Skyler. Lada put her head down with a soft moan that earned her a sharp reprimand from her mother.

Those in the sitting room went still, so still it felt as though the air held its breath. Skyler deliberately picked up the gold inlaid glass set in the gold filigree stand and took another drink of the tea. Even her motion didn't change the way those in the room fixated on Vasilisa. They stared at her, the men with piercing, fanatical eyes and Polina with an overbright, judgmental air.

Vasilisa appeared perfectly calm. Very regal. "That's an interesting question to pose in this day and age, Nikita. I would have to give some thought to it, especially as you grouped several topics together. I would have liked to have heard the discussion you had. Don't you think every few years, this very topic has been a concern? Some parents try to address it, and others refuse to acknowledge there might be a problem. They want to leave it to schools, which is absurd." She pressed her fingers over her mouth. "I'm sorry, I shouldn't have said that."

"Why not?" Barnabas countered. "Why shouldn't you say that schools shouldn't be the ones to teach our youth about sex?"

"I didn't exactly say that, Nikita. That's why I shouldn't have said anything at all. I get misquoted often. Andros says I have a runaway mouth, and I'm not to express my opinions on any subject. The one you're talking about is very controversial."

Barnabas crossed his arms over his chest and leaned back. As he did so, he moved his fingers in a slight gesture toward their two guests. Afanasiv felt the energy rushing toward Skyler and Vasilisa. Dimitri followed the path, making certain to protect both women by staying in front of them. The energy went to the teapot and the cups. For the briefest of moments, the black current tea bubbled and then subsided.

He changed the chemical property, Dimitri reported. *Skyler, I am certain the tea is tainted now.*

Skyler brought the cup to her lips and appeared as if she were drinking. *He did indeed. This would make me very sleepy and compliant.* She put down the cup.

"Why shouldn't you be able to give your own opinion, Vasilisa?" Barnabas asked. His voice had turned very compelling. "Does your brother insist on being the only royal to state what he believes in public? I thought he was more progressive than that."

Now, my lady. As if you are killing a bug that landed on your cheek. Afanasiv slipped under her skin and waited for the moment she complied.

Vasilisa slapped her palm hard over the spot on her left cheek where the terrible little creature had been embedded. She kept her hand there, not looking at anyone in particular but reaching for her teacup. Simultaneously, Afanasiv struck at the hideous demon, incinerating it in a flash of white-hot energy before it had time to even try to run.

"Are you all right, dear?" Polina asked.

"I'm very sensitive to bites," Vasilisa said. "I've got some kind of skin thing." She shrugged. "It's a nuisance, nothing more. I was bitten by something earlier, and the sensation keeps recurring. I apologize."

"Really, there's no need," Stepan said. "I have a daughter. I know how these little things can bother and be so distracting."

She managed to look embarrassed as she replaced her teacup without drinking. "My brother would be mortified that I acted this way in front of all of you. I really am disciplined. It's just that bugs on my skin . . ." She gave a delicate little shudder.

You can let go of your cheek now, sívamet.

Vasilisa rubbed the spot gently with two fingers and then brought her hand almost reluctantly down to her lap. Barnabas's eyes glowed a dark crimson as they bored into her. He wasn't happy at all, and it showed. He stared at her cheek and then lifted his hand to rub at his temple where a vein throbbed.

"You didn't answer the question," he pointed out. "You're not drinking your tea and you're refusing to answer the simplest questions."

"And clearly, I'm upsetting you," Vasilisa said. "Perhaps it is time for us to leave, Skyler. We did interrupt your meeting, Stepan Belov."

Skyler set down her teacup and, with a show of reluctance, put the rest of the scone on the painted plate. "Thank you for your hospitality. It was lovely meeting you. I hope to come back when you have time to talk," she added to Polina. "I really am interested in your recipes and would love to talk about your garden."

She stood up and made a show of swaying a little, reaching out to catch Vasilisa's arm for balance.

The men stood as well. "Polina, show the girls the new garden I have been building for you in the back," Stepan instructed.

Lada made a sound of distress and shook her head adamantly.

"Lada." Barnabas simply said her name.

Lada put her hand over her mouth, but her eyes, when they met Vasilisa's, were wild with distress and warning. She had tears spilling over, and twice she gave small shakes of her head.

Vasilisa gave her a reassuring smile and then turned to follow Polina through the hall toward the back of the house.

The men followed behind them in a little procession.

There is no fighting room with Skyler trapped between the demons in the portal and the men of the Sacred Circle. If that isn't bad enough, Afanasiv, the high mage is bringing up the rear. He would be enough to contend with. Vasilisa sounded worried. *There were others in the room when we first arrived. They didn't show themselves to us, but I knew they were close. I could feel them. We could be in a little bit of trouble.*

Woman, really? Do you think I would allow you to be in real danger?

15

Vasilisa heard the amusement in her lifemate's voice. Her stomach did a slow roll in response. *You are relying on a royal to counter a high mage's spell.*

Naturally. That shouldn't be a problem for my woman. Saving the day is her specialty. In any case, when the princess goes all royal and warrior woman, it seriously wreaks havoc with my body. In a good way, Afanasiv assured her.

Skyler sighed. *You did not just insert sex into this very serious conversation about fighting the high mage, which I'm about to do, and now all I want to do is laugh.*

Laughing at the high mage might get your mouth sewn shut, Dimitri cautioned. *He's very sensitive, and I'm fond of your mouth.*

"Polina." Vasilisa spoke very softly as she dropped one hand gently on the woman's shoulder to halt her progress. "Don't take one more step."

Polina stood in the doorway and turned her head to look over her shoulder at Vasilisa. Her eyes shone with a zealot's fervor. "The greenhouse Stepan is building for me is right over there. Do you see it?" She indicated the long crack that had opened in the backyard.

"Yes, Polina, I see it. I want you to hear me." Vasilisa spoke low, but her voice changed subtly. It was filled with power, with a bright, hot energy. "We are bound together by the Lycan code. By the earth we guard. It is our sacred duty placed above all else. We are bound together by the code of honor we speak every morning and evening. No constraints are put on us in terms of beliefs of religion, but we always follow the code of the Lycan first. We are individuals. But we are part of the tapestry of the earth and were put here as the guardians. Our lives are intertwined, and each is needed for the other. We believe and live by the code. I am a royal, Princess Vasilisa, and I command each of you to see with the eyes of the Lycan."

Polina, closest to Vasilisa and the portal, gave a startled gasp and tried to clutch at the royal's arm. "Get inside. Stepan. Hurry. There's terrible trouble out here. A crack in the ground has opened, and it's horrible. Very large. I think I can see red eyes glowing inside of it." With each word she uttered, the pitch of her tone rose higher and higher until she was shrieking.

The men separating Skyler and Barnabas began talking all at once. Stepan pushed Skyler aside in an effort to get to his wife.

See what I mean? Afanasiv said. *It's sexy when she talks like that.*

Afanasiv, Skyler protested.

He has a point, Dimitri weighed in. *I love to watch you when you work. It gets me in the mood fast.*

Everything gets you in the mood fast. Skyler pretended exasperation. *I have to concentrate. I have to keep the high mage's attention on me. And get these men out of my way.*

"Stepan, Polina, take your company into the study, where it is safe," Vasilisa ordered.

Stepan and his wife immediately rounded up the other members of the Sacred Circle to go to the meeting room.

Barnabas leaned up against the wall, one elegant shoe crossed over the other. He looked Skyler up and down, a sneer of pure contempt on his face. "Why is it you little girls always think you can take on men of great power? What do the two of you think you're going to do?"

Skyler made a show of looking around her. "The two of us? Don't flatter yourself, Barnabas. Vasilisa has no time to speak with you. She has much more important work to do than play games with you." Skyler kept her voice low and compelling, even as she called him by his true name. She had a smile on her face, her features gentle and kind. "Don't worry, I'll do my best to keep up with you."

I hope you realize I can't possibly take on this mage. He's unbelievably powerful. Skyler held on to her smile, but inside she was shaking. *Few could defeat him.*

You do not have to defeat him, beloved, only stall him, Dimitri assured her.

Skyler took a deep breath and let it out. *You have no idea what you're asking.*

Barnabas straightened. "You think it's a game?" As he straightened, he flicked his fingers toward the ceiling. "If you know my true identity, you should know better than to challenge me."

Spiders of all sizes with dripping fangs crawled out of the cracks and began to make the descent down the walls, multiplying until the room was choking with them. Their eyes were fixed on Skyler as they skittered toward her.

I know I'm supposed to look all cool here, but you do know Barnabas is the real deal. He's a high mage and he could crush me in two seconds. Outwardly, Skyler looked bored, lifted one hand and waved rather weakly at the spiders. To her shock they stopped abruptly and reversed direction, swiveling around to face Barnabas.

Did you think I would allow my daughter to face this madman alone? Razvan stood in front of her, unseen. *There isn't a spell he knows that I didn't learn. I spent several lifetimes with Xavier, Xaviero, Xayvion and even Barnabas. They would forget I was in the room. Just stall. Vasilisa needs time to close the portal and seal the demons and mages in it. Once that is done, I'll take over here openly.*

Skyler fought to keep the shock off her face. She didn't realize Razvan was part of their plan to strike at Lilith and her army. She doubted if anyone could match Barnabas—other than Razvan.

Vasilisa stepped off the stairs onto the snow-covered ground, drawing her crystal sword from inside her long coat. The most important thing was to seal the portal so it couldn't be used again. If the demons were caught on this side, they would not be able to return to the underworld until they found another portal. She raised the sword over her head so that it came alive, a blue flame burning hot, so clean and bright the demons cried out, turning away even with the shields over their eyes.

The crystalline sword seemed as bright as the sun, illuminating the entire backyard as if it were day instead of night. An icy gust of wind rushed through the yard, throwing snow into the air and swirling it around so that the light shot through it, highlighting the beauty of the snowflakes and ice.

There was a child's play set a good distance from the fissure, which lay like a sore with several large mounds of snow heaped up around it in an effort to conceal the zigzag open wound in the earth. A playhouse was in the middle of construction. Beside it was a small greenhouse, finished, but no plants had been planted in the soil beds.

The backyard was huge and open to the forest. There was no fence to divide the Belov land from the trees and brush that crept toward the wide-open spaces surrounding the property. The bushes had found their way back, snaking around the pathways so that the backyard appeared to be part of the forest. That meant there were plenty of large rocks, bushes and even trees for any enemy to hide behind.

Vasilisa drew a vial with clear liquid in it from a loop in her coat. Holding the crystalline sword out from her, she turned in a slow circle, ignoring the demons that locked in on her once again. They were the elite and scared her. She knew how difficult they were to kill. Taking her eyes off them was tantamount to suicide, but she didn't dare stop what she was doing. She had to trust in her lifemate and the other ancients to handle the demons while she consecrated the ground and took it away from them. She needed to close the portal and seal it so it couldn't be used again.

She called to the heavens in a soft, angelic voice. The moment she did, overhead, dark clouds tumbled and rolled, boiling ferociously. In the lining of those churning clouds, white-hot lightning forked. Thunder boomed as if in answer, shaking the house. Vasilisa didn't pause, continuing to chant softly, never raising her voice or hesitating despite the raging storm overhead.

She continued her slow, deliberate circle, bathing the ground with droplets from the vial she held in one hand and the bright blue flame from the crystalline sword she held in the other. The drops from the vial compounded in the air so that a rainstorm burst down on the snow. The rain was hot, and when the drops hit, beneath the icy snow something sizzled and burned. Smoke rose and dark blood bubbled up to stain the large smoldering circles a ruddy red and murky brown.

"Show yourselves to me. Come out of your hiding places. I feel your presence. I know your intentions. Reveal yourselves now." Her tone remained the same. Still sweet and angelic but commanding.

Voices rose, shrieking in protest; the thunder boomed louder directly over her head, a constant low one-note counterpoint to her angelic tone. Demons of various rank crawled out of hiding, from the playhouse, from the roof of the main house and greenhouse, from the piles of bricks and boards, from behind trees and every available cover. An army of demons.

Vasilisa continued as if she weren't surrounded by the hideous creatures creeping toward her. "Hear me, pathetic army of Lilith. You cannot have my lifemate. You cannot have Skyler, lifemate to Dimitri. You cannot have any Dragonseeker, though you have been tasked with bringing one to her. You cannot have a royal."

She plunged the blade of her ceremonial sword deep into the

ground. The light should have been extinguished, but it shone through the layers of dirt, ice and snow, once again illuminating brightly as if it were the sun. The moment the blade cut through the soil, more blood bubbled up, and the shrieks intensified.

"This ground is lost to you. This ground is consecrated and is locked to you. Each form is locked to this consecrated earth." She scattered more drops above her head, to the four directions and then onto the ground.

The demons wailed and shrieked. Vasilisa jerked the blade of her sword from the earth and started toward the portal. The five elite demons spread out in front of her about six feet apart from one another, clearly determined that she not reach the portal, or they could have been intent on taking her prisoner.

She was a demon fighter, trained almost from birth, but the elites were difficult to take on, even for her. She gripped the vial of holy water in one hand and levered the point of her sword straight at their eyes. The light coming from the sword was so bright, the shields they wore as protective gear over the sensitive lens of their eyes failed, and it blinded them temporarily.

Afanasiv, Petru, Nicu, Benedek and Zev shimmered for a moment, transparent in the light, and then emerged fully, each in front of one of the elite. Each had their own weapon as they confronted the demon who would stop Vasilisa from sealing the portal.

Vasilisa felt a little guilty leaving the rather large army of demons to the ancient hunters. Aside from the elite demons, so many others had crawled out from every conceivable hiding place and were attempting to get to her before she could close the portal. Fen and Tatijana, as well as Branislava, were fighting the demons.

Dragons were in the air, spraying the demons with their fire. She didn't have the time to look. Not even glance. Vasilisa ran between the fighters with her blue flame, slicing the ankles of the elite demon that Petru had engaged. She dodged the roaring demon's outstretched claw as she weaved between him and the one closest to him.

That demon, the one Afanasiv was in a fierce sword battle with, suddenly clashed his huge broadsword with Afanasiv's and continued the motion as a follow-through, only to drive straight at Vasilisa's stomach. She barely had time to parry the blade away from her. Afanasiv took full advantage of the momentary distraction and drove the tip of his sword into the vulnerable eye of his opponent with enough force that the sword went straight through the skull.

The sight and sounds were horrifying, but Vasilisa refused to look. She took advantage of the opportunity, dodging the staggering demon as he slashed the air with his sword, turning this way and that. Afanasiv kicked him in his armor-plated stomach, and the demon crashed to the ground amid the smoldering circles bubbling with smoke and blood.

Vasilisa found herself on the other side of the fighting and the demons, facing the portal. This one was a gaping hole in the earth, zigzagging for several feet before abruptly coming to an end. It looked very deep. She wished she'd thought to have someone get the things she would need to make certain she closed the portal for good.

When she looked down into the deep, dark hole, countless pairs of glowing red eyes stared up at her with malevolence. She shivered in spite of the fact that they appeared to be some distance from her and not moving toward her. Demon fighter or not, she had a healthy respect for their capabilities.

Tell me what you need to close the portal for good.

Afanasiv. He seemed to always know when she was hesitant and in need. *I can't just close and lock the portal if anyone human is being held prisoner to force compliance with their demands. Who knows what they have done to these families to make them cooperate?*

She wanted there to be a reason other than religious fervor. The Sacred Circle held with many of the same beliefs as the other religions, but they were far stricter when it came to what women could or couldn't do. They demanded that bloodlines stay pure. In their fervor, they evidently thought it was okay to make a pact with the devil to ensure their principles prevailed.

She felt Afanasiv's instant rejection of her hope that Barnabas had taken family members in order to get their cooperation, but all the same, he shed his physical body and, without thought for his own safety, entered the portal before she could protest. Her heart jumped into her throat. Even without his body, he was putting himself in jeopardy.

All around her, the fight raged on between demons and Carpathians. She had no idea how Skyler was faring with Barnabas. She stepped as close as she dared to the opening of the underworld, desperate to guard Afanasiv. For the first time, her hands shook as she held her crystalline sword pointed across the chasm to shed light down into the deep crack.

Stay back, my lady, Afanasiv instructed. *You are a prize they seek. If you are concentrating on me, a demon could sneak up behind you and throw you into the portal. There are demons waiting down here just for such a moment.*

Vasilisa swung her sword around in a circle to ensure no demon dared to come up behind her. The blue flame would cut them down in a moment. The turn took less than half a second, and she couldn't see Afanasiv with her human or Lycan eyes anyway. She was his lifemate, and that was the only way she knew his exact position. He didn't dare put out energy in the hostile environment, which meant he had to examine the steep walls and jagged rocks below for signs of humans or Lycans being held against their will. It seemed to take forever when, in fact, only a minute or two had gone by before her lifemate was back with her.

You can safely close it. If they took anyone, they did not use this portal to bring them through, Afanasiv assured her.

Thank you. Without waiting another moment, Vasilisa poured the hot blue flame along the wound in the earth, running along the opening as she did so. In her other hand was the vial of holy water, and she sprinkled drops of it into the crack. The drops multiplied and became a deluge, raining directly into the long zigzagging fissure.

"Mother Earth, take back this land. Heal the deep laceration with your skills. I invoke the laws older than time. Older than those who would commit such atrocities against all that is good, all that is natural and one with nature."

She ran around the entire crack a second time, shining the blue flame deep into the portal and shaking drops of holy water from the vial into the fissure so that it rained directly down into the dark abyss.

"I close this wound with your aid. I close this portal between the underworld and this realm with your aid. I seal this portal so it can never be used again by anything foul or unnatural. I call on the properties of nourishment. The sun and moon. Water. The elements. Worms. Every living thing needed to supply and enrich the soil."

Demons shrieked at her in madness, redoubling their effort to stop her. The Carpathians refused to give ground, fighting them off, sometimes taking on two or three at a time. They were outnumbered, but it didn't faze them in the least. Afanasiv seemed to be everywhere, keeping a barrier between her and the demons desperate to prevent her from accomplishing her task.

Vasilisa made the run around the large fissure in the ground a third time, pouring the brilliant light into the abyss, along with the drops from the vial as she invoked her mantra. "Mother Earth, I give back to you this scarred region that was taken from you by force. It is precious to you and to us. Let us seal this ground from all who would use it for evil."

The deep crack was closing from the inside, the seams knitting back together as if it were a terrible wound. Soil poured into the ground from the huge piles scattered around to hide the portal from any who might look into the backyard. Between the light, the soil, nutrients Mother Earth provided, and the water, the jagged scar repaired itself rapidly.

As the portal closed, the demons inside either retreated as fast as they could to the underworld or tried to climb out. Vasilisa had already closed the ground to them. There was no saving themselves by making their way into the realm of the human world. They were trapped. Eventually, there were no more places to hide inside the portal, and the blue flames reached where the demons huddled in the shrinking corners of darkness. They burned in the fierce blue-hot flames.

Vasilisa continued to chant and pour water and light into the scarred wound until it was completely closed, and then she turned to join the ancients in the fight. The demon army was particularly vicious and outnumbered them. The Carpathian fighters were methodical and didn't waver in spite of the numbers.

Andros loped out of the forest, a large, graceful fighter, flanked by his brothers. She should have known they would come. The land would call out to them. They were Lycan. Royals. Guardians. They were her brothers. Any one of those things would trigger a call to her siblings, but the combination of those events would have them running to join in the battle.

Andros positioned himself in front of his sister, a move that set her teeth on edge, but she accepted that he would always be her older brother. She was the better fighter when it came to killing demons. All of them knew that, although they didn't understand why. They did readily take any advice she gave to them, and Andros never tried to stop her from going after demons. He seemed to realize it was something she had to do, not to mention he wasn't so egotistical that he would lose an asset when they needed one.

Skyler found herself feeling sick. Very sick. *It feels as if bugs are crawling inside my stomach and eating their way through my skin. It is one of his spells, yet I didn't see his hands move or his lips, either.*

She had to resist wrapping her arms around her middle. There was no stopping the blood draining from her face. As soon as she reported how she was feeling to Razvan, the sensation faded. Barnabas looked shocked. Not only shocked, but admiration mixed with anger flickered in his eyes, telling her Razvan had reversed the spell, and Barnabas felt the bugs eating him from the inside out.

The house began to shake as thunder boomed overhead. Wooden slats were torn from the walls. Beams dropped from the ceiling. Without warning the floor dropped out from under her, and she fell into a hole in the ground. It was extremely deep and narrow, giving her barely enough room for her arms and shoulders. Once down in the hole, she was wedged inside, unable to move. Soil began to pour in on her, burying her alive. She had the sensation of choking to death. Suffocating. Her heart and lungs bursting.

My love, what is wrong? Dimitri was calm. The voice of reason, blowing away the strands of smoke and mirrors. *This mage is tricking you. You are a child of Mother Earth. She welcomes you. You are Carpathian. She heals you. His spell is nonsense, born of desperation.*

Skyler felt a little silly that she had, for one moment, fallen for the mage's spell. Already, Razvan had reversed the spell and dropped Barnabas deep into the ground, deeper even than the mage had dropped Skyler. She was already standing back in the sitting room while the soil poured in on Barnabas.

He will come at you hard when he rises, Razvan said. *Be warned, he will try to attack you in another form.*

Even as Razvan alerted her, dirt and debris spewed into the air like a geyser, and Barnabas rose, taking the shape of a large wolf, the animal rushing straight at her, showing an abundance of teeth. Ivory, Razvan's partner, materialized in front of Skyler, throwing her fur cape to the ground, releasing the wolves that often rode either on the cape or as tattoos on her back. Simultaneously, she drew her bow with the other hand. Her wolves leapt to meet the mage, going for his vulnerable legs and back, using the strength of their Carpathian teeth to bite through bone, hobbling the animal attacking Skyler.

The wolf screamed in anguish and shifted out from under the weight of the wolves as they crushed his spine. Instantly, Ivory called to her wolves, and they leapt on her back, becoming part of her skin as she became vapor and then was gone, fading completely from sight.

Barnabas limped across the room, arms folded across his chest. Once more, he looked very calm, which scared Skyler more than anything.

"Obviously, you are not the only one in this room with me. You have help. I could command them to show themselves, but I have a feeling that spell would not work."

Skyler smiled at him, making certain not to look taunting. She wanted to look as confident as he did. "You're right. The spell would not work."

"I am right. You are not alone."

"Barnabas, I am nowhere near your level of expertise," Skyler assured him. "You are an incredible mage, and quite frankly, I want nothing to do with you. In fact, your very name scares me. I hope that makes you feel better."

"Yet the one aiding you conceals himself or herself as if they are a coward."

She shook her head. "That's beneath you. You assume they have an ego and will come flying out at such a taunt. There was only one reason for me to stand in front of you like this. You're intelligent. You figure it out."

"I do not like riddles." Barnabas sounded impatient and annoyed.

"It isn't a riddle. There is reason behind me standing in this room with you even though it is terrifying. You should know the reason if you're anywhere near as brilliant as I think you are. But being brilliant can also make a person lazy. I've noticed really intelligent people often don't want to put in any time figuring things out."

Barnabas studied her face for what seemed an eternity. "I often teach classes. I like the discussions that take place, but sometimes I find myself bored. I feel as if some generations refuse to think for themselves. Then along comes a student that is different, one who really thinks. Your mind intrigues me. It would be very satisfying to have you in one of my classes for a semester."

Skyler wasn't certain how to take that. She decided she'd treat it as a compliment. She gave him a little half smile. "Thank you. I didn't realize you still taught school. I knew you had in the past, but didn't realize you kept up with it."

"At university level. It keeps me from being bored. I can't spend every waking moment being the mage from hell."

Who knew he had a sense of humor?

He is up to something, Skyler. Never take Barnabas at face value. He isn't a nice man, and he doesn't make small talk idly, Razvan warned.

Rather than laugh at his joke, which she wanted to do, Skyler raised one eyebrow, trying to portray being skeptical. It was Dimitri who laughed. The moment he did, Barnabas struck at him. Skyler felt his triumph, his absolute glee as he closed his hands around Dimitri's neck to strangle him. At the same time, he ordered the demons to attack.

"I may not be able to get to you," Barnabas declared. "But I can get to your lifemate."

Power surged through her. Dark mage power. Dark, dark earth power so old no one could put a name to it. Carpathian ancient power. The power of the Lycan. The *Sange rau*—the mixed blood. The air crackled and snapped with electricity. The hair on their bodies stood straight up and out. The walls of the house bowed out, unable to contain the force.

The windows exploded, the shattered glass bursting outward, stopping in midflight and then reversing. All the pieces slammed into Barnabas's body and buried themselves deep. His face, his chest, his neck and his throat. He screamed, raising his hands in an effort to shield himself, but after the glass came pictures whirling like missiles, hitting him with single-minded force. The walls of the room disintegrated into spears, penetrating his body from all sides, driving the mage first one way and then the next.

"How dare you touch him," Skyler snapped. "You're beneath contempt." She disappeared in a stream of vapor through one of the many shattered windows.

Barnabas had let go of his hold on Dimitri in order to save himself. Hastily extracting his body from the spears, he began to rid himself of the glass when he heard the low laughter. He spun around. The male in the room with him looked familiar and yet not. He was not in the mood for puzzles. Barnabas snapped his fingers, sending the newcomer out to the demons and sure death—only the man didn't move.

"That daughter of mine has a very bad temper when it comes to anyone trying to harm her lifemate," he said.

Barnabas glared at him and tossed several shards of glass his way. The glass stopped in midair and then dropped to the floor. "Who the hell are you?"

"I'm surprised you don't remember me. We are related. Cousins, I believe. When you were being groomed by the three high mages and Anatolie, I was always in the room with you. Whether you were there or not, I was always in the room. While you were learning, I was learning. No one ever thought I would leave that place, so they didn't think to worry about me soaking up every spell. I learned from every high mage. From you. From Anatolie. The worst curse I thought I had was that I could never forget anything. I have since learned it wasn't a curse."

Barnabas slowly dropped his arms to stare in utter shock at Razvan. "You are that girl's father?" He stared out the window as if he could see Skyler in the night air or the fight that raged among Carpathians and demons. He didn't seem in the least to care about the outcome of the fight. "You are Razvan."

"I am."

Barnabas turned back to face him. "How did you escape? Xavier was never going to let you go. You had Dragonseeker blood. He prized that above all else."

Razvan nodded. "He did. I believe he still does. As does Lilith, it seems."

"How is it he could never get the blood he wanted most from you?"

Razvan shrugged. "Why is it he's so set on Dragonseeker blood? Now Lilith is following in his footsteps, or maybe it's the other way around. Lilith most likely wanted the blood first, and that's why Xavier thought it was such an excellent idea. He always did build his best ideas off the backs of others."

Barnabas nodded his agreement, still pulling out glass slivers. "Xavier was so certain that Dragonseeker blood would allow him access to the secrets of the earth. All of the secrets. Lilith convinced him that if they could have the blood running in their veins, the earth would accept them and do anything for them. She's got this beast she wants to control. It's uncontrollable. Not even mage spells work on the thing. She's worried because the gates are breaking down, and she doesn't have control of him. If she loses him and someone else gets control, she loses everything."

Razvan narrowed his eyes, watching Barnabas with a mage's vision. Why was he removing the glass pieces one at a time rather than all at once? That made no sense, not when he could rid his body of all of them quickly. Mages never did anything without a reason. He was disclosing information because he wanted Razvan's attention on the data he was so casually imparting, not on anything else. Mages weren't helpful or casual. Razvan had just told his daughter this very thing. He had been Xavier's prisoner far too long, watching him trick others who thought the mage was their friend, their ally, only to fall as fodder to one of his dark spells. Razvan had seen it all.

There was a distinct pattern to the way Barnabas pulled the glass shards from his body. With each one he tapped the glass first before he tossed it onto the floor. Every third word the mage shifted his body weight from one foot to the other. On the fifth word, he tapped his left foot gently, almost imperceptibly, on the floor. The cadence of his voice was rhythmic, but Barnabas lulled everyone he spoke with into believing his natural speaking voice was low, pleasant and relaxing to listen to.

Razvan began to subtly counter the spell the high mage wove with every word and body movement. He had to keep his every gesture, every motion of his body, so minute it would be undetected by Barnabas.

"This beast you refer to . . ." Razvan trailed off.

"That's the irony." Barnabas sent Razvan a smile that didn't quite hide the cruelty or underlying evil. "He's a demon more vicious and cunning than any other. Nearly indestructible. And do you know where he comes from, Razvan? He was Carpathian. That's the joke. No one can control him, not even Lilith. If he breaks free, he will kill everything— mage, Carpathian, human—everything. No one can stop him."

While he imparted the information almost gleefully, he never broke from his pattern. Razvan continued reversing the spell Barnabas wove. A holding and strangling spell. Razvan recognized it from one of the more deadly spells Xavier had perfected over time. Many young assistants had suffered before he had made actual kills.

Razvan had spent so much time in chains learning to be absolutely still—never moving a muscle, or working on moving one at a time so he wouldn't call attention to himself—that he became extraordinary at it. It was how he exercised even when Xavier kept him nearly drained of blood and so weak he could barely move. He practiced the art of observation. Checking and rechecking details. He forced himself to move each muscle in his body, no matter how much it hurt, until it was second nature to do so.

Razvan knew the spell, but mages often changed a spell to make it their own. With one as deadly as the holding and choking spell, Razvan wasn't about to take chances. Sure enough, Barnabas began to weave added elements into the spell, incorporating the glass shards. It took a moment to realize what the mage's intentions were. Not only was he planning to kill Razvan, but he was including Skyler in his spell.

Razvan took the deviation in stride. He had long ago been made aware of every kind of treachery there was. He wasn't fooled or surprised by it. Barnabas enjoyed hurting women. He liked to lure them in with false kindness and then slowly show his cruelty, conditioning them more and more to his sadistic ways. To have a woman best him at the smallest thing infuriated him. Razvan had felt Barnabas's momentary fear of Skyler's power when she flew into a rage at his attack on her lifemate. She was young and didn't yet have control of all that power, but Barnabas knew that when she did, she would be a force he would want to avoid.

Never had Razvan paid such close attention to any spell as he did to Barnabas's without seeming to.

"That is ironic and a little terrifying. No wonder he is kept locked up if even Lilith is afraid of him. I had heard that a few of the ancients had lived beyond a point of turning vampire, and there was something worse that could happen to them."

Barnabas blinked rapidly, his expression suddenly interested in what Razvan had to say. Even with that interest, he continued weaving his complicated spell. Now that he had introduced even more strands of darkness, he had to be just as careful not to make a mistake.

"I have lived as long as you, or close to it, Razvan. I have heard many things, but until I walked with Xavier in the underworld, I had not heard of this demon-beast. I had no idea this could happen to a Carpathian. There is more than one?"

Razvan cleared his throat twice, the way the assistant mages had done when Xavier had been working out the spell on them. "I have not heard of it happening to others, but I do know several locked themselves away even from other Carpathians, considering themselves too dangerous to be around anyone." He coughed lightly and drew a light film into the room through the open window. "The demolishing of a house puts caustic materials in the air."

Barnabas cleared his throat several times as well. "It is so. Where do these Carpathians secret themselves? Do you know? You seem to be privy to many things." There was a fawning quality to Barnabas's voice.

"The portal has been closed," Razvan announced. "That is one more lost to Lilith. The ground has been consecrated."

Annoyance crossed Barnabas's face. "The royal is busy. I told Lilith she should rid the world of that family, but she wanted to use them. That is what comes of not listening to sound advice. She schemes too much." He coughed. "I do not need to retreat to the underworld. I go only to speak with the high mages."

He coughed and choked, both hands suddenly going to his throat. His eyes widened in horror. "No. You cannot steal my magic. You didn't move or speak."

His voice was strangled, his breathing labored. He tried to pry his fingers from his throat, but they dug into his neck now, actively part of his own chilling demise. He went to his knees, his face swollen and purple. His eyes began to bulge, blood vessels popping. Blood began to trickle from his nose and the corner of his mouth.

Barnabas shook his head over and over. His fingers dug deeper into his throat, helping to choke the life out of him. He fell to the floor and convulsed, but his hands remained locked. The spell remained relentless. Merciless. Crafted by Xavier. Woven by Barnabas to kill Razvan and Skyler. Turned back on him. The spell would never let up until he was dead, the air sucked from his body, and he was dry and withered with nothing left but a shriveled shell.

Razvan stared at him dispassionately. How many lives had this single mage taken over the centuries of his existence? How many cruelties had he performed?

Beside him, Ivory emerged. His lifemate. To Razvan, she was the most beautiful, selfless, wonderful woman who had ever been born. Of course she would come to him when he was witnessing the demise of a cruel mage. He had to stay and see it through to the end. She would not want him to be alone.

"I never thought I would cast a spell of the dark arts."

"You didn't," she assured. "He cast the spell. You simply turned it back on him. Essentially, he did himself in."

Razvan nodded. That didn't lessen the fact that Barnabas had committed far too many atrocities, just as Xavier and his brothers had.

Xavier had used Razvan's body to help commit those atrocities. As he watched the mage slowly and painfully expire, the memories slipped through his mind of those difficult days. Ivory wrapped one slender arm around his waist.

"It is our time, Razvan," she whispered softly.

"Yes, it is," he agreed. "They cannot have any part of me, not as long as I have you."

16

A ndros strode into the study, now turned into the judgment room. He went straight to the six chairs where the five remaining judges sat. He stood in front of them, hands on his hips, blue eyes like twin crystals burning right through the five men.

Grigor and Garald stood at either end of the room in front of the doors, both grim-faced. There were wounds on all three of the royals. Vasilisa had entered with Afanasiv. They stood on either side of Lada, who had walked to the place between the judges and the nine chairs where she had been made to stand while they questioned her.

"What is this?" Stepan demanded from his place in the first row.

Andros slowly turned to face him. "What is this? This is an inquiry, Stepan. A real one. One concerning high treason. Before I ask my questions of those in this room, I want to know where Lada's daughter is. Remember before you answer, I hear lies. My sister and brothers hear lies. If you lie to me even once, I will know you are part of the conspiracy against the royals and all Lycans. You will be put to death immediately. So think very carefully before you make a mistake. It has been a long few days, and I am not in a mood to be trifled with."

He waited. The clock ticked. Outside the wind howled. Someone shifted restlessly in their chair until it creaked in protest.

"Stepan, I asked you a direct question. Where is Lada's daughter?"

Stepan shook his head, glanced at the men facing him in the judges' seats and looked down at his hands. "I don't know, Andros. She was taken from us."

Polina sobbed and hastily covered her mouth with her hands, her eyes downcast.

Vasilisa exchanged a long look with Afanasiv. *Someone on that panel of judges took that child,* she told him. *Maybe more than one of them has knowledge of where she is.*

Easy enough to get the information. Afanasiv didn't really understand why Vasilisa was waiting for her brother to question the group of Lycans. As far as he was concerned, every judge sitting in those five chairs was complicit. He didn't like that an innocent child was involved or that she had been taken from her mother to force her mother to betray Andros.

He scanned the first suspect's mind. He was the one wearing a robe over his clothes. His name was Ira Semenov, and he had lost his wife recently. They had belonged to the Sacred Circle their entire lives. He had recently been asked by Artyom, his close friend, to sit on the council. Ira was certain Artyom had asked him because he'd fallen into such a depression after losing his wife.

Ira had a lot of questions about the new ideas being brought to the Sacred Circle. The ones considered the "old ways" weren't the ways he'd been brought up with, and he considered himself older and very well versed in all things Sacred Circle until recently. He found himself saying and doing things that didn't make sense when he looked back on it later.

The man known as Nikita was inherently cruel. Ira didn't understand why the others didn't seem to see that in him. He acted kind, but he wasn't. Everyone was afraid of him, Ira included. It was just best not to go against him. Every time Ira thought to tell Artyom he wanted to leave the council, Nikita would turn his blazing eyes on him, and Ira would cower like the others and stay silent.

Afanasiv slid out of Ira's mind and into Artyom's. Artyom Morozov was four years older than Ira and somewhat stern. He believed in rules and needed them to navigate through the world. Rules mattered to him. They had made it much easier to understand what he was supposed to do growing up. He didn't have to worry about making mistakes as long as he followed rules. The Sacred Circle made sense to him. Everything he needed to know was laid out in detail for him, from the rules of his marriage to raising his children.

He wasn't a brilliant man by any means. He didn't think for himself. He simply followed the instructions laid out for him. There was no way he could have come up with any kind of conspiracy against the royals, although if the council set new rules for the Sacred Circle, he would follow them blindly.

It wasn't that he was a bad man; he was a weak man. A lazy one, Afanasiv decided. He might be uncomfortable with the way Lada was being questioned, but he went along with it because Nikita and the others decreed she was immoral, although the child was the daughter of her deceased husband. If the others believed she should do as they wished in order to be cleansed, then he believed it, too. The task they asked, to ensnare Andros in marriage, was such a small thing. He was a royal and, as such, should belong to the Sacred Circle. Lada should be punished for not fulfilling that task. If the others thought so, he did as well.

Afanasiv was rather sickened by Artyom's way of thinking. He refused to be responsible for even one small decision. He didn't know where Lada's child was, but he had voted to take the child from her. Disgusted, Afanasiv left his mind.

What happened to the Lycan belief that they are responsible for one another? That they hold women and children close?

There has been a mage working to destroy us, just as Xavier did his best to destroy the Carpathian people and Xayvion worked to bring the Jaguar people to extinction, Vasilisa said. *A few are not all, as you well know, Siv.*

That is true. Forgive me. He voted to take the child from her mother, yet he doesn't want to be held accountable. I find that . . . revolting. The thought of that little girl scared, not understanding what is happening and why she isn't with her mother, infuriates me.

Lada looks so miserable and sad. I know this is breaking Andros' heart. She told him she wouldn't marry him to save him. She didn't tell him about her daughter. It was the first and only time he asked me to read her mind. He said he knew she loved him and wanted to know why she wouldn't accept his marriage proposal.

Afanasiv had known Vasilisa had gone to Lada to console her before she left for home. He also knew she had slipped into her mind to find out why Lada had turned down Andros' proposal of marriage. Vasilisa had been shocked to find out Lada had been given an ultimatum. If she didn't get Andros to propose to her, she would never see her baby daughter again. She had turned him down to save him from whatever the Sacred Circle had in mind. She had already done so much to get her baby girl back, and they hadn't returned her. She didn't believe they would. Andros had put a plan in motion with his family.

Question the one on the end. His name is Grisha Golubev. He is always sweating and smiling. He is young to be on the council. He is a yes man if I ever saw one. He asked me out numerous times, and his mother and father went to Andros twice to ask for my hand in marriage.

Afanasiv didn't have to be told twice. If Andros had been approached twice by Grisha Golubev's parents for Vasilisa's hand in marriage, then he was definitely someone Afanasiv wanted to take a much closer look at.

That's his father, the grinning one sitting beside him, Vasilisa added. *His name is Vovo.* She gave a little shudder. *Even if Grisha had been the nicest man in the world, I wouldn't have married him just because of his parents. His mother is sitting in the front row beside Polina. Her name is Belka. She smiles just like Grisha does. It gives me the creeps.*

Afanasiv slipped easily into Grisha's mind. The man was filled with lewd thoughts of Vasilisa. He was certain he would end up with her. His parents had promised him, and they always came through with their promises. They were getting Andros out of the way. Even if Lada did come through, and Grisha didn't think the woman had a chance in hell of landing the royal, his brilliant parents had already found a way to get rid of Vasilisa's brother. Afanasiv was unfamiliar with some of the visuals in Grisha's mind.

My lady, join me. Ignore his rude ideas of what he would like to do to you. I do not understand what he means by his parents finding a way to get rid of Andros. There is a site where oil can be found, but it isn't one worth pouring money into. Any Lycan would know that.

Vasilisa was too much of a lady to comment on the disgusting visuals Grisha had in his mind when it came to her. She moved right past them and went on to explore the site where the oil had been discovered.

This is an old discovery. It is in the middle of the preserve Dimitri claimed. He had the government inspect it so his permits would be clear. The Golubevs must be the ones who wrote to the government and got them all stirred up again. A government agent, I believe he is an interrogator, Nikolay Sokolov, is staying at the inn with three other agents. Sokolov served with Andros. He mentioned that he thought our family were royals and that many of the people up here followed us. No one would ever say such a thing unless they were trying to get us in trouble. That would be treason. I'm certain Sokolov was sent here to find out if those rumors are true and if there is oil worth collecting.

Grisha didn't send for the agents, Afanasiv said. *Let me check his grinning father. He continues to stare at your brother as if he expects him to fall over in a faint any moment.*

Don't think my brother hasn't noticed. Andros is saving him for last.

Afanasiv entered Vovo Golubev's mind without preamble, sliding in fast. He didn't try to disguise the fact that he was there. He let Vovo feel bees buzzing in his mind as he moved around. Vovo's head came up, and the grin slowly disappeared from his face. A look of alarm replaced that smirk.

"Is something wrong?" Vasilisa asked in an angelic voice. It was the first time she had spoken aloud to anyone in the room, and Andros stopped his interrogation to give her the floor.

She gestured toward Grisha, then Vovo, Belka, and then around the room. "I'm so sorry, I've been so rude not to introduce my husband, Afanasiv Belan Dragonseeker."

There was an audible gasp from the Lycans in the room. She smiled serenely. "He is one of the ancients from the monastery in the Carpathian Mountains. There is little he cannot see or do, so together we make a formidable team to add to the protection of our people. I guarded his soul carefully. It was a shock to my family, but they understand what an honor it is to have him as one of us."

Andros nodded his head, looking more regal than ever. "We hear lies. The land talks to us. The Dragonseeker not only hears lies, the land speaks to him. He is a child of Mother Earth, but he can simply look into your mind to see whether or not you have committed treason. Or stolen a child."

Vasilisa took up the commentary, looking directly at Grisha. "He can read the vile thoughts of a perverted man who would lust after his wife and wish to do rather disgusting things to her. Or he can see into the mind of another man who committed treason by selling out his king to a government agent in order to remove him so there was no obstacle in his son's path to get what he desired most. He could read in a woman's mind that she helped hatch a plot against a sister, another woman and mother, trying to force her to compromise the king by kidnapping her child. The three of you sicken me. You are guilty of treason, and that is punishable by death. I accuse you of this crime against my brother and Lada Belov."

Belka shook her head. "This is lies. All lies. We had nothing to do with such a thing. We would never betray the royal family."

"Belka, do not speak, you only make it worse," Vovo snapped.

"He's correct," Grigor said. "We can hear lies. Everyone in this room can hear them. Siv, please continue with your examination."

"Please find my daughter," Lada pleaded.

Andros put his arm around her. "We'll find her. There are many ways to die, all of them hard. We are Lycans first, and death by silver is an ugly way to die."

"You wouldn't," Vovo protested.

Andros raised an eyebrow. "You chose your own fate. I know every belief of the Sacred Circle. I am not allowed to hold with any religion, but I must respect them. Lycans always come first, as does the guardianship of the land. But your beliefs are sacred to you, and you believe if the transgression is grievous enough, death by silver is the only viable punishment."

Andros sounded perfectly reasonable. Compelling. His voice was one that was calm and soothing. He could stop arguments and persuade an entire army to do his bidding. It was true that the Sacred Circle believed in death by silver if the transgression was immoral.

"You cast your vote to have Dimitri die by silver, Vovo. In fact, you were the primary councilor arguing for him to be hung up in front of the others to suffer in agony solely because you believed him to be of mixed blood. That was his transgression. Not because he had committed treason for personal gain, a far worse crime."

There were murmurs of agreement around the room. Nods. Lada buried her face against Andros' shoulder.

Afanasiv immediately had a feeling of sickness when he entered the remaining judge's mind: Rudlof Drozdov. This was no ordinary Lycan sitting on the council of the Sacred Circle. He had been silent, taking everything in, but he was a big part of the conspiracy against Andros and the other royals. He influenced them by using their beliefs and their vanities, anything that worked to get them to turn on the people who protected them.

He sat silently, contemplating how he could keep Andros—or Afanasiv—from realizing he had anything to do with the plot against the royals. He didn't really believe Afanasiv could read minds. Rudlof was very good at reading body language, and he was certain that was what the ancient Carpathian did. He couldn't possibly have Rudlof's experience in the military or his discipline. No one did. Certainly not the royal family. They indulged themselves at every turn.

He despised freeloaders. Parasites. They didn't deserve to be living in a palace. Living off the backs of the people, not when they threw out family members in need. They looked their people in the eye and lied to them. Acted holier-than-thou and condemned others for the very things they did. Throwing away others who worked hard for them and trusted them.

They were betrayers. Royals. He had nothing but contempt for them. Let them condemn him to death by silver. They would never get what they wanted. Never. The sweetest, most beautiful woman in the world couldn't sway them to do the right thing. How could he? They were evil. They needed to go. To be taken away by the government and put in prison for life. All of them. Even Vasilisa. It was too bad, but she hadn't lifted a finger to help her own flesh and blood.

Afanasiv kept his features like stone, giving nothing away. *Vasilisa, are you sharing my mind? Are you getting any of this? He believes every word. He has utter contempt for all of you. He has gifts, much like Andros. He can use his voice to persuade others, and he has done so. He amplifies what they want and subtly helps them with ideas to get there.*

There was silence. He felt her shock. *He thinks of my aunt Olga. I see her in his mind. They were lovers. He's totally in love with her still.*

I thought you all had a good relationship with her. You had no idea she was consorting with those in the underworld.

I thought we had a good relationship as well, but clearly, she told him we threw her out and she was penniless.

Afanasiv felt her sorrow. She loved her aunt. It was still difficult for her to believe it was the same woman betraying them all. She wanted to hold out hope that someone had cloned her body.

I know that's silly, Siv. Her voice dripped with tears, but outwardly, she appeared serene.

My lady, it is your empathy, that endless compassion, your ability to love the way you do, that makes me marvel. I am in awe that the universe gave me you.

Afanasiv was sincere. He had known the tremendous pull between lifemates because he had witnessed it between Sandu and Adalasia. He hadn't known how Vasilisa would make him feel. He was with her now for some time, most of it sharing her mind. He could see her clearly. He could see into the heart of her. The soul of her.

Stop. I love my aunt. My brothers love my aunt. What she has become? The woman she is now? That woman, I don't know. And, Siv, I feel that same awe that the universe would give you to me.

Right there, that little feedback she gave to him when she didn't have to, was part of the light she shone onto him. She changed him inside for the better.

"Rudlof." Vasilisa spoke gently. "I know that you love my aunt."

"Do not speak of her."

"I must. We love her, too. The things you believe about us, the things she told you about us, they are not true, and I can prove that to you."

Rudlof leapt at her from his seat, a shocking move that was all wolf. One moment he was seated, and the next he was teeth and claws, going straight at Vasilisa. Afanasiv met him in the air, his solid form hitting the fully formed wolf so hard it knocked Rudlof to the floor. Afanasiv went down with him, slamming him back as he tried to bounce up with a roar of rage. Afanasiv caught the thick ropes of silver and bound the struggling wolf tight. He pulled him up by his fur and shoved him against the wall.

"If you ever try to touch her again, I will rip out your throat."

"Is Rudlof part of the conspiracy with the government agents?" Andros asked.

"He influenced the weaker ones, playing on what they wanted for their own gains," Vasilisa said. "He believes we threw Aunt Olga out penniless into the world. He planted the idea into their heads and then sat back and let them run with it."

"Who took Alyona?" Andros demanded. "Belka, I am asking you directly. Who took this three-year-old child away from her mother?"

"She was stolen from the play yard." Belka sobbed, staring at her husband. Her voice had risen to a high-pitched shriek. "They should have watched her closer. They weren't watching her. She was taken."

"Enough, Belka," Vovo snarled. "Stop talking."

Belka clapped her hand over her mouth.

"Vovo, did you take Alyona from the play yard?" Andros asked.

The man narrowed his eyes at him. "Why should I tell you? You have already condemned my family to death by silver. There is no merit in giving you a single word of this child. In fact, I can go to my grave happy that Lada and her family suffer every day wondering where she is."

Lada jammed her fist into her mouth. Andros pulled her closer and leaned down, whispering encouragement to her, and then pressed kisses on her temple.

Afanasiv wasn't in the least bit worried about being dignified as a royal or nice to anyone. He was used to fighting vampires. Evil was evil as far as he was concerned. He entered Vovo's mind with all the finesse of a hard punch, knocking through all barriers and sifting through memories and thoughts fast. Once he found what he was looking for, he passed the information to Vasilisa.

He took the child from the little play set and ran into the forest in wolf form. She was very frightened and screamed, so he kept his hand over her mouth. When she bit him, he slapped her. He ran with her for miles until he came to the middle of Dimitri's preserve. Rudlof waited for him there, and he gave the child to him.

Vasilisa walked right up to Vovo and slapped him hard across the face. "You horrible little toad. You slapped a child because she was terrified and she bit you when you stole her from her mother, and you put your hand on her mouth so she couldn't breathe? Or cry out to her mother or grandmother? You are the most pathetic, horrible excuse for a Lycan I can imagine. I am almost glad you committed treason so I can tell myself you were never one of us."

She turned away from him. "All Lycans are one with the land. With each other. To know that ones such as you exist sickens me."

Afanasiv left behind mirrors reflecting the rot inside him. Vovo could blink several times, but he could never be free of seeing his self-centered life and the sins he'd committed and intended to commit. Afanasiv pulled out of the man's mind, caught the chains of glittering silver and, without a word, caught up the man and his son, one under each arm, and took them out the door and into the forest to one of the oldest trees with thick, sturdy branches.

In spite of the kicking and screaming and both attempting to shift into their wolves, they were stripped and chained with silver hooks so that it could drip into their bodies and kill them slowly. Death by silver was excruciatingly painful to any Lycan. Straight across from the two men, Belka appeared to be hung, as well, so her husband and son could see her painful death. In truth, she was an illusion. Her death had been swift and her body had been incinerated completely. She would not be added to any memorial wall, her name would never be mentioned and the land would not welcome her ashes.

"Polina," Andros said, "I would like you to take Lada into the other room and attend to her wounds. She has several. Before she came home, we cleaned them thoroughly, but she was handled roughly, so the lacerations are deep. The stitches might have opened."

Lada shook her head. "She's my daughter, Andros. I shouldn't leave this to you."

"I want to do this for you," he said, turning her toward her mother. "Please let me do this without you in the room. Some things are not for your eyes."

Polina wrapped her arms around her daughter. "Come with me, Lada. Let them find out what Rudlof knows by whatever means they can. Sometimes it is better to allow them to work without you present."

"In other words," Rudlof said, squirming and struggling against the burn of the silver torture. He panted, his mouth open, gasping for air as he fought for the ability to speak. "They have bound me with silver, and you see how it burns into my flesh. How it torments my wolf. You would feel it if they didn't shield you."

"Lada." Andros framed her face with both hands and looked into her eyes. His voice was very gentle but compelling. "I have asked you to leave the room. Please comply with my wishes."

"Yes, of course, Andros." She brushed her lips against his, feather-light, as if daring to make the move on her own, before allowing her mother to lead her out.

"All others are excused," Andros continued, looking around the room at the practitioners of the Sacred Circle.

"Andros, we had no idea of the conspiracy against you," Stepan said. "We follow the ways of the Sacred Circle, but we are Lycan first."

"I'm aware."

"I would like to stay, if you don't mind," Stepan continued. "I want to know what happened to my granddaughter. It was bad enough to realize that somehow Nikita had allowed demons into our Circle, and they had taken over our minds to the extent we didn't realize they were using us to do their bidding. I have so much to make up to my daughter for."

"She doesn't blame you."

"The conspirators would have used her to harm you and the other royals. That was their goal. I have no idea what the demons wanted with you, but there seemed to be something there, as well," Stepan continued. "To know that I wasn't strong enough to protect my family, the Lycans and the royal family from harm is humbling."

"The man you call Nikita was a mage of great power. He was very well versed in appearing to be a Lycan and a member of the Sacred Circle."

The ancients guarded the surrounding forest in case any demons had been left alive and were in hiding, waiting to attack the unwary. They provided unseen escorts for those going back to their homes, making certain they weren't attacked and taken over.

Andros waited until the room was empty of any others except his family, Afanasiv and Rudlof. "Your time in the chains would be over, Rudlof, unlike the others in this conspiracy, if you cooperated. You may have nudged them on their path, but you believed we were unworthy of leadership. That belief is still in your mind. I can tell you—and you should be able to hear lies—that the woman you trusted is not our aunt and has been corrupted by the high mage and consorts with those in the underworld."

Rudlof erupted into swearing in the Lycan language, spitting his rage at Andros in an insane display. His eyes went from glowing amber to heated red to a mixture of both until he looked like the very devil, his hatred so deep and unbending, his gaze encompassing all of the royals. There was no getting through to him. No reasoning with him. His loathing of the royals was palpable, tangible and so intense that it filled the room and sank into the walls until they breathed with a dark revulsion.

Vasilisa moved closer to Afanasiv. He knew it was an involuntary action on her part. She would have been annoyed at herself had she realized she had done so, but Afanasiv was elated that she had turned to him when the room had grown so hostile. Her sensitive nature felt the hostility and hatred so much more than most would. Afanasiv registered it, but he shut down emotion easily after centuries of no feeling, particularly when it came to treachery and darkness.

How would my aunt be able to get him to believe her to the point he cannot hear her lies, Siv? And Rudlof was always one with a sense of justice. How is it that he cannot even hear us anymore? He shuts down the moment one of us tries to talk to him.

Afanasiv studied the Lycan as Grigor tried next to reach out to the prisoner. The royal appealed to him first as a man and then as a Lycan. He got the same results Andros did—malevolent loathing. This time, the walls rippled and smoldered with animosity. The wolf snarled and snapped with vicious teeth beneath the mask of the man. Was there a shadowing on him? The man or the wolf? A mage shadowing?

Vasilisa, when you look at Rudlof, do you see shading beneath his skin? Or beneath the fur of his wolf?

Her fingers pressed into his arm. He felt each pad of her finger burn her imprint into his muscle and then his bone.

I look at him and only see his deep hatred of us, Siv.

He could tell the escalating feelings Rudlof projected were wearing on her, fraying her nerves. There had to be magic involved. Barnabas was Xaverio's son. He had been born long before Xavier's first-born son. The first children of the triplets had been kept secret from the world of Carpathians. Even then, Xavier had been preparing to wipe out the Carpathian species.

Barnabas had no doubt been influencing those in the Sacred Circle for a long time—years, maybe. He would have taken his time. Been slow and patient. What of Rudlof? Had he been influenced to detest the royals solely through Olga? Or was Barnabas a factor? Rudlof had been at the start of the conspiracy against the royals, and that conspiracy had taken time to grow. It hadn't happened overnight. Or even over weeks. Or months.

Afanasiv continued to watch the Lycan. He was bothered by the silver, constantly moving, which allowed more of the poisonous drops of liquid silver to burn into his pores, but he wasn't screaming in pain or howling in misery. The ancient stepped in front of his lifemate, putting his body solidly between the Lycan and Vasilisa. Something was off. Very off. He was missing a key piece of the puzzle. When it came to Vasilisa's safety, he couldn't afford to miss anything at all.

Once again, he studied the Lycan's expression. The heavy eyebrows betrayed the wolf in him. The snarl showed the sharp mouthful of teeth. Afanasiv's attention returned to Rudlof's eyes. What was different about them? Amber to red. The red ringed the amber at times. Other times, the red ran through the amber and then covered the yellow completely.

"Rudlof, we were friends. We played chess." Garald made his try.

"You came to the palace often in the evenings to talk. You saw that we didn't live extravagantly."

Siv didn't make the mistake of looking away from Rudlof. He wanted to see if the shading he first thought he saw came back when Garald spoke to the Lycan.

"You helped me understand the theory of planning battles after my father was gone. We often clashed over the idea of whether mixed blood could produce the same results in every Lycan, but you were always willing to listen to anything I had to say, even when we disagreed."

The struggle in Rudlof was evident. He was fond of Garald—or had been. The memories were there, and the royal was touching on them, bringing them to the surface. At the same time, there was a trigger—perhaps his voice? Afanasiv tried to figure it out. Rudlof's eyes continued to change from one color to another, and beneath the man's skin was a purplish shading. The wolf would suddenly be present, and he could see beneath the fur that same faint purplish shadow before he slipped back into the skin of the man.

"Rudlof, tell me what happened between us. Why did you stop coming to see me? I went to your home several times and left you notes. Did you get them? I left them pinned to your front door."

There was no compulsion in Garald's voice. He didn't use the royal's compelling tones or in any way try to persuade Rudlof. There was simple sincerity in Garald's questions, from one friend to another. More, from a young man to his mentor.

Rudlof shook his head several times, his glowing eyes fixed on Garald. The wolf's eyes went from amber to yellow and then to the man's eye color of gray. Only his eyes went to a slashing silver as he looked around the room. In the brief perusal, Rudlof took in first Afanasiv and then tried to peer behind him to lock onto Vasilisa. The eyes instantly turned a mixture of red and yellow again. The exchange was so fast, if Afanasiv hadn't been watching so carefully, he would have missed it.

The wolf showed his teeth and made a half-hearted lunge toward Garald. It wasn't near the try he had made for Andros or especially Vasilisa at the very beginning of the conversations with Rudlof.

Even though he is so far gone, are you able to get into his mind? Vasilisa asked.

Afanasiv nodded his head. "It is possible to read what he is unwilling to give on his own. He holds a sliver of the high mage in him. I could not tell if it was Barnabas or his father, Xaviero. It couldn't be Xavier, because Vasilisa closed the ground to him and sealed him in the underworld. Barnabas was killed, but if a sliver of him was planted prior to his death, it would remain. Having said that, I doubt that Barnabas would repeat the mistakes of his uncle. He saw how using even the smallest slivers of themselves could diminish power. Barnabas was about maintaining power. I believe Rudlof has Xaviero in him, just enough to spy when he wishes."

"Vasilisa consecrated the ground. How can he take the information back to the underworld?" Andros asked.

"If I'm correct and it is Xaviero, he is in Rudlof, but he must connect with him to actually use his vision. He did that, but he couldn't sustain that bridge for more than an instant. That means the portal is some distance from here. We have to find it and close it. Not tonight. Vasilisa is exhausted, and the most important thing is to find the child."

"Her name is Alyona," Andros supplied. Instead of talking in his normal compelling voice, he used a tone similar to his younger brother's. He also paced across the room to look out the window into the night, keeping his back to Rudlof.

"Alyona," Afanasiv confirmed.

"How old is she?" Garald asked.

"Three," Andros said. "She's only three."

"Vovo slapped her," Garald informed Rudlof. "You were always so good with children. I know she was much safer in your care. Do you remember the time I was first trying to let my wolf out and father wasn't around? You talked me through it. I was trying to be so brave, but I was very scared. You pretended not to notice that I was shaking. I'll never forget that. I used to think about it and promised myself that I would take the time with my children the way you always did with me."

Rudlof shuddered as if, finally, the silver bindings were getting to him. Afanasiv waved his hand to fade the sensations so the man could better concentrate on Garald's connection with him. They clearly had had a strong relationship in the past. It had been from Garald's childhood.

Afanasiv carefully touched Rudlof's mind. He struggled to hold on to the memories of Garald. Rudlof had no children of his own, and he had regarded Garald as a son. He had been close friends with Garald's parents, the king and queen, before the murders. He often spent time at the palace with them and the children. In his opinion, Garald was often overlooked. He was quieter than his twin. He loved the older weapons, and because Rudlof did as well, they spent hours practicing together until Garald was adept at using them.

"Swords," he whispered. His voice came out a snarl. His eyes wept from the burn behind them.

"Yes, you taught me how to defend myself with a sword," Garald said. "That saved my life more times than I can count."

Why had he stopped responding to Garald's invitation? He had seen his notes asking for games of chess. For more sword lessons. Asking if he needed help with anything. Did he want to go hunting? There were notes pinned to his door indicating that Garald was worried about him.

Rudlof struggled to reach for memories of what he had done with Garald's notes and why he hadn't answered them. The moment he did, his mind was instantly flooded with visions of his lover. The two of them writhing on the bed together. Laughing. Whispering.

"Rudlof, where is Alyona? I know she must be somewhere safe," Garald reiterated. "You would have made certain of that. I'm not at all worried about her, but she should be home with her mother. She's probably frightened. Was she frightened?"

Rudlof frowned. The little girl. She had been scared. He'd done his best to comfort her. Garald was right, though; she did need her mother. "Garald, why would I take a child away from her mother?"

Afanasiv removed the chains of silver altogether and repaired the burns on Rudlof. He was subtle about it, not wanting to draw Rudlof's attention or Xaviero's. He would have to remove the sliver of the high mage and destroy it. To do that, he couldn't allow the mage to know he had caught a glimpse of him.

Andros had been staring out the window. He suddenly stiffened and turned slowly around to face Rudlof. Each of the royals looked toward the door with trepidation.

Petru warned Afanasiv and Vasilisa. *The woman comes with the stench of the demon on her.*

On the heels of the warning, Andros walked right up to Rudlof, uncaring that he was close enough that his enemy could have ripped out his throat.

"Did you give little Alyona to Olga?" This time Andros made it a demand, using his most compelling voice. "I command you to answer me."

Rudlof stared at him in a kind of daze. "I did. I don't know what she did with her. I haven't seen the child since."

PART FIVE

XXI

THE WORLD

The outer door opened and closed. Then the door to the study was flung open, and Olga waltzed in. She wore a crimson button-down-the-front dress that clung to her thin figure. Her hair was pulled back in a long, high ponytail. A crimson headband emphasized the paleness of her face. She looked unhealthy, even anemic.

She sauntered up to Rudlof, her hips swaying. "I see you met my wolfie boy," Olga greeted him, patting his cheek. "He's very sweet, although a bit boring. He does whatever I ask, don't you, wolfie?"

"Can the crap," Andros snapped. "Where's Alyona?"

Olga jutted out one hip and put her hand on it. "I don't think that's any way to talk to your elders, Andros. Or to get what you want. I'm here to negotiate for her return. The terms won't even hurt you in the least. You'll probably thank me."

Andros just stared at her with a look that promised her he would happily end her existence.

Vasilisa intervened. "What is it you want in return for Alyona?"

Afanasiv watched Olga closely. There was no doubt in his mind that Xaviero had informed her they were interrogating Rudlof and would uncover the fact that he had given the child to Olga. It was just a matter of time before they would have that information. Olga had come at once.

She smiled at Vasilisa. When she did, Afanasiv noted that her gums were receding and that her teeth appeared sharper and a shade stained. She turned her head to include Siv in her smile. She gestured toward him. "I want him in exchange for the child. His blood in my veins. Perhaps a child of my own with him. And he has to agree to return to Lilith and stay as long as she requires him to be with her."

Vasilisa raised an eyebrow. "You believe I would hand my husband over to you first and then to Lilith?"

"You were taught that sharing is a good thing, weren't you, Vasi?" Olga taunted. "You wouldn't want that little girl to be fed to the demons, would you? That could happen very easily."

"Olga," Rudlof interrupted. "You don't mean that. She doesn't mean that. She would never hurt a child."

Olga placed her sharp crimson nails on his face and deliberately raked down, scoring four long furrows. She laughed as blood welled up. "You always did love my claws, wolfie. Do you love them now? That horrid little child is worthless to me if Vasilisa stands in the way of my negotiations. She will have to bear the child's death on her conscience for the rest of her life, which will be very long, I'm told. That's nearly as delicious as taking her man from her. She's such a bleeding heart."

"Aunt Olga, why are you doing this? I don't understand," Grigor said. "We were always close. You loved Mom and Dad. You loved us. How could you turn on us?"

Olga's face twisted into an ugly mask, one Afanasiv thought revealed the real woman. "You're supposed to be the royals who know everything about the land, about your people, yet you couldn't see what was right in front of your face. I played my part on the greatest stage there is. My sister *stole* Vasili from me. He wanted me, but Bronya just couldn't let me be happy. She was so jealous of my dancing. Men flocked to me, and she wanted the attention for herself."

Vasilisa shook her head but expressed her denial only to Afanasiv. *That's not so, Siv. My mother loved her. My father loved my mother. I never felt jealousy from my mother. She was proud of Olga's dancing. She always spoke of her with pride.*

Let her talk, my lady. And remember, this is not the woman you loved.

I am beginning to worry that I didn't know my aunt at all.

Afanasiv was certain none of her family really knew their aunt. When he looked at her, he didn't see a woman who had been compromised by a mage or influenced by one the way Rudlof had been. He had been in the world far too long and fought too many battles with evil. He knew rot when it came from the inside out. She had been ripe for corruption. She would have run toward it, wanting every advantage.

Do not respond, Vasilisa, no matter what she says to slander your mother. Your brothers need to hear for themselves what and who she really is. So does Rudlof. He is not an evil man. He has been twisted by mage magic, and I do not believe it was easy for them to do it.

It wasn't Vasilisa who responded to Olga's accusations; it was Grigor.

"Seriously, Aunt Olga? What the hell are you talking about? Our mother was never jealous of you. She admired you and took pride in your accomplishments."

Olga's face darkened with fury. She clenched her fists so tight her nails pierced her palms. "Lies. Those are lies. She reveled in the accident that took away my dancing. She taunted me every chance she had. She made certain to destroy my friendships, especially with Vasili. She pulled away from him, and I tried to comfort him, but she wouldn't even allow us to be friends. She didn't want him anymore, but no one else could have him. She didn't care if he was miserable."

"That's a lie," Andros snapped. "They loved each other. You know they did. If anyone was jealous, clearly it was you or you wouldn't be talking like that."

Olga's harsh laughter seemed to reverberate through the room. The longer Afanasiv looked at her, the more her features began to change subtly. Her perfect complexion was no longer as smooth as it had been.

There were blotches, dark smudges appearing and creases showing around her mouth and eyes. Her eyes appeared to sink in just a little bit.

"How would you know?" She sneered. "You believed everything I said to you. How do you think those men got into the palace that night? How do you think they knew where to find your parents? My precious sister died, but she gave up her secrets to me. Vasilisa carried the soul of a Carpathian male. Of course she did."

She glared at Vasilisa, looking as if she might leap on her and rip out her heart. "You," she accused. "Just like your mother. Everything going to you that should have gone to me. He should have been mine. The Dragonseeker should have been mine." She all but screamed the last.

Afanasiv could feel the shock in the room. Vasilisa and her brothers had never expected Olga to confess to being part of the conspiracy to kill their parents.

"You fought to save us," Garald said. "We saw you."

"Yes, I was so heroic." Olga tossed her head. "That ensured I was always going to be revered by you and everyone else. It was simply a matter of you rounding up the conspirators and killing them quickly before anyone could figure out who allowed them into the palace." She studied her fingernails with a malicious smile.

Grigor stepped toward her, but Andros caught his arm to hold him in place. Grigor tried to shake off his hand. "Didn't you hear what she just admitted to? She was behind our parents being murdered. She let those men into the palace and showed them the secret room."

"So she claims." Andros sneered at his aunt, pure contempt on his face. "Anyone can say anything, Grigor. You must learn that and not believe everything. She wants us to believe she despised our mother, and yet how many years did we have with her showing just the opposite? Either this woman is an impostor, or she is lying to us now. I doubt she has Alyona or even knows where she is."

Olga's dark brows drew together, and her lips drew back in what should have been a Lycan's snarl. Her mouthful of teeth was definitely longer and sharper.

Afanasiv's radar went off. *Brothers, something is wrong other than Olga having traded her soul. She is part demon. I feel that in her. Something foul has taken hold of her. Come into the room to aid me in containing whatever it is she is host to. You must use as little energy as possible.*

"You dare to talk about me that way, Andros? I took that little hellion, and you won't get her back unless Vasilisa meets my terms. There will be no negotiations. Either she wishes to save the child or she wants her dead." She glared at the royal, her eyes twin pits of red-and-yellow malevolence. A small bit of saliva dripped from the corner of her mouth. She didn't seem to notice.

Vasilisa, move behind me and continue all the way to the other side of the room. Do it casually, but get closer to Andros, where you can defend him.

Is she going to attack him?

I fear she might. He didn't know what Olga's intentions were, but she seemed so confident. He had to believe Xaviero had seen who was in the room and had sent Olga in to confront them. They knew Afanasiv was capable of taking Olga's memories from her just as he had Rudlof's. Why was she so certain she had the upper hand? He had allowed her to taunt the royals, and Andros had even helped, but other than catching that she was hosting another, he hadn't yet solved the puzzle.

Vasilisa sighed. "Andros, please stay calm. I know you're upset over Alyona, but accusing Aunt Olga of lying isn't going to help the situation." As she spoke, she looked directly at Andros, turning her back on Olga and walking to him.

As Vasilisa moved past Afanasiv, her body skimmed his. Feather-light. Every nerve ending in his body was on heightened alert and completely aware of her. The chemistry between them felt sizzling. Explosive. Electricity seemed to arc from Vasilisa to him, tiny little forks of what looked like white lightning crackling just for that brief moment, jumping between them.

An ancient symbol blazed hot on Afanasiv's skin, the one he'd been born with, his birthright. A fiery dragon worn on his body, coming alive for his woman in a brief display of bonding with wings spread. As she moved by, the talons gripped, and a long, hot river of fire emerged in a steady stream before the dragon subsided.

Few things shocked the ancient, but the fact that his woman had awakened the protection of his dragon, and the dragon had displayed a warning given thus far only when a vampire was near, managed to do just that.

There is a possibility that she is part vampire or managed to bring a vampire unseen into this house, he cautioned his brethren. *The women are in another part of the house. Olga's claim of despising the royals rings true to me. She might be spiteful enough to have Lada killed while Andros is trying to locate the child.*

He wove a shield of protection around each of the royals, beginning with Vasilisa. He included Rudlof once he managed a good defensive block above, below and from either side of all of them.

Petru, add your safeguards to mine. There is mage in Olga and she feels too confident. Over the years, we changed much of our safeguards so a mage could not so easily bring them down. Two of us working together should make the shield far too strong for any harm to come to them.

Benedek is with the women. He is uneasy. They have no awareness of him. The house feels foul to him.

Where is Nicu? Afanasiv was really concerned now. He stepped back from Olga deliberately. He had her full attention already, and he wanted whatever she was to see that he was ready to do battle.

He is adding his safeguards to mine to protect the women here, Benedek assured him. *Then he will begin to search through the house to find what is hidden.*

Olga stomped over to Afanasiv. "Don't even look at her," she hissed.

He gave her a cool, arrogant stare. "What makes you think even if Vasilisa should say she would give me to you that I would agree? We are lifemates. You cannot break the soul bond."

A sly look came over Olga's face as she turned her head to stare with venom at Vasilisa. "This is about the child. You care, Carpathian, and you have already displayed a self-sacrificing trait, so no doubt you will do whatever is needed to get this horrid child returned."

His warning system went off again, the dragon blazing with fire, wings extended as the steady stream of fire poured from the muzzle before the small birthmark subsided. Where was the danger coming from? He felt it all around him, but that cunning look of Olga's and the way she said "self-sacrificing" reminded him of Lilith's taunting in those days following his parents' death.

Vasilisa, do not respond for any reason. There is a trap here, and I believe it is one with wordplay. He and his father had been so careful of every word and how it could be interpreted in the contract with Lilith. A lifemate bond could not be broken, but he had a code of honor, and it was well known to Lilith. *The brethren are here and will protect your family if anything goes wrong. I am going to attempt to access her mind to see if she really does know where the child is.*

Wait. Vasilisa stopped him. *They would be expecting you to do that. If they know you can just take the information, they would be prepared for that move.*

Afanasiv had to concede that she was right. He would have done so already had he not wanted to observe Olga. The moment she'd walked in with such supreme confidence, he'd felt something was definitely off.

What are you thinking, sívamet? I have to try before she attacks Andros. She's building up to it.

We should do it together. Or I should be the one to try. They wouldn't expect that. You most likely are the trigger to the trap.

He didn't like the idea of Vasilisa taking any chances. He wasn't about to let her into Olga's rotting brain.

Something else resides within her. I will merge with Petru, and they will be unable to feel my presence or his. You, I think they would notice immediately. He included his brethren in his assessment.

Let us do this, then, Petru agreed.

Afanasiv didn't wait, merging with the other ancient. Petru had a light touch. Afanasiv had known him for centuries, and in that time, he had learned many things about the other ancient. He was lightning fast, decisive, a brilliant strategist; he was intrigued with weapons as they were invented and used throughout the ages, so he always became an expert at using them.

The moment Petru slipped into Olga's mind, it was evident she was not alone. Both Petru and Afanasiv had been on the earth for far too long. Both had souls that were scarred deeply, which meant they fought their own demons, ones that would rival the beast locked behind the gates in the underworld. Still, it was the first time either had ever encountered a live host being used as a Trojan horse.

Petru and Afanasiv began to swiftly move through Olga's memories in an effort to find where she had taken the child. They didn't look at any of the newer retentions; that would come after they found what they needed the most if there was time. There was no saving Olga even if they wanted to. There was little of her left. She had willingly traded her wolf, her royal blood, everything she was, for the promise of becoming immortal. For the promise of having every dream she ever wanted. She had sought out Lilith, calling on her night after night, until finally Barnabas had come to her to aid her in bringing the royals to Lilith in a "fair" exchange.

There was the moment when Rudlof brought her Alyona. The little Lycan child fought back, tooth and nail, refusing to go with any of the captors quietly. The moment Rudlof was out of Olga's sight, she had beaten the little girl until she was quiet. Olga took her to the old abandoned oil field and tossed her down one of the larger boreholes, knowing the little body would be coated with oil and dirt, and most likely she would die there.

Petru and Siv hurried back to the most recent memories to see just how the army of demons and vampires had been planted in Olga's body, since they'd never seen such a thing. Xavier, the high mage, was the one most Carpathians were familiar with. He had run a school when they believed mages and Carpathians were allies and friends. No one was aware he was plotting to exterminate the entire Carpathian species. Nor were they aware he was one of triplets. His brother, Xaviero, Barnabas's father, had been tasked with wiping out the Lycan species. The third triplet and the only one left alive, Xayvion, had, for all intents and purposes, brought the Jaguar species to the brink of extinction.

There had been a growing concern for some time that it was Xayvion who was the most powerful of the three brothers. He never seemed to have anything to prove. He was rarely seen. He slipped away when he assessed the danger as being too high. Xayvion seemed to create his own spells from painstaking trial and error, while his brothers often piggybacked their spells on the foundation of their brightest students—students they eventually murdered.

This spell had been created by Xayvion. Had anyone told Afanasiv it was possible to do what the high mage had done, he would have said they were living in a fantasy world. He had shrunk living vampires and demons until they were shadows, and placed them inside Olga's body. The vampires had never been in the underworld. The demons had been caught aboveground when Vasilisa had consecrated the soil, and they could not return to the underworld.

What does Xayvion want? Petru asked, pushing the query into Afanasiv's mind so gently and softly, Siv nearly missed it.

Olga would be programmed to acquire what the mage was after. So would the army waiting inside her for the word to emerge into battle.

We need to count them anyway, Siv said. *We both have demons within us. Mine is dark and thoroughly entrenched in me, and if one of them feels my presence, he will only see me as another demon. I do have my lifemate as my anchor.* He was essentially asking Petru if he could embrace his demon and not fall after so many centuries of honor.

I would not leave you to defend your lifemate when I have given my word to you. Adalasia told me my lifemate is alive. She would never lie. In any case, I ensured that she did not. You know I can hear lies. I would not betray my lifemate after waiting so long for her.

Petru wore the oath to his woman carved into his back. As before, he didn't hesitate once they made up their minds. They counted the shadows planted in Olga's body. At least six vampires and as many demons. Petru moved through her body a second time to ensure they didn't miss any of the shadows clinging to bone, muscle or organs. Two more vampires were revealed.

There must be guidance. One in charge. In her brain, whispering orders. Afanasiv was certain they would find a tiny shadow watching the royals, making certain that Olga did exactly what Xayvion needed her to do.

A splinter, then. Like Rudlof carries in him, Petru agreed.

Rudlof does not have a splinter of Xayvion. If there is one in Rudlof, it is no doubt Xaviero. He is locked in the underworld. This is getting to be very, very dangerous, Petru. I believe Xayvion has his sights set on annihilating the Lycans, as he did the Jaguars. To do that, he must remove the royals. All of them. He has gathered them here in one place. He has an army waiting to take them out. We need to see what his plan is.

Afanasiv was grateful Petru was with him. If there was one ancient who was excellent at strategizing, it was Petru. It was not going to be an easy task to find that sliver in the folds of the brain and slip into it without detection. The only way they could know how the mage planned to kill the royals and wipe out the Lycans was to access his brain. He wasn't actually present at all times in the sliver he had placed in Olga. That would require too much energy to span the distance, but the small piece of himself allowed him to use her sight. He could hear. He could instruct her. Ensure she carried out his orders. He was a powerful mage, and there was no doubt that he could kill given the right circumstances. But it was a two-way path. That sliver of Xayvion, the tiny slice of himself he had planted in Olga's brain, was a direct path to the mage's mind.

There were telltale colonies of microscopic parasites around Olga's organs and quite a few wiggling in her veins. Her heart wasn't blackened as of yet, but it was shadowed, already discolored.

My lady, you know where the child is? You know the army of vampires and demons you will face when word is given for them to attack?

Petru had begun the search for the tiny bump amid the folds and crevices that made up each quadrant of the brain. Afanasiv wanted to make certain that Vasilisa understood what they were facing just in case something went wrong. Xayvion was extremely dangerous and powerful, but Siv and Petru were betting their lives it would never occur to the mage that anyone would be so foolish as to try to access his memories, using his sliver as a portal while he was using it as well.

Yes. She sounded tense. *Siv, don't do it. You have enough information. We can fight them off. We know he wants to kill us all, and he's brought his army to do it.*

Afanasiv had an uneasy feeling that what was inside Olga was only the opening salvo. If this was really the opening gambit to Xayvion's scheme to wipe out the Lycans, there had to be more. A lot more.

Dimitri, reach out to Fen and Zev. Call in everyone close. Have the wolves search. Read the land. I believe there are more vampires and demons hunting us and any Lycans they can find this night. Vasilisa, have one of your brothers send the warning to your people to beware, to arm themselves.

One of us would have to be outside to send a message that would be heard throughout our entire territory.

Find a way without triggering Olga into action.

That will be difficult. She is snarling and going from wolf to woman and railing against us as if we treated her like garbage the entire time she was with us. None of what she is saying is the truth, Siv. None of it.

She is not Olga. She is a Trojan horse with an army of the enemy inside her, waiting for the signal to get out and murder the royals. That includes you, sívamet. All of you must be prepared to fight for your lives.

We have been doing so since we were very young. My mother began my instruction in the art of fighting demons when I was a toddler.

There was confidence in her voice, but he could still feel her fear for him. She was very opposed to the two ancients making an attempt to turn the tables on Xayvion. He sent her reassurance and continued inspecting every fold, looking for the slightest anomaly. Surprisingly, it didn't take them long to find the tiny bump nestled in a crevice of Olga's occipital lobe. The occipital lobe was located at the back of the skull behind the temporal lobe. The occipital lobe had been their first choice to search because it would allow Xayvion to use Olga's vision and also, through the temporal lobe, hear what was being said.

Now would be a good time to create a diversion, one that has Xayvion watching you closely and trying to keep all of you in sight. Try not to trigger Olga, but one of you slip out and warn the Lycans of the possibility of vampires or demons or even humans being used to try to wipe out as many families as possible. Then get back inside as quickly as possible before Olga notices one of you gone.

Benedek interrupted. *Tell me which royal will leave the room, and I will duplicate him. The women are hidden and protected. I can aid you.*

Vasilisa swamped Afanasiv with warmth, and then she spoke to her brothers. *Grigor, you are closest to the door. Benedek will cast an illusion that you are here with us. Slip out and warn our people.*

The room is small to fight adequately, Petru observed. *All of the royals could slip out and we could duplicate them.*

Afanasiv had already considered that possibility. His every instinct told him the mage had thought of that likelihood and had somehow prepared for it. *I think he would know. One, if there is chaos for a moment, he wouldn't feel the difference, especially if Benedek gets weight and feeling exact.* He added the last as a caution to his brother from the monastery.

"Olga, I don't understand you." Vasilisa took a step toward her aunt. "I really don't. You've become so belligerent toward all of us for no reason at all. When did your animosity start? When we were just children? If you really did hate our mother, if she really was that awful to you, and I'm in no way conceding that she was, how could you extend her behavior to us? We all adored you. We put you up on a pedestal. You know we did."

As she spoke, she let her voice go from calm to that edge of anger. The walls of the room expanded and contracted. The floor beneath their feet undulated, the boards creaking and moaning in protest. Vasilisa didn't seem to notice as she took another step toward Olga. Her eyes changed dramatically, becoming a deep blue that seemed to pierce right through her aunt like twin lasers. Her dark hair, the mass of silk that had appeared to be tamed, was suddenly wild, crackling with energy, tendrils rising into the air around her head like antennae.

She appeared so threatening that Olga took a step back, her hands coming up, fingers curling defensively. Fur broke out on the backs of her arms and hands, and her immaculate crimson nails appeared to be hooks that could rend and tear. She snarled and growled in warning.

"Why would you hate us so much when we were just children and couldn't possibly know how our mother treated you?" Vasilisa demanded. "We *loved* you. We loved you before our parents were killed and even more after. How could you not feel that from us?"

Olga tossed her head and then shook it over and over, the growls still rumbling in her throat. As Vasilisa became more belligerent toward Olga, the building reacted to her anger. She was clearly trying to keep it under control, pacing back and forth. The walls continued to breathe in and out. The floor undulated as if a seismic event were occurring. Pieces of plaster fell from the ceiling so that it rained white powder and chunks of mortar.

"Vasi, take a breath, you're losing control," Andros ordered, backing away from his sister, his hands up defensively.

Rudlof cringed away from both Olga and Vasilisa, his movements distracting now that he found he was without silver chains holding him prisoner. He rushed first toward one corner of the room, hands over his head, and then to the other, back and forth, agitated by the way the house appeared to have come alive and was shaking to pieces.

"Why don't you tell *her* she's losing control," Vasilisa demanded, swinging around to confront Andros. Even pacing and throwing her arms wildly into the air, she kept her body solidly between Olga and the ruling king.

It was now or never. Afanasiv had to admire his lifemate. As a diversion, it was perfect. The chaos she created was believable. Benedek had cast the illusion of Grigor pressed up against the far wall between the door and window. The window bulged outward and his head swiveled between watching it and his sister. With Rudlof so agitated and scuddling back and forth, his bulk continuously blocked the royal from Olga's sight, just giving flashes of him.

Petru and Afanasiv waited until they felt the presence of the high mage. The activity drew him, as they were certain it would. He tried to sort out what he was seeing. Tried to force Olga to face in the direction he wanted her to go. She growled continuously and kept shaking her head, which rocked him and gave him very little in the way of assessing the room.

Petru and Afanasiv drifted into the sliver and straight into the open mind of Xayvion. He was so occupied with trying to control his crumbling Trojan horse that he had no chance of feeling their careful entry. It had never occurred to him that he was vulnerable to an attack—or that anyone would be foolish enough to try such an audacious venture. He hadn't erected safeguards.

They had to be very careful as they sorted through his mind, looking through his memories for the purpose behind his need of Dragonseeker blood and his plan for wiping out the Lycan species. Afanasiv caught the first hint of Xayvion studying Xavier as he repeatedly tried experiments with Rhiannon's blood. She was Dragonseeker, a woman he had taken prisoner and had three children by. Each time he took her blood, her blood changed properties. Xavier became furious at the phenomenon. The same thing happened when he took the blood from his children and then his children's children. No matter how he managed to get Dragonseeker blood, the blood changed properties before he could experiment on it—as if it were alive.

Xayvion was fascinated by the idea that the blood recognized an enemy. What else did it do? Were all Dragonseekers children of Mother Earth? Lycans used the ground's warning system to talk to one another, but it wasn't the same thing. Carpathians were rejuvenated in the soil and considered the earth to be healing and a part of them, but that wasn't the same thing, either. A "child" of Mother Earth would be healed by her in a different way, one Xayvion had heard rumors of but hadn't witnessed. He wanted to experiment.

In his mind, there were a number of experiments he wanted to try with a Dragonseeker. He wanted to see how the ground reacted to a wounded child of Mother Earth. He believed that once he could duplicate the blood, he could trick Mother Earth into accepting him as her child, and he would gain even more power. He also felt he could draw a female to him.

He had the Dragonseekers in one place. He believed the women held great power, maybe more so than the males. His idea was to acquire a pair. Skyler would be the perfect prize. There was such power in her, although she had not quite come into her own. The male he wanted was Afanasiv, because he was truly an ancient, and his power was beyond imagining. To control him, he would have to keep Vasilisa alive. That meant not killing all the royals, but studying her, which would yield helpful ways to draw the Lycans back who had left their country.

He knew the royals were the glue that held the Lycans together. No one spoke of them, but they protected their people from demons and vampires and worked to keep them in the modern world. Destroying the Jaguar species had been far easier. The royals actually served their people, and it wasn't easy to turn them against one another.

Lycans had left their homeland to live in other parts of the world. They were loyal to their species and to the royals, but they were spread throughout other countries. That meant finding a way to get them to return. Xayvion had come up with a three-pronged attack. Kill the royals and as many Lycan *families* as possible, leaving no witnesses other than a child or two this night. Those witnesses would speak of Carpathians coming in the dead of night to murder parents and siblings.

Members of the Sacred Circle that Barnabas had gotten to in the various chapters would come forward to add their voices of condemnation to those of the orphaned children. The royals would be killed this night, with the exception of Vasilisa. He needed her alive for his plan to work. He intended for Olga to subdue her right before the wretched woman burst like a ripe fruit, spilling his army into the room to kill the other royals.

The Lycans living abroad would return swiftly to defend their homeland from the Carpathians. By capturing Vasilisa, he would ensure they would come—all of them. They would need the one remaining royal, and they would do anything to get her back. All of them would believe the elders in the Sacred Circle, and they would go to war with the Carpathians.

By bringing in the government agents, making them believe the old oil field was a gold mine and the royals were committing treason, he had hoped to keep the ruling family occupied while he put his army in place. Unfortunately, Xavier, Barnabas and Lilith had no patience. None. Xavier never had.

Lilith was ridiculous thinking she could control the demon behind the gates with Dragonseeker blood. She couldn't control the Dragonseeker. She wasn't clever. But Xayvion had listened carefully to her wailing about how she had lost him, and she had this contract. Xayvion had studied the wording of the contract. He realized Afanasiv had stayed true to his word, never violating it.

Olga just had to get Vasilisa to say she would "lend" her lifemate or "give" her lifemate for the child's whereabouts. Her wording was important. The Dragonseeker could be tricked into giving his word of honor, as well. Once that was accomplished, the pair belonged to Xayvion. They would have to do whatever he said, including keep the blood from changing while he experimented on it.

The two ancients had been in the high mage's mind for far too long. He fascinated Afanasiv. He was a brilliant man. His mind had actually thought out the logistics of such a plan and put it in steps and then put the plan into action. He had taken his time, seeing to every detail, uncaring that time passed by. Time meant nothing to him.

Vasilisa, stay away from Olga. Antagonize her so she does that head shaking again.

Afanasiv didn't send the thought to his lifemate. He built the images in his head, knowing a small part of her had remained merged with him.

"You say our mother stole our father away from you." Vasilisa whirled around, her white fur swirling gracefully around her ankles. "You come here thinking to steal another woman's man from her. *My* man. It seems to me that you are the thief."

More of the ceiling fell, so that white powder eddied around them like a snowstorm. Olga's face turned so red it was purple. She coughed. Her snout elongated. She shook her head back and forth, her snarls and growls rumbling louder and louder in warning.

"You admit to stealing our parents' lives. You stole a child from her mother. You tried to steal Rudlof's dignity and pride. Perhaps the only way you can get a man is to steal one or to use spells on them until they don't know who they are anymore."

"Vasilisa." Andros snapped her name like a command. "Stop this at once. I need to know where little Alyona is." He put his hand on his sister's arm and drew her behind him protectively. It put him in a very vulnerable position. "Olga, please forgive Vasilisa. She's distraught over the revelations you've disclosed. Hearing you say you never loved us has really shaken her. When she was a child, she followed you everywhere, do you remember that? Please tell me where the little one is."

There was no stopping Olga. She was furious. Enraged beyond all comprehension. Her eyes went bright red. Glowing. Fangs dripped long strings of venomous saliva. Her body contorted as her wolf tried to emerge in order to set upon those she considered her mortal enemies. She was so far gone she could no longer form words.

Petru and Afanasiv slipped out of the high mage's mind and made their way quickly out of Olga's unstable brain. Just before they made their exit, both turned at the same time and took aim at the sliver of Xayvion. He was trying to force the command out of Olga to trigger his army to burst out of her. Using white-hot energy, they concentrated the attack like a laser point, aiming ruthlessly at the tiny bump.

Olga shrieked with an agony of torment and horror as the pain in her head exploded. Xayvion roared his command to her, forcing obedience with magic as he retreated, leaving the tiny sliver of himself to die under the ferocity of the Carpathian light. Olga's body twisted and knotted, her flesh pushing out in different directions, stretching as if she were made of rubber. Blood burst from her pores as her skin cracked open. Claws and talons grasped at the seams of the broken flesh and tore from the inside out. Blood poured onto the floor. Olga's body was shredded to pieces as dark shapes began to emerge.

Petru and Afanasiv placed their bodies squarely between the royals and the emerging army. *Get outside, into the open, sívamet. Get your brothers outside.*

The room was far too small, and with so many inside, the blood on the floor making it slippery to take a step, the enemy would have the advantage getting to the royals. The stench was unbearable—a foul smell permeating the air.

Garald managed to get the door open, grabbed Rudlof by the front of his shirt and thrust him outside. Andros all but shoved his sister out the door, following her closely. Grigor moved up to her side and Garald took her other side.

Once in the open, the royals spread out, giving each other room while still being close enough to protect one another.

The wind rose to a fever pitch, howling as it raced toward them, coming down the mountain in a rush of bitter cold. Dark clouds rolled and pitched, black and then gray in an angry boiling mix of icy mist. Lightning veined underneath the edges of the clouds, strobing the dark sky with brief flashes of white-hot energy. A few yards away, the forest seemed alive, thick tree branches beating the air wildly, needles flying like tiny spears in all directions as the wind hit from first one direction and then another.

Afanasiv positioned himself close to his lifemate. "Six demons coming at us from the house. They look to be elites. There are eight vampires. At least three could be master vampires. Xayvion wouldn't have placed lesser vampires who were unable to protect their masters. He wants a decisive victory."

Andros gave a short, brisk nod, acknowledging the information as he tore off his clothes, allowing his wolf freedom. His sister and Garald were the best at fighting demons. Grigor and he would help the ancients with the vampires.

"They want your deaths above all others," Afanasiv reminded him.

Vasilisa drew her sword from beneath her coat. Garald took her back, his sword raised high. They kept their gazes fixed on the large figures with the horns on their heads as they came stomping out of the house, looking like giant bulls standing upright on back legs. At once, the red, glowing eyes locked on the two royals. The demons snorted and stamped their cloven hooves. Gray smoke streamed out of the wide nostrils. They lowered their heads and charged.

Behind the demons came the vampires, hissing and spreading out the moment they were out of the house, taking to the air, going in different directions. Afanasiv kept his attention on them as they burst from the structure, trying to dull their images, still disoriented from being small shadows locked inside Olga. He waited to lock on to one of the master vampires.

The lesser vampires coming out first were to provide distraction so their masters could escape all discovery. The masters waited, hidden, having no idea that the ancients and royals knew anything of their numbers or plans.

As the lesser vampires flew at the royals shrieking, trying to encircle them, Fen and Zev materialized out of the air, slamming their fists deep into the chests of the two vampires closest to Andros and ripping out their hearts. Lightning forked across the sky and slammed down to incinerate the two hearts, immediately jumping to the bodies of the two vampires before they even fell from the sky to the ground.

One lesser vampire had managed to get above Garald and had started his descent, teeth and claws out, his speed increasing as he got closer to the royal. Garald's attention was fully occupied with the demons bearing down on him. The vampire ran full force into a barrier, impaling his chest on wicked talons that drove right through muscle and bone and fastened around his heart. Shrieking, he backpedaled, pulling away, using his hands to tear at the barrier. By pulling away, he assisted in the extraction of his heart. Razvan tossed the heart away from the vampire into the air, right into a jagged vein of lightning. The streak of white-hot energy forked to include the vampire's rotting body, incinerating both body and heart.

The wind shrieked and moaned a warning. The ground beneath their feet shivered, lifted and settled.

"More come," Vasilisa cautioned.

Afanasiv felt the warning coming from both the earth and the wind. They knew Xayvion had assembled an army to attack the Lycans, and this was his night to wipe out as many as possible in one fast raid. Still, he waited without revealing himself. The masters would come like bloated spiders, waiting until chaos took all attention and they could safely exit the house. It mattered little to them that the pawns they'd brought to serve them were being destroyed; more were coming. More would take their place. Xayvion had promised he would provide many vampires to surround the masters to serve them.

The fourth and fifth lesser vampires rushed the king of the Lycans, desperate to get at him. Any who could claim to have killed a royal would be richly rewarded by the high mage. Unlike either of his brothers, Xayvion seemed to keep his word.

Andros had stepped out of the protective circle, a large dark wolf with ice-blue eyes attempting to draw as much danger as possible away from his sister and brother. Both were more vulnerable in their human form. Six feet from him was Grigor, a tall, broad-shouldered wolf with powerful muscles and the same ice-blue eyes.

The vampires came at them, chanting, swaying, doing their best to distract and mesmerize as they approached the wolves. Andros and Grigor allowed them to come closer before they sprang at the two vampires with the incredible speed of a Lycan. The vampires simply took to the air, certain they could get above the wolves and then drop down on them to rip their heads from their shoulders. Lycans could leap incredible distances, but few knew of their abilities unless they had reason to know. The vampires found themselves with jaws that felt like steel clamped around their legs and claws tearing into their chests, digging for their hearts before they'd even been torn from the skies and brought back to earth.

The wolves dragged the vampires to the ground, ignoring the black acid pouring over their muzzles as they held them down while they tried to drag the hearts out of the chests. Vampires and demons rushed from all directions of the forest, bearing down on the group. Andros and Grigor didn't stop. They continued ripping at the chests of the two lesser vampires until they managed to extract the hearts.

Vasi. Andros tossed the heart high. Grigor did the same.

Vasilisa used the blue flame from her sword to incinerate the hearts and then turned the hot flames on the vampire bodies as her brothers sprang away. Choosing two of the vampires closest to their siblings, Andros and Grigor rushed toward them, angling away from Vasilisa and Garald.

Vasilisa turned her attention fully onto the approaching elite demons. There were only so many places on one of these thick-chested, armor-plated demons where one could kill them. Still, they couldn't take the blazing light of her crystalline sword any better than the vampires could. As the lowered heads with the sharpened horns of the demons closed in on her, she waited until the last possible second. Garald never flinched, although he was facing three of the demons, and he could feel the heat of the putrid breath on his face. He waited for his sister to take control.

The blazing light of the crystalline sword turned night into day, as if the sun had suddenly switched places with the moon in the night sky. It was just for a split second that the elite demons were completely disoriented, blinded by the light. They tried skidding to a halt, dust and snow thrown up as their hooves fought for traction.

Garald stepped forward, his sword stabbing deep into the eye of one while his smaller dagger found the eye of the second demon. As he pulled the sword free, he kept the movement continuous, slicing the head from first one and then the second. He danced closer to the third as it righted itself, shaking its massive head. His sword swung under the head, coming up through the throat. The demon jerked its head high off the blade before it could do any real damage. Garald had anticipated the move, having fought the elite on a number of occasions with his sister. As his opponent jerked upward freeing the blade, Garald turned in an elegant, almost ballet move, the sword going up and over, slicing cleanly through the back of the neck, removing the head.

Vasilisa blinded the demons with the blazing light from her sword as their foul breath reached her. The moment they seemed confused, trying to pull up, clearly unable to see, she stabbed deep, one eye after another, with blinding speed. The moment she did, she used the burning hot blade to remove the heads of all three elite demons. Glancing over her shoulder, she saw that her brother had dropped the demons charging him. Together, they moved out and away from the house and circle of protection the hidden ancients provided in order to better protect their brothers from the demons rushing from the forest.

Afanasiv felt his heart nearly stop. *Sívamet. Stay close to me. The master vampires will be exiting. I must stay here in order to stop them.*

This is what I do, Siv. Just as you fight vampires, I fight demons. These are my brothers, my people. Trust in my abilities.

For one terrible moment, Afanasiv fought with himself not to use his considerable powers to force obedience. He couldn't be in two places at one time. Most master vampires had gotten to be in that position because they had fought and killed many hunters. They'd learned how to use lesser vampires as pawns to tire the hunter or wound him and make him vulnerable. Over the centuries, they had acquired battle strategy. Depending on the age and experience of a master vampire, they could be quite deadly to fight.

Splinters of wood on the doorjamb shriveled and peeled off, smoking and falling to the snow in tiny specks of blackened ash. One master slithered across the snow in the wake of the demons attacking the royals.

I do not recognize him, Afanasiv said to his brethren.

I will take him, Benedek announced. *I have run into him before. He calls himself Slayer of Hunters.*

He launched himself straight at the master vampire, full speed, much like a missile. At the last moment, as the master vampire was certain he had made an escape without being seen, Benedek materialized in front of him, slamming his fist deep through the chest wall. His momentum and the speed the master vampire was using to depart aided him in going through the thin armor plate he had encountered before when fighting the vampire.

His fingers closed around the heart. Slayer of Hunters instantly went on the attack, driving his own fist into Benedek's chest, seeking his heart. Simultaneously, the vampire leaned into the ancient hunter and ripped at his throat with serrated spiked teeth. Rich Carpathian blood welled up, spilled from the torn throat down to his chest. Instantly, the vampire inhaled the scent of the blood and began frantically licking with a snakelike tongue. Starved of blood from being shrunken and left for too long, the vampire tried gulping the rare treat. The blood would make him strong. It was rich and hot. He hadn't had Carpathian blood in a century.

Benedek ripped the heart from Slayer of Hunters' chest and flung it on the ground, calling down the lightning as he did so. The master vampire jerked at Benedek's heart, but it was too late for him. He was still partially distracted by the rich blood that he barely noticed until the white-hot flash came that his heart was gone. Shrieking, he threw himself at his heart, trying to get to it before the jagged bolt of lightning reached it. He was too late. The blinding light hit the heart and leapt to the vampire.

The second master vampire had crawled up the doorjamb to cling to the side of the structure as Benedek attacked Slayer of Hunters. He went very still to hide himself. As the vampire and Benedek fought, he hurried up to the rooftop and lay flat, peering over the side to see how Slayer of Hunters fared. He began to back away, slithering like a crab on the roof, when he caught the scent of the rich, hot Carpathian blood. The droplets seemed to float in the air to him. Starved, he hesitated, torn between self-preservation and the terrible need to feed on the amazing and rare treat of ancient Carpathian blood.

Petru stalked the master vampire, hovering just above him. It was very clear Xayvion hadn't realized what being inside his Trojan horse for so long would do to his demons and vampires. It was his first time using this spell, and he hadn't considered the vampires would be weak and not just craving blood but starving for it.

Before Petru struck, the vampire crawled forward again and peered over the roof at Benedek, who seemed to stagger as he turned toward Vasilisa and Garald. He was slow closing his wounds, as if he had been severely injured and it was taking far more strength than he had anticipated. The master vampire growled his appreciation, looked around carefully at the chaos happening below and sniffed the air one more time. The overpowering scent of the ancient blood was too hard to resist. He floated to the ground to stand just out of reach of the hunter.

"You seem to be having trouble healing your wounds, Benedek. Perhaps I can aid you." The sly malice in his voice matched the hideous putrid vapor pouring out of his mouth. The discolored gas appeared green against the white backdrop of Vasilisa's sword's light. The vampire threw up a cloak to shield his body from the brightness, but his eyes wept continuously.

Benedek narrowed his gaze and took a half step to the side to avoid the vapor. His hands dropped from his wounds as he faced the vampire. "Baird. How good of you to worry about me, but I think I can manage. It is best if you seek justice elsewhere this night. In all fairness, I can see that you have been deprived of blood for some time and are too weak to give me any kind of real challenge."

Baird licked at his lips. From the corners of his mouth, tiny parasites wiggled free and dropped to the ground.

"Hunters care nothing for fairness in battle. What is wrong, Benedek?" Baird sent another stream of poisonous vapor toward the ancient. Baird began to sway slightly, inching closer, beginning to drool.

"Actually, Baird," Benedek said. "Nothing at all. I believe your mistake was trusting the mage and all his promises. It sounded like a good idea, didn't it? But mages have a way of making things sound good, especially when you are the one taking all the chances."

Baird's eye twitched, or it could have been the parasites that had begun to crawl over his face. Several had made it to his eyebrow, and two had gotten caught in the sunken sockets. He halted his forward momentum, suddenly suspicious. Something struck him hard in the back. He choked, trying to shape-shift. The fist drove through skin, bones and muscles, tearing everything in its path to reach his heart.

"No, no, no." Where were his servants? Why had he taken such a foolish chance? He was so weak, and the blood he needed was only a few steps away from him. Snarling, he drew back his lips to reveal his teeth, his every intention to fly at Benedek and take what he needed by force.

Benedek began healing the terrible wounds in his neck and chest, all the while watching him with that same impassive, merciless look on his face. If Benedek was in front of him, who had impaled him? Who had wrapped their fingers around his heart and relentlessly dragged it from his body?

Baird shrieked and wailed as he spun around, spewing the poisonous vapor every which way in the hope of getting a direct hit on the hunter behind him. Another ancient. He didn't have time to remember his name; the bolt of lightning was leaving the clouds and slamming into the heart the large Carpathian had flung into the air. Baird tried to crawl away, but without his heart, nothing worked right. The flash was dazzling as the white-hot energy enveloped him, reducing him to ash.

Afanasiv kept his gaze fixed on the third master vampire making his break at the same time as the first two. He recognized him immediately, not from looks but from his movements, although he appeared slow and stiff. At one time, centuries earlier, Gazsi had been considered a legendary Carpathian hunter. He had been a good friend to Prince Vladimer. When the hunters were asked to leave the Carpathian Mountains, Gazsi had done so willingly, and he'd been an efficient destroyer of the undead.

Afanasiv heard the rumors that he had turned. A hunter such as Gazsi had many battles under his belt. He'd also exchanged blood with other hunters when he was wounded. The first thing he'd done was track those hunters through his blood bond and kill them. More than once, Afanasiv had run across his kills and had begun tracking him only to have to break off in order to save a village from a hoard of newly made starving vampires killing everyone in sight. Gazsi became famous for his sacrifices of villages and pawns.

Gazsi started out of the house but was far more careful than the other two master vampires. He wasn't looking at the demons rushing the royals or the Lycans battling the lesser vampires. He stuck his head out the door and sniffed the air. Instead of stepping outside, he remained inside but stretched his neck as he stood cautiously, continuously testing the air. The entire time, his eyes moved restlessly over the battlefield, ensuring that every royal was occupied. It was clear he was uneasy. He extended one foot out the door, his hands grasping the doorjamb in preparation of launching himself skyward.

As Benedek revealed himself to Slayer of Hunters, Gazsi was back inside. Afanasiv knew the other ancients had sealed the windows and doors in an effort to force the army hidden inside the Trojan horse to exit out the back door.

You are certain the women are protected? Afanasiv said.

Gazsi had been a smart hunter. He hadn't lost that intelligence when he chose to give up his soul. If anything, he had become even more cunning. He might feel the safeguards the ancients had woven around the women. If he did, was it possible he would be able to reverse them and use the women as hostages or for the blood he was starving for?

They are, Benedek assured him.

There was no arrogance in Benedek, but it was impossible not to believe him. He was that confident, even while battling Slayer of Hunters.

Even with the reassurance, Afanasiv drifted close to the house, ignoring Petru as he circled to the side of the structure to follow the progress of the one called Baird. Afanasiv's prey was Gazsi, and he couldn't take anything for granted when it came to the master vampire.

Afanasiv assessed the things Gazsi would need for his continual survival. He would be methodical about getting everything in place. He didn't need to be outside fighting the royals or the Lycans. He didn't have anything to prove to anyone. He didn't care about anyone but himself. He would sacrifice anyone to stay alive. He would stay in the house as long as it took for him to feel it was safe enough to leave. In the meantime, he would see to his needs.

Gazsi would search for food, anything to make him stronger. That would be a priority. Benedek could weave the strongest safeguards, and they would keep a vampire out, but a master vampire might be able to compel someone to come to him. The safeguards normally weren't woven to keep someone prisoner. That meant he would call someone to him.

Lycans weren't easily beguiled or tricked, but everyone inside had belonged to the Sacred Circle, including those who worked there. Barnabas had worked for years to get key members to undermine the royals using his insidious preying on their innermost desires. The weaker ones had eventually caved, believing themselves above reproach. If any inside still had ties to Barnabas even after he had been destroyed, Gazsi very well could persuade them to come out of their safeguarded hiding place.

Afanasiv drifted back into the house on a slight wind. He needed every sense, but the stench in the room where the Trojan horse had exploded, expelling Xayvion's army, was overpowering. He shut down all emotion as he had been doing for more time than he had ever had feelings. The moment he did, the demon rose in him, eager to do battle. It was that darkness that aided him now. Darkness called to darkness.

He was aware instantly of Gazsi gliding through the next room, not as graceful as he normally might be. Afanasiv listened to the footsteps. The master vampire wasn't wasting precious energy on flying or trying to camouflage his appearance.

"Aw, now I know where you are. I can smell you."

Afanasiv heard the quiet chuckle in the vampire's voice and he passed through the open archway to catch a glimpse of Gazsi hurrying around a corner.

"Lycans have too much wolf in them to try to hide from anyone with a nose," the vampire went on in a singsong voice. The voice was very compelling. "Come to me, feed me. Be my servant. I can give you immortal life. Come to me now."

Afanasiv circled in front of the master vampire to find the hiding place in the kitchen where the woman who served the family for years had secreted herself in a small space in the wall. Benedek had woven safeguards to keep any vampires out, but the woman could easily walk right through them if she wanted to step back into the kitchen.

Very carefully, Afanasiv threw up a second safeguard, this one blocking the vampire's voice and ensuring the weave prevented the woman from going to anyone evil.

Vasilisa, visualize the woman who works for Lada.

As he waited for her response, he caught a glimpse of her determinedly sprinting toward a small army of demons and vampires as they rushed toward Andros and Grigor. Behind the demons and vampires poured an army of Lycans. Even while he was merged with Vasilisa, several Lycans leapt on the vampires and tore at their chests or backs. Others lifted demons and slammed them over their knees to break their backs. Andros' people had come to protect the royals.

Vasilisa sent him a detailed picture of the woman hidden behind the panel in the kitchen. He cast the illusion over his body, taking the older woman's appearance. *Thank you, my lady. It would please me if you would come back into the yard.*

I am certain it would. Behind the laughter, there was a grim note.

Gazsi was in the kitchen, sniffing at the walls and waving his hands in a revealing spell. He would know that an ancient would think to safeguard any Lycan or human remaining in the house. Gazsi didn't appear as disoriented as the other two master vampires had, but he was weak and very aware of it. He watched his back trail even as he systematically went over each wall, trying to find the hidden room, coax out his prey with his sweet, persuasive voice, or find the right combination of words to reveal woven safeguards. He couldn't keep up his appearance, something all master vampires took great pride in.

He neared the wall where the woman hid in the small room. Afanasiv didn't move, waiting patiently as Gazsi lifted his hands once more and murmured his revealing spell. At once a barricade that looked much like a tapestry of woven threads appeared. The threads blazed with life spinning around one another in various hues.

"There you are," Gazsi said aloud. "Why do you hide from me?" His voice sounded sweeter than ever. "I will give you everything you ever wanted. Come to me. You know you want to be with me."

The tapestry swayed, although there was no wind. Gazsi's smirk widened. "That's right, my lovely. You know me. They do not treat you right here. You should not work for them. Others would work for you.

They would bow before your beauty. Come to me. Whisper your name to me. Just take one small step. One foot in front of the other."

The tapestry swayed again, the threads blazing with colors of protest this time. A woman's low moan could be heard. There was a distinct creak. Behind the tapestry, a crack appeared in the wall as if a door slowly inched open.

"That's it, my dear. Come to me. You must come to me yourself. One foot in front of the other," Gazsi instructed in his mesmerizing voice.

He nearly danced with glee but kept himself under control, staring at the tapestry of safeguards as it fought to warn the woman to stay behind it. A foot inched past the fluttering threads, and then, with infinite slowness, she appeared. She looked to be about sixty, but with Lycans, it was impossible to tell age. They had longevity, so she could have been much older. Her hair was dark with a few silver threads that seemed to take on the glow of the threads in the tapestry. She kept her head down, arms crossed over her chest, and trembled continuously. It was very clear from her body language that she didn't want to obey his voice, but she couldn't stop herself.

Gazsi was careful not to leap on her, but the need was there on his face. His once handsome features were gray and lined with cracks. Those seams had tiny wiggling parasites nestled in them. The creatures were as gray and gaunt as their host but were now awakened at the sight of prey coming toward them.

She halted, one hand braced on the door to her hiding spot, the other looking as if it clutched the tapestry to keep from moving forward. She looked up slowly, horrified, giving Gazsi even more satisfaction. She didn't look at him but at the center of his chest, where his clothes hung on his thin frame.

"Ah, my dear, you are so perfectly delicious, everything I could have wanted or needed." He used his voice and beckoned to her with his long, bony fingers. "Come to me now, all the way, let go of the door." The last was nothing short of a command, so much so that the boom of his voice broke through his sweet beckoning. "Tell me your name."

The woman swallowed nervously but then licked her lips, making them glisten. They weren't pale at all, they were red. Bright against the olive of her skin tone. "Maria," she whispered.

Gazsi's eyes glowed. He held himself in check, so close to victory. One step. That was all that was required, and then she would be his. "Maria, come to me now."

The woman let go of the door and tapestry, obeying the hypnotic, compelling voice as all his victims inevitably did. The battle raged outside, and he didn't care in the least who was winning. He was starved, and this woman was the key to everything—to getting him to full strength and allowing him to leave while the others engaged the Lycans.

Maria kept her head down as she stepped into his open arms. He inhaled her scent. She smelled like Lycan under all that human form. That would give him extra strength. Her heart . . . Gazsi frowned.

"Is something wrong?" Maria asked. "Perhaps you were expecting my heart to be pounding out of control. You want adrenaline in my bloodstream. It would give you such a rush."

She lifted her head finally to stare him straight in the eyes. Her eyes were strangely colored. Blue and then green, the colors swirling and changing rapidly. Gazsi stared, trying to place those eyes. There were only a few people in the world he had come across with those eyes. They mesmerized him.

She moved. It seemed a subtle movement. One arm, the muscles rippling, came alive, the arm not that of a woman but a man. He gasped and hunched as pain exploded through him and his glowing eyes filled with hate.

"Hunter," he hissed, his voice now high-pitched. "You are Dragon-seeker."

Afanasiv gave up all pretense of the illusion of docile Maria. He ripped the heart from the shocked vampire. Clamping his fist around the heart, he streaked through the house toward the back door, calling the lightning as he did so. The heart pulsed and burned, spewing black acid desperate to get back to its master. As he reached the door, it slammed closed, nearly hitting him in the face.

Vines erupted from the floor to wrap around Afanasiv's legs. He'd encountered such vines before, the hooks poisonous as they sank into flesh, holding the hunter nearly paralyzed and unable to shift shapes while the vampires rushed in for the kill. He waved his hand, and the hungry vines burst into flames.

There was no dropping the heart into the flames using the vines as fuel. The wizened organ would never incinerate before the master vampire had gotten to it. Now the heart was tearing at his palm in a frenzy to get back to Gazsi.

"I will burn this house down around you, hunter. There are Lycans here. They think to hide from me, but they cannot. Give me what is mine and I will go quietly."

The vines collapsed back to the floor they'd been made from. The flooring now appeared twisted and scarred. The blood from Olga's body no longer stained the flooring. Instead, there were blackened blemishes on the wood, like wounds.

"Vampires are ever the deceivers." Afanasiv circled back around to the wider part of the room, where he could lead the vampire away from where the mage might have lingering power to aid one of his chosen army.

"And hunters are not? I heard of your contract with Lilith. She told Olga, and the mage heard everything. You did not fulfill your contract."

Gazsi followed Afanasiv slowly, trying to cut him off but not succeeding. That confirmed that the vampire had his ability to work his spells, but his physical body was too much energy to maintain without an infusion of blood. Had Xayvion been watching, he would have learned quite a bit from his experiment.

Afanasiv would have felt guilty had he spoken with anyone about the contract he had made with Lilith, but the other Carpathians, men of honor, had assured him following the contract to the letter was what was expected of him, even with an enemy such as Lilith. His parents hadn't made it out of the underworld, but Lilith's side of the contract hadn't specified the conditions of their health. Technically, Afanasiv had killed his father by ripping out his heart. Lilith hadn't done that. He had made the pact with his father and followed through, even though it was the most difficult thing he'd ever done. He had welcomed losing his emotions after that.

What are you doing? I'm making my way back to you. Stay near the door.

Was there a little bit of panic in his confident lady's mind? *I am an ancient hunter, sívamet,* he soothed. *I need a larger space. Have no worries, I know how to kill a vampire after all these centuries.*

He tried to keep a shield between them in his mind—not because he feared she couldn't take the battle with a vampire, but he disliked her seeing the way the demon in him embraced the battle.

I need to know you are all right, Siv.

Again, there was that note of anxiety. Part of him was happy for it, another part mystified. *Vasilisa, you wanted me to have faith in your abilities. Why are you questioning mine?* That made no sense to him.

I can't touch you.

From out of the walls, more vines attacked. Several dropped from the ceiling, trying to form a cage around him. He couldn't shift to mist, not with the vampire's heart attempting to chew through his palm. Using his free hand, he countered, reversing the direction of the vines back onto the vampire.

Snarling in frustration, Gazsi blocked the wooden vines he'd created as they snapped greedily at him and tried to sink hooks into his body. Afanasiv continued to backtrack through the house, staying off the floors and away from the walls. He didn't get too far ahead of Gazsi, not wanting him to attempt to lure anyone else out of their hidden safe room as a hostage to trade for the shrunken heart.

We are merged, my lady, and yet I can sense you are apprehensive.

The next room was exactly what he was looking for. Oval-shaped. Large. Empty. A fireplace with a good-sized chimney. His dragon had been glowing on his side, a warning that the vampire was near. He hovered close to the fireplace, turned slightly so the dragon faced the firebox with an iron grate on the floor of it. A few logs were piled up, ready to be set on fire. The ashes were already cleaned out for the night. The dragon glowed bright for the briefest of moments, casting a shadow on the opposite wall. Then the fiery red-orange light was gone as the mythical creature traveled up past the damper to the smoke chamber and out into the night.

I feel the vampire's gathering power. He is starving. He is also aware the Lycans have arrived in force to protect us. He knows the plan was somehow thwarted, but he doesn't know how.

Afanasiv didn't like the idea that Vasilisa was anywhere near Gazsi's mind. It was as rotten as the heart he held in his hand. If the vampire sensed she was there, he could show her things that would sicken her. She would never be able to get them out of her mind. The best healers would not be able to aid her.

How do you know these things? You cannot touch his mind, Vasilisa.

Petru and Benedek removed the splinter of Xaviero from Rudlof. Once they were able to destroy the sliver before it found another host, they questioned Rudlof. Lycans put our species first as a rule. Rudlof knows all of those within the Sacred Circle involved in the conspiracy to murder us. He also was connected with the vampire through Xaviero. That sliver was meant to command Rudlof and spy. That gave Xayvion two sets of eyes. Through Rudlof, all Lycans can feel the master vampire's hatred of you and his need to get at your blood.

Afanasiv sent her reassurance. *Have no worries.*

You are Dragonseeker, Siv. They all seem to have this idea about Dragon-seekers. They think you are magic. That the earth will respond in ways to you that it will not to even the Lycan. We are guardians of the earth. I can't help but be afraid for you.

His woman. She had courage. She also thought she needed to protect him, because he must be delusional thinking that a Dragon-seeker could have a stronger connection to the earth than a Lycan. She heard the rumors and legends of ancients and how powerful they were, but he shielded her from just how dangerous he was. Mostly, he did so because he had crossed over to a place where the darkness would al-ways be a part of him, and he didn't want his woman to ever doubt him.

Afanasiv knew Vasilisa was someone who needed to feel in control. She was a warrior, and she had been raised to believe her purpose was the protection of others. He didn't want to take away her belief that she was his equal in power, or even that she might have more power than he did simply because she was both Carpathian and Lycan. What he was about to do would change things. She would know who her lifemate was.

"You are trapped, ancient one. Give me my heart. There is nowhere for you to go." Once more, Gazsi tried using his voice on Afanasiv to compel him to obey.

Light burst through the firebox as the dragon dropped through the chimney and landed on the iron grate, still flapping wings in a fierce display. Outside, thunder rolled and then boomed so loud it shook the house. Gazsi looked nervously out the window to the roiling clouds. Lightning lit up the dark skies, but instead of jagged bolts or forked rods, the white-hot electricity appeared in the shape of a dragon streak-ing toward earth.

Gazsi looked from the fierce dragon in the sky to the tiny glowing one rearing back on two legs, wings flapping as it turned its blue eyes, now swirling with a deep emerald green. He burst into a cackle, point-ing to the small mythical creature.

Without preamble, Afanasiv tossed the heart right to the dragon. Grasping the heart in its talons, the dragon was gone, disappearing up the chimney.

Outside, the fierce dragon made of lightning flicked its tail to send spears of the white-hot energy sizzling across the sky. Screaming, Gazsi watched as the tiny dragon tossed the heart up toward the fierce dragon. Instantly, a stream of fire burst from the huge dragon in the sky, incinerating the vampire's heart. Simultaneously, Gazsi leapt toward the window, reaching up as if he could stop the fire from reaching his heart. Very slowly, his body crumpled and broke apart, spewing insects and acid onto the tiled floor.

Outside the house, the wind howled just as loud as the wolves as they descended on the demons and vampires.

That was . . . Vasilisa hesitated, searching for the right words. *Incredible. Truly incredible.*

A ndros thrust open the door to the Wolf's Retreat, Vasilisa right behind him. There was an urgency to their entry, and those inside turned slowly, one by one, stopping conversations to stare at the two of them. Lycans shared a common pathway. They knew what had transpired this night—a plot to murder the royals and to kill as many Lycans as possible and blame it on the Carpathians. To protect the royals from the speculation from outsiders, those inside the inn were willing to go to any lengths.

Andros held up his hand and Kendal shut off the music. "A child was kidnapped several days ago, and we have been searching for her. A credible anonymous tip has come in that she was thrown into one of the many wellbores in the old oil field. She was alive at the time she was tossed inside. The odds are against her being alive now, but if there's the slightest chance, we have to find her. I need volunteers. It's a big field with quite a few old wellbores."

"Dimitri has organized the search by mapping out the field in grids," Vasilisa added. "We need as many people as possible."

The Carpathians were already searching. All of them. Lycans could feel the earth talking, but down that deep, possibly covered in oil, she doubted if any of them would even hear a whisper. But the Dragonseekers—children of the earth—that might be different. Hopefully, it would be.

The reaction to the call for help was instantaneous. The Lycans in the inn immediately rose, abandoning drinks and food to gather coats. Andros and Vasilisa turned to follow them out.

"Andros, wait." Nikolay Sokolov, the government agent Vasilisa had spoken with, hurried to him. "My friends and I will help you find this child. We might not know the area, but we can search as well as anyone else." He gestured to the other three men who had come up behind him.

Andros' clothes were covered in dirt, blood and rips. It was easy to see he had been in a fight of some kind. He nodded his head. "All help is gratefully accepted, Nikolay. Alyona is my fiancé's daughter. She's only three. We must go. There's a slim chance she's still alive."

Vasilisa knew if the child still lived, it was because she was Lycan. That was the "slim chance" Andros was talking about. She knew he was feeling crazy inside. He was broadcasting his distress so loud she was certain the Lycans could feel it the way she did. He didn't want to be at the inn, he wanted to be at the oil field looking for Alyona. He had to protect the government agents.

Part of the three-pronged attack on the Lycans was to have the government people murdered and Andros and his family implicated so there would be an investigation. Again, Xayvion counted on those he controlled in the Sacred Circle to come forward and tell the investigators Andros had declared himself a king.

They expected an attack on the government agents before the night was over. Andros and Vasilisa were the bodyguards for the four men. They knew Sokolov would want to come with them. He'd been told the oil fields were producing and he would want the chance to be able to inspect the fields without appearing to do so. He would also be in the confines of a vehicle with Andros on the ride to the fields. That meant he could ask questions while trying to appear friendly and casual.

They rushed outside to the waiting vehicle. The engine was still running, and the moment everyone was seated, Andros tapped the driver, the signal to go. The narrow, little used trails were barely open, but that didn't deter their driver from going at breakneck speed. Around them, other vehicles followed. Most of the Lycans had disappeared into the forest already, shifting to make the run fast. They could cut through the forest and get there much quicker than those in cars.

Nikolay glanced uneasily out the window, although he couldn't see much. Dark clouds blotted out the moon, and the cold seemed to just get colder. "You're certain your driver can see to drive at this speed through the trees?"

"Good reflexes," Andros said. He allowed his gaze to slide over the government agent as if really seeing him for the first time. "You've come for a visit at a hell of a time."

"What's going on, my friend?"

Vasilisa thought Nikolay looked as friendly as a tiger.

Andros frowned and rubbed his temples. "It's been a nightmare. There's a belief system here among some people based on old traditions and very strict codes that date back, it feels like, to the beginning of time. I made an enemy out of them because I testified against the son of one of the members. The man had attacked a woman outside the inn. I wasn't the only one that heard her scream. Four of us testified against him. That was a good two years ago, maybe longer. I guess they've been holding a grudge."

"Why would they take a child?"

"My fiancé wasn't married when Alyona was conceived. As I said, this particular sect is very old-fashioned and wanted to punish her. He was Sacred Circle. I am not. They ambushed me when I tried to get to Lada. It's been hell, Nikolay." He leaned forward to look to the driver. "Do you need help driving, Klim? I can switch places."

Vasilisa put a gentle hand on his arm. "He'll get us there. The search has already started. At least you managed to get a tip that might pay off." Her voice was soothing.

"I probably should have turned down your offer," Andros continued. "I believe these people are going to try to kill me again. At least when I was interro—" He broke off and changed his wording. "Speaking with several of those involved in the conspiracy, it seemed as though this sect was very determined to kill me and the other three men who testified against one of their own. They also believe in hanging traitors in trees with hooks in them until they die. Anyone who speaks of their beliefs or talks to outsiders about their plans is considered a traitor."

"Andros," Vasilisa spoke softly, one hand going to her throat. "When your friend first introduced himself to me, he mentioned that old rumor, the one about our family being royalty and ruling over people."

Andros groaned and shook his head. "Nikolay would never fall for that. We still can't afford to fix that old place up. Half of it is modern, the other half needs to be torn down." He looked directly at his friend. "What brings you up this way?"

"A letter, Andros, and now I'm very disturbed, as well." There was speculation in Nikolay's voice. He slid his hand inside his coat and loosened his gun. "The letter said you called yourself king and people here worshiped you. They said you were drilling for oil and selling it privately. I was sent to investigate."

"And we're taking them to the oil field to find the child that was tossed down a wellbore," Vasilisa whispered. She turned on the seat, going up on her knees, pulling a gun from under her coat. "Andros." There was anxiety in her voice.

Andros swore under his breath. "We're taking you straight into an ambush. Klim, stop. We have to turn around."

"No, we're not turning around," Nikolay snapped in an authoritative voice. "Let these madmen come for us."

"You don't understand," Andros said. "If they succeed in killing you, my family and those other men who testified will be blamed. This is my fight. I'm responsible for the safety of these people and you, whether you like it or not."

"You will continue to the oil fields," Nikolay insisted. "I am to inspect them and put it in my report that all is as it was the last time they were inspected."

Andros swore. "Nikolay, there's going to be hundreds of people searching for Alyona. The murderers could be anyone."

"Why would you think you're responsible for us?" another agent demanded.

Vasilisa didn't turn to look at her brother. She was certain these men worked well together. This was another question posed to Andros with just the right hint of disbelief in the agent's voice intending to produce the need in Andros to defend himself. The agents still hoped to trip him up.

Andros didn't deign to answer. He was too busy staring out the window, tension in every line of his body.

Nikolay lifted an eyebrow. "You didn't read anything in the report I sent you on Andros? You wouldn't ask that question if you had, Feliks. He's a cop with a large territory to cover, and he takes his job seriously. He took his work seriously when we served together."

Vasilisa had to acknowledge Nikolay was smooth. He defended Andros when her brother didn't take the bait, making it appear as if his partner had no idea Andros enforced the laws in their territory. Of course he knew. Nikolay was not the kind of man to tolerate any of those working with him not doing their homework. She didn't blame them for trying to trip Andros up, particularly when it was clear he was upset over the missing child.

As if reading her thoughts, Andros reached out to her. *You're certain Afanasiv and the others are looking for Alyona, too.*

You know they are, Andros. All of the Carpathians are looking. She was counting on her lifemate and the other Dragonseekers. She poured confidence into his mind. *They will find her. If she's there, they will find her.*

She knew Andros hated not being with those searching. He had to stop any threat to the agents and convince them everything told to them in the letter was to discredit Andros, as well as set up any government agent sent to investigate to be murdered.

The vehicle bounced hard over several mounds of dirt and snow, and then they were in a tight turn. Andros, Vasilisa and Klim felt the threat instantly. The attackers were Lycan, members of the Sacred Circle, and there was no way to hide their presence from other Lycans. The oil field was just around the curve.

Keep going, Klim, Andros commanded. *Fast.*

As the vehicle swept around the curve to the oil field, there were many other vehicles parked. Klim swore out loud, slamming on the brakes. "It's a trap. First three cars on either side have armed men in them. They've parked one across the road, so we can't move forward. We're at the back of the parking area."

"Let me out," Andros said. "Vasilisa, I'll take the ones on the right. You go left."

Before Nikolay could protest, the two royals rolled out of the car, slamming the doors closed behind them. Klim immediately began backing up as fast as possible to the curve. The locks clicked into place, and no matter how much Nikolay commanded the driver to open the doors, he didn't. He stopped at the bend, engine still running.

Vasilisa crouched low, pulling her weapon as she ran toward the three cars, circling as she did so. She was incredibly fast, so fast that the agents in the car lost sight of her through the bulletproof glass. There was no finding Andros at all. He had disappeared into the night, racing to the right.

Flashes of multiple guns firing came next, pouring out of the vehicles from either side, left and right. There was no hail of bullets in answer from Vasilisa or Andros. Vasilisa had been trained in the art of warfare by her brothers and several of the older Lycans. She wasn't to ever waste bullets and give her position away. Select a target, make it a kill shot, squeeze the trigger and roll or back away from where she was if she were close. Then repeat. Keep it up until she had every opponent down. After that, feel the land around her for signs of one holding back, waiting for his chance to target her.

Vasilisa took her time, firing when she had the kill shot and moving instantly. Her enemies were Lycan, and they had the ability to read the ground just as she did. They had to hurry, whereas she didn't. Lycans in the search party would know two members of the royal family were under attack, and they would come running.

She targeted the lead car first, the one that would be able to get away first and allow the two behind it to do the same. There were three men in it and she hit each one between the eyes. Then she targeted the second car. It also had three men in it. All fired at her and around the ground where she had been when she'd taken the last shot.

One had his foot out the door on the road side in order to better feel where she was. She shot him in the calf and then switched targets to take out one of the two men trying to spray the ground with automatic weapons. Immediately, she rolled down into a small depression she hadn't realized was there before. It was odd that it was suddenly available to her. Bullets sounded like an angry swarm of bees as they flew over her. She waited until the spray of bullets moved to a different section of ground before she cautiously lifted her head, tilting so her gaze was fixed on the shooters while she was still hidden.

Before she fired at her target, she looked around, marking where she would roll or scoot as soon as she pulled the trigger. This time, the earth had provided several options. On either side were depressions with shorter bushes in front of them. Behind her was something similar. It looked like a ditch with a rock partially blocking the front of it and more bushes on the other side. The earth was definitely helping her out. She took her time, found both targets, took a breath and squeezed the trigger, twice, a quick one-two tap, and then she rolled to her left to find the depression in the soil.

She kept her head down as a barrage of automatic fire was sprayed over the entire area where she had been. She'd taken out the six men in the first two vehicles. She knew all six Lycans. She'd been to their homes. Laughed with them over the antics of young Lycans. She had provided care for one of their mothers when she fell and broke her hip and then got a terrible infection. A year later, she'd stayed with him while his mother was dying. It was difficult to believe these men would conspire to kill her entire family.

She recognized the two remaining men in the last vehicle. They were older than the six she'd already killed. They were her father's age. Her father's friends. One of them had worked on self-defense training with all of her siblings and with her. He had sat at their dinner table. Both men had. They had served as Andros' advisers after their parents had been murdered. The betrayal of the two of them hurt nearly as much as her aunt's had.

I am with you, my lady. These men are corrupt and they seek power. They are part of the reason you have felt the dark whisper of conspiracy for some time. It has overshadowed your ability to help keep the gate closed securely and shut down any portals demons have to cause their mischief in your land. You have no choice, Vasilisa. The land will no longer whisper to these Lycans. It has closed itself off to them.

Vasilisa wiped the sweat from her forehead. Dragonseeker. Her man. He had influenced the land in her favor. Hopefully, he was doing the same with her brother.

The sound of gunfire was loud, drowning out the natural sounds of the night. In the distance, beyond the cars, lights lit up areas here and there. She took a deep breath and let it out.

Have you found the child, Siv? Is she alive?

Mother Earth has indicated she is alive. Each Dragonseeker has taken one of the boreholes or wellbores to inspect. I am going to my third one. I believe I feel her. She feels small and vulnerable. Radiating fear and thirst.

I can do this on my own. Find her for us, Siv. I need you to find her. Please let her be alive.

Vasilisa needed the positivity of the little girl being alive after all the betrayal and deceit. She needed it for Lada and Andros. She needed it for herself. She thought that little girl represented redemption for every Lycan desperately searching for her. The fact that the conspiracy to murder the royals had spread and no one had known shook every-one. These were people they all knew—were friends with. The idea that any Lycan had kidnapped a little girl and thrown her down a borehole to die of starvation, if she didn't die on impact or drown in the sludge, was abhorrent to all Lycans.

She's alive, Vasilisa. She's here in this borehole. I will go down first to see her condition and bring her out. Finish and get your brother here. She will need someone she knows.

That was the encouragement she needed. She locked on to the targets, thinking of them only as that, and she squeezed the trigger twice. Both men tumbled from the vehicle they were shooting out of. One hung out the window on the driver's side, his weapon hitting the ground but still in his hand. The other fell backward onto the back seat.

Andros. She is found. She will need you. I'm coming around to take your place so you can go to Alyona. Siv is bringing her out and she will be ter-rified.

Vasilisa had automatically crawled backward on her belly until she felt that depression behind her. A rock and a bush helped to hide her as she secreted herself there. Now, certain the two men were dead, she crawled farther away from the Lycans she'd killed and began to circle back toward the other side of the road.

My targets are dead. Head for the borehole. Give me the coordinates. I'll be right behind you.

The relief in her brother's voice made her want to weep. She gave him the exact location of the borehole and took off running, avoiding the road leading into the area where all the cars were parked. Andros fell in behind her. Once out of sight of the vehicle holding the govern-ment agents, they used Lycan speed to get to the location. Klim would bring the agents to the location as soon as they finished examining the dead and then looking over the oil field. He had been told to guard them.

Andros was done taking care of business, even the kind of business that would ensure he looked like a cop doing his best to cover a large territory, not like a member of a royal ruling family. Vasilisa thought it was the same thing, being a cop and doing what they did to protect their people.

Poor baby is so frightened she is trying to fight me, but she is starved, needs water and is covered in oil. I am bringing her up if Andros is there. I keep saying his name, and that is the only reason she will be calm for a moment.

Afanasiv had to appear as human as the Lycans did in front of the government agents. Vasilisa reminded him. *We don't have time to get ropes in there. Dimitri and his brother Fen have brought them to set up. Zev is here as well, and they're working as fast as they can to make sure it looks as if you climbed down with rope. We have no idea when the government agents will get here, but when they do, everything has to look legitimate.*

Vasilisa and her family dealt with humans, such as the government agents, so she knew what it took to make the rescue operation look very legitimate. Afanasiv, by his own admission, avoided being around humans or even Lycans, for that matter. He might not think or even care about being seen and then disappearing.

Soft laughter slid into her mind. He was as overjoyed at finding Alyona alive as she was, and Vasilisa felt the change in him.

Seriously, my lady, I do take care that my differences are not discovered. Have no worries that I will endanger you, your family or the Lycans. Since you guard the gate of the beast, I will presume that we will make our home here.

She felt a melting sensation around her heart. At the borehole, Dimitri, Fen and Zev tossed anchored ropes into the opening while several Lycans quickly set up lights. Andros peered down, gripping the warm blanket someone thrust into his hands.

"Get her up here," he called down to Afanasiv.

"Bringing her up now," Siv answered. He didn't grip the ropes. He just ascended, his arms around the child, making his body smaller to fit the close confines of the borehole. "I'm bringing you to Andros," he assured her in a soothing voice.

He had reached into the child's mind to help calm her. Vasilisa had stayed partially merged with him and found Alyona was more wild wolf child than human. Afanasiv had gently and skillfully reached the animal in her, allowing it to read his intentions. That also helped to calm her.

When Afanasiv emerged from the borehole with the little girl in his arms, his clothing was stained with oil, as was the gear he wore. He looked like any member of a search-and-rescue team who had volunteered to go into the hole and retrieve the child. She was even messier, the oil covering every inch of her, including her face and hair. The Lycans erupted into wild cheers, some yelling out, "She's alive! She's alive!"

Andros dragged her from Afanasiv, heedless of the oil, and wrapped his arms tightly around her, burying his face in her neck. There was an abrupt silence, with the exception of Andros' choking. When he lifted his oil-smeared face, there were tears running down it.

"Thank you," he said simply. "I don't know what else I can say to you, Siv." He looked around at his people. They had come to his family's aid earlier when they'd been attacked, and they hadn't hesitated to search for Alyona. "All of you, thank you."

He took the bottle of water Vasilisa handed him and held it to the softly crying child's lips. She drank a little and then drank some more. She kept patting Andros' face with her oil-covered hands.

"The medics are here," someone stated.

When Andros tried to set her on the gurney, she clung like a little monkey, refusing to let him go. She buried her face in his neck, so in the end, he held her while they did a quick examination.

"Mommy's going to meet us at the hospital," Andros whispered. "We'll get the oil off you and make you feel so much better."

"I'm so glad you found her alive," Nikolay said.

Andros looked up, his features giving away the fact that the agents had been so far from his mind that he'd all but forgotten them. "I'm sorry, Nikolay." He walked with the medical people to the ambulance. "I'm going to the hospital with her."

"No worries. You do what you have to do. We'll visit another time." Nikolay waved him away.

"I think my driver is around here somewhere." Andros looked distracted.

Klim came forward. "I'll get them back to the inn, Andros."

"Thanks, Klim." Andros accepted the warm, wet towels and began to wipe off the oil as best he could from Alyona's face. She was lying passively in his arms, and Vasilisa could feel fear building in her brother.

I healed every wound she had, or at least from the inside, so if the agents checked, they would find she had been beaten before being thrown in the borehole, Afanasiv said. *I also carried water down with me and gave it to her. Small amounts so her body could handle it. They will find her in surprisingly good shape. Andros does not have to worry.*

Vasilisa relayed the news to her brother, assuring him that the child was merely falling asleep in his arms. Around them, the Lycans were cleaning up the field of all gear and covering the boreholes. She waited until the government agents were safe in the car with Klim before she turned to Afanasiv.

"You look very cute with oil all over you."

He stepped toward her as if he might take her in his arms and hold her close. Laughing, she pushed him away.

"I thought I was cute."

"Not that cute. You just stay over there until we can get you cleaned up."

Afanasiv accepted the towels handed to him by Fen, who shook his head. "Some men will do anything for attention, Dimitri."

Afanasiv wiped his face and noticed the oil came right off.

"You should know, Fen," Dimitri said. "You should see him with Tatijana, Siv. She's so sweet, I don't think it would occur to her that Fen was being a baby when he gets a scratch on him. He gets all dramatic, and she falls all over him to make him better."

Afanasiv flashed his lady a quick grin. She knew she wasn't the type to fall all over him to make his wounds better, at least not in public. She would keep her anxiety to herself.

Have I told you that I have fallen in love with you, Vasilisa? Because if I have not, it is a grave oversight on my part. I do not expect you to feel the same, nor do I expect the words from you, but it is important that you know. I have taken the time to know you. To see you. To see who you are. Everything about you moves me.

Vasilisa couldn't help herself. She knew she was looking at him with her heart in her eyes. In terms of days and nights and long weeks and months, they hadn't known each other for any time at all. But they were in each other's minds. She saw him—who he was—she saw his spirit and the goodness of him. He might have darkness—that was undeniable—but he had a code of honor he didn't deviate from. That was why he had wrestled so long with whether or not he had broken that code.

You know something, Dragonseeker? I find that I've fallen in love with you, too, and I don't even know when it happened. Come home with me to my apartment. Let's see if I can take as good care of you as Tatijana does her lifemate when he's been showing off.

Afanasiv's blue-green eyes met hers, and he tossed the towel to Dimitri before holding out his hand to his woman. The other Carpathians instantly threw up an illusion of the couple walking away to get into a vehicle. They took to the sky together, two night birds winging their way back to the palace.

We're going to have to live around your brothers. He made it a statement.

I suppose I will have to make it worth your while. Vasilisa felt daring teasing him. She poured a sultry note into his mind. She didn't want to have any limits on their relationship. She knew she was more than ready for a complete commitment and wanted him to know she was.

He stroked a caress along the walls of her mind. He made her feel wanted and beautiful. He made her feel like a woman and warrior, giving her respect in both aspects of her life. The palace loomed in front of them, a large, sprawling work of art, sometimes hidden by the snow and foggy air until one was right up on it. The two owls perched on the outside balcony of her private apartment and then, once more taking their own forms, stepped off the wide railing to enter her sitting room.

She took his hand and led him down the hall to her private bath, with the large sunken tub she always enjoyed so much after battles. Aware of the time passing and Siv's inability to stay up when the sun rose, she pulled all the privacy screens to black out any sun that might sneak past the snow that had begun to come down in earnest. They didn't have a tremendous amount of time before they would go to ground together and sleep beneath her bedroom in the chamber she had there. Vasilisa meant to utilize every moment they had.

She waved her hand at the tub to fill it with hot, steamy water and turned to her lifemate. "Let me." She opened his shirt, one old-fashioned square button at a time. With each button she slipped open, her heart accelerated just a little more. She felt his eyes on her face, but she didn't look up at him. Not yet. She knew if she did, she'd want to go too fast. Every nerve ending already reacted to his body heat. To his nearness. She wanted to be the one in charge for just a little while, just enough to show him she was no longer afraid, and she wanted every experience he could give her. She wanted to bring him every pleasure.

It was difficult when she opened his shirt to look at the heavy muscles of his chest and the many raw lacerations, gouges and terrible wounds Afanasiv had. "Siv," she whispered his name and leaned forward to use her tongue to help heal the wounds. As a Carpathian, he was always clean after a battle, making certain no vampire had injected parasites into his blood. He'd taken the time before he went into the borehole to seal the wounds. She kissed every laceration and tear in his chest, neck and throat, using the healing saliva in her tongue in an effort to speed up the recovery process.

Her hands dropped to the waistband of his trousers as she kissed her way down his chest to his abdomen. Opening the material, she pushed it off his hips, down his thighs, and then, with a wave of her hand, she rid him of his clothing and shoes. Her hands found his rock-hard cock and began to stroke and caress. Only then did she look up at him, her gaze meeting his.

Afanasiv looked back at her with stark, raw hunger. With such a mixture of love and lust, her entire body followed the meltdown of her heart. He framed her face with both hands, holding her head still as he bent his head toward hers. His long hair brushed over her skin, feeling like a silken caress. She hadn't realized her clothing was gone. He had done that at some point when she was obsessed with healing his wounds.

Electricity crackled, seemed to sizzle and create little pinpoints of lightning arcing between them. His mouth took hers. So hot—his tongue like a flame, dueling with hers, stroking hunger and need into her. He held her gently, yet his mouth wasn't gentle. His kisses were rough, almost savage, devouring hungrily, possessively.

She gave herself up to his kisses, the storm of need in her rising to a fever pitch. She was only half aware of him using one hand to stop the flow of water into the bathtub. His mouth welded to hers, he lifted her into his arms and carried her straight to the bedroom. She barely felt it when he laid her on the bed because she was kissing him hungrily. Her breasts ached, felt swollen and achy. Her sex wept with need of him, fire exploding in her belly. Hot blood pounded through her clit as his mouth left hers to travel over her chin to her throat.

"Siv," she whispered his name, and it came out an ache.

"I want to taste your skin and then devour you, *sívamet*." He murmured his needs against the swell of her breasts.

His mouth, hot and hungry, closed over her aching left breast. Her breath exploded from her lungs, and a low moan of desire escaped. She couldn't possibly contain the firestorm blossoming in her belly and exploding outward, sending flames scattering in every direction. She cradled his head to her, the sweep of his hair on her sensitive skin adding to the coiling tension building so fast.

The hot cavern of his mouth sent shudders of pleasure through her body. His tongue teased and flicked her nipple while his fingers tugged at her right one. Sensations rushed through her, the flames burning a pathway from her breasts to her sex, igniting another wave of frantic need.

She craved the heat of his mouth and the slow burn his hands created in counterpoint to the wildfire burning in her sex. His mouth was rough but his hands, as they moved over her body, gentle. So intimate. The pads of his fingers explored her the way a blind man might commit every inch of her to memory.

Every strong pull of his mouth was answered by a featherlight touch of his fingers as he stroked caresses over her ribs and belly. He found her hip bones and the indentations around them. His mouth began to follow the path his hands had taken, a slow gentle exploration as if he were memorizing every inch of her—or worshiping her.

Afanasiv parted her thighs as he kissed his way from one hip to the other. He kissed his way lower still, his tongue tasting, his teeth nipping very gently. She moaned, her head thrashing, her dark hair spilling around her flushed face. Just for one moment, before he lowered his head to feast, he stopped to take in the sight of her. The intensity of his stare shook her. That look. Those eyes. There was possession in his wild, almost feral gaze. There was a mixture of lust and love that melted her insides.

Then he bent his head again. That first leisurely swipe of his tongue didn't prepare her for his feasting. His devouring. For the waves of pleasure crashing through her so fast. She couldn't stop sobbing his name, her hips as wild as his mouth. She fisted his hair, her only anchor as he ruthlessly drove her up higher and higher.

There was no thinking, no way to do anything but feel, as her body shuddered from one powerful orgasm to the next. She was barely aware of him kneeling up, lodging the wide head of his cock in her welcoming entrance. As he slowly entered her, forcing her tight sheath to accept his invasion, the burning sensation became part of the contractions rolling through her. He tilted her hips slightly to accommodate his size, and then he surged forward, driving deep, welding them together.

She felt stretched. Full. She felt his heart beat through his cock as he withdrew and then surged forward again, sending streaks of white-hot lightning through her entire body. He felt thick and hot, pulsing with urgent demand, stretching her so she fit tight around him.

He was being careful of her, but she didn't want or need careful. She lifted her hips to meet every stroke, wanting deeper and faster and harder. Eyes on his, she impaled her body on his heavy cock, letting the feel of pleasure wash through and over her. She saw he was fighting for control, and she didn't want him in control. She sensed the rising wildness in him and merged more fully to feel what he was feeling.

His entire body was hot and hard, his groin and belly on fire. The way her breasts jolted at every surge added to his pleasure. Her sheath, surrounding him, was a tunnel of silk and fire, so hot and tight that he could barely breathe. Barely think. With every stroke, the friction increased. Hotter. Wilder.

More, she encouraged him. *Let go. I'm not afraid.* She wasn't. His feral nature only called to the wildness in her.

The pleasure continued to rise with every surge of his hips as he drove into her again and again. Her tight muscles clenched around him, wanting to keep him, reluctant to allow him to slide back. She felt his cock swelling even more, pressing tight against her sheath. The friction was scalding now, searing them both, threatening to take them over the edge. Her muscles clenched in demand as white-hot flames added to the ecstasy of the moment.

There was no holding back, as much as she wanted to. Her fingers dug into the comforter she writhed on as he leaned closer to her, once again changing his angle. Her body clamped down on his, milking and suckling to drag every bit of his essence from him. The orgasm rolled through her like an earthquake, followed by another and another as his hips drove harder and deeper.

His hoarse shout mingled with her sobbing cry of his name. She felt the heat of his release, the rocketing jets of seed coating her walls and triggering more powerful quakes.

His body shuddering with pleasure, Afanasiv collapsed over her, burying his face in her neck. His tongue slid over her pounding pulse, and then his teeth sank deep. Her body went wild again, clamping down, desperate for more.

His cock seemed as full as ever as he moved in her, one hand stroking her breast and then tugging at her nipple. All the while, his hips moved, driving deep again while he took her blood. It was the most erotic moment she could imagine. She sank her fingers into his thick hair, raising her hips to meet his while he sent jagged bolts of lightning flashing through every nerve ending leading straight to her sex.

He closed the twin holes in her neck with a sweep of his tongue and caught her legs, pushing them back so her knees were nearly in line with her head. At the same time, he leaned over her. *Take my blood, sívamet.*

His blood was an aphrodisiac, created just for her. The scent of him surrounded her. She didn't hesitate but sank her teeth into his chest. Immediately his cock hardened more. Swelled more. Pushed against the sensitive tissues, straining her capacity to take him, triggering an expected series of rolling waves all over again. He moved in her, driving through her contracting sheath over and over until it was too much, and she was forced to slide her tongue over the marks on his chest just to breathe. His release was explosive, and she fragmented, taking him with her.

They lay together for a long time, content to hold each other as their heartbeats returned to normal and the fierce heat cooled a little.

"The sun is coming up, Vasilisa," Afanasiv murmured against her breast. "We will have to wait for the bath until next rising."

"I was supposed to do all the exploring." She pretended to grouse.

He laughed softly. "I promise you can have all rising tomorrow to explore as much as you want. We need a few days to ourselves."

"And you need to heal, Siv," she said firmly. "And let me take care of you. I'm sending word to my family not to bother us for several days. Sorina will meet us at the cave of crystals when I put out the call to her, and we can discuss how best to handle the situation with the gates deteriorating then."

Afanasiv nuzzled her throat and then slowly, reluctantly, allowed his body to slip from hers. She felt a little bereft. He reached for her, lifting her into his arms as she waved aside the bed and floor to reveal the stairs leading to the sleeping chamber. Once below the bedroom, she gave a silent order to have the floor and furniture return to the normal position.

Arms around his neck as they floated into the welcoming soil, she decided maybe a week was needed to heal him properly. At the very least. With her overseeing every aspect of his care.

20

D o you have any idea why the gates are breaking down?" Afanasiv asked Vasilisa as he followed her through the underground tunnel leading deeper into the labyrinth of caves.

"Both Sorina and I have speculated on that. According to Sorina, the gates were made of ancient wood and protected by safeguards considered the best at the time they were set," Vasilisa answered. "It's Sorina's blood on my tarot cards that allowed them to stay vital and be handed down from mother to daughter until your lifemate was born. She's very powerful, and she watched as the gates were constructed and the safeguards put in place. You can ask her yourself. She's waiting for us in the cave of crystals."

Afanasiv knew ancient wood didn't break down on its own. Insects couldn't penetrate it. It was nearly impossible to burn. He glanced at Petru, Benedek and Nicu as they moved carefully through the cave system following Vasilisa. It was easy to feel the powerful energy in the walls of earth as they passed through narrow openings and long halls and caught glimpses of shockingly beautiful gems gleaming occasionally as they moved through chambers with vaulted ceilings.

"In those times," Petru said, "Xavier was the instructor for all Carpathians learning how to weave safeguards. If those safeguards put into the gate were of his creation, he could easily unravel them."

"Not all Carpathians relied solely on Xavier," Afanasiv disagreed. "We are ancients, far older than Xavier. The safeguards I learned as a child from my father came in part from the earth itself."

"Your safeguards have always been different from ours," Petru admitted.

"You had safeguards long before those attending Xavier's school ever had them," Afanasiv pointed out. "Where did you learn yours?"

Petru was silent for a moment, trying to look back too many centuries. Finally, he shrugged. "The memory is so far away from me, I cannot find it."

Vasilisa reached for Afanasiv's hand. He felt the instant welling of compassion in her. It was useless to tell her Petru couldn't feel sorrow for his lost memories. He now knew the emotions were somewhere inside each of the ancients. Even though they couldn't acknowledge them, others like Vasilisa, with her sensitive nature, felt the emotions in the ancient Carpathians.

As they walked together, Siv brought her hand to his mouth to kiss her inner wrist. *Do not look so sad, sívamet. Petru cannot feel sorrow the way you do.*

Before Vasilisa could answer him, Petru spoke again. "*Sisarke*, I know my lifemate exists in this time. In this century. Adalasia read the cards for each of us. I will find her, and she will restore my ability to feel the emotions that are buried as deep as many of my memories. It is the same for Benedek and Nicu."

Afanasiv watched Vasilisa closely. Her free hand had crept to her heart. She laid her palm almost gently over it as if protecting something precious. "Perhaps I should give you a reading as well, Petru, in the hope of providing information that may help."

This is not something you have to do, Afanasiv assured her.

The cards wish to feel each of them before they leave this place to hunt for the woman who can restore the light to their worlds.

To judge them? For the first time, a hint of the anger he was capable of slipped out. Wind rushed through the chamber they were in, picking up dust and debris from the floor and swirling it around to create mini towers of stalagmites.

At times the men had to turn sideways in the halls, their shoulders scraping either side of the carved-out earth. Those times, to Afanasiv, it felt much like touching Vasilisa's ancient deck of tarot cards. The cards judged one. He feared what would happen if the system they were going through saw only the demons in them and couldn't detect that they had a code of honor they strictly followed.

To help them, Siv. Do you think I have not seen their struggles? And yet they aided us time and again. She looked up at him from under her long lashes. *They are your family. That makes them my family.*

Vasilisa owned his heart. It was that simple. His woman could disarm him with her gentle nature and then become a fierce guardian in the next heartbeat. He loved every trait. When he was certain it was impossible to feel more, the emotion he had for her became even more overwhelming, growing when she said something so simple, yet eloquent.

"Who wove the safeguards for this labyrinth beneath the earth," Benedek asked.

"Do you feel the power? It's amazing, isn't it?" Vasilisa said. "Sorina and Aura together wove the safeguards. Sorina guards the gate here, and Aura guards the gate in Algeria. Both are Carpathian. Aura has a special affinity with the earth."

Afanasiv raised an eyebrow. "Not another Dragonseeker? I think we're taking over."

Vasilisa chose to take him seriously. "I don't believe she's Dragonseeker. She doesn't talk much about her past. For that matter, neither does Sorina. I consecrated the ground against demons, so anywhere throughout this cave system, Lilith would be unable to establish a portal for her army to slip through."

Afanasiv had wondered why the earth beneath his feet felt so like home to him.

They moved from that chamber into another narrow hallway. The constant dripping of water reverberated through the hallway as they made their way to the end of it. The dirt walls were streaked darker in places where the water trickled down and dropped to the floor. They'd been steadily going downward, heading deeper beneath the earth.

The hallway made a sharp bend and then opened up into an enormous chamber. On one entire side, there was a drop-off. The other three sides of the chamber were lit with candle sconces. The lights reflected off the gems and crystals embedded in the walls.

A woman leaned against the rail surrounding the drop-off. She was tall and slender with thick, long blond hair—unusual for a Carpathian. Her eyes were a dark brown. Her features were delicate and very feminine, but Afanasiv could see the warrior in her. She looked them over, taking in every detail. Her gaze moved over his face as if judging the heart of him for her friend. Her smile welcomed them, but it didn't go to her eyes. She still regarded them warily.

"It is long since I've spoken to a Carpathian male," she greeted. "I've seen Dimitri and his brother Fen in the distance but never had the occasion to talk with them. I am Sorina Vad."

Benedek shook his head. "You are from one of the ancient and respected lineages, and yet you are here alone without any protection or guardian." There was no censure for her, but clearly, he wasn't happy with her family.

Sorina's dark eyes remained on him, but she made no comment.

Vasilisa went right up to her and greeted her warmly. "Thank you for meeting us here. I wanted Afanasiv to get to know you and for you to know him. These men are his family and therefore mine. This is Petru, Benedek and Nicu." She indicated the ancients with a quick smile. "I find them wonderful and scary at the same time. They really need to catch up a bit with modern ways."

Sorina tilted her head just a bit. "Afanasiv, have you caught up with modern ways?"

He felt his lady's breath hitch slightly, but looking at her, she appeared as calm and serene as ever. "She is teaching me. The thing about living so long is you know you have to adapt to each century and the new normal. I have had a bit of reluctance to learn technology when it is so easy to pull information from minds. Lucian explained to me when I ran into him some time ago that there is far more information on the internet than in one person's mind."

Vasilisa had returned to his side. She bumped her hip against his. "Sometimes one person does have an amazing amount of information based on his education and experience."

Sometimes just his education, he teased her.

Color swept up her neck into her face. She turned back to Sorina. "The big question everyone, including me, is asking is, why are the gates breaking down? They shouldn't be, not with the ancient wood and safeguards."

Sorina frowned. "All of the guardians of the gates have asked this question and tried to find the answer. At first, we blamed it on the environment, but when we spoke with Gaia, she didn't think so."

"The mages?" Afanasiv asked. "Although you're an ancient and wouldn't necessary rely on Xavier's spells to weave a safeguard."

"We purposely didn't use anything taught to us by a mage. We knew the safeguards had to last centuries. There are four of us who guard with the aid of others, such as Vasilisa and her family. All four of us wove those safeguards, strand by strand, layering our safeguards between us in no discernible pattern," Sorina explained. "We didn't go in any particular order. We didn't want a mage to figure out a pattern."

The ancients exchanged long looks. It was a puzzle.

"Are you able to get close enough to the gate to see if the safeguards are unraveling?" Benedek asked. "If the strands are worn in places? You might be able to tell if someone has been picking at them."

Sorina sighed and looked over the railing into the dark abyss. "I asked Gaia to look for me. Aura did the same on her gate. Gaia said she could see the strands were thinner in some places, and one or two were actually broken. She checked every gate and found the same thing. None of us knows how it is being done."

"Could it be Lilith?" Vasilisa ventured.

"It's possible," Sorina said. "But not probable. She wouldn't want the beast to escape unless she could control him. What would be the point? Unleashing a terrible weapon without the ability to control it?"

Afanasiv had been studying Sorina's expression carefully. She was really worried. "You have an idea of what might be taking place."

Sorina looked around the chamber of gems before she answered somewhat reluctantly. "Aura and I consulted with Tora. She's been uneasy for some time, she said, aware the safeguards weren't holding up."

"Did you consult with Adalasia and Leona as well?" Afanasiv asked. "We were with her, and she didn't mention concerns."

"We didn't. Leona has never indicated to us that the gate itself was breaking down. There were portals demons were slipping through, but the gate on her side was holding," Sorina explained. "That was what gave Tora the idea that worried all of us. Leona's family has a connection to the beast. He saved their lives and remained behind to give them time to get free of the underworld. He would know everything Leona knows in the way of safeguards. In those days, Afanasiv, the family handed down safeguards from one generation to the next."

The sound of water dripping in the cave was loud. Nicu voiced what they were all thinking. "You believe the beast is the one breaking down the safeguards and opening up the ancient wood to insects and other corrosions."

Sorina nodded slowly. "He's extremely intelligent. The demon may have overtaken him, but he is no vampire with a rotted brain. He has all the cunning and instincts of an animal and retains everything he knew before he was imprisoned behind the gate. According to Gaia, each time anyone—demon, a prisoner, Lilith, anyone at all—comes to visit him, he scans their brain for new information. She has always said he's thirsty for knowledge."

Afanasiv thought that over. If Justice, the ancient Carpathian demon, had an active mind that required knowledge all the time, he would be desperate to get free. No matter what his original motivation was, he had been behind those gates for centuries. That alone could drive someone mad.

"He doesn't need to work so hard at Leona's safeguards," Petru said. "He knows them. So he's taking his time unraveling the other three, leaving Leona's safeguards for last."

Sorina nodded. "That's our best guess, and there doesn't seem to be a way to stop him if we're right. Gaia asked him, but he goes for long periods of time without speaking. When he does speak, it's usually only a few words, and then he's back to pacing away from her."

Benedek continued to look at her. "Your brothers know you are alive?"

Sorina sent him that same smile that didn't quite reach her eyes. "If they knew, I imagine they would have visited some time ago. My father knew I was not suited to be a lifemate. There were things . . ." She broke off and waved her hand as if it didn't matter. "He told me a woman was needed, someone strong enough to guard without knowing how long that position would last. I volunteered, and he brought me to the palace to meet Vasilisa's family. They had the tarot deck and took care of any demons slipping through a portal. We made a good team."

"And your lifemate?" Petru asked. "What of him?"

She tilted her chin. "It isn't as if I'm wandering around the world. I'm in one place. I suspect if he was going to find me, he would have already. That's his duty, not mine."

"Do you mind if I get word to your brothers that you're alive?" Benedek pushed. "The dead were never spoken of in the old days. They believe you have passed from this world."

For the first time, a real smile touched her mouth. "I suspect you would let them know I still live no matter what I said."

Benedek gave a slight bow. "I would stay to persuade you my way is best."

Afanasiv laughed. He couldn't help it. "He would, too. Thank you for meeting with us and giving us your opinion. I will be staying here with Vasilisa, but my friends go out in the world to seek their life-mates. We return to the palace so Vasilisa can give them a reading in the hope that the cards reveal more clues to their whereabouts. Would you care to join us?"

Sorina shook her head. "Thank you, but not this time. Perhaps another."

Afanasiv understood. She was uncomfortable in the company of so many male Carpathians but didn't want to say so.

"It was good to finally meet you."

Vasilisa sat at the table, with Petru across from her. She liked him. She liked the set of his shoulders and his odd-colored eyes. They looked as if they were liquid silver. His hair was almost silvery-white and long, as the other ancients seemed to wear theirs. It was braided and fell nearly to his waist. It didn't make him look at all feminine. Mostly, she liked him because he'd been there unfailingly for Afanasiv.

She simply handed him the cards. He took them without hesitation. Instantly, power clashed against power. A fierce storm brewed. Ice and fire clashed. Lightning seemed to fork from the cards, flashes of white reflected in his eyes. Petru was calm, merely shuffling the cards while the storm raged through them and tried to snap at his palms with flashes of lightning.

When the storm had calmed, he divided the deck and set one half aside. From the remaining half, he chose his six cards.

Vasilisa looked at them, butterflies in her stomach. She wanted so much for these men. She wanted to give them something in return for all they'd given Afanasiv, her and her people. She looked his cards over.

"The six of swords is transition, moving from one situation to another, hopefully a better one. The chariot indicates action, travel, forward movement. The seven of swords indicates an element of danger surrounds the issue, and you should plan carefully. The two of cups tells you there is a love connection between two people that will be successful. The magician has the innate capability of showing you the way." She frowned, waiting for the right reading. "Do you have scars from a particular battle? A map of scars? That battle, those scars, show you the way." She lifted her gaze to his, but his expression was unreadable. "The three of cups indicates a surprise, a wonderful one. I believe that would be the woman you seek."

Petru nodded his head. "You have aided me tremendously, *sisarke*." He stood and bowed to her before stepping back to allow Benedek to take his place.

Vasilisa took her time cleansing the cards, determined to give Benedek as good of a reading as possible. Benedek was a big man, larger even than any of the other ancients. He was intimidating just being outdoors. Inside, up close, Benedek was the one ancient she was fascinated by. He had thick black hair streaked with silver. Afanasiv had told her at one time the hair was to his ankles, but he had cut it to his waist and wore it pulled back at the nape of his neck with a leather cord. His eyes were mesmerizing, a midnight black, so at times, there was a dark blue shimmering behind that black. His shoulders were wide, and where some Carpathians appeared sinewy but lithe, his muscles were very defined.

Afanasiv had told her Benedek was a fierce fighter yet an incredible artist. He had a very dark aura. Petru and Benedek often stayed together to ensure the other didn't succumb to the demon in a weak moment. She couldn't imagine either man having a weak moment, but Afanasiv said it was easy enough to happen, so she wanted to give him hope.

He took the cards, and instantly there was a struggle for power. An eruption of fire, the flames burning out from his palms. Almost immediately, the flames took on various hues. An explosion of colors burst from the fire and then quickly died down. Through it all, Benedek never changed expression or stopped shuffling the cards. When the cards had grown silent, he split the deck and set one half aside before choosing his cards.

"Knight of pentacles, this card represents bravery." She shot him a smile, knowing he wouldn't even consider himself brave. "It also means putting someone else's interest before your own. The moon. There is a warning here. Something is hidden and you need to pay attention, look deeper. Not all are being truthful. There could be deceit involved."

Vasilisa didn't stumble over the reading. To her, the warning was clear. Benedek didn't change expressions, so she went on. "The three of pentacles. You must be able to rely on others. You will succeed with the support of allies. The lovers. At the heart of the matter, there is an intimate connection with another who will have a significant impact on your life. Four of swords. Needing to figure things out. Going to a mental space of neutral observation to get clarity. Chariot. This is action, moving forward, travel." Vasilisa looked up at him. He didn't so much as blink, but then she wasn't certain he ever did.

Benedek rose and gave her a small courtly bow. "Thank you, Vasilisa. I, too, regard you as a little sister."

That admission had tears burning behind her eyes. To cover her emotions, she stood up and stretched before, once again, cleansing the cards. Each reading had to be true. She glanced at Afanasiv, who sat in the shadows, but she could feel his eyes on her. *I love you.* She needed to tell him. Reading for the ancients was stressful, but somehow, he managed to make her feel she wasn't alone, and she could lean on him any time she needed to.

I love you, Vasilisa. What you are doing for my family is a gift. Thank you.

Emboldened by her lifemate, Vasilisa faced Nicu. He was different. A little wild, but like the wolves and other untamed large predators, he was also unbelievably gentle. There were shadows surrounding him, and her heart went out to him. When he took the cards and began to shuffle, animals burst out, raptors flew at him. He didn't flinch away but kept shuffling, his soft voice mesmerizing as he calmed his ferocious adversaries. He chose his cards and laid them out as she directed, then sat back, looking at her with his calm gaze.

"The tower. This is a warning. Danger. Potential for destruction. Endings to lead to new beginnings. Judgment. Being careful not to judge others or jump to conclusions about them. Also, this is about learning to trust yourself and your own instincts. In other words, you can trust yourself and others, and you must do so. The fool. If you're not careful and don't proceed with caution, you could stumble and fall. Don't lose sight of your priorities. Nine of swords." Vasilisa lifted her gaze to Nicu's. "Worrying and fretting about something. Guilt. Is there something in your past you need to resolve that keeps you from trusting anyone?"

Nicu didn't so much as flinch. She continued. "Page of cups. This is not surprising. This signals a being connected to animals. Usually starts from a young age, in childhood. Pay attention to the signs from the animal kingdom. Queen of cups. A romantic partner. A woman who is loving, nurturing and supportive. This is very positive."

Vasilisa sat back in her chair, suddenly feeling exhausted. Nicu rose and, like the others, bowed to her. "Little sister, I cannot thank you enough. Hope can sustain one for centuries."

Afanasiv walked the three ancients out while she watched through the open sliding door. She gathered her tarot cards and shuffled them before pulling one card from the deck. The world. She watched her lifemate grasp the arms of each one of his friends as he told them to stay in the light and thanked them for their aid.

He returned to her, and she settled, realizing a part of her was afraid he would leave to help his friends find their lifemates. She was needed where she was. She couldn't leave Sorina alone to hold the gate.

Lilith would gather her forces and try to create portals. She would need to fight demons and close each portal as it was found. She was very aware she had to be with Afanasiv. She didn't want to be apart from him.

He leaned down and brushed a kiss on the top of her head. "What does that card mean, my lady?" He indicated the world.

She touched the card with her finger and looked up at him, knowing love was shining in her eyes. "Harmony. Completion. A sense of belonging. That was something I never quite felt before. I feel I've found that with you."

Afanasiv reached for her, pulled her out of her chair and into his arms. "And I with you."

CARPATHIAN HEALING CHANTS

To rightly understand Carpathian healing chants, background is required in several areas:

1. The Carpathian view on healing
2. The Lesser Healing Chant of the Carpathians
3. The Great Healing Chant of the Carpathians
4. Carpathian musical aesthetics
5. Lullaby
6. Song to Heal the Earth
7. Carpathian chanting technique

1. THE CARPATHIAN VIEW ON HEALING

The Carpathians are a nomadic people whose geographic origins can be traced at least as far as the Southern Ural Mountains (near the steppes of modern-day Kazakhstan), on the border between Europe and Asia. (For this reason, modern-day linguists call their language "proto-Uralic," without knowing that this is the language of the Carpathians.) Unlike most nomadic peoples, the Carpathians did not wander due to the need to find new grazing lands as the seasons and climate shifted, or to search for better trade. Instead, the Carpathians' movements were driven by a great purpose: to find a land that would have the right earth, a soil with the kind of richness that would greatly enhance their rejuvenative powers.

Over the centuries, they migrated westward (some six thousand years ago), until they at last found their perfect homeland—their *susu*—in the Carpathian Mountains, whose long arc cradled the lush plains of the kingdom of Hungary. (The kingdom of Hungary flourished for over a millennium—making Hungarian the dominant language of the Carpathian Basin—until the kingdom's lands were split among several countries after World War I: Austria, Czechoslovakia, Romania, Yugoslavia and modern Hungary.)

Other peoples from the Southern Urals (who shared the Carpathian language but were not Carpathians) migrated in different directions. Some ended up in Finland, which explains why the modern

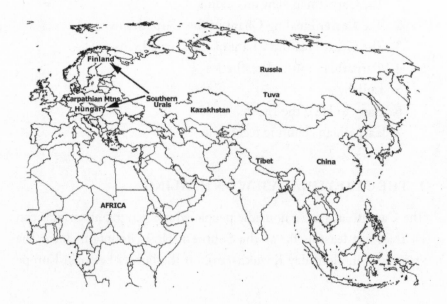

Hungarian and Finnish languages are among the contemporary descendants of the ancient Carpathian language. Even though they are tied forever to their chosen Carpathian homeland, the Carpathians continue to wander as they search the world for the answers that will enable them to bear and raise their offspring without difficulty.

Because of their geographic origins, the Carpathian views on healing share much with the larger Eurasian shamanistic tradition. Probably the closest modern representative of that tradition is based in Tuva (and is referred to as "Tuvinian Shamanism")—see the map on the previous page.

The Eurasian shamanistic tradition—from the Carpathians to the Siberian shamans—held that illness originated in the human soul, and only later manifested as various physical conditions. Therefore, shamanistic healing, while not neglecting the body, focused on the soul and its healing. The most profound illnesses were understood to be caused by "soul departure," where all or some part of the sick person's soul has wandered away from the body (into the nether realms) or has been captured or possessed by an evil spirit, or both.

The Carpathians belong to this greater Eurasian shamanistic tradition and share its viewpoints. While the Carpathians themselves did not succumb to illness, Carpathian healers understood that the most profound wounds were also accompanied by a similar "soul departure."

Upon reaching the diagnosis of "soul departure," the healer-shaman is then required to make a spiritual journey into the netherworld to recover the soul. The shaman may have to overcome tremendous challenges along the way, particularly fighting the demon or vampire who has possessed his friend's soul.

"Soul departure" doesn't require a person to be unconscious (although that certainly can be the case as well). It was understood that a person could still appear to be conscious, even talk and interact with others, and yet be missing a part of their soul. The experienced healer or shaman would instantly see the problem nonetheless, in subtle signs that others might miss: the person's attention wandering every now and then, a lessening in their enthusiasm about life, chronic depression, a diminishment in the brightness of their "aura" and the like.

2. THE LESSER HEALING CHANT OF THE CARPATHIANS

Kepä Sarna Pus (**The Lesser Healing Chant**) is used for wounds that are merely physical in nature. The Carpathian healer leaves his body and enters the wounded Carpathian's body to heal great mortal wounds from the inside out using pure energy. He proclaims, "I offer freely my life for your life," as he gives his blood to the injured Carpathian. Because the Carpathians are of the earth and bound to the soil, they are healed by the soil of their homeland. Their saliva is also often used for its rejuvenative powers.

It is also very common for the Carpathian chants (both the Lesser and the Great) to be accompanied by the use of healing herbs, aromas from Carpathian candles and crystals. The crystals (when combined with the Carpathians' empathic, psychic connection to the entire universe) are used to gather positive energy from their surroundings, which is then used to accelerate the healing. Caves are sometimes used as the setting for the healing.

The Lesser Healing Chant was used by Vikirnoff Von Shrieder and Colby Jansen to heal Rafael De La Cruz, whose heart had been ripped out by a vampire, as described in *Dark Secret*.

Kepä Sarna Pus (The Lesser Healing Chant)
The same chant is used for all physical wounds. "Sívadaba" (into your heart) would be changed to refer to whatever part of the body is wounded.

Kuńasz, nélkül sívdobbanás, nélkül fesztelen löyly.
You lie as if asleep, without beat of heart, without airy breath.

Ot élidamet andam szabadon élidadért.
I offer freely my life for your life.

O jelä sielam jŏrem ot ainamet és soŋe ot élidadet.
My spirit of light forgets my body and enters your body.

O jelä sielam pukta kinn minden szelemeket belső.
My spirit of light sends all the dark spirits within fleeing without.

Pajńak o susu hanyet és o nyelv nyálamet sívadaba.
I press the earth of our homeland and the spit of my tongue into
    your heart.

Vii, o verim soŋe o verid andam.
At last, I give you my blood for your blood.

To hear this chant, visit christinefeehan.com/members/.

3. THE GREAT HEALING CHANT OF THE CARPATHIANS

The most well-known—and most dramatic—of the Carpathian healing chants is *En Sarna Pus* (**The Great Healing Chant**). This chant
is reserved for recovering the wounded or unconscious Carpathian's
soul.

Typically a group of men would form a circle around the sick
Carpathian (to "encircle him with our care and compassion") and begin
the chant. The shaman or healer or leader is the prime actor in this
healing ceremony. It is he who will actually make the spiritual journey
into the netherworld, aided by his clanspeople. Their purpose is to ecstatically dance, sing, drum and chant, all the while visualizing (through
the words of the chant) the journey itself—every step of it, over and
over again—to the point where the shaman, in trance, leaves his body
and makes that very journey. (Indeed, the word *ecstasy* is from the Latin
ex statis, which literally means "out of the body.")

One advantage that the Carpathian healer has over many
other shamans is his telepathic link to his lost brother. Most sha-

mans must wander in the dark of the nether realms in search of their lost brother. But the Carpathian healer directly "hears" in his mind the voice of his lost brother calling to him, and can thus "zero in on" his soul like a homing beacon. For this reason, Carpathian healing tends to have a higher success rate than most other traditions of this sort.

Something of the geography of the "other world" is useful for us to examine in order to fully understand the words of the Great Healing Chant. A reference is made to the "Great Tree" (in Carpathian: *En Puwe*). Many ancient traditions, including the Carpathian tradition, understood the worlds—the heaven worlds, our world and the nether realms—to be "hung" upon a great pole, or axis, or tree. Here on earth, we are positioned halfway up this tree, on one of its branches. Hence, many ancient texts referred to the material world as "middle earth": midway between heaven and hell. Climbing the tree would lead one to the heaven worlds. Descending the tree to its roots would lead to the nether realms. The shaman was necessarily a master of movement up and down the Great Tree, sometimes moving unaided and sometimes assisted by (or even mounted upon the back of) an animal spirit guide. In various traditions, this Great Tree was known as the *axis mundi* (the "axis of the worlds"), Yggdrasil (in Norse mythology), Mount Meru (the sacred world mountain of Tibetan tradition), etc. The Christian cosmos, with its heaven, purgatory/earth and hell, is also worth comparing. It is even given a similar topography in Dante's *Divine Comedy*: Dante is led on a journey first to hell, at the center of the earth; then upward to Mount Purgatory, which sits on the earth's surface directly opposite Jerusalem; then farther upward to Eden, the earthly paradise, at the summit of Mount Purgatory; and then upward at last to Heaven.

In the shamanistic tradition, it was understood that the small always reflects the large; the personal always reflects the cosmic. A movement in the greater dimensions of the cosmos also coincides with an internal movement. For example, the *axis mundi* of the cosmos corresponds with the spinal column of the individual. Journeys up and down the *axis mundi* often coincided with the movements of natural and spiritual energies (sometimes called *kundalini* or *shakti*) in the spinal column of the shaman or mystic.

En Sarna Pus (The Great Healing Chant)

In this chant, ekä ("brother") would be replaced by "sister," "father," "mother," depending on the person to be healed.

Ot ekäm ainajanak hany, jama.
My brother's body is a lump of earth, close to death.

Me, ot ekäm kuntajanak, pirädak ekäm, gond és irgalom türe.
We, the clan of my brother, encircle him with our care and
   compassion.

*O pus wäkenkek, ot oma śarnank, és ot pus fünk, álnak ekäm ainajanak,
   pitänak ekäm ainajanak elävä.*
Our healing energies, ancient words of magic and healing herbs bless
   my brother's body, keep it alive.

*Ot ekäm sielanak pälä. Ot omboće päläja juta alatt o jüti, kinta, és szelemek
   lamtijaknak.*
But my brother's soul is only half. His other half wanders in the
   netherworld.

Ot en mekem ŋamaŋ: kulkedak otti ot ekäm omboće päläjanak.
My great deed is this: I travel to find my brother's other half.

*Rekatüre, saradak, tappadak, odam, kaŋa o numa waram, és avaa owe o
   lewl mahoz.*
We dance, we chant, we dream ecstatically, to call my spirit bird, and
   to open the door to the other world.

Ntak o numa waram, és mozdulak; jomadak.
I mount my spirit bird and we begin to move; we are underway.

Piwtädak ot En Puwe tyvinak, ećidak alatt o jüti, kinta, és szelemek
    lamtijaknak.
Following the trunk of the Great Tree, we fall into the netherworld.

Fázak, fázak nó o śaro.
It is cold, very cold.

Juttadak ot ekäm o akarataban, o sívaban és o sielaban.
My brother and I are linked in mind, heart and soul.

Ot ekäm sielanak kaŋa engem.
My brother's soul calls to me.

Kuledak és piwtädak ot ekäm.
I hear and follow his track.

Saγedak és tuledak ot ekäm kulyanak.
I encounter the demon who is devouring my brother's soul.

Nenäm ćoro, o kuly torodak.
In anger, I fight the demon.

O kuly pél engem.
He is afraid of me.

Lejkkadak o kaŋka salamaval.
I strike his throat with a lightning bolt.

Molodak ot ainaja komakamal.
I break his body with my bare hands.

Toja és molanâ.
He is bent over, and falls apart.

Hän ćaδa.
He runs away.

Manedak ot ekäm sielanak.
I rescue my brother's soul.

Alɔdak ot ekam sielanak o komamban.
I lift my brother's soul in the hollow of my hand.

Alɔdam ot ekam numa waramra.
I lift him onto my spirit bird.

Piwtädak ot En Puwe tyvijanak és saɣedak jälleen ot elävä ainak
    majaknak.
Following up the Great Tree, we return to the land of the living.

Ot ekäm elä jälleen.
My brother lives again.

Ot ekäm weńća jälleen.
He is complete again.

To hear this chant, visit christinefeehan.com/members/.

4. CARPATHIAN MUSICAL AESTHETICS

In the sung Carpathian pieces (such as the "Lullaby" and the "Song to Heal the Earth"), you'll hear elements that are shared by many of the musical traditions in the Uralic geographical region, some of which still exist—from Eastern European (Bulgarian, Romanian, Hungarian, Croatian) to Romany ("gypsy"). These elements include:

- the rapid alternation between major and minor modalities, including a sudden switch (called a "Picardy third") from minor to major to end a piece or section (as at the end of the "Lullaby")
- the use of close (tight) harmonies
- the use of *ritardi* (slowing down the pace) and *crescendi* (swelling in volume) for brief periods
- the use of *glissandi* (slides) in the singing tradition
- the use of trills in the singing tradition (as in the final invocation of the "Song to Heal the Earth")—similar to Celtic, a singing tradition more familiar to many of us
- the use of parallel fifths (as in the final invocation of the "Song to Heal the Earth")
- controlled use of dissonance
- "call-and-response" chanting (typical of many of the world's chanting traditions)
- extending the length of a musical line (by adding a couple of bars) to heighten dramatic effect
- and many more

"Lullaby" and "Song to Heal the Earth" illustrate two rather different forms of Carpathian music (a quiet, intimate piece and an energetic ensemble piece)—but whatever the form, Carpathian music is full of feeling.

5. LULLABY

This song is sung by a woman while a child is still in the womb or when the threat of a miscarriage is apparent. The baby can hear the song while inside the mother, and the mother can connect with the child telepathically as well. The lullaby is meant to reassure the child, to encourage the baby to hold on, to stay—to reassure the child that he or she will be protected by love even from inside until birth. The last line literally means that the mother's love will protect her child until the child is born ("rise").

Musically, the Carpathian "Lullaby" is in three-quarter time ("waltz time"), as are a significant portion of the world's various traditional lullabies (perhaps the most famous of which is Brahms's Lullaby). The arrangement for solo voice is the original context: a mother singing to her child, unaccompanied. The arrangement for chorus and violin ensemble illustrates how musical even the simplest Carpathian pieces often are, and how easily they lend themselves to contemporary instrumental or orchestral arrangements. (A wide range of contemporary composers, including Dvořák and Smetana, have taken advantage of a similar discovery, working other traditional Eastern European music into their symphonic poems.)

Odam-Sarna Kondak (Lullaby)

Tumtesz o wäke ku pitasz belső.
Feel the strength you hold inside.

Hiszasz sívadet. Én olenam gæidnod.
Trust your heart. I'll be your guide.

Sas csecsemõm; kuńasz.
Hush, my baby; close your eyes.

Rauho joŋe ted.
Peace will come to you.

Tumtesz o sívdobbanás ku olen lamt3ad belső.
Feel the rhythm deep inside.

Gond–kumpadek ku kim te.
Waves of love that cover you.

Pesänak te, asti o jüti, kidüsz.
Protect, until the night you rise.

To hear this song, visit christinefeehan.com/members/.

6. SONG TO HEAL THE EARTH

This is the earth-healing song that is used by the Carpathian women
to heal soil filled with various toxins. The women take a position on
four sides and call to the universe to draw on the healing energy with
love and respect. The soil of the earth is their resting place, the place
where they rejuvenate, and they must make it safe not only for themselves but for their unborn children, as well as their men and living children. This is a beautiful ritual performed by the women together, raising
their voices in harmony and calling on the earth's minerals and healing
properties to come forth and help them save their children. They literally dance and sing to heal the earth in a ceremony as old as their species. The dance and notes of the song are adjusted according to the
toxins felt through the healers' bare feet. The feet are placed in a certain pattern, and the hands gracefully weave a healing spell while the
dance is performed. They must be especially careful when the soil is
prepared for babies. This is a ceremony of love and healing.

Musically, the ritual is divided into several sections:

- **First verse:** A "call-and-response" section, where the chant leader
  sings the "call" solo, and then some or all of the women sing the
  "response" in the close harmony style typical of the Carpathian
  musical tradition. The repeated response—*Ai, Emä Maye*—is an
  invocation of the source of power for the healing ritual: "Oh, Mother
  Nature."

- **First chorus:** This section is filled with clapping, dancing, ancient horns and other means used to invoke and heighten the energies upon which the ritual is drawing.
- **Second verse**
- **Second chorus**
- **Closing invocation:** In this closing part, two song leaders, in close harmony, take all the energy gathered by the earlier portions of the song/ritual and focus it entirely on the healing purpose.

What you will be listening to are brief tastes of what would typically be a significantly longer ritual, in which the verse and chorus parts are developed and repeated many times, to be closed by a single rendition of the closing invocation.

Sarna Pusm O Maγet (Song to Heal the Earth)

First verse
Ai, Emä Maγe,
Oh, Mother Nature,

Me sívadbin lañaak.
We are your beloved daughters.

Me tappadak, me pusmak o maγet.
We dance to heal the earth.

Me sarnadak, me pusmak o hanyet.
We sing to heal the earth.

Sielanket jutta tedet it,
We join with you now,

Sívank és akaratank és sielank juttanak.
Our hearts and minds and spirits become one.

Second verse
Ai, Emä Maγe,
Oh, Mother Nature,

Me sívadbin lañaak.
We are your beloved daughters.

Me andak arwadet emänked és me kaŋank o
We pay homage to our mother and call upon the

Põhi és Lõuna, Ida és Lääs.
North and South, East and West.

Pide és aldyn és myös belső.
Above and below and within as well.

Gondank o maγenak pusm hän ku olen jama.
Our love of the land heals that which is in need.

Juttanak teval it,
We join with you now,

Maγe maγeval.
Earth to earth.

O pirä elidak weńća.
The circle of life is complete.

To hear this chant, visit christinefeehan.com/members/.

7. CARPATHIAN CHANTING TECHNIQUE

As with their healing techniques, the actual "chanting technique" of the Carpathians has much in common with the other shamanistic traditions of the Central Asian steppes. The primary mode of chanting was throat chanting using overtones. Modern examples of this manner of singing can still be found in the Mongolian, Tuvan and Tibetan traditions. You can find an audio example of the Gyuto Tibetan Buddhist monks engaged in throat chanting at christinefeehan.com/carpathian_chanting/.

As with Tuva, note on the map the geographical proximity of Tibet to Kazakhstan and the Southern Urals.

The beginning part of the Tibetan chant emphasizes synchronizing all the voices around a single tone, aimed at healing a particular "chakra" of the body. This is fairly typical of the Gyuto throat-chanting tradition, but it is not a significant part of the Carpathian tradition. Nonetheless, it serves as an interesting contrast.

The part of the Gyuto chanting example that is most similar to the Carpathian style of chanting is the midsection, where the men are chanting the words together with great force. The purpose here is not to generate a "healing tone" that will affect a particular "chakra" but rather to generate as much power as possible for initiating "out-of-body" travel and for fighting the demonic forces that the healer/traveler must face and overcome.

The songs of the Carpathian women (illustrated by their "Lullaby" and their "Song to Heal the Earth") are part of the same ancient musical and healing tradition as the Lesser and Great Healing Chants of the warrior males. You can hear some of the same instruments in both the male warriors' healing chants and the women's "Song to Heal the Earth." Also, they share the common purpose of generating and directing power. However, the women's songs are distinctively feminine in character. One immediately noticeable difference is that while the men speak their words in the manner of a chant, the women sing songs with melodies and harmonies, softening the overall performance. A feminine, nurturing quality is especially evident in the "Lullaby."

THE CARPATHIAN LANGUAGE

Like all human languages, the language of the Carpathians contains the richness and nuance that can only come from a long history of use. At best we can only touch on some of the main features of the language in this brief appendix:

1. The history of the Carpathian language
2. Carpathian grammar and other characteristics of the language
3. Examples of the Carpathian language (including the Ritual Words and the Warriors' Chant)
4. A much-abridged Carpathian dictionary

1. THE HISTORY OF THE CARPATHIAN LANGUAGE

The Carpathian language of today is essentially identical to the Carpathian language of thousands of years ago. A "dead" language like the Latin of two thousand years ago has evolved into a significantly different modern language (Italian) because of countless generations of speakers and great historical fluctuations. In contrast, many of the speakers of Carpathian from thousands of years ago are still alive. Their presence—coupled with the deliberate isolation of the Carpathians from the other major forces of change in the world—has acted (and continues to act) as a stabilizing force that has preserved the integrity of the language over the centuries. Carpathian culture has also acted as a stabilizing force. For instance, the Ritual Words, the various healing chants (see Appendix 1) and other cultural artifacts have been passed down through the centuries with great fidelity.

One small exception should be noted: the splintering of the Carpathians into separate geographic regions has led to some minor dialectization. However, the telepathic link among all Carpathians (as well as each Carpathian's regular return to his or her homeland) has ensured that the differences among dialects are relatively superficial (small numbers of new words, minor differences in pronunciation, etc.), since the deeper internal language of mind-forms has remained the same because of continuous use across space and time.

The Carpathian language was (and still is) the proto-language for the Uralic (or Finno-Ugric) family of languages. Today, the Uralic languages are spoken in northern, eastern and central Europe and in Siberia. More than twenty-three million people in the world speak languages that can trace their ancestry to Carpathian. Magyar or Hungarian (about fourteen million speakers), Finnish (about five million speakers) and Estonian (about one million speakers) are the three major contemporary descendants of this proto-language. The only factor that unites the more than twenty languages in the Uralic family is that their ancestry can be traced back to a common proto-language—Carpathian—that split (starting some six thousand years ago) into the various languages in the Uralic family. In the same way, European languages such as English and French belong to the better-known Indo-European family and also evolved from a common proto-language ancestor (a different one from Carpathian).

The following table provides a sense of some of the similarities in the language family.

Note: The Finnic/Carpathian "k" shows up often as the Hungarian "h." Similarly, the Finnic/Carpathian "p" often corresponds to the Hungarian "f."

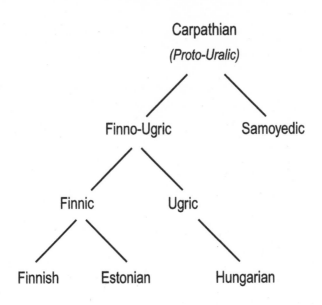

Carpathian
(Proto-Uralic)

Finno-Ugric Samoyedic

Finnic Ugric

Finnish Estonian Hungarian

Carpathian (proto-Uralic)	Finnish (Suomi)	Hungarian (Magyar)
elä—live	*elä*—live	*él*—live
elid—life	*elinikä*—life	*élet*—life
pesä—nest	*pesä*—nest	*fészek*—nest
kola—die	*kuole*—die	*hal*—die
pälä—half, side	*pieltä*—tilt, tip to the side	*fél, fele*—fellow human, friend (half; one side of two) *feleség*—wife
and—give	*anta, antaa*—give	*ad*—give
koje—husband, man	*koira*—dog, the male (of animals)	*here*—drone, testicle
wäke—power	*väki*—folks, people, men; force	*val/-vel*—with (instrumental suffix)
	väkevä—powerful, strong	*vele*—with him/her/it
wete—water	*vesi*—water	*víz*—water

2. CARPATHIAN GRAMMAR AND OTHER CHARACTERISTICS OF THE LANGUAGE

Idioms. As both an ancient language and a language of an earth people, Carpathian is more inclined toward the use of idioms constructed from concrete, "earthy" terms rather than abstractions. For instance, our modern abstraction "to cherish" is expressed more concretely in Carpathian as "to hold in one's heart"; the "netherworld" is, in Carpathian, "the land of night, fog and ghosts"; etc.

Word order. The order of words in a sentence is determined not by syntactic roles (like subject, verb and object) but rather by pragmatic, discourse-driven factors. Examples: *"Tied vagyok."* ("Yours am I."); *"Sívamet andam."* ("My heart I give you.")

Agglutination. The Carpathian language is agglutinative; that is, longer words are constructed from smaller components. An agglutinating language uses suffixes or prefixes whose meanings are generally unique and that are concatenated one after another without overlap. In Carpathian, words typically consist of a stem that is followed by one or more suffixes. For example, *sívambam* derives from the stem *"sív"* ("heart"), followed by *"am"* ("my," making it "my heart"), followed by *"bam"* ("in," making it "in my heart"). As you might imagine, agglutination in Carpathian can sometimes produce very long words, or words that are very difficult to pronounce. Vowels often get inserted between suffixes to prevent too many consonants from appearing in a row (which can make a word unpronounceable).

Noun cases. Like all languages, Carpathian has many noun cases; the same noun will be "spelled" differently depending on its role in a sentence. The noun cases include nominative (when the noun is the subject of the sentence), accusative (when the noun is a direct object of the verb), dative (indirect object), genitive (or possessive), instrumental, final, suppressive, inessive, elative, terminative and delative.

We will use the possessive (or genitive) case as an example to illustrate how all noun cases in Carpathian involve adding standard suffixes to the noun stems. Thus, expressing possession in Carpathian—"my lifemate," "your lifemate," "his lifemate," "her lifemate," etc.—involves adding a particular suffix (such as "-am") to the noun stem ("päläfertiil") to produce the possessive ("päläfertiilam"—"my lifemate"). Which suffix to use depends on which person ("my," "your," "his," etc.) and whether the noun ends in a consonant or a vowel. The following table shows the suffixes for singular nouns only (not plural), and also shows the similarity to the suffixes used in contemporary Hungarian. (Hungarian is actually a little more complex, in that it also requires "vowel rhyming": which suffix to use also depends on the last vowel in the noun, hence the multiple choices in the table, where Carpathian has only a single choice.)

person	Carpathian (proto-Uralic)		Contemporary Hungarian	
	noun ends in vowel	noun ends in consonant	noun ends in vowel	noun ends in consonant
1st singular (my)	-m	-am	-m	-om, -em, -öm
2nd singular (your)	-d	-ad	-d	-od, -ed, -öd
3rd singular (his, her, its)	-ja	-a	-ja/-je	-a, -e
1st plural (our)	-nk	-ank	-nk	-unk, -ünk
2nd plural (your)	-tak	-atak	-tok, -tek, -tök	-otok, -etek, -ötök
3rd plural (their)	-jak	-ak	-juk, -jük	-uk, -ük

Note: As mentioned earlier, vowels often get inserted between the word and its suffix so as to prevent too many consonants from appearing in a row (which would produce unpronounceable words). For example, in the table on the previous page, all nouns that end in a consonant are followed by suffixes beginning with "a."

Verb conjugation. Like its modern descendants (such as Finnish and Hungarian), Carpathian has many verb tenses, far too many to describe here. We will just focus on the conjugation of the present tense. Again, we will place contemporary Hungarian side by side with Carpathian because of the marked similarity between the two.

As with the possessive case for nouns, the conjugation of verbs is done by adding a suffix onto the verb stem:

Person	Carpathian (proto-Uralic)	Contemporary Hungarian
1st singular (I give)	-am (andam), -ak	-ok, -ek, -ök
2nd singular (you give)	-sz (andsz)	-sz
3rd singular (he/she/it gives)	— (and)	—
1st plural (we give)	-ak (andak)	-unk, -ünk
2nd plural (you give)	-tak (andtak)	-tok, -tek, -tök
3rd plural (they give)	-nak (andnak)	-nak, -nek

As with all languages, there are many "irregular verbs" in Carpathian that don't exactly fit this pattern. But the table is still a useful guide for most verbs.

3. EXAMPLES OF THE CARPATHIAN LANGUAGE

Here are some brief examples of conversational Carpathian, used in the Dark books. We include the literal translation in square brackets.

It is interestingly different from the most appropriate English translation.

Susu.
I am home.
["home/birthplace." "I am" is understood, as is often the case in Carpathian.]

Möért?
What for?

csitri
little one
["little slip of a thing," "little slip of a girl"]

ainaak enyém
forever mine

ainaak sívamet jutta
forever mine (another form)
["forever to-my-heart connected/fixed"]

sívamet
my love
["of-my-heart," "to-my-heart"]

Tet vigyázam.
I love you.
["you-love-I"]

    Sarna Rituaali (The Ritual Words) is a longer example, and an example of chanted rather than conversational Carpathian. Note the recurring use of *"andam"* ("I give") to give the chant musicality and force through repetition.

Sarna Rituaali (The Ritual Words)

Te avio päläfertiilam.
You are my lifemate.

Éntölam kuulua, avio päläfertiilam.
I claim you as my lifemate.

Ted kuuluak, kacad, kojed.
I belong to you.

Élidamet andam.
I offer my life for you.

Pesämet andam.
I give you my protection.

Uskolfertiilamet andam.
I give you my allegiance.

Sívamet andam.
I give you my heart.

Sielamet andam.
I give you my soul.

Ainamet andam.
I give you my body.

Sívamet kuuluak kaik että a ted.
I take into my keeping the same that is yours.

Ainaak olenszal sívambin.
Your life will be cherished by me for all my time.

Te élidet ainaak pide minan.
Your life will be placed above my own for all time.

Te avio päläfertiilam.
You are my lifemate.

Ainaak sívamet jutta oleny.
You are bound to me for all eternity.

Ainaak terád vigyázak.
You are always in my care.

To hear these words pronounced (and for more about Carpathian pronunciation altogether), please visit christinefeehan.com/members/.

Sarna Kontakawk (**The Warriors' Chant**) is another, longer example of the Carpathian language. The warriors' council takes place deep beneath the earth in a chamber of crystals with magma far below it, so the steam is natural and the wisdom of their ancestors is clear and focused. This is a sacred place where they bloodswear to their prince and people and affirm their code of honor as warriors and brothers. It is also where battle strategies are born and all dissension is discussed, as well as any concerns the warriors have that they wish to bring to the council and open for discussion.

Sarna Kontakawk (**The Warriors' Chant**)

Veri isäakank—veri ekäakank.
Blood of our fathers—blood of our brothers.

Veri olen elid.
Blood is life.

Andak veri-elidet Karpatiiakank, és wäke-sarna ku meke arwa-arvo,
  irgalom, hän ku agba, és wäke kutni, ku manaak verival.
We offer that life to our people with a bloodsworn vow of honor,
  mercy, integrity and endurance.

Verink sokta; verink kaŋa terád.
Our blood mingles and calls to you.

Akasz énak ku kaŋa és juttasz kuntatak it.
Heed our summons and join with us now.

To hear these words pronounced (and for more about Carpathian
pronunciation altogether), please visit christinefeehan.com
/members/.

See **Appendix 1** for Carpathian healing chants, including the *Kepä
Sarna Pus* (The Lesser Healing Chant), the *En Sarna Pus* (The Great
Healing Chant), the *Odam-Sarna Kondak* (Lullaby) and the *Sarna
Pusm O Mayet* (Song to Heal the Earth).

4. A MUCH-ABRIDGED CARPATHIAN DICTIONARY

This very-much-abridged Carpathian dictionary contains most of the
Carpathian words used in the Dark books. Of course, a full Carpathian dictionary would be as large as the usual dictionary for an entire
language (typically more than a hundred thousand words).

Note: The Carpathian nouns and verbs that follow are word **stems**. They
generally do not appear in their isolated "stem" form. Instead, they usually
appear with suffixes (e.g., *andam—I give*, rather than just the root, *and*).

a—verb negation (*prefix*); not (*adverb*).
aćke—pace, step.

aćke éntölem it—take another step toward me.

agba—to be seemly; to be proper (*verb*). True; seemly; proper (*adj.*).

ai—oh.

aina—body (*noun*).

ainaak—always; forever.

o ainaak jelä peje emnimet ŋamaŋ—sun scorch that woman forever
(*Carpathian swear words*).

ainaakä—never.

ainaakfél—old friend.

ak—suffix added after a noun ending in a consonant to make it plural.

aka—to give heed; to hearken; to listen.

aka-arvo—respect (*noun*).

akarat—mind; will (*noun*).

ál—to bless; to attach to.

alatt—through.

aldyn—under; underneath.

alə—to lift; to raise.

alte—to bless; to curse.

amaŋ—this; this one here; that; that one there.

and—to give.

**and sielet, arwa-arvomet, és jelämet, kuulua huvémet ku feaj és
ködet ainaak**—to trade soul, honor and salvation for momentary
pleasure and endless damnation.

andasz éntölem irgalomet!—have mercy!

arvo—value; price (*noun*).

arwa—praise (*noun*).

arwa-arvo olen gæidnod, ekäm—honor guide you, my brother
(*greeting*).

arwa-arvo olen isäntä, ekäm—honor keep you, my brother (*greeting*).

arwa-arvo pile sívadet—may honor light your heart (*greeting*).

arwa-arvod—honor (*noun*).

arwa-arvod mäne me ködak—may your honor hold back the dark
(*greeting*).

aš—no (*exclamation*).

ašša—no (before a noun); not (with a verb that is not in the imperative); not (with an adjective).

aššatotello—disobedient.

asti—until.

avaa—to open.

avio—wedded.

avio päläfertiil—lifemate.

avoi—uncover; show; reveal.

baszú—revenge; vengeance.

belső—within; inside.

bur—good; well.

bur tule ekämet kuntamak—well met brother-kin (*greeting*).

ćaða—to flee; to run; to escape.

čač3—to be born; to grow.

ćoro—to flow; to run like rain.

csecsemő—baby (*noun*).

csitri—little one (*female*).

csitrim—my little one (*female*).

diutal—triumph; victory.

džinõt—brief; short.

eći—to fall.

ej—not (*adverb, suffix*); *nej* when preceding syllable ends in a vowel.

ek—suffix added after a noun ending in a consonant to make it plural.

ekä—brother.

ekäm—my brother.

elä—to live.

eläsz arwa-arvoval—may you live with honor; live nobly (*greeting*).

eläsz jeläbam ainaak—long may you live in the light (*greeting*).

elävä—alive.

elävä ainak majaknak—land of the living.

elid—life.

emä—mother (*noun*).

Emä Maγe—Mother Nature.

emäen—grandmother.

embε—if; when.

embε karmasz—please.

emni—wife; woman.

emni hän ku köd alte—cursed woman.

emni kuŋenak ku aššatotello—disobedient lunatic.

emnim—my wife; my woman.

én—I.

en—great; many; big.

en hän ku pesä—the protector (literally: the great protector).

én jutta félet és ekämet—I greet a friend and brother (*greeting*).

en Karpatii—the prince (literally: the great Carpathian).

én maγenak—I am of the earth.

én oma maγeka—I am as old as time (literally: as old as the earth).

En Puwe—The Great Tree. Related to the legends of Yggdrasil, the *axis mundi*, Mount Meru, heaven and hell, etc.

enä—most.

engem—of me.

enkojra—wolf.

és—and.

ete—before; in front of.

että—that.

év—year.

évsatz—century.

fáz—to feel cold or chilly.

fél—fellow; friend.

fél ku kuuluaak sívam belső—beloved.

fél ku vigyázak—dear one.

feldolgaz—prepare.

fertiil—fertile one.

fesztelen—airy.

fü—herbs; grass.

gæidno—road; way.

gond—care; worry; love (*noun*).

hän—he; she; it; one.

hän agba—it is so.

hän ku—prefix: one who; he who; that which.

hän ku agba—truth.

hän ku kaśwa o numamet—sky-owner.

hän ku kuula siela—keeper of his soul.

hän ku kuulua sívamet—keeper of my heart.

hän ku lejkka wäke-sarnat—traitor.

hän ku meke pirämet—defender.

hän ku meke sarnaakmet—mage.

hän ku pesä—protector.

hän ku pesä sieladet—guardian of your soul.

hän ku pesäk kaikak—guardians of all.

hän ku piwtä—predator; hunter; tracker.

hän ku pusm—healer.

hän ku saa kuć3aket—star-reacher.

hän ku tappa—killer; violent person (*noun*). Deadly; violent (*adj.*).

hän ku tuulmahl elidet—vampire (literally: life-stealer).

hän ku vie elidet—vampire (literally: thief of life).

hän ku vigyáz sielamet—keeper of my soul.

hän ku vigyáz sívamet és sielamet—keeper of my heart and soul.

hän sívamak—beloved.

hängem—him; her; it.

hank—they.

hany—clod; lump of earth.

hisz—to believe; to trust.

ho—how.

ida—east.

igazág—justice.

ila—to shine.

inan—mine; my own (*endearment*).

irgalom—compassion; pity; mercy.

isä—father (*noun*).

isäntä—master of the house.

it—now.

jaguár—jaguar.

jaka—to cut; to divide; to separate.

jakam—wound; cut; injury.

jalka—leg.

jälleen—again.

jama—to be sick, infected, wounded or dying; to be near death.

jamatan—fallen; wounded; near death.

jelä—sunlight; day, sun; light.

jelä keje terád—light sear you (*Carpathian swear words*).

o jelä peje emnimet—sun scorch the woman (*Carpathian swear words*).

o jelä peje kaik hänkanak—sun scorch them all (*Carpathian swear words*).

o jelä peje terád—sun scorch you (*Carpathian swear words*).

o jelä peje terád, emni—sun scorch you, woman (*Carpathian swear words*).

o jelä sielamak—light of my soul.

joma—to be underway; to go.

joŋe—to come; to return.

joŋesz arwa-arvoval—return with honor (*greeting*).

joŋesz éntölem, fél ku kuuluaak sívam belsö—come to me, beloved.

jŏrem—to forget; to lose one's way; to make a mistake.

jotka—gap; middle; space.

jotkan—between.

juo—to drink.

juosz és eläsz—drink and live (*greeting*).

juosz és olen ainaak sielamet jutta—drink and become one with me (*greeting*).

juta—to go; to wander.

jüti—night; evening.

jutta—connected; fixed (*adj.*). To connect; to join; to fix; to bind (*verb*).

k—suffix added after a noun ending in a vowel to make it plural.

kać3—gift.

kaca—male lover.

kadi—judge.

kaik—all.

käktä—two; many.

käktäverit—mixed blood (literally: two bloods).

kalma—corpse; death; grave.

kaŋa—to call; to invite; to summon; to request; to beg.

kaŋk—windpipe; Adam's apple; throat.

karma—want.

Karpatii—Carpathian.

karpatii ku köd—liar.

Karpatiikunta—the Carpathian people.

käsi—hand.

kaśwa—to own.

kaða—to abandon; to leave; to remain.

kaða wäkeva óv o köd—stand fast against the dark (*greeting*).

kat—house; family (*noun*).

katt3—to move; to penetrate; to proceed.

keje—to cook; to burn; to sear.

kepä—lesser; small; easy; few.

kessa—cat.

kessa ku toro—wildcat.

kessake—little cat.

kidü—to wake up; to arise (*intransitive verb*).

kim—to cover an entire object with some sort of covering.

kinn—out; outdoors; outside; without.

kinta—fog; mist; smoke.

kislány—little girl.

kislány hän ku meke sarnaakmet—little mage.

kislány kuŋenak—little lunatic.

kislány kuŋenak minan—my little lunatic.

köd—fog; mist; darkness; evil (*noun*). Foggy, dark; evil (*adj.*).

köd alte hän—darkness curse it (*Carpathian swear words*).

o köd belső—darkness take it (*Carpathian swear words*).

köd elävä és köd nime kutni nimet—evil lives and has a name.

köd jutasz belső—shadow take you (*Carpathian swear words*).

koj—let; allow; decree; establish; order.

koje—man; husband; drone.

kola—to die.

kolasz arwa-arvoval—may you die with honor (*greeting*).

kolatan—dead; departed.

koma—empty hand; bare hand; palm of the hand; hollow of the hand.

kond—all of a family's or clan's children.

kont—warrior; man.

kont o sívanak—strong heart (literally: heart of the warrior).

kor3—basket; container made of birch bark.

kor3nat—containing; including.

ku—who; which; that; where; which; what.

kuć3—star.

kuć3ak!—stars! (exclamation).

kudeje—descent; generation.

kuja—day; sun.

kule—to hear.

kulke—to go or to travel (on land or water).

kulkesz arwa-arvoval, ekäm—walk with honor, my brother (*greeting*).

kulkesz arwaval, joŋesz arwa arvoval—go with glory, return with honor (*greeting*).

kuly—intestinal worm; tapeworm; demon who possesses and devours souls.

küm—human male.

kumala—to sacrifice; to offer; to pray.

kumpa—wave (*noun*).

kuńa—to lie as if asleep; to close or cover the eyes in a game of hide-and-seek; to die.

kuŋe—moon; month.

kunta—band; clan; tribe; family; people; lineage; line.

kuras—sword; large knife.

kure—bind; tie.

kuš—worker; servant.

kutenken—however.

kutni—to be able to bear, carry, endure, stand or take.

kutnisz ainaak—long may you endure (*greeting*).

kuulua—to belong; to hold.

kužõ—long.

lääs—west.

lamti (or lamt3)—lowland; meadow; deep; depth.

lamti ból jüti, kinta, ja szelem—the netherworld (literally: the meadow of night, mists and ghosts).

lańa—daughter.

lejkka—crack; fissure; split (*noun*). To cut; to hit; to strike forcefully (*verb*).

lewl—spirit (*noun*).

lewl ma—the other world (literally: spirit land). *Lewl ma* includes *lamti ból jüti, kinta, ja szelem*: the netherworld, but also includes the worlds higher up *En Puwe*, the Great Tree.

liha—flesh.

lõuna—south.

löyly—breath; steam (related to *lewl*: spirit).

luwe—bone.

ma—land; forest; world.

magköszun—thank.

mana—to abuse; to curse; to ruin.

mäne—to rescue; to save.

maɣe—land; earth; territory; place; nature.

mboće—other; second (*adj.*).

me—we.

megem—us.

meke—deed; work (*noun*). To do; to make; to work (*verb*).

mić (or mića)—beautiful.

mića emni kuŋenak minan—my beautiful lunatic.

minan—mine; my own (*endearment*).

minden—every; all (*adj.*).

möért?—what for? (*exclamation*).

molanâ—to crumble; to fall apart.

molo—to crush; to break into bits.

moo—why; reason.

mozdul—to begin to move; to enter into movement.

muonì—appoint; order; prescribe; command.

muonìak te avoisz te—I command you to reveal yourself.

musta—memory.

myös—also.

m8—thing; what.

na—close; near.

nä—for.

nâbbŏ—so, then.

ŋamaŋ—this; this one here; that; that one there.

ŋamaŋak—these; these ones here; those; those ones there.

nautish—to enjoy.

nélkül—without.

nenä—anger.

nime—name.

ńiŋ3—worm; maggot.

nó—like; in the same way as; as.

nókunta—kinship.

numa—god; sky; top; upper part; highest (related to the English word *numinous*).

numatorkuld—thunder (literally: sky struggle).

ńůp@l—for; to; toward.

ńůp@l mam—toward my world.

nyál—saliva; spit (related to *nyelv*: tongue).

nyelv—tongue.

o—the (used before a noun beginning with a consonant).

ó—like; in the same way as; as.

odam—to dream; to sleep.

odam-sarna kondak—lullaby (literally: sleep-song of children).

odam wäke emni—mistress of illusions.

olen—to be.

oma—old; ancient; last; previous.

omas—stand.

omboce—other; second (*adj.*).

ŏrem—to forget; to lose one's way; to make a mistake.

ot—the (used before a noun beginning with a vowel).

ot (or t)—past participle (*suffix*).

otti—to look; to see; to find.

óv—to protect against.

owe—door.

päämoro—aim; target.

pajna—to press.

pälä—half; side.

päläfertiil—mate or wife.

päläpälä—side by side.

palj3—more.

palj3 na éntölem—closer.

partiolen—scout (*noun*).

peje—to burn; scorch.

peje!—burn! (*Carpathian swear word*).

peje terád—get burned (*Carpathian swear words*).

pél—to be afraid; to be scared of.

pesä—nest (*literal; noun*); protection (*figurative; noun*).

pesä—nest; stay (*literal*); protect (*figurative*).

pesäd te engemal—you are safe with me.

pesäsz jeläbam ainaak—long may you stay in the light (*greeting*).

pide—above.

pile—to ignite; to light up.

piŋe—little bird.

piŋe sarnanak—little songbird.

pion—soon.

pirä—circle; ring (*noun*). To surround; to enclose (*verb*).

piros—red.

pitä—to keep; to hold; to have; to possess.

pitäam mustaakad sielpesäambam—I hold your memories safe in my soul.

pitäsz baszú, piwtäsz igazáget—no vengeance, only justice.

piwtä—to seek; to follow; to follow the track of game; to hunt; to prey upon.

poår—bit; piece.

põhi—north.

pohoopa—vigorous.

pukta—to drive away; to persecute; to put to flight.

pus—healthy; healing.

pusm—to heal; to be restored to health.

puwe—tree; wood.

rambsolg—slave.

rauho—peace.

reka—ecstasy; trance.

rituaali—ritual.

sa—sinew; tendon; cord.

sa4—to call; to name.

saa—arrive, come; become; get, receive.

saasz hän ku andam szabadon—take what I freely offer.

saγe—to arrive; to come; to reach.

salama—lightning; lightning bolt.

sapar—tail.

sapar bin jalkak—coward (literally: tail between legs).

sapar bin jalkak nélkül mogal—spineless coward.

sarna—words; speech; song; magic incantation (*noun*). To chant; to sing; to celebrate (*verb*).

sarna hän agba—claim.

sarna kontakawk—warriors' chant.

sarna kunta—alliance (literally: single tribe through sacred words).

śaro—frozen snow.

sas—shoosh (*to a child or baby*).

satz—hundred.

siel—soul.

sielad sielamed—soul to soul (literally: your soul to my soul).

sielam—my soul.

sielam pitwä sielad—my soul searches for your soul.

sielam sieladed—my soul to your soul.

sieljelä isäntä—purity of soul triumphs.

sisar—sister.

sisarak sivak—sisters of the heart.

sisarke—little sister.

sív—heart.

sív pide köd—love transcends evil.

sív pide minden köd—love transcends all evil.

sívad olen wäkeva, hän ku piwtä—may your heart stay strong, hunter (*greeting*).

sívam és sielam—my heart and soul.

sívamet—my heart.

sívdobbanás—heartbeat (*literal*); rhythm (*figurative*).

sokta—to mix; to stir around.

sõl—dare, venture.

sõl olen engemal, sarna sívametak—dare to be with me, song of my heart.

soŋe—to enter; to penetrate; to compensate; to replace.

Susiküm—Lycan.

susu—home; birthplace (*noun*). At home (*adv.*).

szabadon—freely.

szelem—ghost.

ször—time; occasion.

t (or ot)—past participle (*suffix*).

taj—to be worth.

taka—behind; beyond.

takka—to hang; to remain stuck.

takkap—obstacle; challenge; difficulty; ordeal; trial.

tappa—to dance; to stamp with the feet; to kill.

tasa—even so; just the same.

te—you.

te kalma, te jama ńiŋ3kval, te apitäsz arwa-arvo—you are nothing but a walking maggot-infected corpse, without honor.

te magköszunam nä ŋamaŋ kać3 taka arvo—thank you for this gift beyond price.

ted—yours.

terád keje—get scorched (*Carpathian swear words*).

tõd—to know.

tõdak pitäsz wäke bekimet mekesz kaiket—I know you have the courage to face anything.

tõdhän—knowledge.

tõdhän lõ kuraset agbapäämoroam—knowledge flies the sword true to its aim.

toja—to bend; to bow; to break.

toro—to fight; to quarrel.

torosz wäkeval—fight fiercely (*greeting*).

totello—obey.

tsak—only.

t'šuva vni—period of time.

tti—to look; to see; to find.

tuhanos—thousand.

tuhanos löylyak türelamak saγe diutalet—a thousand patient breaths bring victory.

tule—to meet; to come.

tuli—fire.

tumte—to feel; to touch; to touch upon.

türe—full; satiated; accomplished.

türelam—patience.

türelam agba kontsalamaval—patience is the warrior's
    true weapon.

tyvi—stem; base; trunk.

ul3—very; exceedingly; quite.

umuš—wisdom; discernment.

und—past participle (*suffix*).

uskol—faithful.

uskolfertiil—allegiance; loyalty.

usm—to heal; to be restored to health.

vár—to wait.

varolind—dangerous.

veri—blood.

veri ekäakank—blood of our brothers.

veri-elidet—blood-life.

veri isäakank—blood of our fathers.

veri olen piros, ekäm—literally: blood be red, my brother; figuratively:
    find your lifemate (*greeting*).

veriak ot en Karpatiiak—by the blood of the prince (literally: by the
    blood of the great Carpathian; *Carpathian swear words*).

veridet peje—may your blood burn (*Carpathian swear words*).

vigyáz—to love; to care for; to take care of.

vii—last; at last; finally.

wäke—power; strength.

wäke beki—strength; courage.

wäke kaða—steadfastness.

wäke kutni—endurance.

wäke-sarna—vow; curse; blessing (literally: power words).

wäkeva—powerful; strong.

wäkeva csitrim ku pesä—my fierce little protector.

wara—bird; crow.

weńća—complete; whole.

wete—water (*noun*).

Do you love fiction with a supernatural twist?

Want the chance to hear news about your favourite
authors (and the chance to win free books)?

Christine Feehan
J.R. Ward
Sherrilyn Kenyon
Charlaine Harris
Jayne Ann Krentz and Jayne Castle
P.C. Cast
Maria Lewis
Darynda Jones
Hayley Edwards
Kristen Callihan
Keri Arthur
Amanda Bouchet
Jacquelyn Frank
Larissa Ione

Then visit the *With Love* website and
sign up to our romance newsletter:
www.yourswithlove.co.uk

And follow us on Facebook for book giveaways,
exclusive romance news and more:
www.facebook.com/yourswithlovex

PIATKUS

CHRISTINE FEEHAN

'The queen of paranormal romance . . .
I love everything she does'
J. R. Ward

PIATKUS